Laura Augu̶s̶t̶ ... ...

.10

, Laura A. Evans

1904.

The Voice of the People

CROWNED MASTERPIECES
OF MODERN FICTION
SPECIAL SUBSCRIPTION EDITION

The Voice of the People

BY

Ellen Glasgow Anderson Gholson

NEW YORK ❧ DOUBLEDAY
PAGE & COMPANY ❧ *1905*

TO REBE GORDON GLASGOW

246595

BOOK I

FAIR WEATHER AT KINGSBOROUGH

THE
VOICE OF THE PEOPLE

BOOK I

FAIR WEATHER AT KINGSBOROUGH

I

The last day of Circuit Court was over at Kingsborough.

The jury had vanished from the semicircle of straight-backed chairs in the old court-house, the clerk had laid aside his pen along with his air of listless attention, and the judge was making his way through the straggling spectators to the sunken stone steps of the platform outside. As the crowd in the doorway parted slightly, a breeze passed into the room, scattering the odours of bad tobacco and farm-stained clothing. The sound of a cow-bell came through one of the small windows, from the green beyond, where a red-and-white cow was browsing among the buttercups.

" A fine day, gentlemen," said the judge, bowing to right and left. " A fine day."

He moved slowly, fanning himself absently with

his white straw hat, pausing from time to time to exchange a word of greeting—secure in the affability of one who is not only a judge of man but a Bassett of Virginia. From his classic head to his ill-fitting boots he upheld the traditions of his office and his race.

On the stone platform, just beyond the entrance, he stopped to speak to a lawyer from a neighbouring county. Then, as a clump of men scattered at his approach, he waved them together with a bland, benedictory gesture which descended alike upon the high and the low, upon the rector of the old church up the street, in his rusty black, and upon the red-haired, raw-boned farmer with his streaming brow.

" Glad to see you out, sir," he said to the one, and to the other, " How are you, Burr? Time the crops were in the ground, isn't it? "

Burr mumbled a confused reply, wiping his neck laboriously on his red cotton handkerchief.

" The corn's been planted goin' on six weeks," he said more distinctly, ejecting his words between mouthfuls of tobacco juice as if they were pebbles which obstructed his speech. " I al'ays stick to plantin' yo' corn when the hickory leaf's as big as a squirrel's ear. If you don't, the luck's agin you."

" An' whar thar's growin' corn thar's a sight o' hoein'," put in an alert, nervous-looking countryman. " If I lay my hoe down for a spell, the weeds git so big I can't find the crop."

Amos Burr nodded with slow emphasis: " I never see land take so natural to weeds nohow as mine do," he said. " When you raise peanuts you're raisin' trouble."

He was a lean, overworked man, with knotted hands the colour of the soil he tilled and an inanely honest face, over which the freckles showed like splashes of mud freshly dried. As he spoke he gave his blue jean trousers an abrupt hitch at the belt.

" Dear me! Dear me! " returned the judge with absent-minded, habitual friendliness, smiling his rich, beneficent smile. Then, as he caught sight of a smaller red head beneath Burr's arm, he added: " You've a right-hand man coming on, I see. What's your name, my boy? "

The boy squirmed on his bare, brown feet and wriggled his head from beneath his father's arm. He did not answer, but he turned his bright eyes on the judge and flushed through all the freckles of his ugly little face.

" Nick—that is, Nicholas, sir," replied the elder Burr with an apologetic cough, due to the insignificance of the subject. " Yes, sir, he's leetle, but ʰe's plum full of grit. He can beat any nigger I ever seed at the plough. He'd outplough me if he war a head taller."

". That will mend," remarked the lawyer from the neighbouring county with facetious intention. " A boy and a beanstalk will grow, you know. There's no helping it."

" Oh, he'll be a man soon enough," added the judge, his gaze passing over the large, red head to rest upon the small one, " and a farmer like his father before him, I suppose."

He was turning away when the child's voice checked him, and he paused.

" I—I'd ruther be a judge," said the boy.

He was leaning against the faded bricks of the old court-house, one sunburned hand playing nervously with the crumbling particles. His honest little face was as red as his hair.

The judge started.

" Ah ! " he exclaimed, and he looked at the child with his kindly eyes. The boy was ugly, lean, and stunted in growth, browned by hot suns and powdered by the dust of country roads, but his eyes caught the gaze of the judge and held it.

Above his head, on the brick wall, a board was nailed, bearing in black marking the name of the white-sand street which stretched like a chalk-drawn line from the grass-grown battlefields to the pale old buildings of King's College. The street had been called in honour of a duke of Gloucester. It was now " Main " Street, and nothing more, though it was still wide and white and placidly impressed by the slow passage of Kingsborough feet. Beyond the court-house the breeze blew across the green, which was ablaze with buttercups. Beneath the warm wind the yellow heads assumed the effect of a brilliant tangle, spreading over the unploughed common, running astray in the grass-lined ditch that bordered the walk, hiding beneath dusty-leaved plants in unsuspected hollows, and breaking out again under the horses' hoofs in the sandy street.

" Ah ! " exclaimed the judge, and a good-natured laugh ran round the group.

" Wall, I never ! " ejaculated the elder Burr, but there was no surprise in his tone ; it expressed rather the helplessness of paternity.

The boy faced them, pressing more firmly against the bricks.

" There ain't nothin' in peanut-raisin'," he said. " It's jest farmin' fur crows. I'd ruther be a judge."

The judge laughed and turned from him.

" Stick to the soil, my boy," he advised.   " Stick to the soil.   It is the best thing to do.   But if you choose the second best, and I can help you, I will —I will, upon my word—Ah! General," to a jovial-faced, wide-girthed gentleman in a brown linen coat, " I'm glad to see you in town.   Fine weather ! "

He put on his hat, bowed again, and went on his way.

He passed slowly along in the spring sunshine, his feet crunching upon the gravel, his straight shadow falling upon the white level between coarse fringes of wire-grass.   Far up the town, at the street's sudden end, where it was lost in diverging roads, there was visible, as through a film of bluish smoke, the verdigris-green foliage of King's College.   Nearer at hand the solemn cruciform of the old church was steeped in shade, the high bell-tower dropping a veil of English ivy as it rose against the sky.   Through the rusty iron gate of the grave-yard the marble slabs glimmered beneath submerging grasses, long, pale, tremulous like reeds.

The grass-grown walk beside the low brick wall of the churchyard led on to the judge's own garden, a square enclosure, laid out in straight vegetable rows, marked off by variegated borders of flowering plants —heartsease, foxglove, and the red-lidded eyes of scarlet poppies.   Beyond the feathery green of the asparagus bed there was a bush of flowering syringa, another at the beginning of the grass-trimmed walk, and yet another brushing the large white pillars of the square front porch—their slender sprays blown from sun to shade like fluttering streamers of cream-coloured ribbons.   On the other side there were lilacs, stately and leafy and bare of bloom, save for a few ashen-hued bunches lingering late amid the heavy foliage.   At the foot of the garden the wall was hidden in raspberry vines, weighty with ripening fruit.

The judge closed the gate after him and ascended the steps.   It was not until he had crossed the wide hall and opened the door of his study that he heard the patter of bare feet, and turned to find that the boy had followed him.

For an instant he regarded the child blankly; then his hospitality asserted itself, and he waved him courteously into the room.

"Walk in, walk in, and take a seat.   I am at your service."

He crossed to one of the tall windows, unfastening the heavy inside shutters, from which the white paint was fast peeling away.   As they fell back a breeze filled the room, and the ivory faces of microphylla roses stared across the deep window-seat. The place was airy as a summer-house and odorous with the essence of roses distilled in the sunshine beyond.   On the high plastered walls, above the book-shelves, rows of bygone Bassetts looked down on their departed possessions—stately and severe in the artificial severity of periwigs and starched ruffles. They looked down with immobile eyes and the placid monotony of past fashions, smiling always the same smile, staring always at the same spot of floor or furniture.

Below them the room was still hallowed by their touch. They asserted themselves in the quaint curves of the rosewood chairs, in the blue patterns upon the willow bowls, and in the choice lavender of the old Wedgwood. Their handiwork was visible in the laborious embroideries of the fire-screen near the empty grate, and the spinet in one unlighted corner still guarded their gay and amiable airs.

" Sit down," said the judge. " I am at your service."

He seated himself before his desk of hand-carved mahogany, pushing aside the papers that littered its baize-covered lid. In the half-gloom of the high-ceiled room his face assumed the look of a portrait in oils, and he seemed to have descended from his allotted square upon the plastered wall, to be but a boldly limned composite likeness of his race, awaiting the last touches and the gilded frame.

" What can I do for you? " he asked again, his tone preserving its unfailing courtesy. He had not made an uncivil remark since the close of the war— a line of conduct resulting less from what he felt to be due to others than from what he believed to be becoming in himself.

The boy shifted on his bare feet. In the old-timed setting of the furniture he was an alien—an anachronism—the intrusion of the hopelessly modern into the helplessly past. His hair made a rich spot in the colourless atmosphere, and it seemed to focus the incoming light from the unshuttered window, leaving the background in denser shadow.

The animation of his features jarred the serenity of the room. His profile showed gnome-like against the nodding heads of the microphylla roses.

"There ain't nothin' in peanut-raisin'," he said suddenly; "I—I'd ruther be a judge."

"My dear boy!" exclaimed the judge, and finished helplessly, "my dear boy—I—well—I——"

They were both silent. The regular droning of the old clock sounded distinctly in the stillness. The perfume of roses, mingling with the musty scent from the furniture, borrowed the quality of musk.

The child was breathing heavily. Suddenly he dug the dirty knuckles of one fist into his eyes.

"Don't cry," began the judge. "Please don't. Perhaps you would like to run out and play with my boy Tom?"

"I warn't cryin'," said the child. "It war a gnat."

His hand left his eyes and returned to his hat— a wide-brimmed harvest hat, with a shoestring tied tightly round the crown.

When the judge spoke again it was with seriousness.

"Nicholas—your name is Nicholas, isn't it?"

"Yes, sir."

"How old are you?"

"Twelve, sir."

"Can you read?"

"Yes, sir."

"Write?"

"Y-e-s, sir."

"Spell?"

The child hesitated. "I—I can spell—some."

"Don't you know it is a serious thing to be a judge?"

"Yes, sir."

"You must be a lawyer first."

"Yes, sir."

"It is hard work."

"Yes, sir."

"And sometimes it's no better than farming for crows."

The boy shook his head. "It's cleaner work, sir."

The judge laughed.

"I'm afraid you are obstinate, Nicholas," he said, and added: "Now, what do you want me to do for you? I can't make you a judge. It took me fifty years to make myself one—a third-rate one at that——"

"I—I'd l-i-k-e to take a bo-b-o-o-k," stammered the boy.

"Dear me!" said the judge irritably, "dear me!"

He frowned, his gaze skimming his well-filled shelves. He regretted suddenly that he had spoken to the child at the court-house. He would never be guilty of such an indiscretion again. Of what could he have been thinking? A book! Why didn't he ask for food—money—his best piece of fluted Royal Worcester?

Then a loud, boyish laugh rang in from the garden, and his face softened suddenly. In the sunscorched, honest-eyed little figure before him he saw his own boy—the single child of his young wife, who was lying beneath a marble slab in the churchyard. Her face, mild and Madonna-like, glimmered against the pallid rose leaves in the deep window-seat.

He turned hastily away.

"Yes, yes," he answered, "I will lend you one. Read the titles carefully. Don't let the books fall. Never lay them face downwards—and don't turn down the leaves!"

The boy advanced timidly to the shelves between the southern windows. He ran his hands slowly along the lettered backs, his lips moving as he spelled out the names.

"The F-e-d-e-r-a-l-i-s-t," "B-l-a-c-k-s-t-o-n-e-'s C-o-m-m-e-n-t-a-r-i-e-s," "R-e-v-i-s-e-d Sta-tu-tes of the U-ni-ted Sta-tes."

The judge drew up to his desk and looked over his letters. Then he took up his pen and wrote several replies in his fine, flowing handwriting. He had forgotten the boy, when he felt a touch upon his arm.

"What is it?" he asked absently. "Ah, it is you? Yes, let me see. Why! you've got Sir Henry Maine!"

The boy was holding the book in both hands. As the judge laughed he flushed nervously and turned towards the door.

The judge leaned back in his chair, watching the small figure cross the room and disappear into the hall. He saw the tracks of dust which the boy's feet left upon the smooth, bare floor, but he was not thinking of them. Then, as the child went out upon the porch, he started up.

"Nicholas!" he called, "don't turn down the leaves!"

II

A facetious stranger once remarked that Kingsborough dozed through the present to dream of the past and found the future a nightmare. Had he been other than a stranger, he would, perhaps, have added that Kingsborough's proudest boast was that she had been and was not—a distinction giving her preëminence over certain cities whose charters were not received from royal grants—cities priding themselves not only upon a multiplicity of streets, but upon the more plebeian fact that the feet of their young men followed the offending thoroughfares to the undignified music of the march of progress.

But, whatever might be said of places that shall be nameless, it was otherwise with Kingsborough. Kingsborough was the same yesterday, to-day, and forever. She who had feasted royal governors, staked and lost upon Colonial races, and exploded like an ignited powder-horn in the cause of American independence, was still superbly conscious of the honours which had been hers. Her governors were no longer royal, nor did she feast them; her races were run by fleet-footed coloured urchins on the court-house green; her powder-magazine had evolved through differentiation from a stable into a church; but Kingsborough clung to her amiable habits. Travellers still arrived at the landing stage some several miles distant and were driven over all but impassable roads to the town. The eastern wall

of the court-house still bore the sign "England
Street," though the street had vanished beneath encroaching buttercups, and the implied loyalty had
been found wanting. Kingsborough juries still sat
in their original semicircle, with their backs to the
judge and their faces, presumably, to the law;
Kingsborough farmers still marketed their small
truck in the street called after the Duke of Gloucester; and Kingsborough cows still roamed at will
over the vaults in the churchyard. In time trivial
changes would come to pass. Tourists would ar-
rive with the railroad; the powder-magazine would
turn from a church into a museum; gardens would
decay and ancient elms would fall, but the farmers
and the cows would not be missed from their accustomed haunts. On the hospitable thresholds of
" general " stores battle-scarred veterans of the war
between the States dealt in victorious reminiscences
of vanquishment. They had fought well, they had
fallen silently, and they had risen without bitterness.
For the people of Kingsborough had opened their
doors to wounded foes while the battle raged
through their streets, succouring while they resisted.
They lived easily and they died hard, but when death
came they met it, not in grim Puritanism, but with
a laugh upon the lips. They made a joy of life while
it was possible, and when that ceased to be, they did
the next best thing and made a friend of death. Long
ago theirs had been the first part in Virginia, and, as
they still believed, theirs had been also the centre of
all things. Now the high places were laid low, and
the greatness had passed as a trumpet that is blown.
Kingsborough persisted still, but it persisted eva-

sively, hovering, as it were, upon the outskirts of modern advancement. And the outside world took note only when it made tours to historic strongholds, or sent those of itself that were adjudged insane to the hospitable shelter of the asylum upon the hill.

It was afternoon, and Kingsborough was asleep.

Along the verdurous, gray lanes the houses seemed abandoned, shuttered, filled with shade. From the court-house green came the chime of cow-bells rising and falling in slow waves of sound. A spotted calf stood bleating in the crooked footpath, which traversed diagonally the waste of buttercups like a white seam in a cloth of gold. Against the arching sky rose the bell-tower of the grim old church, where the sparrows twittered in the melancholy gables and the startled face of the stationary clock stared blankly above the ivied walls. Farther away, at the end of a wavering lane, slanted the shadow of the insane asylum.

Across the green the houses were set in surrounding gardens like cards in bouquets of mixed blossoms. They were of frame for the most part, with shingled roofs and small, square windows hidden beneath climbing roses. On one of the long verandas a sleeping girl lay in a hammock, a gray cat at her feet. No sound came from the house behind her, but a breeze blew through the dim hall, fluttering the folds of her dress. Beyond the adjoining garden a lady in mourning entered a gate where honeysuckle grew, and above, on the low-dormered roof, a white pigeon sat preening its feathers. Up the main street, where a few sunken bricks of a vanished pavement were still visible, an old negro woman, sitting on the stone before her cabin, lighted her replenished pipe with a taper, and leaned back, smoking, in the doorway, her scarlet handkerchief making a spot of colour on the dull background.

The sun was still high when the judge came out upon his porch, a smile of indecision on his face and his hat in his hand. Pausing upon the topmost step, he cast an uncertain glance sideways at the walk leading past the church, and then looked straight ahead through the avenue of maples, which began at the smaller green facing the ancient site of the governor's palace and skirted the length of the larger one, which took its name from the courthouse. At last he descended the steps with his leisurely tread, turning at the gate to throw a remonstrance to an old negro whose black face was framed in the library window.

" Now, Cæsar, didn't I——"

" Lord, Marse George, dis yer washed-out blue bowl, wid de little white critters sprawlin' over it, done come ter pieces——"

" Now, Cæsar, haven't I told you twenty times to let Delilah wash my Wedgwood? "

" Fo' de Lord, Marse George, I ain't breck hit. I uz des' hol'n it in bofe my han's same es I'se hol'n dis yer broom, w'en it come right ter part.   I declar 'twarn my fault, Marse George, 'twarn nobody's fault 'cep'n hit's own."

The judge closed the gate and waved the face from the window.

" Go about your business, Cæsar," he said, " and keep your hands off my china——"

Then his tone lost its asperity as he held out his hands to a pretty girl who was coming across the green.

"So you are back from school, Miss Juliet," he said gallantly. "I was telling your mother only yesterday that I didn't approve of sending our fairest products away from Kingsborough. It wasn't done in my day. Then the prettiest girls stayed at home and gave our young fellows a chance."

The girl shook her head until the blue ribbons on her straw hat fluttered in the wind, and blushed until her soft eyes were like forget-me-nots set in rose leaves. She possessed a serene, luminous beauty, which became intensified beneath the gaze of the beholder.

"I have come back for good, now," she answered in a serious sweetness of voice; "and I am out this afternoon looking up my Sunday-school class. The children have scattered sadly. You will let me have Tom again, won't you?"

"Have Tom! Why, you may have him every day and Sunday too—the lucky scamp! Ah, I only wish I were a boy again, with a soul worth saving and such a pair of eyes in search of it."

The girl dimpled into a smile and flushed to her low, white forehead, on which the soft hair was smoothly parted before it broke into sunny curls about the temples. She exhaled an atmosphere of gentleness mixed with a saintly coquetry, which produced an impression at once human and divine, such as one receives from the sight of a rose in a Bible or a curl in the hair of a saint. The judge looked at her warmly, sighing half happily, half regretfully.

2

" And to think that the young rogues don't realise their blessings," he said.   " There's not one of them that wouldn't rather be off fishing than learn his catechism.   Ah, in my day things were different—things were different."

" Were you very pious, sir? " asked the girl with a flash of laughter.

The judge shook his stick playfully.

" I can't tell tales," he answered, " but in my day we should have taken more than the catechism at your bidding, my dear.   When your father was courting your mother—and she was like you, though she hadn't your eyes, or your face, for that matter—he went into her Bible class, though he was at least five and twenty and the others were small boys under ten.   She was a sad flirt, and she led him a dance."

" He liked it," said the girl.   " But, if you will give my message to Tom, I won't come in.   I am looking for Dudley Webb, and I see his mother at her gate.   Good-bye!   Be sure and tell Tom to come Sunday."

She nodded brightly, lifted her muslin skirts, and recrossed the street.   The judge watched her until the flutter of her white dress vanished down the lane of maples; then he turned to speak to the occupants of a carriage that had drawn up to the sidewalk.

The vehicle was of an old-fashioned make, bare of varnish, with rickety, mud-splashed wheels and rusty springs.   It was drawn by an ill-matched pair of horses and driven by a lame coloured boy, who carried a peeled hickory branch for a whip.

" Ah, General Battle," said the judge to a stout

gentleman with a red face and an expansive shirt front from which the collar had wilted away; " fine afternoon ! Is that Eugenia? " to a little girl of seven or eight years, with a puppy of the pointer breed in her arms, and " How are you, Sampson? " to the coloured driver.

The three greeted him simultaneously, whereupon he leaned forward, resting his hand upon the side of the carriage.

" The young folks are growing up," he said.   " I have just seen Juliet Burwell, and, on my life, she gets prettier every day. We shan't keep her long."

" Keep her! " replied the general vigorously, wiping his large face with a large pocket handkerchief. " Keep her! If I were thirty years younger, you shouldn't keep her a day—not a day, sir."

The little girl looked up gravely from the corner of the seat, tossing her short, dark plait from her shoulder. " What would you do with her, papa? " she asked.   " We've got no place to put her at home."

The general threw back his great head and laughed till his wide girth shook like a bag of meal.

" Oh, you needn't worry, Eugie," he said.   " I'm not the man I used to be.   She wouldn't look at me. Bless your heart, she wouldn't look at me if I asked her——"

Eugenia clasped her puppy closer and turned her eyes upon her father's jovial face.

" I don't see how she could help it if you stood in front of her," she answered gravely, in a voice rich with the blending of negro intonations.

The general shook again until the carriage

creaked on its rusty springs, and the coloured boy, Sampson, let the reins fall and joined in the hilarity.

" She won't let me so much as look at a girl! " exclaimed the general delightedly, stooping to recover the brown linen lap robe which had slipped from his knees. " She's as jealous as if I were twenty and had a score of sweethearts."

The little girl did not reply, but she flushed angrily. " Don't, precious," she said to the puppy, who was licking her cheek with his warm, red tongue.

" What have you named him, Eugie? " asked the judge, changing the subject with that gracious tact which was mindful of the least emergency. " He is nicely marked, I see."

" I call him Jim," replied Eugenia. She spoke gravely, and the gravity contrasted oddly with the animation of her features. " But his real name is James Burwell Battle. Bernard and I christened him in the spring-house—so he'll go to heaven."

" Cap'n Burwell gave him to her, you know," explained the general, who laughed whenever his daughter spoke, as if the fact of her talking at all was a source of amazement to him, " and she hasn't let go of him since she got him. By the way, Judge, you have a first-rate garden spot. I hear your asparagus is the finest in town. Ours is very poor this year. I must have a new bed made before next season. Ah, what is it, daughter? "

" You've forgotten to buy the sugar," said Eugenia, " and Aunt Chris can't put up her preserves. And you told me to remind you of the whip——"

" Bless your heart, so I did. Sampson lost that whip a month ago, and I've never remembered it yet. Well, good-day—good-day."

The judge raised his hat with a stately inclination; the general nodded good-naturedly, still grasping the linen robe with his plump, red hand; and the carriage jolted along the green and disappeared behind the glazed brick walls of the church.

The judge regarded his walking-stick meditatively for a moment, and continued his way. The smile with which he had followed the vanishing figure of Juliet Burwell returned to his face, and his features softened from their usual chilly serenity.

He had gone but a short distance and was passing the iron gate of the churchyard, when the droning of a voice came to him, and looking beyond the bars, he saw little Nicholas Burr lying at full length upon a marble slab, his head in his hands and his feet waving in the air.

Entering the gate, the judge followed the walk of moss-grown stones leading to the church steps, and paused within hearing of the voice, which went on in an abstracted drawl.

" The most cel-e-bra-ted sys-tem of juris-pru-dence known to the world begins, as it ends, with a code——" He was not reading, for the book was closed. He seemed rather to be repeating over and over again words which had been committed to memory.

" With a code. From the commencement to the close of its history, the ex-posi-tors of Ro-man Law con-sistently em-ployed lan-guage which implied that the body of their sys-tem rested on the twelve

De-cem-vi-ral   Tables—Dec-em-vi-ral—De-cem-vi-ral Tables."

" Bless my soul! " said the judge. The boy glanced up, blushed, and would have risen, but the judge waved him back.

" No—no, don't get up. I heard you as I was going by. What are you doing? "

" Learnin'."

" Learning! Dear me! What do you mean by learning? "

" I'm learnin' by heart, sir—and—and, if you don't mind, sir, what does j-u-r-i-s-p-r-u-d-e-n-c-e mean? "

The judge started, returning the boy's eager gaze with one of kindly perplexity.

" Bless my soul! " he said again. " You aren't trying to understand that, are you? "

The boy grew scarlet and his lips trembled. " No, sir," he answered. " I'm jest learnin' it now. I'll know what it means when I'm bigger—— "

" And you expect to remember it? " asked the judge.

" I don't never forget," said the boy.

" Bless my soul! " exclaimed the judge for the third time.

For a moment he stood looking silently down upon the marble slab with its defaced lettering. Of the wordy epitaph which had once redounded to the honour of the bones beneath there remained only the words " who departed," but he read these with a long abstracted gaze.

" Let me see," he said at last, speaking with his

accustomed dignity. " Did you ever go to school,
Nicholas? "

" Yes, sir."

" When? "

" I went 'most three winters, sir, but I had to leave
off on o'count o' pa's not havin' any hand 'cep'n
me."

The judge smiled.

" Ah, well," he returned. " We'll see if you can't
begin again. My boy has a tutor, you know, and
his playmates come to study with him. He's about
your age, and it will give you a start. Come in to-
morrow at nine, and we'll talk it over. No, don't
get up. I am going."

And he passed out of the churchyard, closing
the heavy gate with a metallic clang. Nicholas lay
on the marble slab, but the book slipped from his
hands, and he gazed straight before him at the oriel
window, where the ivy was tremulous with the shining bodies and clamorous voices of nesting sparrows.
They darted swiftly from gable to gable, filling the
air with shrill sounds of discord, and endowing with
animation the inanimate pile, wrapping the dead
bricks in a living shroud.

On the other side swept the long, colourless
grasses, rippling in faint waves like a still lake that
reflects the sunshine and swaying lightly beneath
myriads of gauzy-winged bees that flashed with a
droning noise from blade to blade, to find rest in the
yellow hearts of the damask roses. Across the white
vaults and the low-lying marble slabs innumerable
shadows chased, and from above the gnarled old
locust trees swept a fringe of vivid green, the slender

blossoms hanging in tassels from the branches' ends, and filling the air with a soft and ceaseless rain of fragrant petals. Pale as the ghosts of dead leaves, they fell always, fluttering night and day from the twisted boughs, settling in creamy flakes upon the bending grasses, and outlining in delicate tracery the epitaphs upon the discoloured marbles.

Nicholas lay with wide-open eyes, looking up at the oriel window where the sparrows twittered. On a near vault a catbird poised for an instant, surveying him with bright, distrustful eyes. Then, with an impetuous flutter of slate-gray wings, it fled to the poisonous oak on the far brick wall. A red-and-white cow, passing along the lane outside, stopped before the closed gate, and stood philosophically chewing the cud as she looked within through impeding bars. From the judge's garden came the faint sound of a negro voice as the old gardener weeded the vegetables. Nicholas rolled over again and faced the outstretched wings of the noseless angel on the nearest tombstone. The loss of the nose had distorted the marble smile into a grimace, which gave a leer to the remaining features. As the boy looked at it he laughed suddenly, and his voice startled him amid the droning of bees. Then he sat up and glanced at his brier-scratched feet stretched upon the slab, and laughed again for the sheer joy of discord.

III

Nicholas followed the main street to its sudden end at King's College, and turned into one of the diverging ways which skirted the whitewashed plank fence of the college grounds, and led to what was known in the neighbourhood as the Old Stage Road. Passing a straggling group of negro cabins, it stretched, naked, bleached, and barren, for a good half-mile, dividing with its sandy length the low-lying fields, which were sown on the one side in a sparse crop of grain and on the other in the rich leaves and round pink heads of ripening clover. At the end of the half-mile the road ascended a slight elevation, and the character of the soil changed abruptly into clay of vivid red, which, extending a dozen yards up the rain-washed hillside, appeared, in a general view of the landscape, like the scarlet tongue protruding from the silvery body of a serpent.

Far ahead to the right of the highway and beyond the thinly sown wheat a stretch of pine woodland was darkly limned against the western horizon, standing a gloomy advance guard of the shadows of the night. At its foot the newer green of the late spring foliage took a frivolous aspect, presenting the effect of deep-tinted foam breaking against the impenetrable mass of darkness.

The boy trudged resolutely along the sandy road,

reaching at intervals to grasp handfuls of sassafras leaves from the bushes beside the way. From the ditch on the left a brown toad hopped slowly into the dust of the road. On the worm-eaten rails of the fence, on the other side, a gray lizard glided swiftly like a stealthy shadow of the leaves of the poisonous oak.

Nicholas picked up a stone from the roadside and aimed it at the slimy little body, but his throw erred, and the missile fell harmlessly into the wheat field beyond, startling a blackbird with scarlet marks, which soared suddenly above the bearded grain and vanished, with a tremulous cry and a flame of outstretched wings, into the distant wood.

The sun had gone down behind the pines and a warm mist steamed up from the cooling earth, condensing into heavy dew on the dusty leaves of the plants in the ditch. Above the lowering pines the horizon burned to a deep scarlet, like an inverted brazier at red heat, and one gigantic tree, rising beyond the jagged line of the forest, was silhouetted sharply against the enkindled clouds. Suddenly, from the shadows of the long road, a voice rose plaintively. It was rich and deep and colourific, and it seemed to hover close to the warmth of the earth, weighed down by its animal melody. It had mingled so subtly with the stillness that it was as much a part of nature as the cry of a whip-poor-will beyond the thicket or the sunset in the pine-guarded west. At first it came faintly, and the words were lost, but as Nicholas gained upon the singer he caught more clearly the air and the song.

> *" Oh, de Ark hit came ter res'*
> *On-de-hill,*
> *Oh, de Ark hit came ter res'*
> *On-de-hill,*
> *En' dar ole Noah stood,*
> *En' spread his han's abroad,*
> *Er sacri-fice ter-Gawd*
> *On-de-hill."*

Nicholas quickened his pace into a run and, in a moment, saw the stooping figure of an old negro toiling up the red clay hillside, a staff in his hand and a bag of meal on his shoulder. In the vivid light of the sunset his stature was exaggerated in size, giving him an appearance at once picturesque and pathetic—softening his rugged outline and magnifying the distortion of age.

As he ascended the gradual incline he planted his staff firmly in the soil, shifting his bag from side to side and uttering inaudible grunts in the pauses of his song.

> *" En' dar, mid flame en smoke,*
> *De great Jehovah s-poke,*
> *En' awful thunder b-roke,*
> *On-de-hill."*

"Uncle Ish!" called the boy sharply. The old man lowered the bag from his shoulder and turned slowly round.

"Who dat?" he demanded severely. "Ain't I done tell you dar ain' no ha'nts 'long dis yer road?"

"It's me, Uncle Ish," said the boy. "It's Nick Burr. I heard you singing a long ways off."

"Den what you want ter go a-hollerin' en a-stealin' up on er ole nigger fer des' 'bout sundown?"

" But, Uncle Ish, I didn't mean to scare you. I jest heard——"

" Skeer! Who dat you been skeerin'? Ain't I done tole you dar ain' no ha'nts round dese parts? What I gwine ter be skeered fer uv er little no 'count white trash dat ain' never own er nigger in dere life? Who you done skeer dis time?"

He picked up his bag, slung it over his shoulder and went on his way, the boy trotting beside him. For a time the old man muttered angrily beneath his breath, and then, becoming mollified by the boy's silence, he looked kindly down on the small red head at his elbow.

" You ain't said howdy, honey," he·remarked in a fault-finding tone. " Dar ain' no manners dese days, nohow. Dey ain' no manners en dey ain' no nuttin'. De niggers, dey is gwine plum outer dey heads, en de po' white trash dey's gwine plum outer dey places."

He looked at Nicholas, who flinched and hung his head.

" Dar ain' nobody lef' to keep 'em ter dey places, no mo'. In Ole Miss' time der wa'nt no traipsin' roun' er niggers en intermixin' up er de quality en de trash. Ole Miss, she des' pint out der place en dey stay dar. She ain' never stomach noner der high-ferlutin' doin's roun' her. She know whar she b'long en she know whar dey b'long. Bless yo' life, Ole Miss wuz dat perticklar she wouldn't drink arter Ole Marster, hisself, 'thout renchin' out de gow'd twel t'wuz mos' bruck off de handle."

He sighed and shifted his bag.

" Ef Ole Miss 'ud been yer thoo' dis las' war, dar

wouldn't er been no slue-footed Yankees a-foolin'
roun' her parlour. She'd uv up en show'd 'em de
do'——"

" Are all Yankees slue-footed, Uncle Ish ? "

" All dose I seed, honey—des' es slue-footed. En
dar wuz Miss Chris' en ole Miss Grissel a-makin'
up ter 'em, en a-layin' out er demselves fer 'em en
a-spreadin' uv de table, des' de same es ef dey went
straight on dey toes. Dar wan't much sense in dat
ar war, nohow, an' I ain' never knowed yit what
'twuz dey fit about. Hit wuz des' a-hidin' en a-
teckin' ter de bushes, en a-hidin' agin, en den a-
feastin', en a-curtsin' ter de Yankees. Dar wan't
no sense in it, no ways hits put, but Ise heered Marse
Tom 'low hit wuz a civil war, en dat's what it wuz.
When de Yankees come a-ridin' up en a-reinin' in
dere hosses befo' de front po'ch, en Miss Chris come
out a-smilin' en a-axin' howdy, en den dey stan' dar
a-bowin' en a-scrapin', hit wuz des' es civil es ef
dey'd come a-co'tin'. But Ole Miss wuz dead en
buried, she wuz."

Nicholas shook his head without speaking. There
was a shade of consolation in the thought that the
awful " Ole Miss " was below the earth and beyond
the possibility of pointing out his place.

The brazier in the west snapped asunder suddenly,
and a single forked flame shot above the jagged
pines and went out in the dove-coloured clouds. In
a huge oak beyond the rail fence there was a harsh
rustling of wings where a flock of buzzards settled to
roost.

" Yes, Lord, she wuz dead en buried," repeated
Uncle Ish slowly. " En dar ain' none like her lef'

roun' yer now. Dis yer little Euginny is des' de
spit er her ma, en it 'ud mek Ole Miss tu'n in her
grave ter hear tell 'bout her gwines on. De quality
en de po' folks is all de same ter her. She ain' no
mo' un inspecter er pussons den de Lord is—ef Ole
Miss wuz 'live, I reckon she'd lam 'er twel she wuz
black en blue——"

" Is she so very bad? " asked Nicholas in an awed
voice.

Uncle Ish turned upon him reprovingly.

" Bad! " he repeated.   " Who gwine call Ole
Miss' gran'chile bad?   I don't reckon it's dese yer
new come folks es hev des' sprouted outer de dut
es is gwine ter——"

At this instant the sound of a vehicle reached
them, gaining upon them from the direction of
Kingsborough, and they fell to one side of the road,
leaving room for the horses to pass. It was the
Battle carriage, rolling heavily on its aged wheels
and creaking beneath the general's weight.

" Howdy, Marse Tom! " called Uncle Ishmael.
The general responded good-naturedly, and the carriage passed on, but, before turning into the branch
road a few yards ahead, it came to a standstill, and
the bright, decisive voice of the little girl floated
back.

" Uncle Ish—I say, Uncle Ish, don't you want to
ride? "

" Dar, now! " cried Uncle Ishmael exultantly.
" Ain't I tell you she wuz plum crazy?   What she
doin' a-peckin' up en ole nigger like I is? "

He hastened his steps and scrambled into the seat
beside the driver, settling his bag between his knees ;

and, with a flick of the peeled hickory whip, the carriage rolled into the branch road and disappeared, scattering a whirl of mud drops as it splashed through the shallow puddles which lingered in the dryest season beneath the heavy shade of the wood.

Nicholas turned into the branch road also, for the poor lands of his father adjoined the slightly richer ones of the Battles. He felt tired and a little lonely, and he wished suddenly that a friendly cart would come along in which he might ride the remainder of the way. Between the densely wooded thicket on either side, the road looked dark and solemn. It was spread with a rotting carpet of last year's leaves, soft and damp under foot, and polished into shining tracks in the ruts left by passing wheels. Through the dusk the ghostly bodies of beech trees stood out distinctly from the surrounding wood, as if marked by a silver light falling from the topmost branches. The hoarse, grating notes of jar-flies intensified the stillness.

Nicholas went on steadily, spurred by superstitious terror of the silence. He remembered that Uncle Ish had said there were no " ha'nts " along this road, but the assurance was barren of comfort. Old Uncle Dan'l Mule had certainly seen a figure in a white sheet rise up out of that decayed oak stump in the hollow, for he had sworn to it in the boy's presence in Aunt Rhody Sand's cabin the night of her daughter Viny's wedding. As for Viny's husband Saul, he had declared that one night after ten o'clock, when he was coming through this wood, the " booger-boos " had got after him and chased him home.

At the end of the wood the road came out upon the open again, and in the distance Nicholas could see, like burnished squares, the windows of his father's house. Between the thicket and the house there was a long stretch of clearing, which had been once planted in corn, and now supported a headless army of dry stubble, amid a dull-brown waste of brooms-edge. The last pale vestige of the afterglow, visible across the level country, swept the arid field and softened the harsh outlines of the landscape. It was barren soil, whose strength had been exhausted long since by years of production without returns, tilled by hands that had forced without fertilising. There was now grim pathos in its absolute sterility, telling as it did of long-gone yields of grain and historic harvests.

Nicholas skirted the waste, and was turning into the pasture gate on the opposite side of the road, when he heard the shrill sound of a voice from the direction of the house.

" Nick!—who—a Nick!"

On one of the cedar posts of the fence of the cow-pen he discerned the small figure and green cotton frock of his half-sister, Sarah Jane, who was shouting through her hollowed palms to increase the volume of sound.

" I say, Nick! The she-ep hev' been driv-en u-p! Come to sup-per!"

She vanished from the post and Nicholas ran up the remainder of the road and swung himself over the little gate which led into the small square yard immediately surrounding the house. At the pump near the back door his father, who had just come from work, was washing his hands before going into supper, and near a row of pointed chicken coops the three younger children were " shooing " up the tiny yellow broods. The yard was unkempt and ugly, run wild in straggling ailanthus shoots and littered with chips from the wood-pile.

As he entered the house he saw his stepmother placing a dish of fried bacon upon the table, which was covered with a " watered " oilcloth of a bright walnut tint. At her back stood Sarah Jane with a plate of corn bread in one hand and a glass pitcher containing buttermilk in the other. She was a slight, flaxen-haired child, with wizened features and sore, red eyelids.

As his stepmother caught sight of him she stopped on her way to the stove and surveyed him with sharp but not unkindly eyes.

" You've been takin' your time 'bout comin' home," she remarked, " an' I reckon you're powerful hungry. You can sit down if you want to."

She was long and lean and withered, with a chronic facial neuralgia, which gave her an irritable expression and a querulous voice. For the past several years Nicholas had never seen her without a large cotton handkerchief bound tightly about her face. She had been the boy's aunt before she married his father, and her affection for him was proved by her allowing no one to harry him except herself.

" How's your face, ma?" asked Nicholas with the indifference of habit as he took his seat at the table, while Sarah Jane went to the door to call her father. When Burr came in the inquiry was repeated.

" Face any easier, Marthy?" It was a form that

had been gone through with at every meal since the malady began, and Marthy Burr, while she deplored its insincerity, would have resented its omission.

"Don't you all trouble 'bout my neuralgy," she returned with resigned exasperation as she stood up to pour the coffee out of the large tin boiler. "It's mine, an' I've borne worse things, I reckon, which ain't sayin' that 'tain't near to takin' my head off."

Amos Burr drank his coffee without replying, the perspiration standing in drops on his large, freckled face and shining on his heavy eyebrows. Presently he looked at Nicholas, who was eating abstractedly, his gaze on his plate.

"I got that thar piece of land broke to-day," he said, "an' I reckon you can take the one-horse harrow and go over it to-morrow. Them peanuts ought to hev' been in the ground two weeks ago——"

"They ain't hulled yet," interrupted his wife. "Sairy Jane ain't done more'n half of 'em. She and Nick can do the balance after supper. Hurry up, Sairy Jane, and get through. Nannie, don't you touch another slice of that middlin'. You'll be frettin' all night."

Nicholas looked up nervously. "I don't want to harrow the land to-morrow, pa," he began; "the judge said I might come in to school——"

Amos Burr looked at him helplessly. "Wall, I never!" he exclaimed.

"Did you ever hear the likes?" said his wife.

"I can go, pa, can't I?" asked Nicholas.

"He can go, pa, can't he?" repeated Sarah Jane, looking up with her mouth wide open and full of corn bread.

Burr shook his head and looked at his wife.

"I don't see as I can get any help," he said.
"You're as good as a hand, and I can't spare you."
Then he concluded with a touch of irritation, "I
don't see as you want any more schoolin'. You can
read and write now a heap better'n I can."

Nicholas choked over his bread and his lips trembled.

"I—I don't want to be like you, pa!" he cried
breathlessly, and the unshed tears stung his eyelids.
"I want to be different!"

Burr looked up stolidly. "I don't see as you
want any more schoolin'," he repeated stubbornly,
but his wife came sharply to the boy's assistance.

"I wish you'd stop pesterin' the child, Amos,"
she said, inspired less by the softness of amiability
than by the genius of opposition. "I don't see how
you can be everlastingly doin' it—my dead sister's
child, too."

Nicholas swallowed his tears with his coffee and
turned to his father. "I can get up 'fore day and do
a piece of the land, and I can help you 'bout the
sowin' when I get back in the evening. I'll be back
by twelve——"

"Oh, I reckon you can go if you're so set on it,"
said Amos gruffly. He rose and left the room, stopping in the hall to get a bucket of buttermilk for
the hogs. Nicholas went over to the window and
joined Sarah Jane, who was shelling the peanuts,
carefully separating the outer hulls from the inner
pink skins, which were left intact for sowing.
Marthy Burr, who was clearing off the table, let fall

a china dish and began scolding the younger children.

"I declare, if you don't all but drive me daft!" she said, flinching from a twinge of neuralgia and raising her voice querulously. "Why can't you take yourselves off and give me some rest? Nannie, you and Jake go out to the old oak and see if all the turkeys air up. Be sure and count 'em—and take Jubal (the youngest) 'long with you. If you see your pa tell him I say to look at the brindle cow. She acted mighty queer at milkin', and I reckon she'd better have a little bran mash—Sairy Jane," turning suddenly upon her eldest daughter, "if you eat another one of them peanuts I'll box your jaws——"

Nicholas finished the peanuts and went upstairs to his little attic room. He was not sleepy, and, after throwing himself upon his corn-shuck mattress, he lay for a long time staring at the ceiling, thinking of the morrow and listening to the groans of his stepmother as she tossed with neuralgia.

IV

In the first glimmer of dawn Nicholas dressed himself and stole softly down from the attic, the frail stairway creaking beneath his tread. As he was unfastening the kitchen door, which led out upon a rough plank platform called the "back porch," Marthy Burr stuck her head in from the adjoining room where she slept, and called his name in a high-pitched, querulous voice.

"Is that you, Nick?" she asked. "I declar, I'd jest dropped off to sleep when you woke me comin' down stairs. I never could abide tip-toein', nohow. I don't see how 'tis that I can't get no rest 'thout bein' roused up, when your pa can turn right over and sleep through thunder. Whar you goin' now?"

Nicholas stopped and held a whispered colloquy with her from the back porch. "I'm goin' to drag the land some 'fore pa gets up," he answered. "Then I'm goin' in to town. You know he said I might."

His stepmother shook her bandaged head peevishly and stood holding the collar of her unbleached cotton gown.

"Oh, I reckon so," she responded. "I was thinkin' 'bout goin' in myself and hevin' my tooth out, but I s'pose I can wait on you. The Lord knows I'm used to waitin'."

Nicholas looked at her in perplexity, his arm resting on the little shelf outside, which supported the wooden water bucket and the long-handled gourd.

"You can go when I come back," he said at last, adding with an effort, "or, if it's so bad, I can stay at home."

But, having asserted her supremacy over his inclinations, Marthy Burr relented. "Oh, I don't know as I'll go in to-day," she returned. "I ain't got enough teeth left now to chew on, an' I don't believe it's the teeth, nohow. It's the gums——"

She retreated into the room, whence the shrill voice of Sairy Jane inquired:

"Air you up, ma? Why, 'tain't day!"

Nicholas closed the door and went out upon the porch. The yard looked deserted and desolated, giving him a sudden realisation of his own littleness and the immensity of the hour. It was as if the wheels of time had stopped in the dim promise of things unfulfilled. A broken scythe lay to one side amid the straggling ailanthus shoots; near the woodpile there was a wheelbarrow half filled with chips, and at a little distance the axe was poised upon a rotten log. From the small coops beside the henhouse came an anxious clucking as the fluffy yellow chickens strayed beneath the uneven edges of their pointed prisons and made independent excursions into the world.

In the far east the day was slowly breaking, and the open country was flooded with pale, washed-out grays, like the background of an impressionist painting. A heavy dew had risen in the night, and as the boy passed through the dripping weeds on his way to the stable they left a chill moisture upon his bare

feet. His eyes were heavy with sleep, and to his
cloudy gaze the familiar objects of the barnyard
assumed grotesque and distorted shapes. The
manure heap near the doorway presented an effect
of unreality, the pig-pen seemed to have suffered
witchery since the evening before, and the haystack,
looming vaguely in the drab distance, appeared to
be woven of some phantasmal fabric.

He led out the old sorrel mare and followed her
into the large ploughed field beyond the cow-pen,
where the harrow was lying on one side of the brown
ridges. As he passed the pen the startled sheep
huddled into a far corner, bleating plaintively, and
the brindle cow looked after him with soft, persuasive eyes. When he had attached the clanking
chains of the plough harness to the single-tree, he
caught up the ropes which served for reins and set
out laboriously over the crumbling earth, which
yielded beneath his feet and made walking difficult.

The field extended from the cow-pen and the
bright, green rows of vegetables that were raised for
market to the reedy brook which divided his father's
land from that belonging to General Battle. The
brook was always cool and shady, and silvery with
minnows darting over the shining pebbles beneath
the clear water. As Nicholas looked across the
neutral furrows he could see the feathery branches
of willows rising from the gray mist, and, farther
still up the sloping hillside, the dew-drenched green
of the mixed woodlands.

The land before him had been upturned by shallow ploughing some days since, and it lay now pale
and arid, the large clods of earth showing the de-

tached roots of grass and herbs, and presenting a hint of menacing destruction rather than the prospect of the peaceful art of cultivation. It was the boy's duty to drag the soil free from grass, after which it would be laid out into rows some three feet apart. When this was done two furrows would be thrown together to give what the farmers called a "rise," the point of which would be finally levelled, when the ground would be ready for the peanut-sowing, which was performed entirely by hand.

The boy worked industriously through the deepening dawn, giving an occasional "gee up, Rhody!" to the mare, and following the track of the harrow with much the same concentration of purpose as that displayed by his four-footed friend. He was strong for his years, lithe as a sapling, and as fearless of elemental changes, and as he walked meditatively across the bare field he might have suggested to an onlooker the possible production of a vast fund of energy.

Presently the gray light was shot with gold and a streak of orange fluttered like a ribbon in the east. In a moment a violet cloud floated above the distant hill, and as its ends curled up from the quickening heat it showed the splendour of a crimson lining. A single ray of sunshine, pale as a spectral finger, pointed past the woodlands to the brook beneath the willows, and the vague blur of the mixed forest warmed into vivid tints, changing through variations from the clear emerald of young maples to the olive dusk of evergreens.

Last of all the ploughed field, which had preserved a neutral cast, blushed faintly in the sunrise, glow-

ing to pale purple tones where the sod was newly
turned. From the fugitive richness of the soil a
warm breath rose suddenly, filling the air with the
genial odour of earth and sunshine. The shining,
dark coils of worms were visible like threads in the
bright brown clods.

Nicholas raised his head and stared with unseeing
eyes at the gorgeous east. A rooster crowed shrilly,
and he turned in the direction of the barnyard.
Then he flicked the ropes gently and went on, his
gaze on the ground. His thoughts, which at first
were fixed solely upon the teeth of the harrow, took
tumultuous flight, and he reviewed for the hun-
dredth time his conversation with the judge and
the vast avenue of the future which was opening before him. He would not be like his father, of this
he was convinced—his father, who was always working with nothing to show for it—whose planting was
never on time, and whose implements were never in
place. His father had never had this gnawing desire to know things, this passionate hatred of the
work which he might not neglect. His father had
never tried to beat against the barriers of his ignorance and been driven back, and beat again and wept,
and read what he couldn't understand. The teacher
at the public school had told him that he was far
ahead of his years, and yet they had taken him away
when he was doing his level best, and put him to
dragging the land, and gathering the peanuts, and
carrying the truck to market, and marking the sheep
with red paint, and bringing up the cows, and doing
all the odd, innumerable jobs they could devise. He
let the ropes fall for an instant and dug his fist into

his eye; then he took them up again and went on stolidly. At last the sun came out boldly above the hill, and the hollows were flooded with light. In the centre of the field the boy's head glowed like some large red insect. A hawk, winging slowly above him, looked down as if uncertain of his species, and fluttered off indifferently.

At six o'clock his stepmother came to the back door and called him to breakfast.

When the meal was over Amos Burr went out to the field, and Nicholas was sent to drive the sheep to the pasture. With vigorous wavings of a piece of brushwood, and many darts from right to left, he succeeded finally in driving them across the road and through the gate on the opposite side, after which he returned to assist his stepmother about the house. Not until nine o'clock, when he had seen the Battle children going up the road, was he free to set off at a run for Kingsborough.

As he sped breathlessly along, past the waste-lands, into the woods, down the road to the hillside, and down the hillside to the road again, he went too rapidly for thought. The fresh air brushed his heated face gently, and, at the edge of the wood, where the shallow puddles lingered, myriads of blue and yellow butterflies scattered into variegated clumps of colour at his approach, darting from the moist heaps of last year's leaves to the shining rivulets in the wheel ruts by the way. A partridge whistled from the yellowing green of the wheat, and a rabbit stole noiselessly from the sassafras in the ditch and shot shy glances of alarm; but he did not turn his head, and his hand held no ready stone.

Though he had run half the way, when at last he reached the judge's house, and stood before the little office in the garden where the school was held, his courage misgave him, and he leaned, trembling, against the arbour where a grapevine grew. The sound of voices floated out to him, mingled with bright, girlish laughter, and, looking through the open window, he saw the light curls of a little girl against the darker head of a boy. He choked suddenly with shyness, and would have hesitated there until the morning was over had not the judge's old servant, Cæsar, espied him from the dining-room window.

"Look yer, boy, what you doin' dar?" he demanded suspiciously, and then called to some one inside the house. "Marse George, dat ar Burr boy is a-loungin' roun' yo' yawd."

The judge did not respond, but the tutor came to the door of the office and intercepted the boy's retreat. He was a pale, long-faced young man in spectacles, with weak, blue eyes and a short, thin moustache. His name was Graves, and he regarded what he called the judge's "quixotism" with condescending good-nature.

"Is that you, Nicholas Burr?" he asked in a slightly supercilious voice. "The judge has told me about you. So you won't be a farmer, eh? And you won't stay in your class? Well, come in and we'll see what we can make of you."

Nicholas followed him into the room and sat down at one of the pine desks, while the judge's son, Tom, nodded to him from across the room, and Bernard Battle grinned over his shoulder at his

sister Eugenia, and a handsome boy, called Dudley
Webb, made a face which convulsed little Sally
Burwell, who hid her merriment in her curls. There
were several other children in the room, but Nicholas did not see them distinctly. Something had got
before his eyes and there was a lump in his throat.
He sat rigidly in his seat, his straw hat, with the
shoestring around the crown, lying upon the desk
before him. He looked neither to the right nor to
the left, keeping his frightened gaze upon the tutor's
face.

Mr. Graves asked him a few questions, which he
could not answer, and then, giving him a book,
turned to the other children. As the lessons went
on it seemed to Nicholas that he had never known
anything in his life; that he should never know anything; and that he should always remain the most
ignorant person on earth—unless that lot fell to
Sairy Jane.

The difficulties besetting the path of knowledge
appeared to be insurmountable. Even if he had the
books and the time he could never learn anything—
his head would prevent it.

" Bound Beloochistan, Tom," said the tutor, and
Tom, a stout, fair-haired boy with a heavy face, went
through the process to the satisfaction of Mr. Graves
and to the amazement of Nicholas.

The office was a plain, square room, containing,
besides the desks and tables, an old secretary and
a corner cupboard of an antique pattern, which held
an odd assortment of cracked china and chemist
bottles. There was also a square mahogany chest,
called the wine-cellar, which had been sent from the

dining-room when the last bottle of Tokay was opened to drink the health of the Confederacy.

Before the war the place had been used by the judge as a general business room, but when the slaves were freed and there were fewer servants it was found to be little needed, and was finally given over entirely to the children's school.

When recess came the tutor left the office, telling Nicholas that he might go home with the little girls if he liked. " I shall try to have the books you need by to-morrow," he said, and, his natural amiability overcoming his assumed superciliousness, he added pleasantly :

" I shouldn't mind being backward at first. The boys are older than you, but you'll soon catch up."

He went out, and Nicholas had started towards the door, when Tom Bassett flung himself before him, swinging skilfully over an intervening table.

" Hold up, carrot-head," he said. " Let's have a look at you. Are all heads afire where you come from ? "

" He's Amos Burr's boy," explained Bernard Battle with a grin. " He lives 'long our road. I saw him hoeing potatoes day before yesterday. He's got freckles enough to tan a sheepskin ! "

In the midst of the laugh which followed Nicholas stood awkwardly, shifting his bare feet. His face was scarlet, and he fingered in desperation the ragged brim of his hat.

" I reckon they're my freckles," he said doggedly.

" And I reckon you can keep 'em," retorted Bernard, mimicking his tone. " We ain't going to steal 'em. I say, Eugie, here're some freckles for sale ! "

The dark little girl, who was putting up her books in one corner, looked up and shook her head.

"Let me alone!" she replied shortly, and returned to her work, tugging at the straps with both hands. Dudley Webb—a handsome, upright boy, well dressed in a dark suit and linen shirt—lounged over as he munched a sandwich.

He looked at Nicholas from head to foot, and his gaze was returned with stolid defiance. Nicholas did not flinch, but for the first time he felt ashamed of his ugliness, of his coarse clothes, of his briar-scratched legs, of his freckles, and of the unalterable colour of his hair. He wished with all his heart that he were safely in the field with his father, driving the one-horse harrow across upturned furrows. He didn't want to learn anything any more. He wanted only to get away.

"He's common," said Dudley at last, throwing a crust of bread through the open window. "He's as common as—as dirt. I heard mother say so——"

"Father says he's *un*common," returned Tom doubtfully, turning his honest eyes on Nicholas again. "He told Mr. Graves that he was a most uncommon boy."

"Oh, well, you can play with him if you like," rejoined Dudley resolutely, "but I shan't. He's old Amos Burr's son, anyway, who never wore a whole shirt in his life."

"He had on one yesterday," said Bernard Battle impartially. "I saw it. It was just made and hadn't been washed."

Nicholas looked up stubbornly. "You let my father alone!" he exclaimed, spurred by the desire to resent something and finding it easier to fight for another than himself. " You let my father alone, or I'll make you!"

" I'd like to see you!" retorted Dudley wrathfully, and Nicholas had squared up for the first blow, when before his swimming gaze a defender intervened.

" You jest let him alone!" cried a voice, and the flutter of a blue cotton skirt divided Dudley from his adversary. " You jest let him alone. If you call him common I'll hit you, an'—an' you can't hit me back!"

" Eugie, you ought to be——" began Bernard, but she pushed the combatants aside with decisive thrusts of her sunburned little hand, and planted herself upon the threshold, her large, black eyes glowing like shaded lamps.

" He wan't doin' nothin' to you, and you jest let him be. He's goin' to tote my books home, an' you shan't touch him. I reckon I know what's common as well as you do—an' he ain't—he ain't common."

Then she caught Nicholas's arm and marched off like a dispensing providence with a vassal in tow. Nicholas followed obediently. He was sufficiently cowed into non-resistance, and he felt a wholesome awe of his defender, albeit he wished that it had been a boy like himself instead of a slip of a girl with short skirts and a sunbonnet. At the bottom of his heart there existed an instinctive contempt of the sex which Eugenia represented, developed by the fact that it was not force but weakness that had vanquished his victorious opponent. Dudley Webb was a gentleman, and only a bully would strike a girl,

even if she were a spitfire—the term by which he
characterised Eugenia. He remembered suddenly
her exultant, "an' you can't hit me back!" and it
seemed to him that, even in the righteous cause of
his deliverance, she had taken an unfair and feminine
advantage of the handsome boy for whom he cher-
ished a shrinking admiration.

As for Eugenia herself, she was troubled by no
such misgivings. She walked slightly in front of
him, her blue skirt swinging briskly from side to
side, her white sunbonnet hanging by its strings
from her shoulders. Above the starched ruffles rose
her small dark head and white profile, and Nicholas
could see the determined curve of her chin and the
humorous tremor of her nostril. It was a vivid
little face, devoid of colour except for the warm
mouth, and sparkling with animation which burned
steadily at the white heat of intensity—but to Nicholas she was only a plain, dark, little girl, with an un-
healthy pallor of complexion. He was grateful,
nevertheless, and when his first regret that she was
not a boy was over he experienced a thrill of affection. It was the first time that any one had deliberately taken his part in the face of opposing odds,
and the stand seemed to bring him closer to his
companion. He held her books tightly, and his
face softened as he looked at her, until it was transfigured by the warmth of his emotion. Then, as
they passed the college grounds, where a knot of
students greeted Eugenia hilariously, and turned
upon the Old Stage Road, he reached out timidly to
take the small hand hanging by her side.

" It's better walkin' on this side the road," he said

with a mild assumption of masculine supremacy. " I wouldn't walk in the dust."

Eugenia looked at him gravely and drew her hand away.

" You mustn't do that," she responded severely. " When I said you weren't common I didn't mean that you really weren't, you know; because, of course, you are. I jest meant that I wouldn't let them say so."

Nicholas stood in the centre of the road and stared at her, his face flushing and a slow rage creeping into his eyes.

For a moment he stood in trembling silence. Then he threw the books from him into the sand at her feet, and with a choking sob sped past her to vanish amid a whirl of dust in the sunny distance.

Eugenia looked thoughtfully down upon her scattered possessions. She was all alone upon the highway, and around her the open fields rolled off into the green of far-off forests. The sunshine fell hotly over her, and straight ahead the white road lay like a living thing.

She stooped, gravely gathered up the books, and walked resolutely on her way, a cloud of yellow butterflies fluttering like loosened petals of full-blown buttercups about her head.

4

V

Battle Hall was a square white frame house with bright-green window shutters and a deep front porch, supported by heavy pillars, and reached from the gravelled walk below by a flight of rugged stone steps. In the rear of the house, through which a wide hall ran, dividing the rooms of the first floor, there was another porch similar to the one at the front, except that the pillars were hidden in musk roses and the long benches at either side were of plain, unpainted pine. At the foot of the back steps a narrow, well-trodden path led to the vegetable garden, which was separated from the yard by what was called " Cattle Lane "—a name derived from the morning and evening passage of the cows on their way to and from the pasture.

Beginning at the gate into the garden, where the tall white palings were gay with hollyhocks and heavy-headed sunflowers, a grapevine trellis extended to the farmyard at the end of the lane, whence an overgrown walk led across tangled meadows to the negro " quarters "—a long, whitewashed row of almost deserted cabins. Since the close of the war the " quarters " had fallen partly into disuse and had decayed rapidly, though some few were still tenanted by the former slaves, who gathered as of old in the doorways of an evening to strum upon broken-stringed banjos and to wrap the hair of their small offspring. Beyond this row there was a slight ele-

vation called " Hickory Hill," where Uncle Ishmael
had lived for more than seventy years; and at the
foot of the hill, on the other side, near " Sweet Gum
Spring," there were several neatly patched log
cabins occupied by the house servants, who held in
social contempt the field hands in the neighbouring
" quarters." Overlooking the " Sweet Gum Spring,"
on a loftier hill, was the family graveyard, which was
walled off from the orchard near by, where the
twisted old fruit trees had long since yielded the
larger part of their abundance.

At the front of the Hall the view was vastly different. There the great blue-grass lawn was thickly
studded with ancient elms and maples, whose shade
fell like a blanket upon the velvety sod beneath.
The gravelled walk, beginning at the front steps,
was bordered on either side by rows of closely
clipped box, which ended in the long avenue of
cedars leading from the lawn to the distant turnpike.
To the right of the house there were three pointed
aspens, which shivered like skeletons in silver, holding grimly aloof from the vivid pink of the crêpe
myrtle at their feet. Beyond them was the well-
house, with a long moss-grown trough where the
horses and the cows came to drink, and across the
road began the cornlands, which stretched in
rhythmic undulations to the dark belt of the pine
forest. On the left of the box walk, in a direct line
from the three aspens, towered a huge sycamore,
and from one of its protecting arms, shaded by large
fan-like leaves, a child's swing dangled by a thick
hemp rope. Near the sycamore, where an old oak
had fallen, the rotting stump was hidden by a high

" rockery," edged with conch shells, and over the rough gray rocks a tangle of garden flowers ran wild — sweet-william, petunias, phlox, and the mossy stems of red and yellow portulaca. On the western side of the house there was a spreading mimosa tree, its sensitive branches brushing the green shutters of a window in the second story.

The Hall had been built by the general's father when, because of family dissensions, he had decided to move from a central county to the more thinly settled country surrounding Kingsborough. There the general had passed his boyhood, and there he had left his wife when he had gone to the war. At the beginning of the struggle he had freed his slaves and buckled on his sword.

" They may have the negroes, and welcome," he had said to the judge. " Do you think I'd fight for a damned darkey ? It's the principle, sir—the principle! "

And the judge, who had not freed his servants, but who would as soon have thought of using a profane word as of alluding in disrespectful terms to a family portrait, had replied gravely :

" My dear Tom, you will find principle much better to fight for than to live on."

But the general had gone with much valour and more vehemence. He had enlisted as a private, had risen within a couple of years to a colonelcy, and had been raised to the rank of general by the unanimous voice of his neighbours upon his return home. After an enthusiastic reception at Kingsborough he had mounted a heavy-weight horse and ridden out to the Hall, to find the grounds a tangle of weeds and his wife with the pallor of death upon her brow. She had rallied at his coming, had lingered some sad years an invalid in the great room next the parlour, and had died quietly at last as she knelt in prayer beside her high white bed.

For days after this the empty house was like a coffin. The children ran in tears through the shuttered rooms, and the servants lost their lingering shred of discipline. When the funeral was over, the general made some spasmodic show of authority, but his heart was not in it, and he wavered for lack of the sustaining hold of his wife's frail hand. He dismissed the overseer and undertook to some extent the management of the farm, but the crops failed and the hay rotted in the fields before it was got into the barn. Then, as things were galloping from bad to worse, a letter came from his sister, Miss Christina, and in a few days she arrived with a cartload of luggage and a Maltese cat in a wicker basket. From the moment when she stepped out of the carriage at the end of the avenue and ascended the box-trimmed walk to the stone steps, the difficulties disentangled and the domestic problems dwindled into the simplest of arithmetical sums. By some subtle law of the influence of the energetic she assumed at once the rights of authority. From the master of the house to the field hands in the " quarters," all bent to her regenerating rule. She opened the windows in the airy rooms, cleaned off the storeroom shelves with soda and water, and put the marauding small negroes to weeding the lawn. Before her passionate purification the place was purged of the dust of years. The hardwood floors of the wide old halls began to shine like mirrors, the assortment of odds and ends in the attic was relegated to an outhouse, and even the general's aunt, Miss Griselda Grigsby, was turned unceremoniously out of her apartment before the all-pervading soapsuds of cleaning day.

As for the servants, a sudden miraculous zeal possessed them. Within a fortnight the garden rows were hoed free from grass, the hops were gathered from the fence, and the weeds on the lawn vanished beneath small black fingers. Even the annual threshing of the harvest was accomplished under the overseeing eye of " Miss Chris," as she was called by the coloured population. During the week that the old machine poured out its chaffless wheat and the driver whistled in the centre of the treadmill Miss Chris appeared at the barn at noon each day to warn the hands against waste of time and to see that the mules were well watered.

But the revolutions without were as naught to the internal ones. Aunt Verbeny, the cook, whose tyranny had extended over thirty years, was assisted from her pedestal, and the hen-house keys were removed from the nail of the kitchen wall.

" This will never do, Verbeny," said Miss Chris a month after her arrival. " We could not possibly have eaten three dozen chickens within the last week. I am afraid you take them home without asking me."

Aunt Verbeny, a fat old woman with a shining black skin, smoothed her checked apron with offended dignity.

" Hi! Miss Chris, ain't I de cook? " she exclaimed.

But Miss Chris preserved her ground.

"That is no excuse for you taking what doesn't belong to you," she replied severely. "If this keeps up I shall be obliged to let Delphy do the cooking. There won't be a chicken in the hen-house by the end of the month."

Aunt Verbeny still smoothed her apron, but her authority was shaken, and she felt it. She gave a slow grunt of dissatisfaction.

"Dese ain't de doin's I'se used ter," she protested, and then, beneath the undaunted eyes of Miss Chris, she melted into propitiation.

"Des' let dat ar chicken alont, Miss Chris," she said, skilfully reducing the charge to a single offence. "Des' let dat ar chicken alont. 'Tain' no use yo' rilin' yo'se'f 'bout dat. Hit's done en it's been done. Hit don't becomst de quality ter fluster demse'ves over de gwines on uv er low-lifeted fowl. You des' bresh yo'se'f down an steddy like hit ain' been fool you ef you knowed yo'se'f. You des' let dat ar chicken be er little act uv erdultery betweenst you en me. Ef'n it's gone, hit'll stay gone!"

Whereupon Miss Chris retreated, leaving her opponent in possession of the kitchen floor.

But from this day forth the hen-house was locked at night and unlocked in the morning by the hand of Miss Chris, and Aunt Verbeny's overweening ill-temper diminished with her authority.

Miss Chris had been a beauty in her day, but as she passed middle age the family failing seized upon her, and she grew huge and unwieldy, the disproportion of her enormous figure to her small feet giving her an awkward, waddling walk.

She had a profusion of silvery-white hair, worn in fluffy curls about her large pink face, soft brown eyes, and a full double chin that fell over a round cameo brooch bearing the head of Minerva set in a plain gold band. In winter she wore gowns of black Henrietta cloth, made with plain bodices and full plaited skirts; in summer she wore the same skirts with loosely fitting white linen sacques, trimmed in delicate embroideries, with muslin ruffles falling over her plump hands. When she came to the Hall she brought with her innumerable reminiscences of her childhood, which she told in a musical voice with girlish laughter.

After his sister's arrival the general discontinued his fitful overseeing. He rose early and spent his long days sitting upon the front porch, smoking an old briar pipe and reading the Richmond papers. Occasionally he would ride at a jogging pace round the fields, giving casual directions to the workers, but as his weight increased he found it difficult to mount into the saddle, and, at last, desisted from the attempt. He preferred to sit in peace in his cane rocking chair, looking down the box walk into the twilight of the cedar avenue, or gazing placidly beyond the aspens and the well-house to the streaked ribbons of the ripening corn. It was said that he had never been the same man since the death of his wife. Certainly he laughed as heartily and his jovial face had taken a ruddier tint, but there was a superficiality in his exuberant cheerfulness which told that it was not well rooted below the surface. His jokes were as ready as ever, but he had fallen into an absent-minded habit of repetition, and sometimes repeated the same stories at breakfast and supper. He talked freely of his dead wife, he even made ill-placed jests about his widowerhood, and he never failed to kiss a pair of red lips when the chance offered; but, for all that, his gaze often wandered past the huge sycamore to the family graveyard, where rank periwinkle grew and mocking-birds nested. Through the long summer not a Sunday passed that he did not take fresh flowers to one of the neatly trimmed mounds where the marble headpiece read:

"AMELIA TUCKER,

BELOVED WIFE OF

THOMAS BATTLE,

DIED APRIL 3RD., 18—.

'*I am the Resurrection and the Life, saith
the Lord.*'"

Sometimes the children were with him, but usually he went alone, and once or twice he returned with red eyelids and asked for a julep.

There was little to fill his life now, and he divided it between Bernard and Eugenia, whom he adored, and the negroes, whom he reviled for diversion and spoiled to make amends.

"They will break me!" he would declare a dozen times a day. "They will turn me out of house and home. Here's old Sambo's Claudius come back and moved into the quarters. He hasn't a cent to his name, and he's the most no 'count scamp on earth. It's worse than before the war—upon my soul it is!

Then they lived on me and I got an odd piece of work out of them. Now they live on me and don't do a damned lick!"

"My dear Tom!" Miss Chris cheerfully remonstrated. She had long been reconciled to her brother's swearing propensities, which she regarded as an amiable eccentricity to be overlooked by a special indulgence accorded the male sex, but she never knew just how to meet him in a discussion of the servants.

"What is to be done about it?" she inquired gravely. "Claudius left here at the beginning of the war, Aunt Griselda says, and he has never been back until now. It seems he has brought his family. He has lung-trouble."

"Done about it!" repeated the general heatedly. "What's to be done about it? Why, the rascal can't starve. I've just told Sampson to wheel him down a barrel of meal. Oh, they'll break me! I shan't have a morsel left!"

The next time it was an opposite grievance.

"What do you reckon's happened now?" he asked, marching into the brick storeroom, where his sister was slicing ripe, red tomatoes into a blue china bowl. "What do you think that fool Ish has done?"

Miss Chris looked up attentively, her large, fresh-coloured face expressing mild apprehension. She had rolled back her linen sleeves, and the juice of the tomatoes stained her full, dimpled wrists.

"He hasn't killed himself?" she inquired anxiously.

"Killed himself?" roared the general. "He'll live forever. I don't believe he'd die if he were strung up with a halter round his neck. He's moved off."

" Moved off!" echoed Miss Chris faintly. " Why, I believe Uncle Ish was living in that cabin on Hickory Hill before I was born. I remember going up there to help him gather hickory nuts when I wasn't six years old. I couldn't have been six because mammy Betsey was with me, and she died before I was seven. I declare there were always more nuts on those trees than any I ever saw——"

But the general broke in upon her reminiscences, and she took up a fresh tomato and peeled it carefully with a sharp-edged knife.

" Some idiots got after him," said the general, " and told him if he went on living on my land he'd go back to slavery, and, bless your life, he has gone —gone to that little one-room shanty where his daughter used to live, between my place and Burr's —as if I'd have him," he concluded wrathfully. " I wouldn't own that fool again if he dropped into my lap straight from heaven!"

Miss Chris laughed merrily.

" It is the last place he would be likely to drop from," she returned; " but I'll call him up and talk with him. It is a pity for him to be moving off at his age."

So Uncle Ishmael was summoned up to the porch, and Miss Chris explained the error of his ways, but to no purpose.

" I ain' got no fault ter fine," he repeated over and over again, scratching his grizzled head. " I ain' got no fault ter fine wid you. You've been used me moughty well, en I'se pow'ful 'bleeged ter you—en

Marse Tom, he's a gent'mun ef ever I seed one.   I ain' go no fault ter fine."

The general lost his temper and started up.

" Then what do you mean by turning fool at your age? " he demanded angrily.   " Haven't I given you a roof over your head all these years? "

" Dat's so, suh."

" And food to eat? "

" Dat's so."

" And never asked you to do a lick of work since you got the rheumatism? "

" Dat's es true es de Gospel."

" Then what do you mean by going off like mad to that little, broken-down shanty with half the roof gone? "

Uncle Ishmael shuffled his heavy feet and scratched his head again.

" Hit's de trufe, Marse Tom," he said at last. " Hit's de Gospel trufe.   I ain' had so much ter eat sence I'se gone off, en I ain' had much uv er roof ter kiver me, en I ain' had nuttin' ter w'ar ter speak on—but, fo' de Lawd, Marse Tom, freedom it are er moughty good thing."

Then the general flew into the house in a rage and Uncle Ishmael left, followed by two small negroes, bearing on their heads the donations made by Miss Chris to his welfare.

On the day that Eugenia encountered Nicholas at school the general was sitting, as usual, in his rocking chair upon the front porch, when he saw the flutter of a blue skirt, and Eugenia emerged from the avenue and came up the walk between the stiff rows of box.   It was two o'clock, and the general was peacefully awaiting the sound of the dinner bell, but at the sight of Eugenia his peacefulness departed, and he called angrily:

"Eugie, where's Bernard?"

"Comin'."

"Coming!" returned the general indignantly. "Haven't I told you a dozen times not to walk along that road by yourself? Why didn't you wait for the carriage? Are you never going to mind what I say to you?"

Eugenia came up the steps and threw her books on one of the long green benches. Then she seated herself in a rocking chair and untied her sunbonnet.

"I wa'n't by myself," she said. "A boy was with me."

"A boy? Where is he?"

"He ran away."

The general's great head went back, and he shook with laughter. "Bless my soul! What did he mean by that? What boy was it, daughter?"

Eugenia sat upright in the high rocker, fanning her heated face with her sunbonnet.

"The Burr boy," she answered.

The general gasped for breath, and turned towards the hall.

"Come out here, Chris!" he called. "Here's Eugie been walking home with the Burr boy!"

In a moment Miss Chris's large figure appeared in the doorway, and she handed a brimming mint julep to the general.

"I don't know what Eugie can be made of," she remarked. "Amos Burr was overseer for the Carringtons before he got that place of his own, and I

remember just as well as if it were yesterday old Mr.
Phil Carrington telling me once, when I was on a
visit there, that the more his man Burr worked the
less he accomplished.   But, as for Eugenia, that
isn't the worst about her.   Just the other morning, when I was looking out of the storeroom window, I saw her with her arm round the neck of Aunt
Verbeny's little Suke.   I declare I was so upset I let
the quart pot fall into the potato bin! "

"But there isn't anybody else, Aunt Chris," protested Eugenia, looking up from her father's julep,
which she was tasting.   "And I'm 'bliged to have
a bosom friend."

The general shook until his face was purple and
the ice jingled in the glass.

"Bosom friend, you puss! " he roared.   "Why
can't you choose a bosom friend of your own colour?
What do you want with a bosom friend as black as
the ace of spades? "

"O papa, she ain't black; she's jes' yellow-brown."

"You ought to be ashamed of yourself, Eugie,"
said Miss Chris severely.   "Now go upstairs and
wash your face and hands before dinner.   It is almost ready.   I wonder where Bernard is! "

"Can't I wait twell the bell rings? " Eugenia
asked; but Miss Chris shook her head decisively.

"Eugenia, will you never stop talking like a
darkey? " she demanded.   "How often must I tell
you that there's no such word as ' twell ' ?   Now,
go right straight upstairs."

Eugenia rose obediently and went into the hall.
She had learned from her father and the servants
not to dispute the authority of Miss Chris, though

she yielded to it with a mild surprise at her own docility.

"She don't really manage me," she had once confided to Delphy, the washerwoman, "but I jes' plays that she does."

When Eugenia came downstairs she found the family seated at dinner, Miss Chris and her father beaming upon each other across a dish of fried chicken and a home-cured ham. Bernard was on Miss Chris's right hand, and on the other side of the table Eugenia's seat separated the general from Aunt Griselda, who sat severely buttering her toast before a brown earthenware teapot ornamented by a raised design of Rebecca at the well. Aunt Griselda was a lean, dried-up old lady, with a sharp, curved nose like the beak of a bird, and smoothly parted hair brushed low over her ears and held in place by a tortoise-shell comb. There were deep channels about her eyes, worn by the constant falling of acrid tears, and her cheeks were wrinkled and yellowed like old parchment.

Twenty years ago, when the general had first brought home his young wife, before her buoyancy had faltered, and before the five little head-boards to the five stillborn children had been set up amid the periwinkle in the family graveyard, Aunt Griselda had written from the home of her sister to say that she would stop over at Battle Hall on her way to Richmond.

The general had received the news joyfully, and the best chamber had been made ready by the hospitable hands of his young wife. Delicate, lavender-

scented linen had been put on the old tester-bed and
curtains of flowered chintz tied back from the window seats.   Amelia Battle had placed a bowl of tea-
roses upon the dressing table and gone graciously
down to the avenue to welcome her guest.   From
the family carriage Aunt Griselda had emerged
soured and eccentric.   She had gone up to the best
chamber, unpacked her trunks, hung up her bombazine skirts in the closet, ordered green tea and toast,
and settled herself for the remainder of her days.
That was twenty years ago, and she still slept in the
best chamber, and still ordered tea and toast at the
table.   She had grown sourer with years and more
eccentric with authority, but the general never failed
to treat her crotchets with courtesy or to open the
door for her when she came and went.   To the mild
complaints of Miss Chris and the protestations of
Eugenia he returned the invariable warning: " She
is our guest—remember what is due to a guest, my
dears."

And when Miss Chris placidly suggested that the
privileges of guestship wore threadbare when they
were stretched over twenty years, and Eugenia fer-
vently hoped that there were no visitors in heaven,
the general responded to each in turn:

" It is the right of a guest to determine the length
of his stay, and, as a Virginian, my house is open as
long as it has a roof over it."

So Aunt Griselda drank her green tea in acrid silence, turning at intervals to reprove Bernard for
taking too large mouthfuls or to request Eugenia
to remove her elbows from the table.

To-day, when Eugenia descended, she was gazing

5

stonily into Miss Chris's genial face, and listening constrainedly to a story at which the general was laughing heartily.

"Yes, I never look at these forks of the bead pattern that I don't see Aunt Callowell," Miss Chris was concluding.   "She never used any other pattern, and I remember when Cousin Bob Baker once sent her a set of teaspoons with a different border, she returned them to Richmond to be exchanged.   Do you remember the time she came to mother's when we were children, Tom ?   Eugie, will you have breast or leg?"

"I don't think I could have been at home," said the general, his face growing animated, as it always did, in a discussion of old times; "but I do remember once, when I was at Uncle Robert's, they sent me eighteen miles on horseback for the doctor, because Aunt Callowell had such a queer feeling in her side when she started to walk.   I can see her now holding her side and saying: 'I can't possibly take a step!   Robert, I can't take a step!'   And when I brought the doctor eighteen miles from home, on his old gray mare, he found that she'd put a shoe on one foot and a slipper on the other."

The general threw back his head and laughed until the table groaned, while Miss Chris's double chin shook softly over her cameo brooch.

Aunt Griselda wiped her eyes on the border of her handkerchief.

"Aunt Cornelia Callowell was a righteous woman," she murmured.   "I never thought that I should hear her ridiculed in the house of her great-nephew.   She scalloped me a flannel petticoat with her own hands. Eugenia, in my day little girls didn't reach for the butter. They waited until it was handed to them."

Congo, the butler, rushed to Eugenia's assistance, and the general shook his finger at her and formed the word " guest " with his mouth. Miss Chris changed the subject by begging Aunt Griselda to have a wing of chicken.

" I don't believe in so much dieting," she said cheerfully. " I think your nerves would be better if you ate more. Just try a brown wing."

" I know my nerves are bad," Aunt Griselda rejoined, still wiping her eyes, " though it is hard to be accused of a temper before my own nephew. But I know I am a burden, and I have overstayed my welcome. Let me go."

" Why, Aunt Griselda? " remonstrated Miss Chris in hurt tones. " You know I didn't accuse you of anything. I only meant that you would feel better if you didn't drink so much tea and ate more meat——"

" I am not too old to take a hint," replied Aunt Griselda. " I haven't reached my dotage yet, and I can see when I am a burden. Here, Congo, you may put my teapot away."

" O Lord! " gasped the general tragically; and rising to the occasion, he said hurriedly: " By the way, Chris, they told me at the post-office to-day that old Dr. Smith was dead. It was only last week that I met him on his way to town with his niece's daughter, and he told me that he had never been in better health in his life."

" Dear me! " exclaimed Miss Chris, holding a

large spoonful of raspberries poised above the dish to which she was helping. "Why, old Dr. Smith attended me forty years ago when I had measles. I remember he made me lie in bed with blankets over me, though it was August, and he wouldn't let me drink anything except hot flax-seed tea. They say all that has been changed in this generation——"

"Leave me plenty of room for cream, Aunt Chris," broke in Bernard, with an anxious eye on Miss Chris's absent-minded manipulations. She reached for the round, old silver pitcher, and poured the yellow cream on the sugared berries without pausing in her soft, monotonous flow of words.

"But even in those days Dr. Smith was behind the times, and he has been so ever since. He used to say that chloroform was invented by infidels, and he would not let them give it to his son, Lawrence, when he broke his leg on the threshing machine. It was a mania with him, for, when I was nursing in the hospitals during the war, he told me with his own lips that he believed the Lord was on our side because we didn't have chloroform."

"He had a good many odd ideas," said the general, "but he is dead now, poor man."

"He raised up my dear father when he was struck down with paralysis," murmured Aunt Griselda.

When dinner was over the general returned to the front porch, and Eugenia and the puppy went with Bernard to the orchard to look for green apples.

They started out in single file; Bernard, a bright-faced, snub-nosed boy with a girlish mouth, a little in advance, Eugenia following, and the puppy at her heels. On the way across the meadow, where myr-

iads of grasshoppers darted with a whirring noise
beneath the leaves of coarse mullein plants or the
slender, unopened pods of milkweed, the puppy
made sudden desperate skirmishes into the tangled
pathside, pointing ineffectually at the heavy-legged
insects, his red tongue lolling and his short tail
wagging. Up the steep ascent of the orchard a
rocky trail ran, bordered by a rail fence. From the
point of the hill one could see the adjoining country
unrolled like a map, olive heights melting into
emerald valleys, bare clearings into luxuriant crops,
running a chromatic scale from the dry old battlefields surrounding Kingsborough to the arable
" bottoms " beside the enrichening river.

After an unsuccessful search for cherries Bernard
climbed a tree where summer apples hung green,
and tossed the fruit to Eugenia, who held up her
blue skirt beneath the overhanging boughs. The
puppy, having dodged in astonishment a stray apple,
went off after the silvery track of a snail.

" That's enough," called Bernard presently, and
he descended and filled his pockets from Eugenia's
lap. " They set my teeth on edge, anyway. Got
any salt? "

Eugenia drew a small folded envelope from her
pocket. Then she threw away her apple and pointed
to the little brook at the foot of the hill. " There's
that red-winged blackbird in the bulrushes again. I
believe it's got a nest."

And they started in a run down the hillside, the
puppy waddling behind with shrill, impertinent
barks.

At the bottom of the hill they lost the blackbird

and found Nicholas Burr, who was lying face downwards upon the earth, a fishing line at his side.

"He's crying," said Eugenia in a high whisper.

Nicholas rolled over, saw them, and got up, wiping his eyes on the sleeve of his shirt.

"There warn't nobody lookin'," he said defiantly.

"You're too big to cry," observed Bernard dispassionately, munching a green apple he had taken from his pocket. "You're as big as I am, and I haven't cried since I was six years old. Eugie cries."

"I don't!" protested Eugenia vehemently. "I reckon you'd cry too if they made you sit in the house the whole afternoon and hem cup-towels."

"I'm a boy, Miss Spitfire. Boys don't sew. I saw Nick Burr milking, though, one day. What made you milk, Nick?"

"Ma did."

"I'd like to see anybody make me milk. You're jes' the same as a girl."

"I ain't!"

"You are!"

"I ain't!"

"'Spose you fight it out," suggested Eugenia, with an eye for sport, settling herself upon the ground with Jim in her lap.

Nicholas picked up his fishing line and wound it slowly round the cork. "There's a powerful lot of minnows in this creek," he remarked amicably. "When you lean over that log you can catch 'em in your hat."

"Let's do it," said Eugenia, starting up, and they went out upon the slippery log between the reedy banks. Over the smooth, pebbly bed of the stream flashed the shining bodies of hundreds of minnows, passing back and forth with brisk wriggles of their fine, steel-coloured tails. On the Battle side of the bank a huge, blue-winged dragonfly buzzed above the flaunting red and yellow faces of three tiger-lilies.

Jim sat on the brookside and watched the minnows, having ventured midway upon the log, to retreat at the sight of his own reflection in the water.

"He's a coward," said Bernard teasingly, alluding to the recreant Jim. "I wouldn't have a dog that was a coward."

"He ain't a coward," returned Eugenia passionately. "He jes' don't like looking at his own face, that's all. Here, Nick, hand me your hat."

Nick obediently gave her his hat, and Eugenia leaned over the stream, her bare arms and vivid face mirrored against the silvery minnows, when a shrill call came from the house.

"Nick! Who-a Ni-ck!"

"That's Sairy Jane," said Nicholas, reaching for his hat. "Ma wants me."

"Who is Sairy Jane?"

"Sister."

Eugenia handed him his dripping hat, and stood shaking her fingers free from the sparkling drops.

"Will you come and fish with me to-morrow?" she asked.

"If I ain't got to work in the field——"

"Don't work."

"Can't help it."

The call was repeated, and Nicholas sped over the

mossy log and across the ploughed field, while Bernard and Eugenia toiled up the hillside.

As they passed the Sweet Gum Spring they saw Delphy, the washerwoman, standing in her doorway, quarrelling with her son-in-law, Moses, who was hoeing a small garden patch in the rear of an adjoining cabin. Delphy was a large mulatto woman, with a broad, flat bosom and enormous hands that looked as if they had been parboiled into a livid blue tint.

" 'Tain' no use fer to hoe groun' dat ain' got no richness," she was saying, shaking her huge head until the dipper hanging on the lintel of the door rattled, " en 'tain' no use preachin' ter a nigger dat ain' got no gumption. Es de tree fall, so hit' gwine ter lay, en es a fool's done been born, so he gwine ter die. 'Tain' no use a-tryin' fer to do over a job dat de Lawd done slighted. You may ding about hit en you may dung about hit, but ef'n it won't, hit won't."

Moses, a meek-looking negro with an honest face, hoed silently, making no response to his mother-in-law's vituperations, which grew voluble before his non-resistance.

" Dar ain' no use er my frettin' en perfumin' over dat ar nigger,"she concluded, as if addressing a third person. " He wuz born a syndicate en he'll die er syndicate. De Debbil, he ain' gwine tu'n 'm en de Lawd he can't. De preachin' it runs off 'im same es water off er duck's back. I'se done talked ter him day in en day out twell dar ain' no breff lef' fer me ter blow wid, an' he ain' changed a hyar f'om what de Lawd made 'im. Seems like he ain' got de sperit uv——"

"Why, Delphy!" exclaimed Bernard, interrupting the flow of speech. "What's the matter with Moses?"

Delphy snorted contemptuously and took breath for procedure, when the sharp cry of a baby came from Moses' cabin, and Eugenia broke in excitedly:

"Why, there's a baby in there, Delphy! Whose baby is that?"

"Git er long wid you, chile," said Delphy. "You knows er plum sight mo' now'n you ought ter." Then she added with a snort: "Hit's es black es er crow's foot."

"Is it Betsey's baby?"

"I reckon 'tis. Moses he says ez what 'tis, but he's de mos' outlandish nigger on dis yer place. Dar ain' no relyin' on him, noways."

"When did it come, Delphy? Who brought it? I saw Dr. Debs yesterday, an' his saddle-bag bulged mightily."

"De Lawd didn't brung hit," returned Delphy emphatically. "De Lawd wouldn't er teched hit wid er ten-foot pole. Dis yer Moses, he ain' wuth de salt dat's put in his bread. He's de wuss er de hull lot——"

"Why doesn't Betsey get rid of him?" asked Bernard, eyeing the shrinking Moses with disfavour. "I heard Aunt Chris say that Mrs. Willie Wilson in Richmond got a divorce from her husband for good and all——"

"Lawdy, chile! Huccome you think I'se gwine ter pay fer a dervoge fer sech er low-lifeted creetur ez dat? He ain' wuth no dervogin', he ain'. When

it come ter dervogin', I'll dervoge 'im wid my fis'
en foot——"

Here the baby cried again, and the irate Delphy
disappeared into Moses' cabin, while the meek-
looking son-in-law hoed the garden patch and muttered beneath his breath.

The children passed the spring, crossed the meadow, and followed the grapevine trellis to the back
steps, when Eugenia rushed through the wide hall
with an impetuous flutter of short skirts.

" Papa! " she cried, bursting upon the general as
he sat smoking upon the front porch. " What do
you think has happened?   There's a new baby
came to Moses' cabin, an' Delphy says it's as black
as——"

" Well, I am blessed! " groaned the general,
knocking the ashes from his pipe. " Another mouth
to feed.   Eugie, they'll ruin me yet."

" I reckon they will," returned Eugenia hopelessly.   She seated herself upon the topmost step
and made a place for Jim beside her.

The general was silent for some time, smoking
thoughtfully and staring past the aspens and the
well-house to the waving cornfield.   When he spoke
it was with embarrassed hesitation.

" I say, daughter."

Eugenia looked up eagerly.

" Didn't that spotted cow of Moses' die last
week? "

" That it did," replied Eugenia emphatically. " It
got loose in your clover pasture and ate itself too
full.   Moses says it bu'st."

" Pish! " exclaimed the general angrily. " Mv

clover! I tell you, they won't leave me a roof over my head. They'll eat me into the poorhouse. But I'll turn them off. I'll send them packing, bag and baggage. My clover!"

"Moses ain't got much of a garden patch," said Eugenia. "It looks mighty poor. The potato-bugs ate all his potatoes."

The general was silent again.

"I say, daughter," he began at last, blowing a heavy cloud of smoke upon the air, "the next time you go by Sweet Gum Spring you had just as well tell Moses that I can let him have a side of bacon if he wants it. The rascal can't starve. But they won't leave me a mouthful—not one. And Eugie——"

"Yes, sir."

"You needn't mention it to your Aunt Chris——"

At that instant a little barefooted negro came running across the lawn from the spring-house, a large tin pail in his hand.

"Here, boy!" called the general. "Where're you off to? What have you got in that pail?"

"It's Jake," said Eugenia in a whisper, while Jim barked frantically from the shelter of her arms. "He's Delphy's Jake."

The small negro stood grinning in the walk, his white eyeballs circling in their sockets. "Hit's Miss Chris, suh," he said at last.

"Miss Chris, you rascal!" shouted the general. "Do you expect me to believe you've got Miss Chris in that pail? Open it, sir; open it!"

Jake showed a shining row of ivory teeth and stood shaking the pail from side to side.

"Miss Chris, she gun hit ter me, suh," he explained. "Hit's Miss Chris herse'f dat's done sont me ter tote dish yer buttermilk ter Unk Mose."

"Bless my soul!" cried the general wrathfully. "Get away with you! The whole place is bent on ruining me. I'll be in the poorhouse before the week's up." And he strode indoors in a rage.

VII

Twice a year, on fine days in spring and fall, Aunt Griselda's bombazine dresses were taken from the whitewashed closet and hung out to air upon the clothesline at the back of the house, while pungent odours of tar and camphor were exhaled from the full black folds. On these days Aunt Griselda would remain in her room, sorting faded relics which she took from a cedar chest and spread beside her on the floor. The door was kept locked at such times, but once Eugenia, who had gone with Congo to carry Aunt Griselda her toast and tea, had caught a glimpse of a yellowed swiss muslin frock and the leather case of a daguerreotype containing the picture of a round-eyed girl with rosy cheeks. Aunt Griselda had hidden them hastily away at the child's entrance—hidden them with that nervous, awkward haste which dreads a dawning jest of itself; but Eugenia had seen that her old eyes were red and her voice more rasping than usual.

Sixty years ago Aunt Griselda had had her romance, and she still kept her love-letters tied up with discoloured ribbons and laid away in the cedar chest. It was but the skeleton of a love story—the adolescent ardours of a high-spirited country girl and the high-spirited son of a neighbouring farmer. When the quarrel came the letters were overlooked when the ring went back. Griselda Grigsby had tossed them carelessly into the cedar chest and gone out to

forget them. Her heart had not been deeply touched
and it soon mended. No other lovers came, and she
lived her quiet life in her father's house, gathering
garden flowers for the great, blue bowls in the
parlour, teaching the catechism to small black
slaves, and making stiff, old-fashioned samplers in
crewels. The high-spirited lover had loved elsewhere and died of a fever, and, beyond a passing regret, she thought little of him. There were nearer
interests, and she was still the petted daughter of
her father's house—the eldest and the best beloved.
Then the crash came. The old people passed away,
the house changed hands, Aunt Griselda was
stranded upon the high tide of hospitality—and
crewel work went out of fashion.

In her sister's home she became a constant guest
—one to be offered the favoured share and to be
treated with tender, increasing tolerance—not to be
loved. Since the death of her parents none had
loved her, though many had borne gently with her
spoiled fancies. But her coming in had brought
no light, and her going out had left nothing dark.
She was old and ill-tempered and bitter of speech,
and, though all doors opened hospitably at her approach, all closed quickly when she was gone. Her
spoiled youth had left her sensitive to trivial stings,
unforgivable to fancied wrongs. In a childish over-
sight she detected hidden malice and implacable
hate in a thoughtless jest. Her bitterness and her
years waxed greater together, and she lost alike her
youth and her self-control. When she had yearned
for passionate affection she had found kindly tolerance, and the longings of her hidden nature, which

none knew, were expressed in rasping words and
acrid tears. Once, some years after Bernard's birth,
she had called him into her room as she sat among
her relics, and had shown him the daguerreotype.

" It's pitty lady," the child had lisped, and she
had caught him suddenly to her lean old breast, but
he had broken into peevish cries and struggled free,
tearing with his foot the ruffle of the swiss muslin
gown.

" Oo ain't pitty lady," he had said, and Aunt Griselda had risen and pushed him into the hall with
sharp, scolding words, and had sat down to darn
the muslin ruffle with delicate, old-fashioned stitches.

It was only when all living love had failed her that
she returned to the dead. She had gathered the letters of nearly sixty years ago from the bottom of the
cedar chest, reading them through her spectacles
with bleared, watery eyes. Those subtle sentimen-
talities which linger like aromas in a heart too aged
for passion were liberated by the bundle of yellow
scrawls written by hands that were dust. As she
sat in her stiff bombazine skirts beside the opened
chest, peering with worry-ravaged face at the old
letters, she forgot that she was no longer one with
the girl in the muslin frock, and that the inciter of
this exuberant emotion was as dead as the emotion
itself.

When the dresses were brought up to her she
would put them on again and go down to flinch
before kindly eyes and to make embittered speeches
in her high, shrill voice. Outwardly she grew more
soured and more eccentric. On mild summer evenings she would come down stairs with her head

wrapped in a pink knitted "nubia," and stroll back and forth along the gravelled walk, her gaunt figure passing into the dusk of the cedar avenue and emerging like the erratic shadow of one of the sombre trees.

Sometimes Eugenia joined her, but Bernard, her favourite, held shyly aloof.   In her exercise she seldom spoke, and her words were peevish ones, but there was grim pathos in her carriage as she moved slowly back and forth between the straight rows of box.

After supper the family assembled on the porch and talked in a desultory way until ten o'clock, when the lights were put out and the house retired to rest. Eugenia slept in a great, four-post bedstead with Aunt Chris, and the bed was so large and soft and billowy that she seemed to lose herself suddenly at night in its lavender-scented midst, and to be as suddenly discovered in the morning by Rindy, the house-girl, when she came with her huge pails of warm water.

Those fresh summer dawns of Eugenia's childhood became among her dearest memories in after years. There were hours when, awaking, wide-eyed, before the house was astir, she would rise on her elbow and look out across the dripping lawn, where each dewdrop was charged with opalescent tints, to the eastern horizon, where the day broke in a cloud of gold. The song of a mocking-bird in the poplars of the little graveyard came to her with unsuspected melody—a melody drawn from the freshness, the loneliness, the half-awakened calls from hidden nests and the lyric ecstasy of dawn.

Then, with the rising of the sun, Aunt Chris would turn upon her pillow and open her soft, brown eyes.

" It is not good for little folks to be awake so early," she would say, and there would rush upon the child a sense of warmth and tenderness and comfort, and she would nestle closer to her sweet, white pillow. With the beginning of day began also the demands upon the time of Miss Chris. First the new overseer, knocking at her door, would call through the crack that a cow had calved, or that one of the sheep was too ill to go to pasture. Then Rindy, entering with her pails, would shake a pessimistic head.

" Lawd, Miss Chris, one er dem ole coons done eat up er hull pa'cel er yo' chickens." And Miss Chris, at once the prop and the mainstay of the Battle fortunes, would rise with anxious exclamations and put on her full black skirt and linen sacque.

When breakfast was over Miss Chris went into the storeroom each morning and came out with a basin of corn-meal dough, followed by Sampson bearing an axe and Aunt Verbeny jingling the hen-house keys. The slow procession then filed out to the space before the hen-house, the door of which was flung back, while Aunt Verbeny clucked at a little distance. Miss Chris scattered her dough upon the ground and, while her unsuspecting beneficiaries made their morning meal, she pointed out to Sampson, the executioner, the members of the feathered community destined to be sacrificed to the carnivorous habits of their fellow mortals.

" Feel that one with the black spots, Sampson,"

6

she said with the indifference of an abstract deity. " Is it fat? And the domineca pullet, and the two roosters we bought from Delphy."

And when Sampson had seized upon the victims of the fiat she turned to inspect the bunches of fowls offered by neighbouring breeders.

To-day it was Nicholas Burr who stood patiently in the background, three drooping chickens in each hand, their legs tied together with strips of a purple calico which Marthy was making into a dress for Sairy Jane.

Seeing that Miss Chris had delivered her judgments, he came forward and proffered his captives with an abashed demeanour.

" How much are they worth? " asked Miss Chris in her cheerful tones, while Aunt Verbeny gave a suspicious poke beneath one of the flapping wings, followed by a grunt of disparagement.

Nicholas stammered confusedly:

" Ma says the biggest ought to bring a quarter," he returned, blushing as Aunt Verbeny grunted again, " and the four smallest can go for twenty cents."

But when the bargain was concluded he lingered and added shamefacedly: " Won't you please let that red-and-black rooster live as long as you can? I raised it."

" Why, bless my heart! " exclaimed Miss Chris, " I believe the child is fond of the chicken."

Eugenia, who was hovering by, burst into tears and declared that the rooster should not die.

" Twenty cents is s-o ch-ea-p for a li-fe," she sobbed. " It shan't be killed, Aunt Chris. It shall

go in my hen-h-ou-se." And she rushed off to get
her little tin bank from the top bureau drawer.

When the arrangements were concluded Nicholas started empty-handed down the box walk, the
money jingling in his pocket. At the end of the
long avenue of cedars there was a wide, unploughed
common which extended for a quarter of a mile
along the roadside. In spring and summer the
ground was white with daisies and in the autumn
it donned gorgeous vestments of golden-rod and
sumach. In the centre of the waste, standing alike
grim and majestic at all seasons, there was the
charred skeleton of a gigantic tree, which had been
stripped naked by a bolt of lightning long years ago.
At its foot a prickly clump of briars surrounded
the blackened trunk in a decoration of green or red,
and from this futile screen the spectral limbs rose
boldly and were silhouetted against the far-off
horizon like the masts of a wrecked and deserted
ship. A rail fence, where a trumpet-vine hung
heavily, divided the field from the road, and several
straggling sheep that had strayed from the distant
flock stood looking shyly over the massive crimson
clusters.

When Nicholas came out from the funereal dusk
of the cedars the field was almost blinding in the
morning glare, the yellow-centred daisies rolling in
the breeze like white-capped billows on a sunlit
sea. From the avenue to his father's land the road
was unbroken by a single shadow—only to the right,
amid the young corn, there was a solitary persimmon tree, and on the left the gigantic wreck stranded
amid the tossing daisies.

The sun was hot, and dust rose like smoke from the white streak of the road, which blazed beneath a cloudless sky.

The boy was tired and thirsty, and as he tramped along the perspiration rose to his forehead and dropped upon his shoulder. With a sigh of satisfaction he came upon the little cottage of his father and saw his stepmother taking the clothes in from the bushes where they had been spread to dry. It was Saturday, and ironing day, and he hoped for a chance at his lessons before night came, when he was so tired that the facts would not stick in his brain. He thought that it must be very easy to study in the mornings when you were fresh and eager and before that leaden weight centred behind your eyeballs.

When Marthy Burr saw him she called irritably:

" I say, Nick, did they take the chickens? "

Nicholas nodded, and, crossing the weeds in the garden, gave her the money from his pocket.

" They didn't say nothing 'bout wantin' more, I 'spose? Did you tell 'em I was fattenin' them four pairs of ducks? "

Nicholas shook his head. No, he hadn't told them.

" Well, your pa wants you down in the peanut field. You'd better get a drink of water first. You look powerful red."

An hour later, when work was over, he carried his book to the orchard and flung himself down beneath the trees. The judge had given him a biography of Jefferson, and he had learned his hero's life with lips and heart. The day that it was finished he put the volume under his arm and went to the rector's house.

"I want to join the church," he said bluntly.

The rector, a kindly, middle-aged man, with a love for children, turned to him in half-puzzled, half-sympathetic inquiry.

"You are young, my child," he replied, "to be so zealous a Christian."

"'Tain't that, sir," said the boy slowly. "I don't set much store by that. But I've got to go to heaven—because I can't see Thomas Jefferson no other way."

The rector did not smile. He was wiser than his generation, for he left the great man's own religion to himself and God. He said merely:

"When you are older we shall see, my boy—we shall see."

Nicholas left with a chill of disappointment, but as he passed along the street his name was called by Juliet Burwell, and she fluttered across to him in all her mystifying flounces and her gracious smile.

"I was at the rector's," she said, "and he told me that you wanted to be confirmed—and I want you to come into my Sunday-school class."

Nicholas met the kind eyes and blushed purple. Her beauty took away his breath and made his pulses leap. The slow, musical drawl of her speech soothed him like the running of clear water. He felt the image of Thomas Jefferson totter upon its pedestal, but it was steadied with a tremendous lurch. Jefferson was a man, after all, and this was only a woman.

"Will you come?" asked the soft voice, and he stammered an amazed and awkward assent.

VIII

On the Saturday after the day upon which Nicholas had pledged himself to attend Sunday-school Juliet Burwell asked him to come into Kingsborough and talk over the lesson for the following morning. At five o'clock in the afternoon he dressed himself with trembling hands and a perturbed heart; and for the first time in his life turned to look at his reflection in the small, cracked mirror hanging above the washstand in his stepmother's room.

As a finishing touch Marthy Burr tied a flaming plaid cravat beneath his collar.

"You ain't much on looks," she remarked as she drew back to survey him, "but you've got as peart a face as I ever seed. I reckon you'll be plenty handsome for a man. I was al'ays kind of set against one of these pink an' white men, somehow. They're pretty enough to look at when you're feelin' first-rate, but when you git the neuralgy they sort of turns yo' stomach. I've a taste for sober colours in men and caliky."

"I think he looks beautiful," said Sairy Jane, her eyes on the cravat, and Nicholas felt a sudden glow of gratitude, and silently resolved to save up until he had enough money to buy her a hair ribbon.

"I ain't sayin' he don't," returned Marthy Burr with a severe glance in the direction of her eldest daughter, who was minding Jubal in the kitchen doorway. " Thar's red heads an' red heads, an' his ain't no redder than the reddest. But he came honestly by it, which is more than some folks can say as is got yellow. His father had it befo' him, an' thar's one good thing about it, you've got to be born with it or you ain't goin' to come by it no other way. I never seed a dyer that could set hair that thar colour 'cep'n the Lord Himself—an' I ain't one to deny that the Lord has got good taste in His own line."

Then, as Nicholas took up his hat, she added : " If they ask after me, Nick, be sure an' say I'm jes' po'ly."

Nicholas nodded and went out, followed to the road by Sairy Jane and Jubal, while his stepmother called after him to walk in the grass and try to keep his feet clean.

When he reached Kingsborough and crossed the green to the Burwell's house, which was in the lane called " Back Street," he fell to a creeping pace, held back by the fluttering of his pulses. Not until he saw Juliet standing at the little whitewashed gate did he brace himself to the full courage of approaching. When he spoke her name she opened the gate and gave him her hand, while all sense of diffidence fell from him.

" I've been looking at you for a long ways," he said boldly, " an' you were just like one of them tall lilies bordering the walk."

She blushed, turning her clear eyes upon him, and he felt a great desire to kiss the folds of her skirt or the rose above her left temple. He had never seen any one so good or so kind or so beautiful, and

he vowed passionately in his rustic little heart that
he would always love her best—best of all—that he
would fight for her if he might, or work for her if
she needed it.   There was none like her—not his
stepmother—not Sairy Jane—not even Eugenia.
She was different—something of finer clay, made to
be waited upon and worshipped like the picture of
the goddess standing on the moon that he had seen
in the judge's study.

Juliet smiled upon his ardour, and, leading him to
a bench beneath a flowering myrtle, made him sit
down beside her, while she spoke pious things about
Adam and the catechism and the salvation of the
world—to all of which he listened with wide-opened
eyes and a fluttering heart.   He wondered why no
one had ever before told him such beautiful things
about God and the manifold importance of keeping
a clean heart and loving your neighbour as yourself.   It seemed to him that he had been living in
sin for the twelve years of his life and he feared that
he should find it impossible to purge his mind of evil
passions and to love the coloured boy Boss who had
stolen his best fishing line.   He asked Juliet if she
thought he would be able to withstand the assaults
of Satan as the minister told him to do; but she
laughed and said that there was no Satan who went
about like a roaring lion—only cruelty and anger
and ill-will, and that he must be kind to his brothers
and sisters, and to animals, and not rob birds' nests,
which was very wrong.   Then she added as an
afterthought, with a saintly look in her eyes, that he
must love God.   He promised that he should try to
do so, though he wished in his heart that she had

told him to love herself instead. As he sat in the
soft light, watching her beautiful face rising against
a background of lilies, his young brain thrilled with
the joy of life. It was such a glorious thing to
live in a great, kind world, with a big, beneficent
God above the blue, and to love all mankind—not
harbouring an angry thought or an ill feeling! He
looked into the kind eyes beside him and felt that
he should like to be a saint or a minister—not a
lawyer, which might be wicked after all. Then he
remembered the waxen-faced, choleric clergyman
of the church his stepmother attended, but he put
the memory away. No, he would not be like that;
he would not preach fire and brimstone from a
white-pine pulpit. He would be large and just and
merciful like God; and Juliet Burwell would come
to hear him preach, looking up at him with her
blue, blue glance. In the meantime he would not
rob that marsh hen's nest which he had found. He
would never steal another egg. He wished that he
didn't have that drawerful at home. He would
give them to Sairy Jane if she wanted them—all
except the snake's egg, which he might keep, because
serpents were an accursed race. Yes, Sairy Jane
might have them all, and he wouldn't pull her hair
again when he caught her looking at them on the
sly.

Presently Juliet called Sally and took him into
the quaint old dining-room and gave him cakes
and jam on a table that shone like glass. There he
saw Mr. Burwell—a pink-cheeked, little gentleman
who wore an expansive air of innocence and a white
piqué waistcoat—and Mrs. Burwell, a pretty, gray-

haired woman, who ruled her husband with the velvet-pawed despotism which was the heritage of the women of her race and day. She had never bought a bonnet without openly consulting his judgment; he had never taken a step in life without unconsciously following hers.

"Really, my dear Sally," he had said when he heard of Nicholas's reception by his daughter, "Juliet must a—a—be taught to recognise the existence of class. Really, I cannot have her bringing all these people into my house. You must put a stop to it at once, my dear."

Mrs. Burwell had smiled placidly as she patted her gray fringe.

"Of course you know best, Mr. Burwell," she had replied with that touching humility which forbade her to address her husband by his Christian name. "Of course you know best about such matters, and I'll tell Juliet what you say. Poor child, she has such confidence in your judgment that she will believe whatever you say to be right; but she does love so to feel that she is exerting a good influence over the boys, and, perhaps, helping them to work out their future salvation. She thinks, too, that it is so well for them to have a chance of talking to you. I heard her tell Dudley Webb that he must take you for an example——"

"Ah!—ahem!" said Mr. Burwell, who worshipped the ground his daughter trod upon. "I suppose it would be a pity to interfere with her, eh, my dear?"

"Well, I can't help wishing myself, Mr. Burwell, that she would select children of her own class in

life, but, as you say, she has taken a fancy to that
Burr boy, and he seems to be a decent, respectful
kind of child. Of course I know it is your soft heart
that makes you look at it in this way—but I love you
all the better for it. I remember the day you pro-
posed to me for the sixth time, I had just seen you
bandage up the head of a little darkey that had cut
himself—and I accepted you on the spot."

"Yes, yes, my love," Mr. Burwell had responded,
kissing his wife as they left the room. " I am convinced that I am right, and I am glad that you
agree with me. We won't speak of it to Juliet."

In the hall below they met Nicholas Burr, and
greeted him with hospitable kindness.

"So this is your new scholar, eh, Juliet? You
must do justice to your teacher, my boy."

Juliet laughed and went out into the yard to meet
several young men who were coming up the walk,
and Nicholas noticed with a jealous pang that she
sat with them beneath the myrtle and talked in the
same soft voice with the same radiant smile. She
was not speaking of heaven now. She was laughing merrily at pointless jokes and promising to em-
broider a handkerchief for one and to make a box
of caramels for another.

He knew that they all loved her, and it gave him
a miserable feeling. He felt that they were unworthy of her—that they would not worship her always and become ministers for her sake, as he was
going to do. He even wondered if it wouldn't be
better, after all, to become a prize fighter and to
knock them all out in the first round when he got
a chance.

In a moment Juliet called him to her side and laid her hand upon his arm. "He has promised not to rob birds' nests and to love me always," she said.

But the young men only laughed.

"Ask something harder," retorted one. "Any of us will do that. Ask him to stand on his head or to tie himself into a bow knot for your sake."

Nicholas reddened angrily, but Juliet told the jester to try such experiments himself—that she did not want a contortionist about. Then she bent over the boy as he said good-bye, and he went down the walk between the lilies and out into the lane.

He recrossed the green slowly, turning into the main street at the court-house steps. As he passed the church, a little further on, the iron gate opened and the rector came out, jingling the heavy keys in his hand as he talked amicably to a tourist who followed upon his heels.

"Yes, my good sir," he was saying in his high-pitched, emphatic utterance, "this dear old church-yard is never mowed except by living lawn-mowers. I assure you that I have seen thirty heads of cattle upon the vaults—positively, thirty heads, sir!"

But the boy's thoughts were far from the church and its rector, and the words sifted rapidly through his brain. He touched his hat at the tourist's greeting and smiled into the clergyman's face, but his actions were automatic. He would have nodded to the horse in the street or have smiled at the sun.

As he passed the small shops fronting on the narrow sidewalk and followed the whitewashed fence of the college grounds until it ended at the Old Stage Road, he was conscious of the keen, pulsating harmony of life. It was good to be alive—to feel the warm sunshine overhead and the warm dust below. He was glad that he had been born, though the idea had never formulated itself until now. He would be very good all his life and never do a wicked thing. It was so easy to be good if you only wanted to. Yes, he would study hard and become learned in the law, like those old prophets with whom God spoke as man with man. Then, when he had grown better and wiser than any one on earth, his tongue would become loosened, and he would go forth to preach the Gospel, and Juliet would listen to him for his wisdom's sake. Oh, if she would only love him best—best of all!

This evening the road through the wood did not frighten him, though the sun was down. He thought neither of the ghosts that Uncle Dan'l had seen, nor of the bug-a-boos that had chased Viney's husband home. He was too old for these things now. He had grown taller and stronger in a day. When he reached the pasture gate opposite the house he opened it and went in to look for the sheep.

The west was fast losing colour, like a bright-hued fabric that has been drenched in water, and a thick, blue mist, shot with fireflies, shrouded the wide common. A fresh, sharp odour rose from the dew-steeped earth, giving place, as he gained upon the flock, to the smell of moist wool. As he brushed the heavy, purple tubes of Jamestown weeds long-legged insects flew out and struck against his arm before they fell in a drunken stupor to the grass below.

The boy made his way cautiously, his figure becoming blurred as the mist wrapped him like a blanket. The darkness was gathering rapidly. From the far-off horizon clouds of lavender were melting, and the pines had gone gray.

Presently a white patch glimmered in the midst of the pasture, and he began to call softly:

"Coo-sheep! Coo-sheep!"

A tremulous bleat answered, but as he neared the flock it scattered swiftly, the errant leaders darting shyly behind the looming outlines of sassafras bushes. Again he called, and again the plaintive cry responded, growing fainter as several fleeter ewes sped past him to the beech trees beside the little stream.

The space before the boy was suddenly spangled with fireflies, and the mist grew denser.

He broke off a branch of sassafras and started at a brisk run, rounding by some dozen yards the startled ewes. The scattered white blotches closed together as he ran towards them, and fled, bleating, to the flock where it clustered at the pasture gate.

In a moment he had driven them across the road and behind the bars of the cow-pen.

When he entered the house a little later he found that the family had had supper, a single plate remaining for himself. His stepmother, looking jaded and nervous, was putting salted herring to soak in an earthenware bowl, while she scolded Sairy Jane, who was patching Jubal's apron.

"It's goin' on ten years sence I've stopped to draw breath," said Marthy Burr, "an' I'm clean wore out. 'Tain't no better than a dog's life, no-how—a woman an' a dog air about the only creeturs as would put up with it, an' they're the biggest pair of fools the Lord ever made. Here I've been standin' at the tub from sunrise to sunset, with my jaw a'most splittin' from my face, an' thar's yo' pa a-settin' at his pipe as unconsarned as if I wa'nt his lawful wife—the more's the pity! It's the lawful wives as have the work to do, an' the lawfuller the wives the lawfuller the work. If this here government ain't got nothin' better to do than to drive poor women till they drop I reckon we'd as well stop payin' taxes to keep it goin'."

Nicholas wiped his heated brow on his shirt-sleeve and hung his hat on the back of a bottomless chair. Jubal, who was rolling on the floor, gave a gurgle and made a grab at it, to be soundly boxed by his mother as she reseated him at Sairy Jane's feet. His gurgle wavered dolorously and rose into a howl.

"Have you been to supper, ma?" asked Nicholas cheerfully.

"Lord, Nick, it's a long ways past supper-time," answered Sairy Jane, relieved by the interruption. "The things air all washed up, ain't they, pa?"

Amos Burr scowled heavily upon the boy's head, his phlegmatic nature goaded into resentment by his wife's ill-temper and the lamentations of Jubal.

"I don't reckon you expect supper to keep waitin' till breakfast," he said. "You've given your ma trouble enough 'thout makin' her do an extra washin' up on your o'count. You've gone clean crazy sence you've been loafin' round with them Battles. I don't see as you air much o'count, nohow."

Nicholas raised his eyes to his father's face and

looked at him fixedly. For a moment he did not speak, and then he said slowly :

"I'm as good as a hand to you."

He was thinking doggedly that he had never hated any one so much as he hated his own father, and that he liked the sensation. He wished he could do him some real harm—hit him hard enough to hurt or make the peanuts rot in the ground. He should like also to choke Jubal, who never left off yelling.

Amos Burr spat a mouthful of tobacco juice through the open window, flinching before the boy's steady glance. He was a mild-natured man at best, whose chief sin was his softness. It would not have entered his slow-witted head to protest against the accusations of his wife. When they stung him into revolt he revolted in the opposite direction.

But his failures were faults in his son's eyes. To the desperate determination of the boy, weakness became as contemptible as crime. What was a man worth who worked from morning until night and yet achieved nothing? Of what account was the farmer whom the crows outwitted and the weather made a mockery? Did not the very crops cry out as they rotted that his father was a fool, and the un-ploughed land proclaim him a coward? Had he ever dared a venture in his life or risked a season? And yet what had ever returned at his bidding or brought forth at his planting?

"You've been mighty little use of late," repeated Amos Burr stubbornly when his wife placed the earthenware bowl on the shelf and came to the table —her arm outstretched.

"Now, you jes' take yourself right off, Amos Burr," she said. "If you can't behave decently to my dead sister's child you shan't hang round them as was her own flesh and blood kin. Sairy Jane, you bring that plate of hot corn pones from the stove. Here, Nick, set right down an' eat your supper! There's some canned cherries if you want 'em."

Nicholas sat down, but the cornbread stuck in his throat and the coffee was without aroma. He looked at the figured oilcloth on the table and thought of the shining glass and silver at Juliet Burwell's. The flavour of the cake she had given him seemed to intensify his distaste for the food before him. He felt that he cared for nobody—that he wanted nothing. He looked at his stepmother and thought that she was dried and brown like a hickory nut; he looked at Sairy Jane and wondered why she didn't have any eyelashes, and he looked at Jubal and saw that he was all gums.

When he went up to his little attic room after supper he sat on his shucks pallet in the darkness and thought of all the evil that he should like to do. He should like to pull Sairy Jane's plait and to slap Jubal. He should even like to tell Juliet Burwell that he didn't want to keep a clean heart, and to call God names. No, he would not become a minister and preach the Gospel. He would be a thief instead and break into hen-houses and steal chickens. If his father planted watermelons he would steal them from the vines as soon as they were ripe. Perhaps Eugenia would help him. At any rate he would go halves with her if she would be his partner in wicked-

7

ness.   He had just as soon go to hell, after all—if
it were not for Thomas Jefferson.

He leaned his head on his hands and looked
through the narrow window to where the peanut
fields lay in blackness.   From the stable came the
faint neigh of the old mare, and he remembered
suddenly that he had forgotten to put straw in her
stall and to loosen her halter that she might lie
down.   He rose and stole softly downstairs and out
of the house.

IX

One evening in late autumn Nicholas went into
Delphy's cabin after supper and found Eugenia
seated upon the hearth, facing Uncle Ish and Aunt
Verbeny. Between them Delphy's son-in-law,
Moses, was helping Bernard mend a broken hare
trap, while Delphy, herself, was crooning a lullaby
to one of her grandchildren as she carded the wool
which she had taken from a quilt of faded patchwork.
On the stones of the great fireplace the red flames
from lightwood splits leaped over a smouldering
hickory log, filling the cabin with the penetrating
odour of burning, resinous pine. From the wall
above the hearth a dozen roasting apples were suspended by hemp strings, and as the heat penetrated
the russet coats the apples circled against the yawn-
ing chimney like small globes revolving about a sun.

Eugenia was sitting silently in a low, split-bot-
tomed chair, her hands folded in her lap and her
animated eyes on the dark faces across from her,
over whose wrinkled surfaces the dancing firelight
chased in ruddy lights and shadows.

Uncle Ish had stretched his feet out upon the
stones, and the mud adhering to his rough, home-
made boots was fast drying before the blaze and
settling in coarse gray dust upon the hearth. His
gnarled old palms lay upward on his knees, and his
grizzled head was bowed upon his chest. At inter-

vals he muttered softly to himself, but his words were inaudible—suggested by some far-off and disconnected vision. Aunt Verbeny was nodding in her chair, arousing herself from time to time to give a sharp glance into the face of Uncle Ish.

"Huccome dey let you out ter-night, honey?" asked Delphy suddenly, turning her eyes upon Eugenia as she drew a fresh handful of wool from between the covers of the quilt.

"I ran away," replied the child gravely. "I saw Bernard with his hare trap, and Bernard shan't do nothin' that I can't do."

"Yes, I shall," rejoined Bernard without looking up from his trap. "You can't wear breeches."

"I like to know why I can't," demanded Eugenia. "I put on a pair of your old ones and they fit me just as well as they do you—only Aunt Chris made me get out of them."

"Sakes er live!" exclaimed Aunt Verbeny, awaking from her doze.

Uncle Ish stared dreamily into the flames. "Ole Miss wuz in her grave, she wuz," he muttered, while Delphy looked at him and shook her head mysteriously.

Then, as Nicholas entered, they made a place for him upon the hearthstones, treating him with the forbearing tolerance with which the well-born negro regards the low-born white man.

"Pa wants you all to help him in peanut-picking to-morrow," said Nicholas, addressing the group indiscriminately. "He's late at it this year, but he's been laid up with rheumatism."

"Dar ain' nuttin' ez goes on two foot er fo' ez

won' len' er han' at a pickin'," remarked Uncle Ish
as the boy sat down. " Dar ain' nuttin' in de shape,
er man er crow ez won't he'p demse'ves w'en dey's
lyin' roun' loose, nuther."

"Dar's gwine ter be er killin' fros' fo' mawnin',"
said Moses, his teeth chattering from the draught
let in by the opening door. " Hit kilt all Miss Chris'
hop vines las' year, en it'll kill all ez ain't under
kiver ter-night. Hit seems ter sort er lay holt er
yo' chist en clean grip hit."

"You ain' never had no chist, nohow," remarked
Delphy disdainfully. " Hit don't take mo'n er spit
er fros' ter freeze thoo you. You de coldest innered
somebody I ever lay eyes on. Dar mought ez well
be er fence rail er roun' on er winter night fer all
de wa'mth ez is in yo' bones."

"Dat's so," admitted Moses shamefacedly.
"Dat's so. Dese yer nights, when de fire is all gone,
is moughty near ter freezin' me out er house en
home. I ain' never seed ne'r quilt ez wuz made fur
er hull fambly yit. Wid me ter pull en Betsey ter
pull en de chillun ter pull, whar de quilt?"

"Dar ain' no blankets dese days," said Uncle Ish
sadly. " Dey ain' got mo'n er seasonin' er wool in
dese yer sto' stuff. Dey wa'nt dat ar way in ole
times, sis Verbeny. Bless yo' soul, sis Verbeny, dey
wan't dat ar way."

"Ole Miss she use ter have eve'y stitch er her
wool carded fo' her own eyes," said Aunt Verbeny.
"What wa'nt good enough fer her wuz good enough
fer de res', en we got hit. Ef'n de briars wouldn't
come out'n it soon ez she laid her han' on 'em, Ole
Miss she turnt up her nose en thowed de wool on

ter de niggers' pile.   Hit had ter be pisonous white en sof' fo' hit 'ud tech Ole Missusses skin.   Noner yo' nappy stuff done come near her."

Uncle Ish chuckled and hung his head on his breast.

" Doze wuz times! " he cried, " doze wuz times, en dese ain't times! "

Then he looked at Nicholas, who was watching the apples spinning in the heat.

" De po' white trash ain' set foot inside my do'," he added, " en de leetle gals ain' flirt roun' twell dar wa'nt no qualifyin' der legs f'om der arms."

" I don't care! " said Eugenia, looking defiantly at Uncle Ish.

" Lor', chile, don't teck on dat way," remonstrated Aunt Verbeny.   " You ain't had no raisin' noways, en dar ain' been nobody ter brung you up 'cep'n yo' pa.   Hit's de foolishness uv Miss Chris ez has overturnt de hull place."

" She's a-settin' moughty prim now," continued Uncle Ish, his eyes on the little girl.   " She des' es prim es ef she wuz chiny en glass, but I'se had my eye on 'er afo' dis.   I'se done tote 'er in dese arms when she wa'nt knee high ter Marse Tom's ole mule Jenny, en she ain't cut nairy er caper dat I ain't 'sperienced hit."

" I don't care," retorted Eugenia.

" Ain't I done see her plump right out whar sis Delphy wuz a-wallopin' her leetle nigger Jake, en holler out dat Jake ain' done lay han's on her pa's watermillion—'case she done steal 'em herse'f? "

" I don't care! " repeated Eugenia with tearful defiance.

"An' she ain' no mo' steal dat ar watermillion den I is," finished Uncle Ish triumphantly.

"It was just a lie," said Bernard. "Eugie, you know where liars go."

"Des' ez straight ter de bad place ez dey kin walk," added Aunt Verbeny severely. "Des' ez straight ez de Lord kin sen' 'em dar."

"It was a good lie," declared Nicholas, in manful defence of the weak. "I don't believe she's goin' to be damned for a good lie and a little one, too."

"Well, dar's lies en dar's lies," put in Delphy con- solingly, "an' I 'low dat dar's mo' in de manner uv lyin' den in de lie. Some lies is er long ways sweeter ter de tas' den Gospel trufe. Abraham, he lied, en it ain't discountenance him wid de Lord. Marse Tom, he lied when he wuz young, en it spar'd 'im er whoppin'. Hit's er plum fool ez won't spar' dere own hinder parts on er 'count uv er few words."

"George Washington didn't," said Bernard.

"I wish he had," added Eugenia. "Aunt Chris made me read about him and his old cherry tree when I told her the red rooster was setting, because I didn't want her to kill him."

"Ma asked me once if I had been fishin' when she told me to clean out the spring," said Nicholas thoughtfully, "an' I said yes."

"What did she say?" asked Bernard.

"Nothin'. She whacked me on the head."

Just then Betsey came in with her baby in her arms, and Moses shuffled aside to give place to her, cowed by an admonishing glance from his mother-in-law.

"Bless de Lord!" exclaimed Uncle Ish, lifting his

withered, old hands. " Ef dar ain' anur er Betsey's babies! How many is de, Mose? "

Moses scratched his head and shrank into the corner.

" I ain' done straighten 'em out yit, Unk Ish," he returned slowly. " 'Pears like soon es I done add 'em all up anur done come, an' I has ter kac'late f'om de bottom agin. I ain' got no head fer figgers, nohow. Betsey, she lays dat dar's ten uv 'em, but ter save my soul I can't mek out mo'n eight."

" Dar's nearer er dozen," rejoined Betsey with offended pride, " dar's nearer er dozen 'cordin' ter de way I count."

" Dar now! " cried Aunt Verbeny. " I ain' never trus' no nigger's cac'lations yit, en I ain' gwine ter now. When I wants countin', I want white folks' countin'."

" Dey tell me," said Delphy, glancing sternly at the head on Betsey's knee, " dat de quality don' set demse'ves up on er pa'sel er chillun no mo'. De time done gone by. My Mahaly, she went up ter some outlandish place wid er wild Injun name, like Philadelphy, en she sez de smaller de fambly de mo' stuck up is de heads er it. She sez ef Ole Miss had gone up dar a-puttin' on airs 'case er her fifteen chillun, she wouldn't never have helt up 'er head no mo'. Mahaly, she ain' mah'ed no man, she ain't. She sez en ole maid in Philadelphy des' looks right spang over all de heads, she's so sot up."

" 'Tain' so yer," said Aunt Verbeny feelingly. " 'Tain' so yer. Hit seems like de 'oman nairy a man is laid claim ter ain' wuth claimin'. Ain' dat so, bro' Ish? "

But Uncle Ish only grunted in retort, his head
nodding drowsily. The tremulous tracery the wood-
fire cast upon his face gave it an expression of dumb
intensity which adumbrated all the pathos and the
patience of his race.

" Mahaly wuz er likely gal," went on Aunt Verbeny, " an' when she las' come home, she wuz a-war-
in' spike-heeled shoes en er veil uv skeeter net-
tin'. 'Tain' so long sence Rhody's Viney went to
Philadelphy, too, but she ain' had no luck sence
she wuz born er twin. Hit went clean agin 'er."

" Lord a-mercy, Aunt Verbeny, she ain't a-comin'
back dis way? " asked Betsey, probing the apples
with a small pine stick and giving the softest to
Eugenia.

Aunt Verbeny shook her head.

" She ain' never had no luck on er 'count er bein'
er twin," she said. " When she sot herse'f on
a-gwine up ter de Yankees, Marse Tom, he tuck er
goose quill en wrote out 'er principles* des' es plain
es writin' kin be writ—which ain't plain enough fer
my eyes—en he gun' 'em ter Viney wid his own
han's. Viney tuck 'n put 'em safe 'way down in de
bottom uv 'er trunk en went 'long ter de Yankees.
But she ain' been dar mo'n er week when one night
she went a-traipsin' out on de street en lef' er principles behint 'er, en, bless yo' life, oner dem ar
Yankees breck right in en stole 'em smack 'way f'om
'er. Yo' trunk is a moughty risky place ter kyar
yo' principles, but Viney, she wuz dat sot up."

A nod of assent passed round the group. The
children ate their apples silently, and Moses got up

* Recommendations.

to put fresh wood on the fire. As the green log fell among the smouldering chips vivid tongues of flame shot up the smoked old mortar of the chimney, and the remaining apples burst their brown peels and sent out little rivulets of juice. The crackling of the fresh bark made a cheerful accompaniment to the chirping of a cricket hidden somewhere in the hearthstones.

" Dar now, bro' Ish! " exclaimed Aunt Verbeny, watching Eugenia as she sat in the dull red glare. " Ef dat chile ain't de patt'en er young Miss Meeley, I'se clean cracked in my head, I is. I 'members Miss Meeley des' ez well ez 'twuz yestiddy de day Marse Tom brung her home en de niggers stood a-bowin' en axin' howdy at de gate. She wuz all black en white en cold lookin' twell she smiled, en den it wuz des' like er lightwood blaze in 'er eyes."

Uncle Ish nodded dreamily.

" I use ter ride erlong wid Marse Tom ter co'te 'er," he said, " en de gent'men wuz a-troopin' ter see her in vayous attitudes. Dey buzzed roun' 'er de same ez bees, but she ain' had no eyes fer none 'cep'n Marse Tom."

At that instant the door opened, and Rindy rushed in, breathlesly pursuing Eugenia.

"Miss Chris is pow'ful riled," she announced, "an' Marse Tom is a-stampin' roun' same ez er bull. I reckon you'se gwine ter ketch it when dey once gits dere han's on you." Then, as her eye fell on Nicholas, she assumed an indignant air. " Dis ain't de place fer po' folks," she added.

Eugenia rose and put a roasted apple in her pocket.

"I ain't goin' to catch anything that Bernard doesn't catch," she said. "When he goes I'm goin' too."

And she went out, followed by Rindy and the boys.

The first breath of the chill atmosphere brought a glow to Nicholas's cheek, and he started at a brisk run across the fields. He had gone but a few yards when he was checked by Eugenia's voice.

"Nick!" she called.

Her small, dark shadow was falling on the ground beside him, and by the light of the pale moon he could see the fog of her breath.

As he went towards her she held out her hand.

"Here's an apple I saved for you," she panted. "And—and I don't mind about your being poor white trash!"

He took the apple, but before the reply left his lips she had darted from him and was speeding homeward across the glimmering whiteness of the frost.

BOOK II

A RAINY SEASON

BOOK II

A RAINY SEASON

I

Mrs. Jane Dudley Webb was a lady who supported an impossible present upon an important past. She had once been heard to remark that if she had not something to look back upon she could not live: and, as her retrospective view was racial rather than individual, the consolation attained might be considered disproportionate to the needs of the case. The lines of her present had fallen in a white frame house in the main street of Kingsborough; those of her past began with the first Dudley who swung a lance in Merry England, to end with irascible old William of the name, who slept in the family graveyard upon James River.

Mrs. Webb herself was straight and elegant, and inclined to the ironical, when, as Jane Dudley, the belle of the country-side, she fired the fancy of young Julius Webb, an officer in the cavalry of the United States. He danced a minuet with her at a ball in Washington, was heard to swear an oath by her eyes at punch before the supper was over; and proceeded the following week to spur his courtship upon old William as daringly as he had ever spurred his horse upon an Indian wigwam.

The last Dudley of the Virginian line withstood, through several stormy years, the united appeals of his daughter and her lover. In the end he yielded, subdued by opposition and gout, retaining the strength to insert but a single stipulation in the marriage contract, to the effect that his daughter should drop the name of Jane and be known as Dudley in her husband's household. To this the dashing bridegroom acquiesced with readiness, and when, within a year of the wedding, his wife presented him with a son, he called the boy, as he called the mother, by her maiden name.

He was a jovial young buck, who lived in his cards and his cups and loathed a quarrel as he loved a fight.

When the war between the States arose he went with Virginia, caring little for either cause, but conscious that his heart was where his home was. So he kissed the young mother and the boy at her side and rode lightly away with a laugh upon his lips, to fall as lightly in the mad charge of cavalry at Brandy Station.

When the news came Jane Dudley listened to it in silence, her hands clasping the worsteds she was winding. After the words were spoken she laid the worsteds carefully aside, stooping to pick up a fallen ball. Then she crossed the room and went upstairs.

She said little, refusing herself alike to consolation and to acquaintances, spending her days in the shuttered house with her boy beside her. When he fretted at the restraint she tied a band of crêpe on his little jacket and sent him to play on the green, while she took up her worsteds again and finished the muffler she had been crocheting. If she wept it was in secret, when the lights were out.

Some years later the house was sold over her head, but when she stood, penniless, upon the threshold it was to cross it as haughtily as she had done as a bride. The stiff folds of her black silk showed no wavering ripple, the repose of her lips betrayed no tremor. The smooth, high pompadour of her black hair passed as proudly beneath the arched doorway as it had done in the days of her wifehood and Julius Webb.

Her neighbours opened their wasted stores to her need, and out of their poverty offered her abundance, but she put aside their proffered assistance and undertook, unaided, the support and education of her child, maintaining throughout the struggle her air of unflinching irony. She moved into a small white frame house opposite the church, and let out her spare rooms to student boarders. Her pride was never lowered and her crêpe was never laid aside. She sat up far into the night to darn the sleeves of her black silk gown, but the stitches were of such exquisite fineness that in the dim light of her drawing-room they seemed but an added gloss.

From behind the massive coffee urn at the head of her table she regarded her boarders as so many beneficiaries upon her bounty. When she passed a cup of coffee she seemed to confer an honour; when she returned a receipted bill it was as if she repulsed an insult. People said that she had been born to greatness and that she had never adapted herself to the obscurity that had been thrust upon her—but they said it when her back was turned. To her face

8

the subject was never broached, and her former prosperity was ignored along with her present poverty. Of her own sorrows she, herself, made no mention. When she spoke from the depths of her bitterness of the war and the ruin it had left, her resentment was general rather than personal. Above the mantel in her room hung the sword of Julius Webb, sheathed under the tattered colours of the Confederate States. At her throat she wore a button that had been cut from a gray coat, and, once, after the close of the war, she had pointed to it before a Federal officer, and had said: " Sir, the women of the South have never surrendered!" The officer had looked at the face above the button as he answered: " Madam, had the women of the South fought its battles, surrender would have been for the men of the North." But Jane Webb had smiled bitterly in silence. To her the Federal officer was but an individual member of a national army of invasion, and the rights of the victors, the wrongs of Virginia.

Her neighbours regarded her with almost passionate pride—rebuking their more generous natures by the sight of her unbowed beauty and her solitary revolt. When young Dudley grew old enough to attend school the general and the judge called together upon his mother and offered, with hesitancy, to undertake his education.

" He is only a year or two older than my Tom," began the judge, tripping in his usually steady speech. " I assure you it will give me pleasure to have the boys thrown together."

Mrs. Webb bowed in unaffirmative fashion.

" On my life, ma'am, I can't forget that Julius

Webb fell at Brandy Station," put in the general
hotly. " Your husband died for Virginia, and your
boy shall not want while I have a penny in my
pocket. I'll send him to college with Bernard. and
feel it to be a privilege!"

Mrs. Webb bowed again.

"A great privilege, ma'am," protested the general,
uneasily.

Mrs. Webb smiled.

" The greatest privilege of my life, ma'am!"
cried the general, his face flushing and his eyes
growing round with agitation.

In the end they gained their point, and Mrs. Webb
consented, but with a reluctance of reserve which
caused the general to choke with embarrassment and
the judge to become speechless from perplexity.
When they rose to leave both thanked her with effu-
sion and both bowed themselves out as gratefully as
if it were a royal drawing-room and they had received the honours of knighthood.

" She is a remarkable woman!" exclaimed the
general, wiping his eyes on his white silk handkerchief as they descended the steps. " A most unusual
woman! Why, I feel positively unworthy to sit in
her presence. Her manner brings all my past in-
discretions to mind. It is an honour to have such
a character in the community, sir!"

The judge acquiesced silently.

The interview had tried his Epicurean fortitude,
and he was wondering if it would be necessary to
repeat the call before Christmas.

" If Julius Webb had lived she would have made
a man of him," continued the general enthusiasti-

cally, the purple flush slowly fading from his flabby face. "A creature who could live with that woman and not be made a man of wouldn't be human; he'd be a hound. There is dignity in every inch of her, sir. I will allow no man to question my respect for our immortal Lee—but if Jane Webb had been the commander of our armies, we should be standing now upon Confederate soil——"

"Or upon the ashes of it," suggested the judge, adding apologetically, "she is indeed a woman in a thousand."

He held it to be a lack of courtesy to dissent from praise of any woman whose chastity was beyond impeachment, as he held it to be an absence of propriety to unite in admiration of one who was wanting in the supremest of the feminine virtues. His code was an obvious one, and he had never seen cause to depart from it.

"I hope the boy will be worthy of her," he said. "It is a good name that he bears."

The general took off his straw hat and mopped his brow.

"Worthy of her!" he exclaimed. "He's got to be worthy of her, sir. If he takes any notion in his head not to be, I'll thrash him within an inch of his life. Let him try it, the young scamp!"

The judge laughed easily, having regained his self-possession. "Well, well, there's no telling," he said; "but he's as bright as a steel trap. I wish Tom had half his sense." Then he turned past the church on his way home, and the general, declining an invitation to dinner, went on to the post-office, where he awaited his carriage.

From this time Dudley Webb attended classes at the judge's house and became the popular tyrant of his little schoolroom. He was a dark, high-bred looking boy, with a rich voice and a nature that was generous in small things and selfish in large ones. There was a convincing air of good-fellowship about him, which won the honest heart of slow-witted Tom Bassett, and a half-veiled regard for his own youthful pleasures, which aroused the wrath of Eugenia.

"I can't abide him," she had once declared passionately to Sally Burwell. "Somehow, he always gets the best of everything."

When, after the first few years, Nicholas Burr entered the schoolroom and took his place upon one of the short green benches, Mrs. Webb called upon the judge in person and demanded an explanation.

"My boy has been carefully brought up," she said; "he is a gentleman, and he will not submit to association with his inferiors. His grandfather would not have done so before him."

The judge quailed, but it was an uncompromising quailing—a surrender of the flesh, not the spirit.

"My dear lady," he began in his softest voice, "your son is a fine, spirited fellow, but he is a boy, and he doesn't care a—a—pardon me, madam—a continental whether anybody else is his inferior or not. No wholesome boy does. He doesn't know the meaning of the word—nor does Tom—and I shan't be the one to teach him. Amos Burr's son is a clever, hard-working boy, and if he will take an education from me, he shall have it."

The judge was firm. Mrs. Webb was firm also.

The judge assumed his legal manner; she assumed her hereditary one.

" It is folly to educate a person above his station," she said.

" Men make their stations, madam," replied the judge.

He sat in his great armchair and looked at her with reverent but determined eyes. His head was slightly bent, in deference to her dissenting voice, and his words wavered, but his will did not. In his attitude his respect for her sexually and individually was expressed, but he had argued the opposing interests in his mind, and his decision was judicial.

" I am deeply pained, my dear lady," he said, " but I cannot turn the boy away."

Mrs. Webb did not reply. She gathered up her stiff skirt and departed with folded lips.

After she had gone the judge paced his study nervously for a half-hour, giving uncertain glances towards the hall door, as if he expected the advent of an incarnate thunderbolt. In the afternoon he sent over a bottle of his best Madeira as a peace-offering. Mrs. Webb acknowledged the Madeira, not the truce. The following day General Battle called upon the judge and requested in half-hearted tones the withdrawal of Amos Burr's son. He looked excited and somewhat alarmed, and the judge recognised the hand of the player.

" My dear Tom Battle," he said soothingly, " you do not wish the poor child any harm."

" 'Fore God, I don't, George," stammered the general.

"He's a quiet, unoffending lad."

The general fingered his limp cravat with agitated plump fingers. "I never passed him on the road in my life that he didn't touch his hat," he admitted, "and once he took a stone out of the gray mare's shoe."

"He has a brain and he has ambition. Think what it is to be born in a lower class and to have a mind above it."

The general's great chest trembled.

"I wouldn't injure the little chap for the world George; on my soul, I wouldn't."

"I know it, Tom."

"My own great-grandfather Battle raised himself, George."

The judge waved the fact aside as insignificant.

"Of course, Mrs. Webb is a woman," he said with sexual cynicism, "and her views are naturally prejudiced. You can't expect a woman to look at things as coolly as we do, Tom."

The general brightened.

"'Tisn't nature," he declared. "You can't expect a woman to go against nature, sir."

"And Mrs. Webb, though an unusual woman (the general nodded), is still a woman."

The general nodded again, though less emphatically.

"On my soul, she's wonderful!' he exclaimed. "Why, damme, sir, if I had that woman to brace me up I shouldn't need a julep."

And the judge, flinching from his friend's profanity, called Cæsar to bring in the decanters.

Some time later the general left and Mr. Burwell

appeared, to be met and dispatched by the same arguments.

"Naturally my instincts prompt me to side with an unprotected widow," said Mr. Burwell.

"No Virginian could feel otherwise," admitted the judge in the slightly pompous tone in which he alluded to his native State.

"But as I said to my wife," continued Mr. Burwell with convincing earnestness, "these matters had best be left to men. There is no need for our wives and daughters to be troubled by them. It is for us, who are acquainted with the world and who have had wide experience, to settle all social barriers."

The judge agreed as before.

"I am glad to say that my wife takes my view of it," the other went on. "Indeed, I think she has expressed what I have said to Mrs. Webb."

"Your wife is an honour to her sex," said the judge, bowing.

Then Mr. Burwell left, and the judge spent another half-hour walking up and down his study floor. He had gained the victory, but he would have felt pleasanter had it been defeat. It was as if he had taken some secret advantage of a woman—of a widow.

But the future of Amos Burr's son was sealed so far as it lay in the judge's power to settle with circumstances, and each morning during the school term Mrs. Webb frowned down upon his hurrying figure as it sped along the street and turned the corner at the palace green. Sometimes, when snow was falling, he would shoot by like an arrow, and Dudley would say with quick compassion, as he

looked up from his steaming cakes: "It's because
he hasn't any overcoat, mother. He runs to keep
warm."

But Mrs. Webb's placid eyes would not darken.

When the boys grew too old for school Tom and
Dudley went to King's College for a couple of years,
while Nicholas returned to the farm. The judge
still befriended him, and the contents of Tom's class
books found their way into his head sooner or later,
with more information than Tom's brain could
hold. One of the instructors at the college—a consumptive young fellow, whose ambitions had leaned
towards the bar—gave the boy what assistance he
needed, and when the work of the class-room and
the farm was over, the two would meet in the dim
old library of the college and plod through heavy,
discoloured pages, while the portraits of painted aris-
tocrats glowered down upon the intrusive plebeian.

Despite the hard labour of spring ploughing and
the cold of early winter dawns, when he was up and
out of doors, the years passed happily enough. He
beheld the future through the visions of an imagina-
tive mind, and it seemed big with promise. Sitting
in the quaint old library, surrounded by faded relics
and colourless traditions, he felt the breath of hushed
oratory in the air, and political passion stirred in the
surrounding dust. There was a niche in a small alcove, where he spent the spare hours of many a day,
the words of great, long-gone Virginians lying before him; behind him, through the small square window, all the blue-green sweep of the college grounds
ending where the Old Stage Road led on to his
father's farm.

He plodded ardently and earnestly, the consumptive young instructor following his studies with the wistful eyes of one who sees another striving where he has striven and failed. The students met him with tolerant hilarity, and Tom Bassett, who would have kicked the Declaration of Independence across the campus in lieu of a ball, watched him with secret mirth and open championship. There had sprung up a strong friendship between the two—one of those rare affections which bend but do not break. Dudley Webb, the most brilliant member of his class and the light of his mother's eyes, began life, as he would end it, with the ready grasp of good-fellowship. He had long since outgrown his artificial, childish distrust of Nicholas, and he had as long ago forgotten that he had ever entertained it. As for Nicholas himself, he had not forgotten it, but the memory was of little moment. He had a work to do in life, and he did it as best he might. If it were the ploughing of rocky soil, so much the worse; if the uprooting of dead men's thoughts, so much the better. He slighted neither the one nor the other.

As he grew older he became tall and broad of chest, with shoulders which suggested the athlete rather than the student. His hair had darkened to a less flaming red, his eyes had grown brighter, and the freckles had faded into a general gray tone of complexion.

"He will be the ugliest man in the State," said Mr. Burwell, inflating his pink cheeks, with a return of youthful vanity, "but it is the ugliness that attracts."

Nicholas had not heard, but, had he done so, the

words would have left a sting. He possessed an inherent regard for physical perfection, rendered the greater by his own tormented childhood. He was strong and vigorous and of well-knit sinews, but he would have given his muscle for Dudley Webb's hands and his brains for the other's hair.

Once, as a half-grown boy, in a fit of jealousy inspired by Dudley's good looks, he had called him "Miss Nancy," and knocked him down. When his enemy had lain at his feet on the green he had raised him up and made amends by standing motionless while Dudley lashed him with a small riding-whip. The jealousy had vanished since then, but the smart was still there.

At last the college days were over. Dudley was sent to the university of the State; Tom Bassett and Bernard Battle soon followed, and Nicholas, still plodding and still hopeful, was left in Kingsborough.

Then, upon his nineteenth birthday, the judge, who had left the bench and resumed his legal practice, sent for him and offered to take him into his office while he prepared himself for the bar.

II

When Nicholas descended the judge's steps he lingered for a moment in the narrow walk. His head was bent, and the books which he carried under his arm were pressed against his side. They seemed to contain all that was needed for the making of his future—those books and his impatient mind. His success was as assured as if he held it already in the hollow of his hand—and with success would come honour and happiness and all that was desired of man. It seemed to him that his lot was the one of all others which he would have chosen of his free and untrammelled will. To strive and to win; to surmount all obstacles by the determined dash of ambition; to rise from obscurity unto prominence through the sheer forces that make for power—what was better than this?

Still plunged in thought, he passed the church and followed the street to the Old Stage Road. From the college dormitories a group of students sang out a greeting, and he responded impulsively, tossing his hat in the air. In his face a glow had risen, harmonising his inharmonious features. He felt as a man feels who stands before a closed door and knows that he has but to cross the threshold to grasp the fulness of his aspiration. Yes, to-day he envied no one—neither Tom Bassett nor Dudley Webb, neither the general nor the judge. He held the books tightly under his arm and smiled down upon the road. His clumsy, store-made boots left heavy tracks in the dust, but he seemed to be treading air.

It was three o'clock in the afternoon of a murky day in early November, and the clouds were swollen with incoming autumnal rains. The open country stretched before him in monotonous grays, the long road gleaming pallid in the general drab of the landscape. As he passed along, holding his hat in his hand, his uplifted head struck the single, high-coloured note in the picture—all else was dull and leaden.

A farmer driving a cow to market neared him, and Nicholas stopped to remark upon the outlook. The farmer, a thickset, hairy man, whose name was Turner, gave a sudden hitch to the halter to check the progress of the cow, and nodded ominously.

" Bad weather's brewin'," he said. " The wind's blowin' from the northeast; I can tell by the way that thar oak turns its leaves. It's a bad sign, and if thar ain't a-shiftin' 'fore mornin', we're likely to hev a spell."

Nicholas agreed.

" There hasn't been much rainfall lately," he added. " I reckon it has come at last and for a long stretch." His eyes swept the western horizon, where the clouds hung heavily above the pines.

" Yo' pa got his crops in?"

" Pretty much. The peanuts were harvested after the last frost."

" He ain't had much luck this year, I hear."

Nicholas shook his head.

"No less than usual. Last year he lost the brindle cow that was calving. This season the mare died."

"Well, well! He never was much for luck, nohow. Seems like he worked too hard to have Providence on his side. I allers said that Providence had ruther you'd leave a share of the business to Him. Got through school yet?"

"Yes; I'm reading law."

"Reading what?"

"I am going to study law in the judge's office— Judge Bassett, you know."

"So you can keep a tongue in yo' head when those plagued cusses come 'bout the mortgage?"

"So I can take cases to court and earn a living."

"Why don't you stick to the land and make yo' bread honest?"

"The law's honest."

Turner shook his hairy head.

"It cheated me out o' twelve bushels of 'taters las' year," he said. "Don't tell me 'bout yo' law. I know it."

Nicholas laughed.

"Come to me when I've set up, if you get in trouble," he rejoined, "and I'll get you out."

The cow gave a lunge at the ropes, and the farmer went on his way. When the man and cow had passed from sight Nicholas stopped and laughed again. He wondered if he could be really of one flesh and blood with these people—of one stuff and fibre. What had he in common with his own father—hard-working, heavy-handed Amos Burr? No, he was not of them and he had never been.

He had turned from the main road into the wood, when a girl on horseback dashed suddenly towards him from the gray perspective. She was riding rapidly, her short skirts flying, her hair blown darkly across her face. A brown-and-white pointer ran at her side.

As she caught sight of Nicholas she half rose in her saddle, giving a loud, clear call.

"Hello, Nick Burr! Hello!"

Nicholas stood aside and waited for her to come up, which she did in a moment, panting from her exercise, her face flushing into a glowing heat.

"I was looking for you," she said, waving a small willow spray in her brown hand. "I went by the farm, but you weren't there. So, you are nineteen to-day!" Her eyes shone as she looked at him. There was a singular brilliance of expression in her face, due partly to the exercise, partly to the restless animation of her features. She was at the unbecoming age when the child is merging into the woman, but her lack of grace was redeemed by her warmth of personality.

Nicholas laid his hand upon the bridle.

"Why, Genia, if I'd known you wanted me I'd have been hanging round somewhere. What is it?"

"Let me look at you."

Nicholas flushed, turning his face away from her.

"God knows, I'm ugly enough," he said.

She leaned nearer, shaking back her straight, black hair, which fell from beneath the small cap.

"I want to see if you have changed since yesterday."

He turned towards her.

" Have I ? " he asked hopefully.

She regarded him gravely, though a smile played over her changeful lips.

" Not a bit.   Not a freckle."

" Hang it all!   I lost my freckles long ago."

" Then they've come back.   There are one—two —three on your nose."

" Hold on!   Let my looks alone, please."

Eugenia whistled softly, half grave, half gay.

" Down, darling!" she said to the pointer, and " be still, beauty!" to the horse.   Then she turned to Nicholas again.

" I've really and truly got something to tell you, Nick Burr."

" Out with it, then.   Don't worry."

She swung her long legs idly from the saddle. " Suppose I don't."

" Then don't."

" Suppose I do."

" I'll be hanged if I care!"

" Oh, you do, you story.   You're just dying to know—but it's serious."

She patted the horse's neck, watching Nicholas with child-like eagerness.

" Well, I'm—I'm—there!   I told you you were dying to know!"

" I'm not."

" Guess, anyway."

" Somebody coming on a visit?"

She shook her head.

" Try again, stupid."

" Miss Chris going to be married?"

" Oh, Lord, no.   You aren't really a fool, Nick."

"Betsey got a baby?"

"Why, Tecumsey only came last June!"

"Then I give it up. Tell me."

"Say please."

"Please, Genia!"

"Say 'please, dear, good Genia.'"

"Please, dear, darling Genia."

"I didn't say 'darling.' I said 'good.'"

"It's the same thing."

She smiled at him with boyish eyes.

"Am I really a darling?"

"Do you really know something?"

"You bet I do."

"What is it?"

She laughed teasingly.

"It'll make you cry."

"Hurry up, Genia!"

"You'll certainly cry very loud."

"I'll shake you in a moment."

"It isn't polite to shake ladies."

"You aren't a lady. You're a vixen."

"Aunt Verbeny says I'm a limb of Satan. But will you promise not to weep a flood of tears, so I can't cross home?"

She leaned still nearer, resting her hand upon his shoulder.

"I'm going away."

"What?"

"I'm going away to-morrow at daybreak. I'm going to school. I shan't come back for a whole year. I'm—I'm going to leave papa and Aunt Chris and Jim and you."

She began to sob.

9

" Don't," said Nicholas sharply.

" And—and you don't care a bit. You're just a stone. Oh, I don't want to go to school!"

" I'm not a stone. I do care."

" No, you don't. And I may die and never come back any more, and you'll forget all about me."

" I shan't. Don't, I say. Do you hear me, Genia, don't."

She looked for a handkerchief, and, failing to find one, wiped her eyes on the horse's mane.

" What are you going to do when I am gone?"

" Work hard so you'll be proud of me when you come back."

" I shall be sixteen in two years."

" And I, twenty-one."

" You'll be a man—quite."

" You'll be a woman—almost."

" I don't think I shall like you so much then."

" I shall like you more."

" Why?" she asked quickly.

" Why? Oh, I don't know. Am I so awfully ugly, Genia?"

" Turn this way."

He obeyed her, flushing beneath her scrutiny.

" I shouldn't call you—awful," she replied at last.

" Am I so ugly, then?"

" Honour bright?"

" Of course," impatiently.

" Then you are—yes—rather."

He shook his head angrily.

" I didn't think you'd be mean enough to tell me so," he returned.

" But you asked me."

" I don't care if I did. You might have said something pleasant."

Her sensitive mouth drooped. " I never think of your being ugly when I'm with you," she said. " It's a good, strong kind of ugliness, anyway. I don't mind it."

He smiled again.

" Looks don't matter, anyway," she went on soothingly. " I'd rather a man would be clever than handsome;" then she added conscientiously, " only I'd rather be handsome myself."

He looked at her closely.

" I reckon you will be," he said. " Most women are. It's the clothes, I suppose."

Eugenia looked down at him for an instant in silence; then she held out her hands.

" I am going at daybreak," she said. " Will you come down to the road and tell me good-bye?"

" Why, of course."

" But we must say good-bye now, too. Did we ever shake hands before?"

" No."

" Then, good-bye. I must go."

" Good-bye, dear—darling."

She touched her horse lightly with the willow, but promptly drew rein, regarding Nicholas with her boyish eyes.

" Do you think it would make it any easier if we kissed?" she asked.

" Gerimniy! I should say so!"

He caught her hands; she leaned over and he kissed her lips. She drew back with the same frank laugh, but a flush burned his face and his eyes were sparkling.

" More, Genia," he said, but she laughed and let the bridle fall.

" No—no—but it made me feel better. There, good-bye, dear, dear Nick Burr, good-bye! "

Then she dashed past him, and a whirl of dust filled the solitary air.

He looked after her until she turned her horse into the Old Stage Road, and the clatter of the hoofs was gone. When the stillness had fallen again he went slowly on his way.

In the woods the pale bodies of the beeches seemed to melt into the cloudy atmosphere. There was no wind among the trees, and the pervading dampness had robbed the yellowed leaves of their silken rustle. They fluttered softly, hanging limp from the drooping branches as if attached by invisible threads. As he went on a deep bluish smoke issued from among some far-off poplars where a farmer was burning brush in a clearing. The smoke hung low above the undergrowth, assuming eccentric outlines and varied tones of dusk. Presently the fires glimmered nearer, and he saw the red tongues of the flames and heard the parched crackling of consuming leaves. The figures of the workers were limned grotesquely against the ruddy background with a startling and unreal absence of detail. They looked like incarnate shadows—stalking between the dim beeches and the blazing brush heaps. A few drops of rain fell suddenly, and the fires began slowly to die away. At the foot of the crumbling " worm " fence, skirting the edges of the wood, deep wind-drifts of russet leaves stirred mournfully. Later they would be hauled away to assist in the winter dressing of the fallows; now they beat helplessly against the retarding rails like a vanquished army of invasion.

Nicholas left the wood and passed the field of broomsedge on his way to the house. Beyond the barnyard he saw the long rows of pine staves that had supported the shocks of peanuts, and from the direction of the field he caught sight of his father, driven homeward by the threatening rain.

Sairy Jane, who was bringing a string of dried snaps from the outhouse, called to him to hurry before the cloudburst. She was a lank, colourless girl, with bad teeth and small pale eyes. Jubal, at the churn in the hall, rested from his labours as Nicholas entered, and grinned as he pointed to his mother in the kitchen. Marthy Burr was ironing. As Nicholas crossed the threshold, she stopped in her passage from the stove and looked at him, a flash of pride softening her pain-scarred features.

"Lord, what a man you are, Nick!" she exclaimed with a kind of triumph. "When I heard yo' step on the po'ch I could have swo'ed it was yo' pa's."

Nicholas nodded at her abstractedly as he took off his hat.

"Where's pa?" he asked carelessly. "I thought he'd have got in before me. I saw him as I came up."

"I reckon he won't git in befo' he gits a drenchin'," responded his stepmother, glancing indifferently through the back window. "If he does it'll be the first time sence he war born. 'Twarn't nothin' to be done in the fields, nohow, an' so I told him, but he ain't never rested yet, an' I don't reckon he's goin' to till I bury him."

As she spoke the rain fell heavily, and presently Amos Burr came in, shaking the water from his head and shoulders.

" I told you 'twarn't no use yo' goin' to the fields befo' the rain," began his wife admonishingly. " But you're a man all over, an' it seems like you're 'bliged to go yo' own way for the sheer pleasure of goin' agin somebody else's. If I'd been pesterin' you all day long to go down thar to look at that ploughin', you'd be settin' in yo' chair now, plum dry."

Amos Burr crossed to the stove and turned his dripping back to the heat.

" Gimme a rubbin' down, Sairy Jane," he pleaded, and his daughter took a dry cloth and began mopping off the water.

Marthy Burr placed an iron on the stove and took one off.

" Whar'd you git dinner, Nick? " she inquired suddenly.

" At the judge's."

" What did they have? " demanded Jubal from the hall, ceasing the clatter of the churn. " Golly! Wouldn't I like a bite of something! "

" I shouldn't mind some strange cookin', myself," said Marthy Burr, shaking her head at one of the children who had come into the kitchen with muddy feet. " I ain't tasted anybody else's vittles for ten years, an' sometimes I feel my mouth waterin' for a change of hand in the dough."

She took one of her husband's shirts from the

pile of freshly dried clothes, spread it on the ironing-board, and sprinkled it with water. Then she moistened her finger and applied it to the iron.

Amos Burr looked up from before the stove, where he still sat drying.

"You're a man now, Nick," he said slowly, as if the words had been revolving in his brain for some time and he had just received the power of speech.

"Yes, pa."

"Whatever he is, he don't git it from his pa," put in Marthy Burr as she bent over the shirt. "He ain't got nothin' of yo'rn onless it's yo' hair, an' that's done sobered down till you wouldn't know it."

Amos waited patiently until she had finished, and then went on heavily as if the pause had been intentional, not enforced.

"You've got as much schoolin' as most city chaps," he said. "Much good it'll do you, I reckon. I never saw nothin' come of larnin' yet, 'cep'n worthlessness. But you'd set yo' mind on it, an' you've got it."

"Thar warn't none of yo' hand in that, Amos Burr," cried his wife, checking him again before he had recovered breath from his last sentence. "Many's the night I've wrastled with you till you war clean wore out with sleeplessness, 'fo' you'd let the child keep on at his books."

"I ain't never seen no good come of it," repeated Burr stolidly; then he returned to Nicholas.

"I reckon you'll want to do somethin' for the family, now," he said, "seein' yo' ma is well wore out an' the brindle cow died calvin', an' Sairy Jane is a hard worker."

Nicholas looked at him without speaking.

"Yes?" he said inquiringly, and his voice was dull.

"I was talkin' to Jerry Pollard," continued his father, letting his slow eyes rest upon his son's, "an' he said you war as likely a chap as thar was roun' here, and he reckoned you'd be pretty quick in business."

"Yes?" said Nicholas again in the same tone.

Amos Burr was silent for a moment, and his wife filled in the pause with a series of running interjections. When they were over her husband took up his words.

"He wants a young fellow about his store, he says, as can look arter the books an' the business. He's gittin' too old to keep up with the city ways an' look peart at the ladies—he'll pay a nice little sum in cash every week."

"Yes?" repeated Nicholas, still interrogatively.

"An' he wants to know if you'll take the place— you're jest the sort of chap he wants, he says— somebody as will be bright at praisin' up the calicky to the gals when they come shoppin'. Thar's nothin' like a young man behind the counter to draw the gals, he says."

Nicholas shook his head impatiently, clasping the books tightly beneath his arm. His gaze had grown harsh and repellent.

"But I am going into the judge's office," he answered. "I am going——" Then he checked himself, baffled by the massive ignorance he confronted.

Amos Burr drew one shoulder from the fire and offered the other. A slow steam rose from his smoking shirt, and the room was filled with the odour of scorching cotton.

"Thar ain't much cash in that, I reckon," he said.

Nicholas took a step forward, still facing his father with obstinate eyes. One of the books slipped from his arm and fell to the floor, with open leaves, but he let it lie. He was watching his father's jaws as they rose and fell over the quid of tobacco.

"No, there is not much cash in that," he repeated.

"Things have gone mighty hard," said Amos Burr. "It's been a bad year. I ain't sayin' nothin' 'bout the work yo' ma an' Sairy Jane an' me have done. That don't seem to count, somehow. But nothin' ain't come straight, an' thar ain't a cent to pay the taxes. If we can't manage to tide over this comin' winter thar'll have to be a mortgage in the spring."

Sairy Jane began to cry softly. One of the children joined in.

"Give me time," said Nicholas breathlessly. "Give me time. I'll pay it all in time." Then the sound of Sairy Jane's sobs maddened him and he turned upon her with an oath. "Damn you! Can't you be quiet?"

It seemed to him that they were all closing upon him and that there was no opening of escape.

Marthy Burr put down her iron and came to where he stood, laying her hand upon his sleeve.

"Don't mind 'em, Nick," she said, and her sharp voice broke suddenly. "Go ahead an' make a man of yo'self, mortgage or no mortgage."

Nicholas lifted his gaze from the floor and looked

into his stepmother's face.   Then he looked at her
hand as it lay upon his arm.   That trembling hand
brought to him more fully than words, more clearly
than visions, the pathos of her life.

"Don't you worry, ma," he said quietly at last.
"It'll be all right.   Don't you worry."

Then he let her hand slip from his shoulder and
left the room.

He passed out upon the back porch and stood
gazing vacantly across the outlook.

It rained heavily, the drops descending in hori-
zontal lengths like a fantastic fall of colourless pine
needles.   Overhead the clouds were black, impenetrable.

Through the falling rain he looked at the view
before him, at the overgrown yard, at the manure
heaps near the stable, at the grim rows of staves in
the peanut field, at the sombre and deserted landscape.   A raw wind blew in gusts from the northeast, and the distorted ailanthus tree in the yard
moaned and wrung its twisted limbs.   Sharp, unpleasant odours came from the pig-pen in the barnyard, where the rain was scattering the slops in the
trough.   A bull bellowed in a far-off pasture.   Before the hen-house door several dripping fowls
strutted with wilted feathers.

He saw it all in silence, with the dogged eyes of
one whose gaze is turned inward.   He made no
gesture, uttered no exclamation.   He was as motionless as the lintel of the door on which he leaned.

Suddenly a gust of wind whipped the rain into
his face.   He turned, reëntered the house, closed
the door carefully, and went upstairs.

III

The next morning Nicholas went into the judge's study and declined the offer of the day before.

"I shan't read law, after all," he said slowly. "There is a business opening for me here, and I'll take advantage of it." He spoke in set phrases, as if he had rehearsed the sentences many times.

"Business!" echoed the judge incredulously. "Why, what business is going on in Kingsborough?"

Nicholas flushed a deep red, but his glance did not waver.

"Jerry Pollard wants me in his store, sir."

The judge removed his glasses, wiped them deliberately on his silk handkerchief, put them on again, and regarded the younger man attentively.

"And you wish to go into Jerry Pollard's store?" he inquired.

"I think it is the best thing I can do."

"The best paying thing, I presume?"

"Yes, sir."

"Bless my soul!" exclaimed the judge testily. "What is the world coming to? I suppose Tom will be writing me next that he intends to keep a stall in market. Well, you know best, of course. You may do as you please; but may I ask if you are going to bargain in Latin and multiply by criminal law in Jerry Pollard's store?"

" No, sir."

" Then, what in the—what in the—I really feel the need of a strong expression—what in the world did you take the trouble to educate yourself for?"

Nicholas was looking at the floor, and he did not raise his eyes. His face was hard and set.

" Because I was a fool," he answered shortly.

" And now, if I may ask?"

" A fool still—but I've found it out."

The judge leaned back in his chair and tapped the ledge of his desk meditatively.

" Have you fully decided?" he asked.

Nicholas nodded.

" I have thought it over," he said quietly.

" Then there's nothing to be done, I suppose. I hope the compensation will satisfy you. Jerry Pollard is said to be somewhat tight-fisted, but your business instincts may be equal to his acquirements. Now, I have a number of letters, so, if you don't mind, I will bid you good-day."

He bowed, and Nicholas left the study and went out of the house.

Rain was still falling, and small pools of water had formed on the palace green. Straight ahead the lane of maples stretched like a line of half-extinguished fires, and the ground beneath was strewn with wet, red leaves. The slanting sheets of rain gave a sombre aspect to the town—to the time-beaten buildings along the unpaved streets and to the commons, where the water stood in grassy hollows. Beneath the gray sky the scene assumed a

spectre-like suggestion of death and decay—the
death of laughter that seemed still to echo faintly
from the vanished stones—the decay of royal charters and of kingly grants. The very air 'was reminiscent of a yesterday that was perished; the
red, wet leaves painted the brown earth in historic
colours.

Nicholas turned the corner at the church and
passed on to Jerry Pollard's store—a long, low
structure fronting on the main street—and entered
by a single step from the sidewalk. The show windows on either side the entrance displayed a motley
selection from the varied assortment of a " general "
store—cheap silks and high-coloured calicos, men's
shirts and women's shoes, cravats and hairpins, sus-
penders and corsets. On the sidewalk near the doorway there was a baby carriage, a saddle, and a collection of farming implements. As Nicholas crossed
the threshold a pink-cheeked girl passed him, her
arms filled with bundles, and at the counter an old
negro woman was pricing red flannel.

Jerry Pollard, a coarse-featured, full-bearded man
of sixty years, was behind the counter. Nicholas
caught his persuasive tones as he leaned over, holding the end of the bolt of flannel in his hands.

" Now, look here, Aunty, you ain't going to find
such a bargain as this anywhere else in town. Take
my oath on that. Every thread wool and forty-four
inches wide. Only thirty cents a yard, too. I got
it at an auction in Richmond, or I couldn't let it go
at double that price. How much? All right."

The flannel was measured off with skilful manipulations of the yardstick and the scissors, the parcel

was handed to the old negro woman, and the change was dropped into the till. Then Jerry Pollard came from behind the counter and slapped Nicholas upon the shoulder.

"Hello, my boy!" he said. "So your pa has taken me at my word, and here you are. Well, Jerry Pollard's word's his bond, and he ain't going back on it. So, when you feel like it, you can step right in and get to business. When'll you begin? To-day? No time like the present time's my motto."

"To-morrow!" returned Nicholas hastily. "I've got some things to wind up. I'll come to-mor-row."

"All right. I'm your man. To-morrow at seven sharp?"

Then a purchaser appeared, and Jerry Pollard went forward, his business smile returning to his face.

The purchaser was Mrs. Burwell, and, as Nicholas passed out, she looked up from a pair of waffle-irons she was selecting and nodded pleasantly.

"I am glad to see you, Nicholas," she said. "Ju-liet was asking after you in her last letter. You were always a favourite of Juliet's. I was telling Mr. Burwell so only last night."

"She was very kind," returned Nicholas, and added: "Is Miss Juliet—Mrs. Galt well?"

Juliet Burwell had married five years before, and he had not seen her since.

Mrs. Burwell nodded cheerily. She was still fresh and youthful, her pink cheeks and bright eyes giving the gray of her hair the effect of powder sprinkled on her brown fringe.

" Yes, Juliet is well," she answered. " They are living in Richmond now. Mr. Galt had to give up his practice in New York because the climate did not suit Juliet's health. I told him she couldn't stand transplanting to the north, and I was right. They had to move south again. Yes, Mr. Pollard, the middle-size irons, please. I think they'll fit my stove. If they don't, I'll exchange them for the small ones. What did you say, Nicholas ? Oh! good-morning."

She turned away, and Nicholas stepped over her dripping umbrella and went out into the rain.

When he was once outside he shook the water from his shoulders and walked rapidly in the direction of the old brick court-house, isolated upon the larger green. The door and windows were closed, but he ascended the stone steps and stood beneath the portico, looking back upon the way that he had come.

The street was deserted, save for a solitary ox-cart rolling heavily through the mud. In the distance the gray drops made a sombre veil, through which the foliage of King's College showed in a blurred discolouration. From the branches of trees a double fall of water descended with a melancholy sound.

Presently the ox-cart neared him, and the driver nodded, eyeing him with apathetic interest.

When the cart had passed Nicholas came down the steps and started up the street at the same rapid walk. He was not thinking of his way, but the impulse of action had seized upon him, and he was walking down the ferment in his brain. He did not formulate the thought that with bodily fatigue would come mental indifference; he merely felt that when he was tired—dead tired—he would go home and sit down to dinner and face his father and discuss Jerry Pollard's terms.   He would do that when he was too tired to care—not before.

When he reached the heavy iron gate of the college he swung it open and entered the grounds.   In the centre of the walk stood the statue of a great Colonial governor, and he paused before it for an instant, staring up into the battered features of the marble face.   He realised suddenly that he had never looked at it before.   Daily, for twelve years, he had passed the college campus, sometimes crossing it so that he might have brushed the effigy of the great Englishman with a careless hand—but he had never seen the face before.   Then he looked through the falling rain at the deserted archway of the old brick building.   For the first time those grim walls, which had been thrice overthrown and had arisen thrice from their ashes, impressed him with the triumphant service they had rendered in the culture of his kind. He saw it as it was—a sacred skeleton, an honourable decay.   The long line of illustrious hands that had procured its ancient charter seemed to wave a ghostly benediction over its ancient learning. Clergy and burgesses, council and governor, planters of Virginia and bishops of London had stood by its birth.   It was the fruit of the union of the old world and the new, and it had waxed strong upon the milk of its mother ere it turned rebel.   Later, to its younger country, it had sent forth its sons as statesmen who gave glory to its name.   And through all its history it had overcome calamity and defied assault.   Thrice it had fallen and thrice it had re-arisen.

He recalled next the sheltered alcove in the dim library, where he had studied with the consumptive young instructor, who was dead.   The creepers upon the wall were encroaching stealthily upon the alcove window.   Scarlet tendrils, like forked flames, licked the narrow ledge.   Several wet sparrows fluttered in and out among the leaves.

He turned hastily away, passed the great English-man with unseeing eyes, clanged the iron gate heav-ily behind him, and went on towards the house of his father.

The family were at dinner when he entered, and he took his seat silently in the empty chair at his stepmother's right hand.

As he sat down she reached out and felt his coat sleeve.

" I declar, Nick, you air soaked clean through," she said.   " Anybody'd think you'd been layin' out in the rain all night.   You go up and change your clothes an' I'll keep your dinner hot on the stove."

Nicholas went upstairs mechanically, and when he came down his father had gone to the stable and his stepmother was alone in the kitchen.

She brought him his dinner, standing beside the table while he ate it, watching him with an intentness that was almost wistful.

" Would you like some molasses on your corn pone? " she asked as he finished and pushed his plate away.   Then, as he shook his head, she added hesitatingly, " It come from Jerry Pollard's store."

But he only shook his head again, following with his eyes the wave-like design on the mahogany-coloured oilcloth that covered the table.

Marthy Burr set the jug aside, nervously clearing her throat.

" I reckon Jerry Pollard has got one of the finest stores anywhar 'bouts," she said suddenly.

Nicholas looked up quickly and met her eyes. She was holding a dish of baked potatoes in one hand and the other was resting for support upon the edge of the table. Her face was yellow and inter-lined, and a faint odour of camphor came from the bandage about her cheek.

" Yes," he replied indifferently. " He does a very good business."

His stepmother put the dish of potatoes back upon the table and took up the pitcher of buttermilk. Her hand was trembling nervously. There was a slight gasp in her voice when she spoke.

" I don't know but what it's as big a thing to be in a fine store like that as 'tis to be a lawyer," she said.

For a moment Nicholas did not answer. His eyes grew darker as she stood before him, and a shadow closed upon his face. As in a frame, he saw the out-line of her figure defined against the square of falling rain between the window sashes. Her shoulders, bent slightly forward as if crushed by the bearing of heavy burdens, reminded him of a domestic animal, full of years and labour.

His face softened and he smiled into her eyes.

" Yes, I don't know but what it is just as well," he responded cheerfully.

The next day he went into Jerry Pollard's store
and began his winter's work. He measured off unbleached cotton cloth for a servant girl; sold a pair
of shoes to a farmer, a cravat to a young fellow from
the grocery shop next door, and a set of garden
tools to an elderly lady who lived in the street facing
the asylum and had a greenhouse. At odd times he
looked over Jerry Pollard's books, and after dark he
dunned several debtors for unpaid bills. He did it
quietly and thoroughly, neither shirking nor over-
elaborating the minutest detail. There are men who
have an immense capacity for taking pains that is
rarer than genius, and he was one of them. Whether
he made a success or a failure of life, he would do it
with a conscientious use of opportunities, good or
bad. An eye that is trained to detect the values of
circumstances, and a hand that is quick to adjust
them, have produced the mental forces that make
or unmake the race.

When the day was over he went home and ascended to his room in silence. The work had left
him with a curious irritating sense of its distasteful-
ness. The second day was as the first—the week
was as the month. There were no variations, no
difficulties, no advancement. With the round of
monotony his irritation sharpened. When Jerry
Pollard spoke he responded in monosyllables; when
Jerry Pollard's pretty daughter, Bessie, smiled in
from the doorway, he kept his eyes on the counter.
At home he was even less responsive. The impulse
which had prompted him to return a cheering falsehood to his stepmother passed quickly. He sacrificed himself to the family interests, but he sacrificed

himself begrudgingly. His face assumed lines of sullen repression; the tones of his voice were full of subdued resentment. He found satisfaction in meeting their overtures with irony, their constraint with callousness. Since he had given the one thing they required and he valued, he justified himself in a series of petty tyrannies. He met his stepmother with avoidance, his father with aversion. The children he swore at or ignored. Amos Burr, gathering his slow wits together, regarded him with a chuckle of self-congratulation. His sensibilities were not susceptible to slight friction, and his son's attitude seemed to him of small significance. He had got what he wanted, and that was sufficient unto the hour.

After the first two months, Nicholas underwent a dogged and indifferent adaptation. He ceased to think of the judge, of Juliet, of Eugenia. He laughed at Jerry Pollard's jokes and he winked at Jerry Pollard's daughter. His horizon narrowed to the four walls of the shop; he told himself that he had a roof above his head and fuel for his stomach —that Bessie Pollard had skin that was fairer than Eugenia's and lips as red. What did it matter, after all?

Sometimes Mrs. Webb entered the store, sweeping him, as she swept the counter, with her clear, cold glance, and once Sally Burwell ran in to do an errand for her mother and nodded with distant pleasantness as she met his eyes. At such times he flushed and ground his teeth, but after Mrs. Webb came farmer Turner, who shook his hand and said:

" Wall, I'm proud of you, Nick Burr."

And after Sally Burwell pretty Bessie Pollard threw him a kiss from the doorway.   It was not that he was ashamed of his work.   He knew that at the close of the war better men than he sought and accepted gratefully such a livelihood as he disdained— that women in whose veins ran good old English blood left their wasted homes to teach in public schools, or turned their delicate hands to the needle for support.   He was ashamed of his past ambition —of his vaunted aspiration—and he was ashamed of Jerry Pollard and his service.

The winter wore gradually to spring.   A brilliant April melted into a watery May.   Nicholas, coming to Kingsborough in the early mornings, would feel the long spring rains in his face as he splashed through the puddles in the road.   In the wood the white blossoms of dogwood showed through interlacing branches like stars in a network of closely wrought iron.   On their hardy shrubs the pale pink clusters of mountain laurel were beaten into shapeless colour-masses by the wind-blown rains.   Sometimes, up above, where the fiery points of redbud trees shot skyward, a thrush sang or a blue jay scolded—and the bird-notes were laden, like the air, with the primal ripeness of spring.

Underfoot the earth was fecundating in dampness. Chill blue violets emerged from beneath the spread of rotting leaves, and where the washed-out sunlight had last shone it had left rays of wandering dandelions straying from the open roadside to the edges of the wood.

And the spring passed into Nicholas also.   The wonderful renewal of surrounding life thrilled through the repression of his nature. With the flowing of the sap the blood flowed more freely in his veins. New possibilities were revealed to him; new emotions urged him into fresh endeavours. All his powerful, unspent youth spurred on to manhood.

IV

At last the rains were over. The sun came out
again, and with it the growth of the season burst into
abundance. There were bird-notes on the air,
fragrance in the stillness, bloom on the trees. In
the thicket dogwood massed itself in clouds of dead-
white stars, like an errant trail from the Milky Way,
lighting the wooded twilight. Wild azalea, so
deeply rose that the hue seemed of the blood, wafted
its sharp, unearthly scent across the underbrush to
the road. The woods were vocal with the mating
songs of their winged inhabitants. The music of
the thrush welled from the sheer forceful joy of living. " It is good—good—good to be a lover ! " he
sang again and again with amorous repetition and
a full-throated flourish of improvisation. In the
pauses of the thrush sounded the cheery whistle of
the redbird, the crying of the catbird, the liquid
tones of the song sparrow, and the giddy exclamations of the pewee. Sometimes an oriole darted
overhead in a royal flash of black and yellow, a robin
stood in the road and delivered a hearty invitation,
or a hawk flew past, pursued by martins.

With the spring planting came a chance of outdoor work, and Nicholas would sometimes rise at
dawn and do a piece of ploughing before breakfast.
He had driven the team out one morning across
the brown, bare earth, which the plough had ripped
open in a jagged track, when something in the

silence and the scents of nature smote him suddenly
as with a vital force. Dropping the reins to the
ground, he threw back his head and breathed a keen,
quick sense of exaltation. A warm mist, sweet and
fresh as the breath of a cow, overhung hill and
field, road and meadow. In a black-browed cedar
tree a mocking-bird was singing.

With a sudden shout Nicholas voiced the glorifi-
cation of toil—of honest work well done. He felt
with the force of a revelation that to throw up the
clods of earth manfully is as beneficent as to revolu-
tionise the world. It was not the matter of the
work, but the mind that went into it, that counted—
and the man who was not content to do small
things well would leave great things undone. The
beasts before him did not shirk their labour because
it was clay and not gold dust that trailed behind the
plough; why should he? And where was happiness
if it sprung not from the soil? Where contentment
if it dwelt not near to Nature? For what was better
than these things—the clear air of sunrise, the keen,
sweet smell of the fertile earth, the relaxation of tired
muscles? Why should he, who had been born to the
soil, struggle forth to alien ends as a sightless earth-
worm to the harrow's teeth?

On his way in from the fields he stopped an instant at the gate of the barnyard to look at the red-
and-white cow that was licking her little, tottering
calf. Some rollicking lambs were skipping near a
dignified group of ewes, that looked on with half-
fearful, half-disapproving faces.

At the pump he saw his stepmother filling a water
bucket, and he took it from her hands.

" I reckon it is too heavy for you to carry," he said
timidly.

" 'Tain't much to tote," returned Marthy Burr
opposingly.   " If I'd never had nothin' more'n that
to bear I'd have as straight a back as yo' pa's got.
'Tain't the water buckets as bends a woman, nohow;
it's the things as the Lord lays on extry."

She relinquished the bucket and followed Nicholas resentfully to the house.

" I never did care 'bout havin' folks come 'round
interferin' with my burdens," she murmured half-
aggrievedly.   " I ain't done for yet, an' when I is
I reckon I'll know it as soon as anybody—lessen it's
yo' pa, who's got powerful sharp eyes at seein' the
failin's of other people—an' powerful dull ones when
it comes to recognisin' his own."

Then she set about preparing breakfast, and
Nicholas flung himself into a chair on the porch.
Nannie, a pretty, auburn-haired girl, was grinding
coffee in a small mill, and he looked at her thoughtfully; then Jubal came out, whittling a stick, and he
turned his gaze inquiringly upon him.

" What would you like to do in the world,
Jubal ? " he asked, " best of all ? "

Jubal looked up in perplexity, his fat forehead
wrinkling.

" You ain't countin' in eatin', I s'pose? " he replied doubtfully.

Nicholas shook his head.

" No, leave out eating," he said.

" An' the splittin' open of that durn livered Spike
Turner ? "

" Yes, that too."

Jubal whittled slowly, his forehead wrinkling more deeply.

"Then I don't know whether it's to give ma a rest or to own Billy Flinders's coon dog, Boss," he said.

Nicholas laughed for an instant, but the laugh softened into a smile.

At the table he asked his stepmother and Sairy Jane about the spring chickens, and they answered with surprised eagerness.

"I am going to mark the lambs to-morrow," he said. "They're a nice lot." And he added: "Some day I'll take the farm and make it pay."

"I don't see what you want to go steppin' in yo' pa's shoes for," put in Marthy Burr. "When toes have got p'inted down-hill they ain't goin' no other way. Don't you come back to raisin' things on this land. I ain't never seen nothin' thrive on it yet, cep'n weeds, an' the Lord knows they warn't planted."

Nicholas shook his head.

"Why, look at Turner," he said. "His land is as poor as this, and he makes an easy living."

"A Turner ain't a Burr," returned his stepmother with uncompromising logic, "an' a Burr ain't a Turner. Whar the blood runs the man follows, an' yours ain't runnin' towards the farm. Jeb Turner can fling a handful of corn in poor groun', an' thar'll come up a cornfield, an' yo' pa may plant with the sweat of his brow an' the groanin' of his spirit, an' the crows git it. A farmer's got to be born, same as a fool. You can't make a corn pone out of flour dough by the twistin' of it."

"That's so," admitted Amos Burr, laying down his knife and meeting his wife's eyes. "That's so.

You can't make a corn pone out of flour dough, noways you turn it."

"Perhaps I'll try some day," said Nicholas with a laugh; and he rose and went out of the house.

When he had reached the little gate he heard a voice behind him, and turned to find his half-sister Nannie, her cheeks flushed like a damp, wild rose above her faded dress.

"I want you to bring me something from the store, Nick," she stammered. "I want a blue ribbon for my hair, it's—it's so worrisome."

She shook her auburn locks, and Nicholas realised suddenly that she must be very good to look at—to men who were only in a Scriptural sense her brothers. He felt a vague pride in her.

"Why, of course I will," he answered. "Blue let it be."

And he opened the gate and went on his way, leaving Nannie, still flushed, in the path.

When he took down Jerry Pollard's shutters a half-hour later he stood for an instant looking thoughtfully down upon the assortment in the window. Then he leaned over and conscientiously set upright a blue-glass vase before going behind the counter to unpin the curtains hanging across the dry-goods shelves.

After breakfast Bessie Pollard came in and stood with her elbow resting on the showcase as she flirted a small feather duster. She had just released her hair from curl paper, and it hung in golden ringlets over her forehead. Her face was ripe and red, like a well-sunned peach, and the firm curves of her bosom swelled the gathers of her gown.

" You look real spry this morning," she said coquettishly; but he turned from her in sudden distaste. Her tawdry refinement irritated the more serious manner of his mood.

Presently she went back to her dusting, and he completed his daily setting to rights of the shop before he drew up to the desk and made out the bills that were due for the month. It was not until some hours later that he looked up upon hearing a step on the threshold. At first he stood up mechanically at the sight of a girl in a riding-habit. Then he started and drew back, for the girl lifted her head, and he saw that it was Eugenia Battle. In the same glance he saw also that there was a keen surprise in her face.

" Why, Nick Burr!" she said breathlessly. She tripped over her long riding-skirt and caught it hastily in one hand; in the other she carried a small switch. She had grown tall and straight, and her hair was gathered up from her shoulders.

For a moment they were both silent. In Eugenia's face the surprise gave place to gladness, and the warmth of her personality gathered to her eyes. She held out her ungloved hand.

" Why, Nick Burr!" she said again.

But Nicholas looked at her in silence. All the dogged bitterness of the last six months welled to his lips—all his new-found philosophy evaporated at the sting of wounded pride. He remembered with a start the gray road on the afternoon in November, the sullen cast of the sky, the hopeless trend of the wind among the trees, the leaping of the light into Eugenia's face. She laughed now as she had laughed then—a hearty little burst of surprise in the suddenness of the meeting.

He turned quickly from the outstretched hand.

" What can I do for you? " he asked, and his tone was like Jerry Pollard's.

Eugenia's hand fell to her side, closing upon the folds of her skirt. She caught her lip between her teeth with a petulant twitch. Then she came forward and laid a small brown bit of cloth upon the counter.

" A spool of silk this shade," she said briskly. " Please match it very carefully."

Nicholas pulled open the small drawers containing the silk, and compared the sample with the row of spools. He made his selection, showing it to Eugenia before wrapping it in brown paper.

" Is that all? " he asked grimly.

Eugenia nodded. He gave her the spool, and she lifted her skirt and went out of the shop. A moment more, and she passed the door swiftly on the brown mare. Nicholas closed the drawer and laid the torn sheet of wrapping paper back in its place. A little girl came in for a card of hooks and eyes for her mother, a dressmaker, and he gave them to her and dropped the nickel in the till. When she went out he followed her to the door and stood looking out into the gray dust of the street.

Across the way a lady was gathering roses from a vine that clambered over her piazza, and the sunlight struck straight at her gracious figure. From afar off came the sound of children laughing. Down the street several mild-eyed Jersey cows were driven by a little negro to the court-house green.

In a near tree a wood-bird sang a score of dreamy notes. Gradually the quiet of the scene wrought its spell upon him—the insistent languor drugged him like a narcotic. On the wide, restless globe there is perhaps no village of three streets, no settlement that has been made by man, so utterly the cradle of quiescence. From the listless battlefields, where grass runs green and wild, to the little white-washed gaol, where roses bloom, it is a petrified memory, a perennial day dream.

The lady across the street passed under her rose vine, her basket filled with creamy clusters. The cows filed lazily on the court-house green. The wood-bird in the near tree sang over its dreamy notes. The clear black shadows in the street lay like full-length figures across the vivid sunlight.

The bitterness passed slowly from his lips. He turned, and was reëntering the shop, when his name was called sharply.

"Why, Nick Burr!"

The words were Eugenia's, but the voice was Tom Bassett's. He had come up suddenly with the judge, and as Nicholas turned he caught his hand in a hearty grasp.

"Well, I call this luck!" he cried. "I say, Nick, you haven't grown bald since I saw you. Do you remember the time you shaved every strand of hair off your head so we'd stop calling you 'Carrotty'?"

"I remember you called me 'Baldy,'" said Nicholas, running his hand through his thick, red hair. Then he looked at the judge. "I hope you are well, sir," he added.

The judge bowed with his fine-flavoured courtesy.
"As I trust you are," he returned graciously.

"Well, all I've got to say," put in Tom, as his
father finished, "is that it's a shame—a confounded
shame.   What good will Nick's brains do him in old
Pollard's store?   Old Pollard's a skinflint, anyway,
and he cuffed me once when I was a small chap."

Nicholas glanced back uncertainly into the shop.
"Oh, he isn't so bad when you know him," he
said.   "Most folks aren't."

"He seems to value Nicholas's services," added
the judge politely.

Nicholas flushed.   "I don't know about that," he
returned awkwardly.

"I know one thing, though," said Tom with
slow wrath, "and that is that I'm not green enough
to be fooled by Nick Burr, if other people are.
Father told me last night that it was Nick's own
choice that took him to Jerry Pollard's.   Choice,
the Dickens!   Why, it's those blasted people of his
that put him here."

Tom was very red in the face, so was Nicholas.
They looked at the judge, and the judge looked
back at them with a humorous twinkle in his eyes.

"My dear Tom," he said at last, "I never gave
you credit for being a Solomon, but some day your
wit may put your father to shame."

Then he held out his hand to Nicholas.

"When you're a little older, my boy," he remarked, "you may learn that, though an old fool
may be the biggest fool, he's not the only one.
Come to see us when you feel like it, eh, Tom?"

They passed on together, and Nicholas stood

looking after them until a man came in to exchange a pair of shoes.

"They're a leetle too skimpy 'cross the toes," he said deprecatingly. "The heels air first-rate, but the toes sorter seem to be made fur a three-toed somebody. 'Tain't as if I could jest set aroun' in 'em, of course; then they'd be a fine fit, but when I go ter stan' up they pinches."

Nicholas gave him a larger size and put the box back upon the shelf. He was thinking of Tom Bassett and the twinkle in the judge's eyes, and he did not hear the man's rambling speech. It seemed to him that his friendship with Tom and his father had been restored—that he might once more go freely in and out of the judge's house.

When the day was over he walked slowly homeward along the deserted road, his mind still busy with recollections of the morning. Yes, life was decidedly endurable at worst. If he might not become celebrated, he might at least become content. He was *not* Tom Bassett, but he had Tom Bassett's friendship. He would live a simple life in his own class among his own people, and he would grow to be respected by those who were above him.

He had entered the wood, when he remembered suddenly that he had forgotten the ribbon for his sister Nannie. He turned quickly and retraced his steps through the thickening twilight.

V

So Nicholas's first fight for his manhood was fought and won. He went back to his books—went back because his intellect ordained it, and the ordinance of intellect is fate—but bitterness had gone out of him, and he had come into his own. From the stress of the last year he had found security in acceptance. His life might not be such as he had planned it—whose was?—his work might not be the thing he wanted—again, whose was?—but life and work were with him, and it remained for him to make the best of them. Fate might make him a shopkeeper; he would see to it that it made him a successful one. Success read backwards spelt work, and work was his inheritance—a heritage of sweat and labour.

He went to Jerry Pollard's an hour earlier that he might rearrange to advantage the shelves. His employer had secured, below cost, a supply of dry goods, and preparations were in the making for the first summer sale in Kingsborough. Nicholas conducted the arrangements as conscientiously as he might have conducted a legal argument. It was the thing before him, and it must not fail.

But at night he found his greater hour. When supper was over and he had helped his father with the odd jobs of the farm, he would take the smoky kerosene lamp to his room and plunge into the pages of " The Federalist." From his sharp, retentive memory nothing passed.   He held his knowledge with the same vital grip with which he held his friends.

He had the judge's library now and the judge's assistance.   Evening after evening he sat in the dim, ghost-hallowed room, the shining calf-bound volumes girdling the walls, and absorbed the judge as the judge, in his own time, had absorbed the men who were gone.   From that rich storehouse of high principles and simple deeds Nicholas's future was drawing nourishment.   Judge Bassett had lived his life in a village, but he had lived it among statesmen. His book-shelves were green with their inspiration, his memory fresh from their impress.   In his youth he himself had been one of the hopes of his State; in his age he was one of her consolations.

He treated the younger man with that quaint courtliness which knew not affectation.   When he talked to him, as he often did, of the great legal minds, it was always with the courtesy of their titles. He spoke of " Mr. Chancellor Kent," of " Mr. Justice Blackstone," as he spoke of " President Davis " or of "General Lee."   To have alluded to them more familiarly he would have held to be a breach of etiquette of unpardonable grossness.

One day he had started in Nicholas his old political dreams of Jeffersonian lustre.

" Virginia is not dead but sleepeth," the judge had said, as a prelude to denunciation of the Readjuster party then in power.

Nicholas was looking at a collection of autograph letters that lay on the judge's desk.   He glanced up with an impulsive start.

" Oh, but I should like to have lived then!" he exclaimed.

The older man shook his head.

" It is not the times, but the man," he answered. " The time makes the man, the great man makes his time."

He leaned his massive old head against the carved back of his chair and looked at the other in his kindly, unambitious optimism. He had lost most that the world accounts of worth, but life had dealt gently by him, on the whole, since it had never infringed upon the sensitiveness of his self-esteem.

" It's rough on the man," Nicholas returned brusquely, and a little later he went out into the night. He had his periods of depression, when desire seemed greater than duty, as he had his periods of exaltation, when duty seemed greater than desire. Neither affected, to outward seeming, the course of his life, but each left its mark upon his mental forces. The chief thing was that he did the work he hated as thoroughly as he did the work he loved.

The spring ripened into summer and the summer chilled into autumn. He had kept rigidly to his way and to his resolutions. From neither had he swerved in one regard. His stepmother, fixing sharp, tired eyes upon him mentally drafted, " Arter all's said an' done, the Lord knows best." She believed him to be content, as she had reason to, for he gave no outward uneasy sign. When his small savings had paid off Amos Burr's little debt, and they started, unhandicapped, upon their shaky progress, it seemed to her that she was justified in commending, for the second time, the visible methods of Providence—a commendation which faltered only before a threatening twinge of neuralgia.

Early in October the judge, whose practice was drawn largely from other sections of the State, left home for an absence of several weeks. Upon his return he sent for Nicholas in the early afternoon, an unusual happening. The young man, dropping in at two o'clock, found him at work in his library before the early dinner, a generous mint julep upon a silver tray on his desk. Cæsar was an acknowledged artist in the mixing of the beverage, and Mrs. Burwell had once exclaimed that " the judge was prouder of Cæsar's fame at the bar than of his own."

" It is an art that is becoming extinct, madam," the judge had replied sadly. " I should wager there are more men in the State to-day who can make a speech than can mix a julep. Cæsar's distinction is greater than mine."

To-day, as Nicholas entered, the judge greeted him hospitably and called for another concoction. When Cæsar brought it, frosted and clear and odorous, the judge raised his own goblet and bowed to his caller.

" To your future, my boy," he said graciously; then, as Nicholas blushed and stammered, he asked kindly:

" How are you getting on now? "

" Very well."

" So well that you wouldn't like a change? "

Nicholas threw a startled look upon him. His pulse beat swiftly, and his skin burned. By these physical reactions he realised the fluttering of his hopes.

" A change ! " he said slowly, holding himself in hand. " Yes, I—should—like a change."

The judge sipped his julep, breathing with enjoyment the strong fragrance of the mint.

" I have just seen my friend, Professor Hartwell, of the University," he said, "and he mentioned to me that in the work of compiling his law-book he found great need of a secretary. It at once occurred to me that it was a suitable opening for you, and I ventured to suggest as much to him——"

He paused an instant, gazing thoughtfully into his glass.

" And he ? " urged Nicholas hurriedly.

" He would like some correspondence with you, I believe; but, if the prospect pleases you, and you would care to undertake the work——"

" Care? " gasped the younger man passionately; " care! Why I—I'd sell my soul for the chance."

The judge laughed softly.

"Such extreme measures are unnecessary, I think. No doubt it can be arranged. I understand from your father that he has tided over his last failures."

But Nicholas did not hear him; the words of release were ringing in his ears.

. . . .

The year that Nicholas Burr "worked " his way to a degree at the University of the State Tom Bassett returned to Kingsborough and took up that portion of the judge's practice which he termed " local"; and his fellow citizens, whose daily existence was proof of their belief in hereditary virtues, brought their legal difficulties to his door. He was a stout, flaxen-haired young fellow, with broad shoulders and hon-

est, light-blue eyes, holding an habitual shade of perplexity. People said of him that his heart outran
his head, but they loved him not the less for this—
perhaps the more.

Upon his return to Kingsborough he applied himself conscientiously to his cases, paid a series of
social calls, and fell over head and ears in love with
Sally Burwell.

"There are two things which every respectable
young man in Kingsborough goes through with,"
remarked the rector's wife as she sat at breakfast
with her husband. "He becomes confirmed and he
goes mad about Sally Burwell. For my part it does
not surprise me. She's not pretty, but no man has
ever found it out, and no man ever will. Did you
notice that muslin she had on in church last Sunday
—all frills and tucks——"

"My mind was upon my sermon, dear," murmured the rector apologetically.

"But we've eyes as well as minds, and those of
every man in the congregation were on that dress of
Sally's."

The rector meekly stirred his coffee.

"I have no doubt of it," he answered. "But what
do you think of Tom's chances, my dear?"

"They aren't worth a candle," returned his wife
with an emphasis which settled the question in the
rector's mind.

Within a month Tom's chances were the topic of
Kingsborough. They were discussed at the post-
office, at sewing societies, at church festivals. Not
a soul in the congregation but knew the number of
times he had accompanied her to evening services;

not an inhabitant of the town but was aware of the
hour and the afternoon upon which they had last
walked through Lover's Lane.

When the state of affairs had gone the rounds of
the community until they were worn threadbare,
they effected a final lodgment in the mind of Mr.
Burwell.

" I have made a little discovery," he announced
one evening to his wife as she was brushing her
hair for the night.

Mrs. Burwell was all delighted attention.

" Why, what can it be? " she murmured with
gratifying feminine curiosity.

" You may have noticed, my dear," began Mr.
Burwell with a nervous glance at Sally's chamber
door across the hall, " that our friend Tom Bassett
has called frequently of late."

His wife nodded smilingly.

" Well, it has occurred to me from something I
observed this evening that it is Sally who attracts
him."

Mrs. Burwell threw back her pretty head and
laughed.

" Why, Mr. Burwell! " she exclaimed, " did you
think that it was you—or I—or your grandfather's
portrait? "

Her husband looked slightly abashed.

" So you have observed it? " he asked in an in-
jured tone.

Mrs. Burwell laid her brush aside and crossed the
room to where he stood.

" Everybody knows you are a very clever man,
Mr. Burwell," she said. " I have never pretended

to have as much sense as a man, and I hope nobody has ever accused me of anything so unwomanly— but there are some things you can't teach your wife, with all your experience."

Mr. Burwell stroked the plump hand on his arm and smiled in returning self-esteem.

"And you are quite sure he fancies Sally?" he inquired.

"I know it," replied his wife decisively.

"Would it not be wise to prepare her, my dear?"

"Prepare Sally?" gasped Mrs. Burwell, and she went back to her mirror with dancing eyes.

VI

"I have learned all they can teach me here," wrote Eugenia from school on her eighteenth birthday, "so I'll be home to-morrow."

"Bless my soul!" exclaimed the general, holding the letter above his cakes and coffee. "The child's mad—clean mad! We must put a stop to it."

"Write her to stay where she is," said Miss Chris decisively.

"I'll write her, the young puss!" returned the general angrily. "Giving herself airs at her age, is she? Why, she's just left her bottle!"

"What else does she say, Tom?" inquired his sister as she passed him the maple syrup.

The letter fluttered helplessly in the general's hand. "I can't stay away any longer from my dear, bad-tempered, old dad," he read in a breaking voice; then he added hesitatingly, "I don't reckon she's right about knowing enough, eh, Chris?"

"Certainly not," responded Miss Chris severely. "The child's as headstrong as a colt. Get that letter off in time for the train, and I'll let Sampson carry it to town."

The general finished his breakfast and went to the old secretary in the library to write his letter. When he had given it to Sampson he came back to Miss Chris, who was washing the teacups in the pantry.

"I s'pose we might as well get her room ready," he suggested. "She may come, anyway, you know."

Miss Chris looked up with a laugh from the delicate saucer she was wiping.

"I know it," she admitted; "and I'll see to her room. But your letter was positive, I hope?"

"Y-e-s," answered the general lamely, and he returned to the Richmond papers with an eager flush in his face.

The next day when Eugenia reached Kingsborough she found the dilapidated carriage awaiting her, with Sampson upon the driver's seat. With an impetuous flutter she threw her arms about the necks of the old horses. "Why, you dear things!" she cried; then she held out her hand to Sampson. "I'm glad to see you, Sampson," she said. "But why didn't papa come to meet me?"

Her animated eyes glanced joyously from side to side and her lips were brimming with the delight of homecoming.

Sampson turned the wheel for her as she got into the carriage, and gave her the linen lap-robe.

"You sho is growed, Miss Eugeny," he observed, and then in reply to her question, "Marse Tom hev got pow'ful stiff-jinted recentelly. Hit seems like he'd ruther sot right still den ease hisse'f outer his cheer. Sence Ole Miss Grissel done drop down dead uv er political stroke, he ain' step 'roun' mo'n he bleeged ter."

The carriage jolted through Kingsborough, and Eugenia bowed smilingly to her acquaintances. Once she stopped to shake hands with the rector and again to kiss Sally Burwell, who flew into her arms.

"Why, Eugie! you—you beauty!" she cried. Eugenia laughed delightedly, her black eyes glowing.

"Am I good-looking?" she asked. "I'm so glad. But I'll never be as pretty as you, you dear, sweet thing. I'm too big."

They laughed and kissed again, and Eugenia stepped from the carriage to greet the judge, who was passing.

"This is a sight for sore eyes, my dear," said the judge, his fine old face wreathed in smiles. Then, as his gaze ran over her full, straight figure, "they make fine women these days," he added. "You're as tall as your father—though you're your mother's child. Yes, I can see Amelia Tucker in your eyes."

"Thank you—thank you," said the girl in a throaty voice. There was a glow, a warmth, a fervour in her face which harmonised the chill black and white of her colouring. Her expression was as a lamp to illumine the mask of her features.

"I couldn't stay away," she went on breathlessly. "I love Kingsborough better than the whole world."

"And Kingsborough loves you," returned the judge. "Yes, it is a good old town and well worth dying in, after all."

He assisted Eugenia into the carriage, shook hands again, and the lumbering old vehicle jogged on its way. In a moment another halt was called, and Mrs. Webb came from her gate to give the girl welcome.

"This is a surprise," she said as she kissed her.

·" I dined at Battle Hall last week, and they didn't tell me you were coming."

"They didn't know it," laughed Eugenia. "I come like a bolt from the blue."

Mrs. Webb smiled coldly. She was just as the girl had known her in childhood—only the high black pompadour was now white. She still wore her stiff black silk gown, fastened at the throat by a Confederate button set in a brooch.

"You are like yourself and no one else," said Eugenia simply. "But tell me of Dudley—where is he?"

Mrs. Webb's face softened slightly.

"His practice is in Richmond now," she answered. "You know he studied law and took great honours at college. But his ambitions, I fear, are political. I don't like politics. They aren't for honest men."

Eugenia did not smile. She merely nodded assent and, saying good-bye pleasantly, jolted out of Kingsborough into the Old Stage Road.

"When did Mrs. Webb dine at home, Sampson?" she asked suddenly after a long silence.

"Hit wa'n' onc't en it wa'n' twice," said Sampson thoughtfully. "Mo' like hit wuz tree times. She done been dar monst'ous often dis yer winter, an' de mo' she come de mo' 'ristocratical she 'pear ter git. Dar wa'n' no placin' her, nohow. We done sot 'er by Ole Mis' Grissel w'en she wuz 'live, an' we done sot 'er by Miss Chris, an' we done sot 'er by Marse Tom hisse'f, an', fo' de Lawd, I ain' never seen 'er congeal yit."

But Eugenia was seeking other information. " Is

Uncle Ish well? And Aunt Verbeny, and the dogs? and did you bury Jim in the graveyard?"

"Dey's all well," replied Sampson, flicking at a horsefly on the sorrel's back, "an' Jim, he's well en buried. Marse Tom sot up er boa'd des' like you tell 'im."

A little later they turned into the cedar avenue, and Eugenia could see the large white pillars of the porch.

"There they are!" she cried excitedly, and before the carriage stopped she was up the narrow walk and in the general's arms.

"Well, daughter! daughter!" said the general. His eyes were watery, and when Eugenia fell upon Miss Chris, he blew his nose loudly with a nervous wave of his silk handkerchief.

"I was obliged to come," explained Eugenia. "When I got your letter saying I might, I was so happy."

"Tom!" murmured Miss Chris reproachfully, but her eyes were shining and she laid an affectionate hand on her brother's arm.

The general blushed like a boy.

"I told her if she'd fully made up her mind to come, I'd—I'd let her," he stammered shamefacedly.

"Oh, I was coming anyway!" announced Eugenia cheerfully as she was clasped upon the bosom of Aunt Verbeny.

"Ain't you des' yo' ma all over?" cried Aunt Verbeny enthusiastically. "Is you ever see anybody so w'ite en' so black in de same breff 'cep'n Miss Meeley? Can't I see her now same ez 'twuz

yestiddy, stannin' right dar in dis yer hall en' sayin',
' You b'longs ter me, Verbeny, en' I'se gwine ter
take cyar you de bes' I kin.' "

Aunt Verbeny fixed her eyes upon the general
and he quailed.

" Don't I take care of you, Aunt Verbeny ? " he
asked appealingly ; but Eugenia, having greeted the
remaining servants, drew him with her into the
dining-room. When he sat down at last to the
heavily laden table, he seemed to have grown twenty
years younger. As Eugenia hung over him with
domineering devotion, the irritable expression faded
from his face and he grew almost jovial. When she
weakened his coffee, he protested delightedly, and
when she refused to allow him his nightly dole of
preserved quinces, he stormed with rapture. " She
wants to starve me, the tyrant," he declared. " She'll
take the very bread from my mouth next."

Then his enthusiasm overcame him.

" That's the finest girl in the world, Chris ! God
bless her, her heart's as warm as her eyes. Why,
she'd damn herself to do a kindness."

Miss Chris appeared to remonstrate.

" I am surprised, Tom," she said disapprovingly,
though why she was surprised or what she was surprised at the general never knew.

When Eugenia went upstairs that night, she blew
out her candle and undressed by the full light of the
moon as it shone through the giant sycamore. Outside, the lawn lay like a sheet unrolled, rent by sharp
black shadows. All the dear, familiar objects were
draped by the darkness as by a curtain ; the body of
the sycamore assumed a spectral pallor, and the

small rockery near by was as mysterious as a tomb. From the dusk beneath the window the fragrance of the mimosa tree floated into the room.

Eugenia, in her long, white nightgown, fell upon her bed and slept.

The next day she went the rounds of the farm. " I'm coming back to take you for exercise," she remarked to the general as she stood before him in her sunbonnet.

The general, who was placidly smoking, groaned in protest.

" Then you'll kill me, Eugie," he urged. " Exercise doesn't suit me.   I'm too heavy."

" You'll get lighter," returned Eugenia reassuringly. " You don't move about half enough, but I'll make you."

The general groaned again, and Miss Chris, pink and fresh in her linen sacque, came out upon the porch.

" Bless the child! " she exclaimed. " Where on earth did she lay hands on that bonnet? Don't stay out too long in the sun, Eugie, or you'll burn black."

The general caught at the straw.

" I wish you'd tell her she ought to sit in the house, Chris. She wants to drag me—me out in that heat." But Eugenia drew the sunbonnet over her dark head and disappeared across the lawn.

Having inspected the farmyard and the stables, she crossed the ragged field to the negro cabins, where she was received with hilarity.

" Ain't I al'ays tell you she uz de fines' lady in de

lan'?" demanded Delphy of the retreating Moses. "Ain't I al'ays tell you dar wa'n't her match in dese yer parts or outer dem? I ax you, ain't I?"

"Dat's so," admitted Moses meekly.

"Where's Betsey?" inquired Eugenia, twirling her sunbonnet. "Aunt Verbeny told me the baby died. I am so sorry."

"De Lawd He give, en' de Lawd He teck," returned Delphy piously, "en' He done been moughty open-handed dis long time. He done give er plum sight mo'n He done teck, en' it ain' no use'n sayin' He ain'."

"So the others are well?" ventured Eugenia, and as a bow-legged crawler emerged from beneath the doorstep she added: "Is that the youngest?"

Delphy snorted.

"Dat ar brat, Miss Euginney? He ain' Betsey's, nohow. He's Rindy's Lije, en' he's de mos' out'n out pesterer sence Mose wuz born."

"Rindy!" exclaimed Eugenia in surprise, lightly touching the small black body with her foot. "Why, I didn't know Rindy was married. She's working at the house now."

Delphy seized the child and held him at arm's length while she applied a sounding box. "Go 'way f'om yer, honey," she said. "Rindy ain' mah'ed. He's des' an accident. Shet yo' mouth, you imp er darkness, fo' I shet hit fur you."

"Don't hurt him, Delphy," pleaded the girl. "Rindy ought to be ashamed of herself, but it isn't his fault. I'm going to send him some clothes. He looks fat enough, anyhow."

"He's fitten ter bus'," retorted Delphy sternly.

" He don't do nuttin' fur his livin' but eat all day,
en' den when night come he don't do nuttin' but
holler kaze de time ter leave off eatin' done come.
He ain' no mo' use'n a weazel."

Eugenia promised to befriend the baby, and left
with Delphy's pessimism ringing in her ears. " He
ain' wuth yo' shoestring, he ain'," called the woman
after her.

The girl was as popular among the negroes as
she had been as a small tomboy in pinafores. Her
impulsive generosity and, above all, her cordial
kindness, had not abated with years. She was as
ready to serve as be served, her heart was as open as
her hand; and the shrewd, childish race received
her as a benignant providence. Her sweetness of
disposition became a proverb. " As sunshiny ez
Miss Euginny," said Aunt Verbeny of a clear day—
and the general raised her wages.

During the early summer Bernard came home on
a vacation. For several years he had held a position
in a bank in Lynchburg, and his visits to Kingsborough took place at uncertain intervals. He was
a slight, insignificant young fellow, with complacent
eyes and a beautiful, girlish mouth. His temper
was quicker than Eugenia's, and he was in continual
friction with the general, who had grown absent-
minded and irritable. He not only forgot his own
opinions as soon as he expressed them, but, what is
still more annoying, he was apt to offer them as
some one's else in the course of a few hours.

" That young Burr's a scamp," he remarked one
morning at breakfast, " a regular scamp. Here he's
setting up as a lawyer under George Bassett's eye,

12

when I happen to know that Jerry Pollard wouldn't have him in his store if you paid him."

" My dear Tom," breathed the placid voice of Miss Chris, " I'm quite sure you're mistaken. Why, Judge Bassett——"

" Mistaken! " persisted the general angrily. " Am I the man to make a statement without authority? I tell you he's a scamp, ma'am—a regular scamp! If you please to doubt my word——"

" That's rather rough on a chap, isn't it? " put in Bernard indifferently. " He isn't a gentleman, but I shouldn't call him a scamp."

" Why should you call him anything, sir? " demanded the general. " It's no business of yours, is it? If I choose to call him a——"

" Now, father," said Eugenia, and at her decisive tones the general broke off and turned upon her round, inquiring eyes. " Now, father, you don't mean one word that you're saying, and you know it." And she proceeded to butter his cakes.

The general was suppressed, and after breakfast he got into the carriage beside his daughter and drove slowly into town. When he returned to dinner he met Miss Chris with triumphant eyes.

" By the way, Chris, you were mistaken this morning about that Burr boy. He's quite a decent person. I don't see how you got it into your head there was something wrong about him."

" I'm glad to hear it," responded Miss Chris good-humouredly. She had never uttered a harsh word about anybody in her life, but she was a long-suffering woman, and she philosophically accepted the accusation.

Twenty-four hours later the general had a passage at arms with Bernard.

"You can watch the threshing this morning, my boy," he remarked as he sat down to breakfast. "You won't go in to town, I suppose?"

Bernard shook his head.

"I thought of riding in for the mail," he answered; "there's a letter I'm looking for."

The general flushed and put out a preliminary feeler. "How are you going?" he inquired; "not on one of my horses, I hope?"

Eugenia shook her head at Bernard, but he went on recklessly:

"Why, yes, I thought I'd take the gray mare."

The general shook his head until his flabby face grew purple.

"The gray mare!" he thundered. "You mean to take out my gray mare, do you? Well, I'd like to see you, sir. Not a step does the gray mare stir —not a step, sir."

"Oh, all right," agreed Bernard so quietly that the general's rage increased. "Keep her in the stables, for all I care." And, having finished his breakfast, he bowed to Miss Chris and left the table.

But an hour later, as he passed through the hall, he found the general waiting. "Aren't you ready?" he asked irascibly. "Are you going to waste the whole morning? Why aren't you in town?"

Bernard's temper was well enough as long as there was no reason it should be better; but he couldn't stand his father, and he knew it.

"I'm not going," he returned sullenly.

" Not going!" cried the general hotly, "not going after all the fuss you've raised? What do you mean by changing your mind every minute?"

Bernard took his hat from the old mahogany rack. " I've nothing to ride," he replied irritably, " and I don't choose to walk—that's what I mean."

But his answer only exasperated his hovering parent.

" Damme, sir, do you want to make me lose my temper?" he demanded. " Isn't the stable full of horses? Where's the gray mare, I'd like to know, sir?"

" Eugie!" called Bernard angrily, " come here." And as the girl appeared he made a break from the house. He possessed an abiding faith in the endurance of Eugenia's clannish soul that was proof against even the suggestion that it might succumb. His father was unquestionably trying, but Eugie was unquestionably strong, and she loved her people with a passion which he felt to be romantically unsurpassable. Yes, Eugie was the hope of the family, after all.

As for the girl, she put her arm about the general and drew him to his chair. He was failing rapidly; this she saw and suffered at seeing. There were wrinkles crossing and recrossing his hanging cheeks, and swollen bluish pockets beneath his eyes. When he moved he carried his great weight uneasily. During the day she hung over him with multiplied caresses; as he sat upon the porch in the afternoon she read to him from the Bible and Shakespeare, the only books his library contained.

" After God and Shakespeare, what was left for

any man to write?" the general had once demanded
of the judge.

Now he asked the question of Eugenia, and she
smiled and was silent. Her eyes passed from the
porch to the lawn and the walk and the immemorial
gloom of the great cedars. Sunshine lay over all
the warm, sleepy land, and sunshine lay across her
white dress and across the senile droop of the general's mouth.

"For He maketh sore, and bindeth up," read the
girl slowly. "He woundeth and His hands make
whole."

"He shall deliver thee in six troubles;—yea, in
seven there shall no evil touch thee."

"In famine He shall redeem thee from death : and
in war from the power of the sword."

She stopped suddenly and looked up, for the
general's eyes were full of tears.

BOOK III

WHEN FIELDS LIE FALLOW

BOOK III

WHEN FIELDS LIE FALLOW

I

On an October afternoon Nicholas Burr was walking along the branch road that led to his father's farm. He carried a well filled bag upon his shoulder, the musty surface of which betrayed that it contained freshly ground meal, but, despite the additional weight, his figure was unflinchingly erect. There was a splendid vigour in his thick-set frame and in the swinging strides of his hardy limbs. His face—the square-jawed, large-featured face of a philosopher or a farmer—possessed, with its uncompromising ugliness, a certain eccentric power. Rugged, gray, alert-eyed as it was, large-browed and overhung by his waving red hair—it was a face to attract or to repel—not to be ignored.

Now, as he swung on vigorously in the October light, there was about him a joyousness of purpose which belonged to his age and his aspirations. It was an atmosphere, an emanation thrown off by respiring vitality.

Across the road the sunshine fell in long, level shafts. The spirit of October was abroad in the wood—veiling itself in a faint, bluish haze like the smoke of the greenwood when it burns. Overhead,

crimson and yellow ran riot among the trees, the
flame of the maple extinguishing the dull red of the
oak, the clear gold of the hickory flashing through
the gloss of the holly.　As yet the leaves had not
begun to fall; they held tenaciously to the living
branches, fluttering light heads in the first autumn
chill.　In the underbrush, where the deerberry
showed hectic blotches, a squirrel worked busily,
completing its winter store, while in the slanting
sun rays a tawny butterfly, like a wind-blown,
loosened tiger lily, danced its last mad dance with
death.

To Nicholas the scene was without significance.
With a gesture he threw off the spell of its beauty,
as he shifted the " sack " of corn meal upon his
shoulder.　He had found Uncle Ish tottering homeward with the load, and he had taken it from him
with a careless promise to leave it at the old negro's
cabin door—then, passing him by a stride, he had
gone on his kindly, confident way.　He forgot Uncle
Ish as readily as he forgot the bag he carried.　His
mind was busily reviewing the points of his last case
and the possible facts of a more important one he
believed to be coming to him.　In this connection
he went back to his first fight in the little court-
house, and he laughed with an appreciation of the
humour of his success.　It was Turner, after all, who
had given it to him; Turner, who, having bought a
horse that died upon the journey home, wanted revenge as well as recompense.　He remembered his
perturbation as he rose to cross-examine the defendant—the nervousness with which he drove his
weapons home.　It had all seemed so important to

him then—the court, his client, the great, greasy horse dealer forced into the witness stand.

He had proved his case by the defendant, and he had won as well a mild reputation among the farmers who had assembled for the day. Since then he had done well, and the judge's patronage had placed much in his hands that, otherwise, would have gone elsewhere.

Beyond the wood, the uncultivated wasteland sported its annual carnival of golden rod and sumach, and across the brilliant plumes a round, red sun hung suspended in a quiet sky. In the corn field, where the late crop was fast maturing, negro women chanted shrilly as they pulled the "fodder," their high-coloured kerchiefs blending, like autumn foliage, with the landscape. Around them the bared stalks rose boldly row on row, reserving their scarred and yellow husks for the last harvest of the year.

When Nicholas reached his father's house he did not enter the little whitewashed gate, but kept on to the log cabin on the edge of General Battle's land, where Uncle Ish was passing his declining years in poverty and independence. The cabin stood above a little gully which skirted the dividing line of the pastures, facing, in its primitive nudity, the level stretch of the shadowless highway. It was a rotting, one-room dwelling, with a wide doorway opening upon a small, bare strip of ground where a gnarled oak grew. In the rear there was a small garden, denuded now of its modest vegetables, only the leafy foliage of a late pea crop retaining a semblance of fruitfulness.

Nicholas went up the narrow path leading from the road to the hut, and placed the bag on the smooth, round stone which served for a step. As he did so, the doorway abruptly darkened, and a girl came from the interior and paused with her foot upon the threshold. He saw, in an upward glance, that it was Eugenia Battle, and, from the light wicker basket on her arm, he inferred that, in the absence of Uncle Ish, she had been engaged in supplying his simple wants. That the old negro was still cared for by the Battles he was aware, though upon the means of his livelihood Uncle Ish, himself, was singularly reticent.

As Eugenia saw him she flushed slightly, as one caught in a secret charity, and promptly pointed to the bag of meal.

" Whose is that? "

He looked from the girl to the bag and back again, his own cheek reddening. At the instant it occurred to him that it was a peculiar greeting after a separation of years.

" It belongs to Uncle Ish," he answered, with unreasonable embarrassment. " I believe your father gave it to him."

" He might have brought it home for him," was her comment, and immediately:

" Where is he? "

" Uncle Ish? He's on the road."

Her next remark probed deeper, and he winced.

" What were you doing with it? "

Her gaze was warming upon him. He met it and laughed aloud.

" Toting it," he responded lightly.

She was still warming. He saw the glow kindle in her eyes and illumine her sombre face; it was like the leaping of light to the surface. As she stood midway of the entrance, in a frame of unpolished logs, her white and black beauty against the smoky gloom of the interior, the red sunset before her feet, he recalled swiftly an allegorical figure of Night he had once seen in an old engraving. Then, before the charm of her smile, the recollection passed as it had come.

"You may bring in the bag," she said, with the authority of one accustomed to much service. "I found he had very little left to eat. We have to bring him things secretly, and he pretends the Lord feeds him as He fed the prophet."

She reëntered the hut, and Nicholas, stepping lightly in the fear that his weight might hasten the fall of the logs, deposited the bag upon a pine table, where an ash cake lay ready for the embers. In a little cupboard he saw the contents of Eugenia's basket—a cold fried chicken and some coffee and sugar. Before the hearth there was a comfortable rocking chair, and a bright coloured quilt was upon the bed. As he turned away the girl spoke swiftly:

"It *was* good of you," she said.

"Good of me?" He met her approbation almost haughtily; then he impulsively added: "I always liked Uncle Ish—and he reminds me of old times."

She turned frankly to him. In the noble poise of her head she had seemed strangely far off; now she appeared to stoop.

"Of our old times?"

Her cordial eyes arrested him.

"Of yours and mine," he answered. "Do you remember the hare traps he set for us and the straw mats he taught us to plait? Once you said you had stolen a watermelon to save Jake a whipping, and he found you out—do you remember?"

He pressed the recollections upon her eagerly, almost violently.

Eugenia shook her head, half laughing.

"No, no," she said; "but I remember you carried me home once when I had hurt my foot, and you jumped into the ice pond to save my kitten, and——"

"You shared your lunch with me at school," he broke in.

"And you dug me a little garden all yourself——"

"And you bought me a Jew's harp on my birthday——"

"And you always left half the eggs in a bird's nest because I begged you to——"

"And you were an out and out angel," he concluded triumphantly.

"An angel, black-haired and a tomboy?"

He assented. "A little tyrannical angel with a temper."

Her confessions multiplied.

"I scratched your face once."

"Yes."

"I got mad and smashed your best hawk's egg."

"You did."

"I threw your fishing line into the brook when you wouldn't let me fish."

"I have never seen it since."

"I was horrid and mean."

"Such were your angelic characteristics."

She thoughtfully swung the basket on her arm, her white sleeve fluttering above her wrist. Her head, with its wave, from the clear brow, of dead-black hair, was bent frankly towards him.

"It has been so long since I saw you," she said suddenly, "and when I last saw you, you were horrid, not I."

He flushed quickly.

"I was a brute," he admitted.

"And you hurt me so, I cried all night."

"Not because you cared?" he asked breathlessly.

"Of course not—because I didn't care a—a rap. I cried for the fun of it."

He was sufficiently abashed.

"If I had known——" he began, and stopped.

"You might have known!" she flashed out.

He was at a disadvantage, which he admitted by a blank regard.

"But things were desperate then, and——"

"So were you."

"Not as desperate as I might have been."

In her equable unconsciousness she threw off the meaning of his retort.

"But I like desperateness."

She had crossed the threshold and stood now in the ambient glow, gazing across the quiet pasture, where a stray sheep bleated. She reached up and broke a bunch of red leaves from the oak, fastening them in her belt as they descended the narrow path.

In the road they came upon Uncle Ish, who was hobbling slowly towards them. He was wrinkled with age and bent with rheumatism, and his voice sounded cracked and querulous.

" Is de Lawd done sont dem vittles? " he demanded suspiciously. " Ef He ain', I dunno how
I'se gwine ter git mo'n a'er ash cake fur supper.
'Pears like He's gittin' monst'ous ondependible dese
yer las' days. I ain' lay eyes on er dish er kebbage
sence I lef' dat ar patch on Hick'ry Hill, en all de
blackeye peas I'se done seen is what I raise right
dar behint dat do'. Es long es Gord A'mighty
ondertecks ter feed you, He mought es well feed you
ter yo' tase."

" There are some eggs in the cupboard," said Eugenia seriously. " You must cook some for supper."

Uncle Ish grunted.

" En egg's er wishwashy creeter es ain' got ernuff
tase er its own ter stan' alont widout salt," he remarked contemptuously; after which he grew hospitable.

" Ain' you gwine ter step in es you'se passin'? "
he inquired.

Eugenia shook her head.

" Not to-day, Uncle Ish," she responded cheerfully. " I know you're tired—and how is your rheumatism? "

" Wuss en wuss," responded the old negro gloomily. " I'se done cyar'ed one er dese yer I'sh taters
in my pocket twell hit sprouted, en de rhematiks
ain' never knowed 'twuz dar. Hit's wuss en wuss."

As they passed on, he hobbled painfully up the
rocky path, leaning heavily upon his stick and grunt-
ing audibly at each rheumatic twinge.

Nicholas and Eugenia followed the highway and
turned into the avenue of cedars. When the house
was in sight, he stopped and held out his hand.

" May I see you sometimes? " he asked diffidently.
She spoke eagerly.

" Oh, do come to see us," she said. " Papa would enjoy talking about Judge Bassett. He half worships him."

" So do I."

She nodded sympathetically.

" I know—I know. He *is* splendid! And you are doing well, aren't you? "

" I have work to do, thank God, and I do it. I can't say how."

" What does Judge Bassett say? "

He laughed boyishly. " He says silence."

She was puzzled.

" I don't understand—but I must go—I really must. It is quite dark."

And she passed from him into the box-bordered walk. He watched her tall figure until it ascended the stone steps and paused upon the porch, whence came the sound of voices. Through the wide open doors he could see the swinging lamp in the centre of the great hall and the broad stairway leading to the floor above. For a moment he stood motionless; then, turning back into the avenue, he retraced his steps to his father's house.

In the kitchen, where the table was laid for supper, his half-sister, Nannie, was sewing on her wedding clothes. She was to be married in the fulness of the winter to young Nat Turner—one of the Turners of Nicholas's boyhood. By the light of the kerosene lamp she looked wonderfully fair and fresh, her auburn curls hanging heavily against her cheek as she bent over the cambric in her lap.

13

As Nicholas entered she looked up brightly, exclaiming: "Oh, it's you!" in disappointed accents.

Nicholas looked about the kitchen inquiringly.

"Where's ma?" he asked, and at the instant Marthy Burr appeared in the doorway, a pat of butter in her hand.

"Air you home, Nick?" was her greeting, as she placed the butter upon the table. Then she went across to Nannie and examined the hem on the cambric ruffle.

"It seems to me you might have done them stitches a little finer," she observed critically. "Old Mrs. Turner's got powerful sharp eyes for stitches, an' she's goin' to look mighty hard at yours. If thar's one stitch shorter'n another, it's goin' to stand out plainer than all the rest. It's the nater of a woman to be far-sighted at seeing the flaws in her son's wife, an' old Mrs. Turner ain't no better'n God made her, if she ain't no worse. 'Tain't my way to be wishin' harm to folks, but I al'ays said the only thing to Amos Burr's credit I ever heerd of is that he's an orphan—which he ain't responsible for."

"But the sewing's all right," returned Nannie in wounded pride. "Nat ain't marrying me for my sewing, anyway."

Her mother shook her head.

"What a man marries for's hard to tell," she returned; "an' what a woman marries for's past findin' out. I ain't never seen an old maid yet that ain't had a mighty good opinion of men—an' I ain't never seen a married woman that ain't had a feelin' that a few improvements wouldn't be out of place. I don't want to turn you agin Nat Turner—he's a man an' he's got a mother, an' that's all I've got agin him. No talkin's goin' to turn anybody that's got their mind set on marryin', any more than it's goin' to turn anybody that's got their mind set on drink. So I ain't goin' to open my mouth."

Here Amos Burr appeared, and as he seated himself beside Nannie she drew her ruffles away. "You're so dusty, pa," she exclaimed half pettishly.

He fixed his heavy, admiring eyes upon her, receiving the reproof as meekly as he received all feminine utterances. He might bully a man, but he would always be bullied by a woman.

"I reckon you're pretty near ready," he observed cheerfully, rubbing his great hairy hands. "You've got 'most a trunk full of finery. I reckon Turner'll know I ain't in the poorhouse yet—or near it."

It was a speech of unusual length, and, after making it, he slowly settled into silence.

"Nat wouldn't mind if I was in the poorhouse, so long as he could get me out," said his daughter, taking up the cudgels in defence of her lover's disinterestedness.

Amos Burr chuckled.

"Don't you set no store by that," he rejoined.

"An' don't you set about judgin' other folks by yourself, Amos Burr," retorted his wife sharply. "'Tain't likely you'd ever pull anybody out o' the poorhouse 'thout slippin' in yourself, seein' as I've slaved goin' on twenty years to keep you from landin' thar at last. The less you say about some things the better. Now, you'd jest as well set down an' eat your supper."

II

The next day Nicholas went into Tom Bassett's office, where he met Dudley Webb, who was spending a dutiful week in Kingsborough. He was a genial young fellow, with a clear-cut, cleanly shaven face and a handsome head covered with rich, dark hair. His hands were smooth and white, and he gesticulated rapidly as he talked. It was already said of him that he told a poor story better than anybody else told a good one—a fact which was probably the elemental feature of his popularity.

As Nicholas looked in, he raised himself lightly from Tom's desk chair and gave him a hearty handshake.

"Hello, Burr! We were just talking of you. I was telling Tom a jolly thing I heard yesterday. Two farmers were discussing you at the post-office, and one of them said: ' 'Tain't that he's got so much sense—I had a sight more at his age—but he's so blamed sure of himself, he makes you believe in him.' How's that for fame?"

"Not so bad as it is for me," returned Nicholas with a laugh. "If you win one or two small cases, there's obliged to be undue influence of the devil."

"Which, occasionally, it is," added Tom seriously.

Dudley threw himself back into his chair and crossed his shapely legs. For a moment he smoked in silence, then he removed his cigar from his mouth and flecked the ashes upon the uncarpeted floor.

"Oh! the mystery to me is," he said, "that you exist down here and live to tell the tale—or at least that you earn enough crumbs to feed the crows."

"Kingsborough crows aren't high livers," remarked Nicholas as he threw himself into the remaining chair.

Dudley laughed softly—a humorous laugh that fell pleasantly on the ear.

"That reminds me," he began whimsically. "I met a tourist with spectacles walking along Duke of Gloucester Street. 'Sir,' he said courteously, 'I am looking for Kingsborough. I am told that it is a city.' 'Sir,' I responded, with a bow that did honour to my grandfather's ghost, 'it was once a chartered city; it is now only a charter.'"

Then he turned to Tom.

"We haven't got used to the railroad yet, have we?" he asked.

Tom shook his head.

"General Battle's still protesting," he replied. "He swears it makes Kingsborough common."

Dudley thoughtfully examined his cigar, an amused smile about his mouth.

"My mother doesn't want the cows turned out of the churchyard," he observed, "because it would abolish one of Kingsborough's characteristics. She's right, too, by Jove."

"They're having a fight over it now," put in Nicholas with the gravity he rarely lost. "The people who own cows call it an 'ancient right.' The people who don't, call it sacrilege. The rector leads one faction, and the congregation has split."

"And split we smash," added Dudley. "Well, these are exciting times in Kingsborough's history; it is almost as lively as Richmond. There we had a religious convention and an elopement last week. I don't suppose you come up to that?"

Nicholas ran his hand through his hair with a habitual gesture. He was idly watching the light of Dudley's cigar and noting the quality by the aroma. He could not afford cigars himself, and he wondered how Dudley managed to do so.

"We are a people without a present," he returned inattentively. "You've heard, I take it, that an old elm has gone near the court-house."

"My mother told me. I believe she knows every brick that used to be and is not. I'm trying to get her away with me, but she won't come."

"Sally Burwell was telling me," said Tom, a dawning interest in his face, "she had tried to persuade her."

"Yes, we tried and failed. By the way, is it true that Sally's engaged to Jack Wyth? I hear it at every turn."

"I—I shouldn't be surprised," gasped Tom painfully.

"I don't believe a word of it," protested Nicholas.

"He isn't much good, eh?"

"Why, he's a brick," said Nicholas.

"He's a cad," said Tom.

Dudley laughed and blew a cloud of smoke in the air.

"Well, she's a daisy herself, and as good as gold. She's the kind of woman to flirt herself hoarse and then settle down into dove-like domesticity. But

what about Eugie? Is she really grown up? My
mother declares she's splendid."

Nicholas was silent.

" Oh, she's handsome enough," Tom carelessly
replied.

" But not like Sally, eh? "

" Oh, no! not like Sally."

Dudley tossed the stump of his cigar through the
open window, lit a cigarette, and changed the subject. He talked easily, relating several laughable
stories, referring occasionally to himself and his
success, illustrating his remarks by his experience
at the bar, giving finally the exclamation of a fellow-
lawyer at the close of an argument he had made:
" You may be a muff of a jurist, Webb," he had
cried, " but, by George! you're a devil of an advocate! "

He was, withal, so affable, so confident, so thoroughly a good fellow, that an hour passed before
Nicholas remembered he had looked in only for a
moment.

When he rose to go, Dudley gripped his hand
again, slapped him on the shoulder, declared him
to be a " first-rate old chap," and ended by pressing
him to drop in on him when he ran up to Richmond.

Nicholas gave back the friendly grasp and pledged
himself to the " dropping in." He resistingly succumbed before the inherent jovial charm.

The afternoon being Saturday, he left town earlier
than usual and spent a couple of hours with his
father in the fields. The peanuts were being harvested. Amos Burr, with a peanut " share " attached to the plough, was separating the yellowed

plants from the ripe nuts underground, and Nicholas, lifting the roots upon a pitchfork, shook them free from earth and threw them over the pointed staves which were the final supports of the " shocks." A negro hand went before him, driving the sticks into the sandy soil.

" I should say you might count on forty bushels an acre," remarked Nicholas cheerfully, as he lifted a detached root from a broken hill. " It's a fair yield, isn't it ? "

Amos Burr shook his head and muttered that there was " no tellin'. Peanuts air one of the things thar's no countin' on," he added. " Wheat air another, corn air another, oats air another."

" Life is another," concluded Nicholas lightly. " Still we live and still we raise wheat and oats and corn. But I wish you'd look into market gardening. I believe it would pay you better."

" 'Tain't no use," returned Amos, with his accustomed pessimism. " 'Tain't no use my plantin' as long as the government ain't goin' to move, nohow. It's been promisin' to help the farmer ever since the war, an' it ain't done nothin' for him yet but tax him."

But Nicholas, to avoid his father's political drift, fell to talking with one of the negro workers.

Several hours later, when he had changed his farm clothes, he joined Eugenia in the pasture and walked with her to Battle Hall, where the general received him with ready, if condescending, hospitality. Eugenia had instructed her family upon the changed conditions of Nicholas's social standing, but her logic was powerless to convince her father

that Amos Burr's son was any better than Amos
Burr had been before him.

"Pish! Pish!" he exclaimed testily, "the boy's
not a lawyer—only gentlemen belong to the bar,
but there's nobody too high or too low to be a
farmer. Polite to him? Did you ever see me
impolite in my own house even to a chimney
sweep?"

"I never saw a chimney sweep in your own
house," Eugenia retorted, whereupon he pinched
her cheek and accused her of "making fun of her
old father."

Now, when Nicholas sat down on one of the long
green benches on the porch, the general conversed
with him as he conversed with the chicken sellers
who came of an afternoon to receive payment for
their luckless fowls.

"This'll be a busy season for you," he observed
cheerfully, in the slightly elevated voice in which he
addressed his inferiors. "You'll be cutting your
corn before long and seeding your winter crops.
What are you planting this fall?"

He could not be induced to engage upon social
topics with the young man or to allude in the most
distant manner to his legal profession. He was
a Burr, and a Burr was a small farmer, nothing
more.

"We're ploughing for oats now, sir," responded
Nicholas diffidently, "and we're going to seed a
little rye with clover—if the clover's killed, the rye'll
last."

"I should advise you to look after the land," said
the general, stuffing the tobacco into the bowl of his

pipe and pressing it down with his fat thumb. " What you need is to plant it in cow-peas and turn them down. There's nothing like them for fertilising."

Nicholas, who was listening attentively, rose to shake hands with Miss Chris who appeared in the doorway.

" The fall comes earlier than it used to," she remarked, drawing a light crocheted shawl about her shoulders. " Why, I remember when it used to be summer up to the middle of November. I was talking to Judge Bassett about it yesterday, and he said he certainly thought the seasons had changed since he was a boy."

" I don't reckon your father has much opinion of fertilisers," broke in the general, reverting to his pleasant patronage.

Nicholas answered before Eugenia could interpose. " No, sir, he doesn't believe in them much," he replied.

" Well, you tell him it's lime he needs," continued the general. " The most successful peanut grower I ever knew put about a thousand pounds of lime to an acre, and he cleared——"

" Have you seen Dudley Webb? " asked Eugenia, shaking her head at the general's frown.

" For an hour this morning. He was in Tom Bassett's office. He told some good stories."

Miss Chris heaved a reminiscent sigh.

" That's poor Julius Webb all over again," she said. " He could keep a dinner table laughing for two hours and fight a duel at daybreak. I remember at his own wedding, when they drank his health,

he told such a funny story that old Judge Blitherstone, who was upwards of eighty, had to have cold
bandages put to his head."

The general took his pipe from his mouth.
"Dudley's a fine young fellow," he said. "I saw
him yesterday when I went to the post-office. They
tell me he's making a name for himself in Richmond."

Eugenia laughed lightly.

"Papa adores Mrs. Webb, so he thinks Dudley
splendid," she said.

"That lady is one of the noblest of her sex,"
loyally asserted the general.

"And one of the most trying of either sex," added
his daughter. "When I came home my last holi-
day, she asked me what I learned at school, and I
danced a skirt dance for her."

"I always told you you spoiled Eugie to death,
Tom," said Miss Chris in justification of her own
responsibility. "In my day no young lady knew
what a skirt dance was."

"But that's what I learned at school," protested
Eugenia.

The general, feeling that the conversation ex-
cluded Nicholas, renewed his attack.

"What do you think of raising garden products?"
he inquired affably. Then Eugenia rose, and he
submissively retired.

"We aren't going to talk farming any more," said
the girl. "Nick and I are going into the garden
for roses," and she descended the steps, followed
by Nicholas, who was beginning for the first time
to breathe freely.

" Tell your father to look into the truck-growing," was the general's parting shot.

The garden was flushed with the riot of autumn. Over the little whitewashed fence double rows of hollyhocks and sunflowers nodded their heavy heads, and bordering the narrow walk were lines of chrysanthemums and dahlias. October roses, the richest of the year, bloomed and dropped in the quaint old squares where the long vegetable rows began. At the end of the straight, overgrown walk the hop vines on the fence threw out a pungent odour.

" Papa wants to have the garden ploughed," said Eugenia. " He says it takes too much time to hoe it. Give me your knife, please."

He opened the blade, and she stooped to cut off a crimson dahlia while the Indian summer sunshine slanted from the west upon her dark head and white dress. Over all was the faint violet haze of the season, hanging above the gay old garden like a delicate effluvium from autumns long decayed.

" There aren't many old-time gardens left," said Nicholas regretfully, " but I like this one best of all. I always think of you in the midst of it."

" Yes, we used to gather calacanthus blossoms and trade them for taffy at school. The bushes are almost all dead now. That is the only one left."

She laid the knife upon the grass and raised her arms to fasten a yellow chrysanthemum in her hair. As it lay against her ear it cast a clear, golden light upon her cheek, as warm as the late sunshine.

" Flowers suit you," he said.

"Do they?" she smiled in a quick, pleased way. "Is it because I love them?"

"It is because you are beautiful," he answered bluntly.

Some one had once called Eugenia's besetting vanity the love of giving pleasure; it was, perhaps, in reality, the pleasure of being loved. It was not the fact that she might be beautiful that now warmed her so gratefully, but the evidence that Nicholas was good enough to consider her so.

"You have seen so few girls," she remarked reasonably enough.

"I may see many, but it won't alter my view of you."

"How can you tell?"

He shook his head impatiently.

"I shan't tell. I shall prove it."

"And when you have proved it where shall I be? —old and toothless?"

"May be—but still beautiful."

There was a glow in her face, but she did not reply. His eyes and the last, long ray of sunshine were upon her. He was revoking from an old October a dark-haired, clear-eyed girl amid the dahlias, and it seemed to him that Eugenia had shot up in a season like one of the stately flowers. As she stood in the grass-grown walk, her skirt half-filled with blossoms, her white hands lifting the thin folds above her ruffled petticoat, she appeared to be the vital apparition of the place—a harbinger of the vivid sunlight and the dark shadows of the passing of the year.

"See how many!" she exclaimed, holding her

lapful towards him. " You may take your choice—
only not that last pink papa loves."

He plunged his hands amid the confusion of colours and drew out a yellow chrysanthemum.

" I like this," he said simply.

She laughed. " But it doesn't suit your hair,"
she suggested.

He met her sally gravely.

" It is my favourite flower," he returned.

" Since when, pray ? "

" Since—since a half-hour ago."

He stooped and picked up his knife from the
grass.

" Are you going away ? " he asked, " or shall you
stay here always ? "

" Always," she promptly returned. " I'm going
to live here with this old garden until I grow to be
an ancient dame—and you may walk over on
autumn afternoons and I'll be sympathetic about
your rheumatism. Isn't that a picture that delights
your soul ? "

" No," he said bluntly ; " I see a better one."

" Tell me."

" I can never tell you," he replied gravely—" not
even when you are an ancient dame and I rheumatic."

She was merry again.

" Then I fear it's wicked," she said, " and I'm
amazed at you. But my day-dreams are all common ones. I ask only the country and my home
and horses and cows and chickens—and a rheumatic
friend. You see I must be happy, I ask so little."

" And you argue that he who demands little gets

it," he returned lightly. " On the other hand, I
should say that he who is content with less gets
nothing. I ask the biggest thing Fate has to give,
and then stand waiting for——"

He paused for a breathless instant while he looked
at her, and then slowly finished:

" For the skies to fall."

They swung open the gate into cattle lane, and
stood waiting while the cows trooped by to the barnyard.

Eugenia called them by name, and they turned
great stupid eyes upon her as they stopped to munch
the hollyhocks.

" She was named after you," said the girl suddenly.

" She? Who? " he turned a helpless look upon
the two small negroes who drove the cows.

" Why, Burr Bess, of course—that Jersey there.
You know we couldn't name her Nick because she
wasn't a boy, so Bernard called her Burr Bess. You
don't seem pleased."

" She's a fine cow," observed Nicholas critically.

" Oh! she was the most beautiful calf! I thought
you remembered it. One was named after me, but
it died, and one was named after Bernard, but it
went to the butcher. Bernard was so angry about
it that he waylaid the cart on the road and let it out.
But they caught it again. It was too bad, wasn't
it? "

The garden gate closed behind them with a click,
and they crossed the lane to the lawn.

Miss Chris, who stood shading her eyes in the
back porch, was giving directions to Aunt Verbeny

in the smoke-house.   When she saw Nicholas she
broke off and asked him to stay to supper, but he
declined hastily, and, with an embarrassed good-
evening, turned back into the lane.   The hollyhocks
over the whitewashed fence brushed him as he
passed, and the spices of the garden came to him like
the essence of the eternal Romance.

III

Over all hung Indian summer and the happy sunshine. Eugenia, rising at daybreak for a gallop across country, would feel the dew in her face and the autumn in her blood. As she dashed over fences and ditches to the unploughed pasture, the morning was as desolate as midnight—not a soul showed in the surrounding fields and the long road lay as pallid as a streak of frost. The loneliness and the hour set her eyes to dancing and the glad blood to bounding in her veins. When a startled rabbit shied from the brushwood she would slacken her speed to watch it, and when, as sometimes chanced, she frightened a covey of partridges from their retreat, she went softly, rejoicing that no shot was near.

At this time she was possessed, perhaps, of a spirit too elastic, of a buoyance almost insolent—she turned, as it were, too round a cheek to Fate. In her clear purity romanticism held no part, and her soul, strong to adhere, was slow to conform. Her nature was straight as an arrow that would not fall though it overshot the mark. She dreamed scant dreams of the future because she clove tenaciously to the past—to the rare associations and the old affections—to the road and the cedars and the Hall as to the men and women whose blood she bore and whose likeness she carried. She loved one and all with a fidelity that did not swerve. Riding home

14

along the open road that led to the cedars, she marked each friendly object in its turn—on one side the persimmon tree where the fruit ripened—on the other the blackened wreck of the giant oak, towering above the shining spread of life-everlasting. She noted that the rail fence skirting the pasture sagged at one corner beneath a weight of poisonous oak, that a mud hole had eaten through the short strip of " corduroy " road, and that where Uncle Ish's path led to his cabin the plank across the gully was rapidly rotting. She saw these things with the tender eyes with which we mark decay in one beloved.

Then, pacing up the avenue to the gravelled walk, she would call " good-morning " to the general and leap lightly to the ground, fresh as the day, bright as the autumn.

It was on one of these early rides that she saw Nicholas again. She was returning leisurely through the stretch of woodland, when, catching sight of him as he swung vigorously ahead, she quickened her horse's pace and overtook him as he glanced inquiringly back.

" Divide the worm, early bird," she cried gaily.

He paused as she did, laying his hand on the horse's neck.

" There wasn't but one and you got it," he retorted lightly. " Have you been far? "

" Miles, and I'm as hungry as two bears. Have you anything in your pocket? "

Her glowing face rose against a background of maple boughs, which surrounded her like a flame. The mist of the morning was on her lips and her eyes were shining. He felt her beauty leap like wine to his brain, and he set his teeth and looked blankly down the road.

She laughed as she plunged her hand into the pocket of his coat. " You used to have apples," she complained, " or honeyshucks, at least—now there's only this."

It was a worn little Latin text book, with frayed edges and soiled leaves.

" Give it to me," he said quickly, but as he reached to take it from her the leaves fell open and she saw her own name written and rewritten across the crumpled pages.

She closed it and gave it back to him.

" You used that long ago," she remarked carelessly; " very long ago."

He replaced the book in his pocket, his steady eyes upon her.

" That's what we get for rifling our neighbour's pockets," he said quietly, " and what we deserve."

" No," she returned with equal gravity, " sometimes we get apples—or even peanuts, which we don't deserve."

He took no notice of the retort, but answered half-absently a former question.

" Yes; I used that long ago," he said. " You don't think I would write your name ' Genia ' now, do you?"

There was a dignity in his assumption of indifference—in his absolute refusal to betray himself, which bore upon her conception of his manhood. There was strength in his face, strength in his voice, strength in his quiet hand that lay upon her bridle. She looked down on him with thoughtful eyes.

" If you wrote of me at all," she returned. " It is my name."

" But I am not to call you by it."

" Why not? "

" Why not? " He laughed with a touch of bitterness, and held out his hand, fresh from the soil, hardened by the plough. It was a powerful hand, brown and sinewy, with distorted knuckles and broken nails. " Oh, not that," he said. " I don't mean that. That shows work, but I know you—Genia— you will tell me work is manly. So it is, but is ignorance and poverty and—and all the rest——"

She leaned over and touched his hand lightly with her own. " All the rest is courage and patience and pride," she said; " as for the hand, it is a good hand, and I like it."

He shook his head.

" Good enough in its place, I grant you," he answered; " good enough in the fields, at the plough, or in the barnyard—good enough even to keep this poor farm from collapse and to lift a few of its burdens—but not good enough to——"

He raised her hand lightly, regarding it with half-humorous eyes.

" How strong it is to be so light! " he added.

" Strong enough to hold fast to its friends," returned Eugenia gravely.

He let it fall and looked into her face.

" May its friends be worthy ones," he said.

She rode slowly through the wood, and he walked with his hand on her bridle. The bright branches struck them as they passed, and sometimes he stopped to hold them aside for her. His eyes followed her as she rode serenely above him, and he thought, in his folly, of the lady in the old romance who was, to the desire of her lovers, as " a distant flame, a sword afar off."

" It was here that you told me good-bye when you went off to school," he said recklessly.

" Was it? " she asked. " I was very miserable that day and you gave me no comfort. You didn't even come down to the road next morning to see me go by."

" Yes, I know," he admitted.

" I thought you were asleep, and I was angry."

" No, I was not asleep. I was at work."

" But you might have come."

" Yes, I might have come," he repeated absently, and quickly corrected himself. " No, I mean I couldn't come, of course. If you were to go away to-morrow, I couldn't come. Something would rise and prevent. I have a presentiment that I shall never say good-bye to you."

She dissented. " I've a feeling that I shall say ' God speed ' to you when you go off to become a great man."

" A great man? Do you mean a rich man? " he asked quickly.

" Oh, dear, yes," she mocked; " a great, gouty gentleman, who owns a couple of railroads and wears an electric light in his shirt-front."

His lips laughed, but his eyes were grave.

" And when I came back to you with such trophies," he objected, " you would tell me that the railroads belonged to the people and that the electric light only served to illuminate my ugliness."

"And I should take it to wear on my forehead," she added. "What prophetic insight!"

"But 'going off' does not always mean railroads and electric light," he went on half seriously. "Suppose I came back poor, but honest, as they say?"

Laughter rippled on her lips. He watched the humorous tremor of her nostrils.

"Then I should probably kill the fatted chicken for you," she said.

There was a touch of bitterness in his answer. "Only in that case I should stay away." As he spoke he stopped to break off a drooping branch from a sweet-gum tree that grew near the road.

"You once called this your colour," he said quietly as he fastened the leaves on her horse's head. "There is no tree that turns so clear and so fiery."

Then, as she rode on with the branch waving like a banner before her, he laughed with a keen delight in the savage brilliance.

"You remind me of—who is it?" he asked— "'*Clear as the sun and terrible as an army with banners.*'"

Her smile was warm upon him.

"But my banners fall before the wind," she said as several loosened leaves fluttered to the road. "So I am not terrible, after all." The glow of the gum-tree was in her face. His eyes fell before it, and he did not speak. The soft footfalls of the horse on the damp ground sounded distinctly. Overhead the wind rustled among the trees.

As they emerged from the wood and passed the Burr farm they saw Amos leaning on his gate, looking moodily upon the morning.

" Good-morning, Mr. Burr ! " said Eugenia with the pleasant condescension of the general in her manner. " Fine weather, isn't it? "

He nodded awkwardly and admitted, with a muttered reservation, that the weather might be worse. Then he looked at Nicholas. " If you ain't got nothin' better to do I reckon you might lend a hand at the ploughin'," he surlily suggested.

" Why, so I might," assented Nicholas good-humouredly. " I've a couple of hours free."

He fastened more securely the branch in the horse's bridle; then, raising his hat, he turned and vaulted the whitewashed fence, while Eugenia, touching her horse into a gallop, vanished in the distance of the open road, blazing her track with scarlet gum leaves that scattered royally in the wind.

As Nicholas passed the peanut field he nodded pleasantly to the congregation of negroes assembled for the annual festival called " a picking." They ranged in degrees from Uncle Ish, the oldest representative of his race, to Betsey's five-year-old Jeremiah, who had already been detected in an attempt to filch the nuts from an overturned shock, and was being soundly admonished by his mother's avenging palm. The ground was strewn with baskets and buckets of varying dimensions, into which the nuts were gathered before being consigned to the huge hamper guarded by Amos Burr. A hoarse clamour, like that produced by a flock of crows, went up from the animated swarm as it settled to work.

Nicholas crossed to the adjoining field and ploughed deep furrows in the soil, going into breakfast with the smell of the warm earth about him and

the glow of exercise in his blood.   He ate heartily
and listened without remark to the political vagaries
of his father.   Amos Burr had been " looking into
politics " of late, and his stubborn wits had been
fixed by a grievance.   " If he was a fool befo' now,
he's a plum fool now," Marthy Burr had observed
dispassionately.   " I ain't never seen no head so
level that it could bear the lettin' in of politics.   It
makes a fool of a man and a worse fool of a fool.
The government's like a mule, it's slow and it's
sure; it's slow to turn, and it's sure to turn the way
you don't want it."

" I tell you it's done promised to help the farmer,"
put in Amos heavily, bringing his large red hand
down upon the table.   " Ain't it been helpin' the
manufacturer all these years?   Ain't it been lookin'
arter the labourer, black an' white?   Ain't it time for
it to keep its word to the farmer? "

" In the meantime I'd finish that piece of ploughing, if I were you," suggested Nicholas.   " The more
work in the fall the less in the spring—that's a proverb for you."

" I don't want no proverb," returned Amos sullenly.   " I want my rights, an' I want the country
to give 'em to me."

" I ain't never seen no good come of settin' down
an' wishin' for rights," remarked his wife tartly.
" It's a sight better to be up an' plantin'.'"

Nicholas finished his breakfast, and a little later
walked in to town.   He was in exuberant spirits,
and his thoughts were high on the scaffolding where
his future was building.   Success and Eugenia
startled, allured, delighted him.   He was at the age

of sublime self-confidence, but his eyes were not bandaged by it. He knew that without success—such success as he dreamed of—there could be, for him, no Eugenia. He believed in her as he believed in the sun, and yet he was not sure of her—he could not be until he possessed her and she bore his name. That she might not love him he admitted; that she might even love another he saw to be dimly possible; but he was determined that so long as no other man held her his arms should be open. In the first ardour of his mood his relative position to that society of which she formed a part was lost sight of, if not obscured. Now he realised bitterly that he might work for a lifetime in the class in which he was born, and at the end still find Eugenia far from him. He must rise above his work and his people, he must cut his old name anew, he must walk rough-shod where his mind led him—among men who were his superiors only in the accident of a better birthright. And if on that higher plane his ambitions did not betray, he would bring honour to his State and to Eugenia.

Here the two loves of the boy and the man stood out boldly. The old romantic fervour with which he had longed for the days of Marshall and Madison, of Jefferson and Henry, still lingered on as an exotic patriotism in an era of time-servers and unprofitable servants. There was an old-fashioned democracy about him—a pioneer simplicity—as one who had walked from the great days of Virginia into her lesser ones. A century ago he might have left his plough to fight, and, having fought, might have returned thereto; but the battle would have tingled in his blood and the furrows have gone crooked. He would have ploughed, not for love of the plough, but because the time for the sowing of the grain had come.

Now he walked rapidly to his work, seeing Eugenia in the woods, in the sunshine, in the very clouds lifted high above. The thought of her surrounded him as an atmosphere.

As for the girl, she rode home and spent the long day in the garden potting plants for the winter. When she came into the hall in the early afternoon, with her trowel in her hand and her sleeves rolled back from her white arms, her father called her to the porch, and, going out, she found Dudley Webb in one of the cane chairs. He sprang to his feet as she reached the threshold, and held out his hand, but she laughed and showed the earth that clung to her wrists. "Unclean! unclean!" she cried gaily. Her face had flushed from its warm pallor and her hair hung low upon her forehead. A long streak of clay lay across her skirt where she had knelt in the flower-bed.

He seized her protesting hand, admiration lighting his eyes. "Why, little Eugie is a woman!" he exclaimed. "Can you grasp it, General?"

The general shook his head.

"If she wasn't almost as tall as I, I shouldn't believe it," he declared, "though she's as old as her mother was when I married her."

Eugenia seated herself upon the bench, still holding the trowel in her hand. She was watching the interest in her father's face, and she realised, half resentfully, that it was evoked by Dudley Webb.

He had drawn the general's favourite anecdotes from him, and they had plunged together into a discussion of the good old days. After a few light words she sat silent, listening with tender attention to the threadbare stories on the one side and the hearty applause of them on the other. She wondered wistfully why Dudley and herself were the only persons who understood as well as loved the general. Why was it Dudley, and not Nicholas, who brought that youthful look to his face and the heartiness to his voice?

"Some one was telling me the other day—I think it was Colonel Preston—that he fought beside you at Seven Pines," Dudley was saying with that absorption in his subject which won him a friend in every man who told him a joke.

"Jake Preston!" exclaimed the general. "Why, bless my soul! I've slept under the same blanket with Jake Preston twenty times. I was standing by him when he got that bullet in his thigh. Did he tell you?"

Eugenia rose in a moment and went back to her flowers. As she passed she threw a grateful glance at Dudley, but when she reached the garden it was of Nicholas she was thinking. There was a glow at her heart that kept alive the memory of his eyes as he looked at her in the wood, of his voice when he called her name, of his hand when it brushed her own.

She fell happily to work, and when Dudley came out, an hour later, to find her, she was singing softly as she uprooted a scarlet geranium.

He smiled and looked down on her with frank

enjoyment of her ripening womanhood, but it did
not occur to him to join in the transplanting as
Nicholas would have done. He held off and absorbed the picture.

"You do papa so much good!" said Eugenia
gratefully. "I hope you will come out whenever
you are in Kingsborough."

She was kneeling upon the ground, her hands
buried in the flower-bed, her firm arms rising white
above the rich earth. The line of her bosom rose
and fell swiftly, and her breath came in soft pants.
There was a flush in her cheeks.

"If you wish it I will come," he answered impulsively. "I will come to Kingsborough every week
if you wish it."

His temperament responded promptly to the appeal of her beauty, and his blood quickened as it did
when women moved him. There was about him,
withal, a fantastic chivalry which succumbed to the
glitter of false sentiment. He would have made the
remark had Eugenia been plain—but he would not
have come to Kingsborough.

"It would please your mother," returned the girl
quietly. She had the sexual self-poise of the Virginia woman, and she weighed the implied compliment at its due value. Had he declared he would
die for her once a week, she would have received the
assurance with much the same smiling indifference.

"I'll run down, I think, pretty often this winter,"
he went on easily. "It's a nice old town, after all—
isn't it?"

"It's the dearest old town in the world," said
Eugenia.

"Well, I believe it is—strange, I used to find it dull, don't you think? By the way, will you let me ride with you sometimes? I hear you are as great a horsewoman as ever."

Eugenia looked up calmly.

"I go very early," she answered. "Can you get up at daybreak?"

He laughed his pleasant laugh.

"Oh, I might manage it," he rejoined. "I'm not much of an early riser, I never knew before what charms the sunrise held."

But Eugenia went on potting plants.

IV

During the following week Sally Burwell came to spend the night with Eugenia, and the girls sat before the log fire in Eugenia's room until they heard the cocks crow shrilly from the hen-house. The room was a large, old-fashioned chamber, full of dark corners and unsuspected alcoves; and the lamp on the bureau served only to intensify the shadows that lay beyond its faint illumination.

Sally, her pretty hair in a tumble on her shoulders and the light of the logs on her bare arms, was stretched upon the hearth-rug, looking up at Eugenia, who lay in an easy-chair, her feet almost touching the embers. A waiter of russet apples was on the floor beside them.

" This is my idea of comfort," murmured Sally sleepily as she munched an apple. " No men and no manners."

" If you liked it, you'd come often, chick," returned Eugenia.

" Bless you! I'm too busy. I made over two dresses this week, trimmed mamma a bonnet, and covered a sofa with cretonne. One of the dresses is a love. I wore it yesterday, and Dudley said it reminded him of one he'd seen on the stage."

" He says a good deal," observed Eugenia unsympathetically.

" Doesn't he? " laughed Sally. " At any rate, he

said that he found you reading Plato under the trees, and that any woman who read Plato ought to be ostracised—unless she happens to be handsome enough to make you overlook it. Is that your Plato? What is he like?"

Eugenia savagely shook her head.

"It's no affair of his," she retorted promptly, meaning not Plato, but Dudley.

"Oh! he said he knew it wasn't. I think he even wished it were. You're too unconventional for him —he frankly admits it—but he admits also that you're good-looking enough to warrant the unconventionality of a Hottentot—and you are, you dear, bad thing, though your forehead's too high and your chin's too long and your nose isn't all that a nose should be."

"Thanks," drawled Eugenia amicably. "But Dudley's a nice fellow, all the same. He gets on splendidly with papa—and I bless him for it."

"He gets on well with everybody—even his mother—which makes me suspect that he's a Job masquerading as an Apollo. By the way, Mrs. Webb wants you to join some society she's getting up called the ' Daughters of Duty.' "

"Oh, I can't! I can't!" protested Eugenia distressfully. " I detest ' Daughter ' things, and I have a rooted aversion to my duty. But if she comes to me I'll join it—I know I shall! How did you keep out of it?"

"I didn't. I'm in it. It seems that our duty is confined to ' preserving the antiquities ' of Kingsborough—so I began by presenting a jar of pickled cucumbers to Uncle Ish. I trust they won't be the

death of him, but he was the only antiquity in
sight."

She gave the smouldering log a push with her
foot, and it broke apart, scattering a shower of
sparks. " I don't know any other woman so much
admired and so little loved," she mused of Mrs.
Webb.

" Papa worships her," said Eugenia. " All men
do—at a distance. She's the kind of woman you
never get near enough to to feel that she is flesh.
Now, Aunt Chris is just the opposite. No one ever
gets far enough away from her to feel that she's a
saint—which she is."

" It's odd she never married," wondered Sally.

" She never had time to." Eugenia clasped her
hands behind her head and looked up at the high,
plastered ceiling. " She never happened to be in a
place where she could be spared. But you know
her lover died when she was young," she added. " It
broke her heart, but it did not destroy her happiness.
She has been happy for forty years with a broken
heart."

" I know," said Sally. " It seems strange, doesn't
it ? But I've known so many like her. The happiest woman I ever knew had lost everything she
cared for in the war. That war was fought on
women's hearts, but they went on beating just the
same. I'm glad I wasn't I then."

" And I'm sorry. I like stirring deeds and shot
and shell and tattered flags. They thrill one."

" And kill one," added Sally. " But you've got
that kind of pluck. You aren't afraid."

" Oh ! yes, I am," protested Eugenia. " I'm

afraid of bats and of getting fat like my fore-
fathers."

Sally shook a reassuring head.

" But you won't, darling.   Your mother was thin,
and you're the image of her—everybody says so."

" But I'm afraid—horribly afraid.   I don't dare
eat potatoes, and I wouldn't so much as look at a
glass of buttermilk.   The fear is on me."

" It's absurd.   Why, your grandma Tucker was a
rail—I remember her.   I know your other grand-
mother was—enormous; but you ought to strike
the happy medium—and you do.   You're splendid.
You aren't a bit too large for your height."

Eugenia laughed as she twisted Sally's curls about
her fingers.   " You're the dearest little duck that
ever lived on dry land," she said.   " If I were a
man I'd be wild about you."

" A few of them are," returned Sally meekly, casting up her eyes, " but I——"

" How about Gerald Smith?"

" He's too tall.   I look like an aspiring grass-
hopper beside him."

" And Jack Wyth?"

" He's too short."

" And Sydney Kent?"

" He's too stupid."

" And Tom Bassett?"

Sally yawned.

" He's too—everything.   There's cock crow, and
I'm going to bed."

The next afternoon Eugenia drove Sally in to
town, and stopped on her outward trip to pay a visit
to Mrs. Webb.   She found that lady serenely seated

in her drawing-room, as unruffled as if she had not just dismissed a cook and cooked a dinner.

"Oh, yes, thank you, dear, all is well," she replied in answer to the girl's question; for she held it to be vulgarity to allude, in her drawing-room, to the trials of housekeeping. She was not touched by such questions because she ignored that she was in any way concerned in them. She spent six hours a day with her servants, but had she spent twenty-four she would have remained secure in her conviction that they did not come within the sphere of her life.

"I have wanted to see you to ask you to join my society, the 'Daughters of Duty,'" she went on, her eyes on a piece of fine white damask she was hem-stitching. "Its object is to preserve our old landmarks, and when I spoke to your father he told me he was quite sure you would care to become an active member."

"I'm afraid I don't have much time," began Eugenia helplessly, when Mrs. Webb interrupted her, though without haste or discourtesy.

"Not have time, my dear?" she repeated with her slow, fine smile. "If I can find time, with all my other duties, don't you think that you might be able to do so?"

Eugenia was baffled. "Of course I love Kingsborough," she said, "and I'd preserve every inch of it with my own hands if I could—but I can't bear meetings—and—and things."

Mrs. Webb took a careful stitch in the damask. "I thought you might care enough to assist us," she remarked tentatively; and Eugenia succumbed.

"I'll do anything I can," she declared. "I will, indeed—only you mustn't expect much."

In a few moments she rose to go, lingering with a courteous appearance of being unwilling to depart, which belonged to her social training. As she stood in the doorway, her hand in Mrs. Webb's, the older woman looked at her almost affectionately.

"I had a letter from Dudley this morning," she said. "He is coming down next week for Sunday."

A flush crossed Eugenia's face, evoking an expression of irritation.

"You must miss him," she observed sympathetically.

"I do miss him, but he comes often. He is a good son. He sent a message to you, by the way, but it was not important."

"No, it was not important," repeated Eugenia with a feeling that her carelessness appeared to be assumed.

She lightly kissed Mrs. Webb and ran down the steps and into the carriage, which was waiting in the road. Her visit had left her with a curious sense of oppression, and she breathed a long draught of the invigorating air.

As she drove down the street she saw Nicholas coming out of his office and offered him a "lift" to his home. He said little on the way, and his utterances were forced, but Eugenia talked lightly and rapidly, as she always did when with him.

She told him of Sally Burwell, of the last letter from Bernard—who was coming home soon—of Mrs. Webb and the "Daughters of Duty."

"The truth is, I like her, but I'm afraid of her—dreadfully."

"She disapproves of your—your liking for me," he said bitterly. "But every one does that—even the judge, though he doesn't say anything. And they are right—I see it. You know from what I came and what I am."

"Yes, I know what you are," she returned defiantly, "and they shall all know some day."

He turned and looked at her as she sat beside him, but he was silent, nor did he speak until he said "good-bye" before his father's gate.

It was some days later that she saw him again. She had gone out to gather goldenrod for the great blue vases that stood on the dining-room mantel-piece, and was standing knee-deep in the ragged field, when he leaped the fence that divided the farms and crossed to where she stood.

The sun was going down behind the blackened branches of the dead oak, and the wide common, spread with goldenrod and life-everlasting, lay like a sea of flame and snow. Eugenia, standing in its midst, a tall woman in a dress of brown, fell in richly with the surrounding colours. Her arms were filled with the yellow plumes and her dress was tinselled with the dried pollen that floated in the air. As Nicholas reached her she was seeking to free herself from the clutch of a crimson briar that crawled along the ground, and in the effort some of the broken stalks slipped from her hold.

Without speaking, he knelt beside her and released her skirt. "You have torn it," he said quietly, but he was looking up at her, and there was a quality in his voice which thrilled her.

" Have I ? " she returned quickly. " Well, I can mend it—but there! it's caught again. I've been trying to get free for—hours."

He smiled.

" You came into the field only twenty minutes ago. I saw you. But, hold on. I'll uproot this blackberry vine while I'm about it."

He tore it from its tenacious hold to the earth and flung it into the field. Then he examined the rent in Eugenia's dress.

" If you had waited until I came you might have spared yourself this—patch," he observed.

" I shan't patch it—and I didn't know you were coming."

" Don't I always come—when there's a patch to be saved ? " he asked. " I hate to see things ruined."

" Then you might have come sooner. There, give me my goldenrod. It's all scattered."

He began patiently to gather up the stalks, arranging them in an even layer of equal lengths.

Eugenia watched him, laughing.

" How precise you are ! " she said.

" Aren't they right ? " He looked up for her approval, and she saw that he had grown singularly boyish. His face was less rugged, more sensitive. He wore no hat, and his thick red hair had fallen across his forehead. She felt the peculiar power of his look as she had felt it before.

" No, they're wrong. They aren't Chinese puzzles. Don't fix them so tight. Here."

She took them from him, and as his hands touched

hers she noticed that they were cold. "You're shaking them all apart," he protested, "and I took such a lot of trouble."

As she bent her head his eyes followed the dark coil of hair to the white nape of her neck where her collar rose. Several loose strands had blown across her ear and wound softly about the delicate lobe. He wanted to raise his hand and put them in place, but he checked himself with a start. With his eyes upon her he recalled the warmth of her woollen dress, and he wished that he had put his lips to it as he knelt. She would never have known.

Then, by a curious emotional phenomenon, she seemed to be suddenly invested with the glory of the sunset. The goldenrod burned at her feet and on her bosom, and her fervent blood leaped to her face. The next moment he staggered like a man blinded by too much light—the field, with Eugenia rising in its midst, flamed before his eyes, and he put out his hand like one in pain.

"What is it?" she asked quickly, and her voice seemed a part of the general radiance. "You have been looking at the sun. It hurts my eyes."

"No," he answered steadily, "I was looking at you."

She thrilled as he spoke and brought her eyes to the level of his. Then she would have looked away, but his gaze held her, and she made a sudden movement of alarm—a swift tremor to escape. She held the sheaf of goldenrod to her bosom and above it her eyes shone; her breath came quickly between her parted lips. All her changeful beauty was startled into life.

"Genia!" he said softly, so softly that he seemed speaking to himself. "Genia!"

"Yes?" She responded in the same still whisper.

"You know?"

"Yes, I know," she repeated slowly. Her glance fell from his and she turned away.

"You know it is—impossible," he said.

"Yes, I know it is impossible."

There was a gasp in her voice. She turned to move onward—a briar caught her dress; she stumbled for an instant, and he flung out his arms.

"You know it is impossible," he said, and kissed her.

The sheaf of goldenrod loosened and scattered between them. Her head lay on his arm, and he felt her warm breath come and go. Her face was upturned, and he saw her eyes as he had never seen them before—light on light, shadow on shadow. He looked at her in the brief instant as a man looks to remember—at the white brow—the red mouth, at the blue veins, and the dark hair, at the upward lift of the chin and the straight throat—at all the perfect colouring and the imperfect outline.

"You know it is impossible," he repeated, and put her from him.

Eugenia gathered herself together like one stunned. "I must go," she said breathlessly. "I must go."

Then she hesitated and stood before him, her hands on her bosom, a single spray of goldenrod clinging to her dress.

He folded his arms as he faced her.

"I have loved you all my life," he said.

She bowed her head; her face had gone white.

"I shall always love you," he went on. "You may as well know it. Men change, but I do not. I have never really loved anybody else. I have tried to love my family, but I never did. When I was a little, God-forsaken chap I used to want to love people, but I couldn't—I couldn't even love the judge—whom I would die for. I love you."

"I know it," she said.

"If you will wait I will work for you. I will work until they let me have you. I don't mean that I shall ever be good enough for you—because I shall not be. I shall always be a brute beside you —but if you will wait I will win you. I swear it!"

She had not moved. She was as still as the dead oak that towered above them. The sunset struck upon her bowed head and upon the quiet bosom, where her hands were clasped.

"I will wait," she answered.

He came nearer and kissed the hands upon her breast. His face was flushed and his lips were hot.

"Thank you," he said simply as he drew back.

In a moment he stooped to pick up the scattered goldenrod, heaping it into her arms. "This is enough to fill the house," he protested. "You can't want so much."

He had regained his rational tone, and she responded to it with a smile.

"I never know when I'm satisfied," she said. "It is my weakness. As a child I always ate candy until it made me ill."

They crossed the field, the long plumes brushing against them and powdering them with a feathery

gold dust. At the fence she gave him the bunch
and lightly swung herself over the sunken rails. It
did not occur to him to assist her; she had always
been as good as he at vaulting bars. Now her long
skirts retarded her, and she laughed as she came
quickly to the ground on the opposite side.

" One of the many disadvantages of my sex," she
said. " The best prisons men ever invented are
women's skirts. Our wings are clipped while we
wear them."

" It is hard," he returned as he recalled her school-
girl feats. " You were such a mighty jumper."

" Those halcyon days are done," she sighed. " I
can never stray beyond my ' sphere ' again."

They had reached the end of the avenue, so he
left her and went homeward along the road. The
sun had gone slowly down and the western horizon
was ripped open in a deep red track. The charred
skeleton of the oak loomed black and sinister
against the afterglow, and at its feet the glory went
out of the autumn field. Straight ahead the sound
of shots rang out where a flock of bats circled above
the road. On the darkening landscape the lights
began to glimmer in farmhouses far apart, and to
Nicholas they seemed watchful, friendly eyes that
looked upon him. All Nature was watchful—all the
universe friendly. The glow which irradiated his
outlook with an abrupt transfiguration was to him
the glow of universal joy, though he knew it to be
but the vanishing beam of youth and the end thereof
age.

It seemed to him that he was singled out—securely set apart by some beneficent hand for some

supreme good which, in his limited observation, he had never seen put forth in the lots of others. His own life lay so much nearer the Divine purpose than did the lives of his neighbours—the purpose of Nature, whose end is the happiness that conforms to sane and immutable laws. His kiss on Eugenia's lips was to him God-given; the answer in her eyes had flamed a Scriptural inspiration. In the tumultuous leaping of his thoughts it seemed to him that the meaning of existence lay unrolled—a meaning obscured in all religions, overlooked in all philosophies—a meaning that could be read only by the lamp that was lit in the eyes that loved.

So in his ignorance and his ecstasy he went on his confident way, while passion throbbed in his pulses and youth quickened in his brain.

From the far-off pines twilight came to meet him, the lights glimmered clearer in distant windows, the afterglow drifted from the west, and the shots ceased where the black bats circled above the road.

Eugenia arranged the goldenrod in the great blue vases and sat in the deserted dining-room thinking of Nicholas. Where the damask curtains were drawn back from the windows a gray line of twilight landscape was visible, and a chill, transparent dusk filled the large room. Outside she would see the box-walk, a stretch of lawn, broken by flower-beds, and the avenue of cedars leading to the highway. From the porch floated the smoke of the general's pipe.

Her brow was on her hand and she sat so motionless that the place seemed deserted, save for an errant firefly that vainly palpitated in the gloom. The glow that had flamed beneath Nicholas's kiss still lingered in her face, and she was conscious of a faint, almost hysterical impulse to weep. The fever in her veins had given place to a still tremor which ran through her limbs. At first she felt rather than thought. She lapsed into an emotional reverie as delicate as the fragrance of the October roses on the table. There was a sensation of softness as when one lies full length in sunshine or is caressed by firelight. She felt it pervade her body even to the palms of her hands. Then her quick mind stirred, and she recalled the pressure of his arms, the light in his eyes, the quiver of his lips as they touched her hands. His strength had dominated her and it still held her—the firm note in the voice that trembled,

the power in the hand that appealed, the almost
savage vigour in the arms that he folded on his
breast. She had succumbed less to his gentleness
than to the knowledge that it was she alone who
evoked that gentleness out of a nature almost ada-
mantine, wholly masculine. His faults she knew to
be the faults of one who had hewn his own road in
life—a rugged surface—a strain of rigidity beneath
—at worst a tendency to dogmatise—and knowing
as she did her own control over them, they attracted
rather than repelled her.

And yet in this pulsating recognition of his manhood there was mingled with an emotion half-
maternal the memory of her own guardianship of
his stunted childhood. To a woman at once rashly
spirited and profoundly feminine the pathos of his
boyish struggle appealed no less forcibly than did
the virility of his manhood. She might have loved
him less had her thought of him been untouched by
pity.

She sat quietly in the twilight until Congo
brought in the lamp and a prospect of supper. Then
she rose and went to join her father on the porch.

"Why did you tell Mrs. Webb I would be a
'Daughter,' papa?" she gaily demanded.

The general took his pipe from his mouth and
stared up at her.

"It's a good cause, Eugie," he replied, "and
she's a remarkable woman. Her executive ability
is astounding—absolutely astounding."

"I joined," said Eugenia. "I had to, after you
said that. You know, I called on her the day I
took Sally in."

The general lowered his eyes and thoughtfully regarded the light that was going gray in his pipe.

"Did she happen to say anything about—Dudley?" he inquired.

"Oh, yes. She said he sent me a message in a letter."

"Did she tell you what 'twas?"

"No. I didn't ask her."

He put the stem of his pipe between his teeth and hung on it desperately for a moment; then he took it out again.

"He's a fine young fellow," he said at last. "I don't know a finer—and, bless my soul! I'd see you married to him to-morrow."

But Eugenia laughed and beat his shoulder.

"You don't want to see me married to anybody," she said, "and you know it."

At the end of the ensuing week Dudley came to Kingsborough, and upon the first evening of his visit he walked out to Battle Hall. He was looking smooth and well groomed, and the mass of his thick dark hair waving over his white brow gave him an air of earnestness and ardour. Eugenia wondered that she had never noticed before that he was like the portrait of an old-time orator, and that his hands were finely rounded.

His voice, with its suggestion of suavity, fell soothingly on her nerves. She had never liked him so much, and she had never shown it so plainly. Once as she met his genial gaze she held her breath at the marvel that he should grow to love her, and in vain. Was it that beside his splendid shal-

lows the more luminous depths of Nicholas's nature
still showed supreme?   Or was it a question of fate
—and of first and last?   Had Dudley come upon her
in the red sunset, in the little shanty beside the road,
would she have gone out to him in the mere leaping
of youth and womanhood?   Was it the moment,
after all, and not the man?   Or was it something
more unerring still—more profound—the prophetic
call of individual to individual, despite the specious
pleading of the race?   But she put the thought aside
and returned casually to Dudley.

His heartiness was a tonic, and her vanity responded to the unaffected admiration in his eyes;
but his chief claim to her regard lay in the fact that
it was the general, and not herself, whom he en-
deavoured to propitiate.

"Well, my dear General!" he exclaimed cordially as he threw himself upon the worn horsehair
sofa in what was called the "sitting-room," "I find
your story about the fighting Texans capped by one
Major Mason was telling me last night about the
North Carolinians——" He got no farther.

"I've fought side by side with North Carolina
regiments, and I tell you, sir, they're the best
fighters God ever made!" cried the general.   "Did
you ever hear that story about 'em when I was
wounded?"

Dudley shook his head and leaned forward, his
hands clasped between his knees and an expression
of flattering absorption on his face.

"I can't recall it now, sir," he delightfully lied.

The general cleared his throat, laid his pipe aside,
and drew up his chair.

" It was in my last battle," he began. " You know I got that ball in my shoulder and was laid up when Lee surrendered—well, sir, I was propped up there close by a company of those raw-boned mountaineers from North Carolina, and they stood as still as the pine wood behind 'em, while their colonel swore at 'em like mad.

" ' Damn you for a troop of babies!' he yelled. ' Ain't you goin' into the fight? Can't you lick a blamed Yankee?' And, bless your soul! those scraggy fellows stood stock still and sung out:

" ' We ain't mad!'

" Well, sir, they'd no sooner yelled that back than a bullet whizzed along and took off one of their own men, and, on my oath, the bullet hadn't ceased singing in my ears before that company charged the enemy to a man—and whipped 'em, too, sir— whipped 'em clean off the field!"

He paused, clapped his knee, and roared.

" That's your North Carolinian," he said. " He's a God Almighty fighter, but you've got to make him mad first."

Miss Chris brought her knitting to the lamp, and Eugenia, sitting with her hands in her lap, followed the conversation with abstracted interest.

It was not until Dudley rose to go that he came over to her and took her hand.

" Good-night," he said, his ardent eyes upon her. " I'm to have that ride to-morrow? You know I came for it."

The unreasoning blood beat in her face as she turned away, and she was conscious that he had seen and misconstrued the senseless blush. It was her misfortune to go red or pale without cause and to show an impassive face above deep emotion.

The next morning she rode with Dudley, and the day after he came out before returning to Richmond. She experienced a certain pleasure in the contact with his bouyant optimism, but it was not without a sensation of relief that she watched him depart after his last visit. It seemed to leave her more to herself—and to Nicholas.

That afternoon she walked with him far across the fields, and they laid together phantasmal foundations of their future lives. Perhaps the chief thing to be said of their intercourse was that it was to each a mental stimulant as well as an emotional delight. Eugenia's quick, untutored mind, which had run to seed like an uncultivated garden, blossomed from contact with his practical, unpolished intellect. He taught her logic and a little law; she taught him poetry and passion. He argued his cases to her and swept her back into the days of his old political dreams—dreams from which he had awakened, but which still hovered as memories in his waking hours. Sometimes he brought his books to Battle Hall, and they read together beneath the general's unseeing eyes; but more often they sat side by side in the pasture or the wood, the volume lying open between them. He was the first man who had ever spurred her into thought; she was the first woman he had ever loved.

As they walked across the fields this afternoon they drifted back to the question of themselves and their own happiness. It was only a matter of waiting, she said, of the patient passage of time; and

they were so sure of each other that all else was unimportant—to be disregarded.

" But am I sure of you? " he demanded.

It was not a personal distrust of Eugenia that he
voiced; it was the hardened state of disbelief in his
own happiness which showed itself when the first
intoxication of passion was lived out.

" Why, of course you are," she readily rejoined.
" Am I not sure of you? You are as much mine as
my eyes—or my hand."

" Oh, I am different! " he exclaimed. " A beggar
doesn't prove faithless to a princess—but what do
you see in me, after all? "

She laughed. " I see a very moody lover."

They had reached a little deserted spring in the
pasture called " Poplar Spring," after the six great
poplars which grew beside it. Eugenia seated herself on a fallen log beside the tiny stream which
trickled over the smooth, round stones, bearing
away, like miniature floats, the yellow leaves that
fell ceaselessly from the huge branches above.

" I don't believe you know how I love you," he
said suddenly.

" Tell me," she insatiably demanded.

" If I could tell you I shouldn't love you as I do.
There are some things one can't talk about—but you
are life itself—and you are all heaven and all hell
to me."

" I don't want to be hellish," she put in provok-
ingly.

" But you are—when I think you may slip from
me, after all."

The yellow leaves fluttered over them—over the

16

fallen log and over the bright green moss beside the little spring. As Eugenia turned towards him, a single leaf fell from her hair to the ground.

"Oh! You are thinking of Dudley Webb!" she said, and laughed because jealousy was her own darling sin.

"Yes, I am thinking——" he began, when she stopped him.

"Well, you needn't. You may just stop at once. I—love—you—Nick—Burr. Say it after me."

He shook his head. Her hand lay on the log beside him, and his own closed over it. As it did so, she contrasted its hardened palm with the smooth surface of Dudley Webb's. The contrast touched her, and, with a swift, warm gesture, she raised the clasped hands to her cheek.

"I told you once I liked your hand," she said. "Well—I love it."

He turned upon her a hungry glance.

"I would work it to the bone for you," he answered. "But—it is long to wait."

"Yes, it is long to wait," she repeated, but her tone had not the heaviness of his. Waiting in its wider sense means little to a woman—and in a moment she cheerfully returned to a prophetic future.

A few days later Bernard came, and she saw Nicholas less often. Her affection for her brother, belonging, as it did, to the dominant family feeling which possessed her soul, was filled with an almost maternal solicitude. He absorbed her with a spasmodic, half selfish, wholly insistent appeal. She received his confidences, wrote his letters, and tied his cravats. Upon his last visit home he had spent the greater part of his time in Kingsborough; now he rode in seldom, and invariably returned in a moody and depressed condition.

" You're worth the whole bunch of them," he had said to her of other girls, " you dear old Eugie."

And she had warmed and laid a faithful hand on his arm. It was characteristic of her that no call for affection went disregarded—that the sensitive fibres of her nature quivered beneath any caressing hand.

" Do you really like me best? " she asked.

" Don't I?" He laughed his impulsive, boyish laugh—" I'll prove it by letting you go in for the mail this afternoon. I detest Kingsborough!"

" Oh! No, no, I love it, but I suppose it is dull for you."

She ordered the carriage and went upstairs to put on her hat. When she came down Bernard was not in sight, and she drove off, wondering why he or any one else should detest Kingsborough.

She performed her mission at the post-office, and was mentally weighing the probabilities of Nicholas having finished work for the day, when, in passing along the main street, she saw him come to the door of his office with a round, rosy girl, whom she recognised as Bessie Pollard.

She had intended to take him out with her, but as she caught sight of his visitor she gave them both a condescending nod and ordered Sampson to drive on. She felt vaguely offended and sharply irritated with herself for permitting it. Her annoyance was not allayed by the fact that Amos Burr stopped her in the road to inform her that his wife was fattening a brood of turkeys which she would like to deliver into the hands of Miss Chris. As he stood before her, hairy, ominous, uncouth, she realised for the first time the full horror of the fact that he was father to the man she loved. Hitherto she had but dimly grasped the idea. Nicholas had been associated in her thoughts with the judge and her earlier school days; and she had conceived of his poverty and his people only in the heroic measures that related to his emancipation from them. Now she felt that had she, in the beginning, seen him side by side with his father, she could not have loved him. She flinched from Amos Burr's shaggy exterior and drew back haughtily.

" I have nothing to do with the housekeeping," she said. " You may ask Aunt Chris."

He spat a mouthful of tobacco juice into the dust and fingered the torn brim of his hat.

" I wish you'd jest speak to Miss Chris about 'em," he returned, " an' send me word by Nick." He gave an awkward lurch on his feet.

The colour flamed in Eugenia's face.

" Aunt Chris will send for the turkeys," she said hurriedly. " Drive on, Sampson."

She sat splendidly erect, but the autumn landscape was blurred by a sudden gush of tears.

An hour later she remembered that she had promised to let Nicholas join her in the pasture, and she left the house with the grievance still at her heart.

When she saw him it broke out abruptly.

" I am surprised that you keep up with such people," she said.

He looked at her blankly.

" If you mean Bessie Pollard," he rejoined, " she
was in trouble and came to me for advice.   I couldn't
help her, but I could at least be civil.   She was kind
to me when I was in her father's store."

" I do not care to be reminded that you were ever
in such a position."

He flinched, but answered quietly:

" I am afraid you will have to face it," he said.
" If you become my wife, you will, unfortunately,
have to face a good deal that you might escape by
marrying in your own class—I am not in your class,
you know," he slowly added.

She was conscious of a cloudy irritation which was
alien to her usually beaming moods.   The figure
of Amos Burr loomed large before her, and she
hated herself for the discovery that she was tracing
his sinister likeness in his son.   No, it was only the
hair—that was all, but she loathed the obvious
colour.

Her lip trembled and she set her teeth into it.

" You might at least allow me to forget it," she
retorted.

" Why should you wish to forget it?   I think I
shall be proud of it when I have risen far enough
above it to claim you.   It is no small thing to be
a self-made man."

She resented the assurance of his tone.

" It is strange that you do not consider my view
of it."

" Your view—what is it? "

" That I do not wish the man I love to—to speak to that Pollard girl," she gasped.

" Since you wish it, I will avoid her in future. She is nothing to me; but I can't refuse to speak to her. You are unreasonable."

She was regarding the hovering shade of Amos Burr.

" If you think me unreasonable," she returned, " we may as well——"

He reached her side by a single step and flung his arm about her. Then he looked into her face and laughed softly.

" May as well what—dearest? " he asked.

She shook an obstinate head.

" You don't love me," was her inevitable feminine challenge.

He laughed again. " Do I love you? " he demanded as he looked at her.

She did not answer, but the shade of Amos Burr melted afar.

Nicholas bent over her with abrupt intensity and kissed her lips until his kisses hurt her.

" Do I love you—now? " he asked.

" Yes—yes—yes." She freed herself with a laugh that dispelled the lingering cloud. " You may convince me next time without violence," she affirmed radiantly.

As he watched her his large nostrils twitched whimsically. " You were saying that we might as well——"

" Go home to supper," she finished triumphantly. " The sun has set."

When she left him a little later at the end of the

avenue she flew joyously up the narrow walk. She was softly humming to herself, and as she stepped upon the porch the song ran lightly into words.

> "I love Love, though he has wings,
>   And like light can flee——"

she sang, and paused within the shadow of the porch to glance through the long window that led into the sitting-room. The heavy curtains obstructed her gaze, and she had put up her hand to push them aside, when her father's voice reached her, and at his words her outstretched arm fell slowly to her side.

"It's that girl of Jerry Pollard's," he was saying. "She's gotten into trouble, and that Burr boy's mixed up in it; the young rascal!"

Miss Chris's placid voice floated in.

"I can't believe it," she charitably murmured; and Bernard, who was on the hearth rug, turned at the sound.

"It's all gossip, you know," he said.

Eugenia pushed aside the curtains and stepped into the room. Her hands hung at her sides, and the animation had faded from her glance. Her face looked white and drawn.

"It is not true," she said steadily. "Papa, it is not true."

"I—I'm afraid it is, daughter," gasped the general. There was an abashed embarrassment in his attitude and his hands shook. He had hoped to keep such facts beyond the utmost horizon of his daughter's life.

Eugenia crossed to the hearth rug and stood look-

ing into Bernard's face. She made an appealing
gesture with her hands.

" Bernard, it is not true," she said.

He turned away from her and, nervously lifting the
poker, divided the smouldering log. A red flame
shot up, illuminating the gathered faces that stood
out against the dusk. The glare lent a grotesque
irony to the flabby, awe-stricken features of the general, brightened the boyish ill-humour in Bernard's
eyes, and played peaceably over Miss Chris's tranquil countenance.

" Bernard, it is not true," she said again.

The poker fell with a clatter to the hearth; and
the noise irritated her. Bernard put out a sudden,
soothing hand.

" It is what they say in Kingsborough," he answered.

She turned from him to the window, pushed the
curtains aside, and went out again into the sunset.

VI

She ran swiftly along the walk, into the gloom of the avenue, and out again to the open road. The sunset colours were flaming in the west, and above them a solitary star was shining. The fields lay sombre and deserted on either side, but straight ahead, in the lighter streak of the road, she saw Nicholas's figure swinging onward. She might have called to him, but she did not; she sped like a shadow in his path until, hearing her footfalls in the dust, he looked back and halted.

" You! " he exclaimed.

She came up to him, her hand at her throat, her face turned towards the sunset. For a moment her breath failed and she could not speak; then all the words that she had meant to say—the appeal to him for truth, the cry of her own belief in him—rang theatrical and ineffectual in her brain.

When at last she spoke, it was to voice the mere tripping of her tongue—to utter words which belied the beating of her thoughts.

" You must marry her," she said, and it seemed to her that it was a stranger who spoke. She did not mean that—she had never meant it.

He looked at her blankly, and made a sudden movement forward, but she waved him off.

" For God's sake, whom? " he demanded.

She wished that he had laughed at her—that he

had laid bare the whole hideous farce, but he did not; he regarded her gravely, with a grim inquiry.

"Whom do you mean?" he repeated.

A light wind sprang up, blowing across the pasture and whirling the dead leaves of distant trees into their faces. Overhead other stars came out, and far away an owl hooted.

"Oh! you know, you know," she said, with a desperate anger at his immobility. "When I saw you with her to-day, I did not—I did not——"

"Do you mean Bessie Pollard?" he asked. His voice was hard; it was characteristic of him that, in the supreme test, his sense of humour failed him. He met grave issues with a gravity that upheld them.

She bowed her head. At the same time she flung out a despairing hand for hope, but he did not notice it. She was softening to him—if she had ever steeled herself against him—and a single summons to her faith would have vanquished the feeble resistance. But he did not make it—the inflexible front which she had seen turned to others she now saw presented to herself. He looked at her with an austere tightening of the mouth and held off.

"And they have told you that I ruined her," he said, "and you believe them."

"No—no," she cried; "not that!"

His eyes were on her, but there was no yielding in them. The arrogant pride of a strong man, plainly born, was face to face with her appeal. His features were set with the rigidity of stone.

"Who has told you this?" he demanded.

"Oh, it is not true—it is not true," she answered;

" but Bernard—Bernard believed it—and he is your friend."

Then his smouldering rage burst forth, and his face grew black. It was as if an incarnate devil had leaped into his eyes. He took a step forward.

"Then may God damn him," he said, "for he is the man!"

She fell from him as if he had struck her. Her spirit flashed out as his had done. The anger of her race shot forth.

"Oh, stop! stop! How dare you!" she cried; "for he tried to shield you—he tried to shield you —he would shield you if he could."

But he crossed to where she stood and caught her outstretched hands in a grasp that hurt her. She winced, and his hold grew gentle; but his voice was brutal in its passion.

"Be silent," he said, "and listen to me. They have lied to you, and you have believed them—you I shall never forgive—you are nothing to me—nothing. As for him—may God, in his mercy, damn him!"

He let her hands drop and went from her into the silence of the open road.

When the thud of his footsteps was muffled by the distance Eugenia turned and went back through the cedar avenue. She walked heavily, and there was a bruised sensation in her limbs as if she had hurt herself upon stones. A massive fatigue oppressed her, and she stumbled once or twice over the rocks in the road. Her happiness was dead, this she told herself; telling herself, also, that it had not perished by anger or by disbelief. The slayer loomed intangible and yet inevitable—the shade that had arisen from the gigantic gulf between separate classes which they had sought, in ignorance, to abridge. The pride of Nicholas was not individual, but typical—the pride of caste, and it was against this that she had sinned —not in distrusting his honour, but in offending it. It was in the clash of class, after all, that their theories had crumbled. He might come back to her again—she might go forth to meet him—but the bloom had gone from their dreams—in the reunion she saw neither permanence nor abiding. The strongest of her instincts—the one that made for the blood she bore—had quivered beneath the onslaught of his accusation, but had not bent. Wherever and whenever the struggle came she stood, as the Battles had always stood, for the clan. Be it right or wrong, true or false, it was hers and she was on its side.

As she went beneath the great cedars, their long branches brushed her face, like the remembering touch of familiar fingers, and she put up her cheek to them as if they were sentient things. Long ago they had soothed her as a troubled child, and now their caresses cooled her fever. Underfoot she felt the ancient carpet they had spread throughout the century—and it smoothed the way for her heavy feet. She was in the state of subjective passiveness when the consciousness of external objects alone seems awake. She felt a tenderness for the twisted box bushes she brushed in passing, a vague pity for a sickly moth that flew into her face; but for herself she was without pity or tenderness—she had not brought her mind to bear upon her own hurt.

Indoors she found the family at supper. The

general, hearing her step, called her to her seat and gave her the brownest chicken breast in the dish before him.   Miss Chris offered her the contents of the cream jug, and Congo plied her with Aunt Verbeny's lightest waffles; but the food choked her and she could not eat.   A lump rose in her throat, and she saw the kindly, accustomed faces through a gathering mist.   She regarded each with a certain intentness, a peculiar feeling that there were hidden traits in the commonplace features which she had never seen before—a complexity in the benign candour of Miss Chris's countenance, in the overwrought youthfulness of Bernard's, in the apoplectic credulity of the general's.   Familiar as they were, it seemed to her that there were latent possibilities—obscure tendencies, which were revealed to her now with microscopic exaggeration.

The general put his hand to her forehead and smoothed back the moist hair.

"Ain't you well, daughter?" he asked anxiously. "Would you like a toddy?"

"It's nothing," said Miss Chris cheerfully. "She's walked too far, that's all.   Eugie, you must go to bed early."

"I had her out all the morning in the sun," put in Bernard, with an affectionate nod at Eugenia, "and she's such a trump she wouldn't give out."

"You must learn to consider your sister," said his father testily. .

"Oh! I liked it, papa," declared Eugenia.   "I'm well and—I'm hungry."

Congo brought more waffles, and she ate one with grim determination.   The alert affection which surrounded her—which proved sensitive to a change of colour or a tremor of voice, filled her with a swift sense of security. She felt a sudden impulse to draw nearer in the shelter of the race—to cling more closely to that unswerving instinct which had united individual to individual and generation to generation.

As they rose from the table, she slipped her arm through her father's and went with him into the hall.

" I'm tired," she said, stopping him on his way to the sitting-room, " so I'll go to bed."

The general held her from him and looked into her face.

" Anybody been troubling you, Eugie? " he asked.

She shook her head.

" You dear old goose—no! "

He patted her shoulder reassuringly.

" If anybody troubles you, you just let me hear of it," he said. " They'll find out Tom Battle wasn't at Appomattox. You've got an old father and he's got an old sword——"

" And he's hungry for a fight," she gaily finished. Then she rubbed her cheek against his brown linen sleeve, which was redolent of tobacco. The firm physical contact inspired her with the courage of life; it seemed to make for her a bulwark against the world and its incoming tribulations.

She threw back her head and looked up into the puffed and scarlet face where the coarse veins were congested, her eyes seeing only the love which transfigured it. She was his pet and his pride, and she would·always be the final reward of his long life.

As she mounted the stairs, he blew his nose and called cheerfully after her:

" Just remember, if anybody begins plaguing you, that I'm ready for him—the rascal."

Once in her room she threw open the window and sat looking out into the night, the chill autumn wind in her face. Far across the fields a pale moon was rising, bearing a cloudy circle that betokened rain. It flung long, ghostly shadows east and west, which flitted, lean and noiseless and black, before the wind. Overhead the stars shone dimly, piercing a fine mist. Eugenia leaned forward, her chin on her clasped hands. Beyond the gray blur of the pasture she could see, like benighted beacons, the lights in Amos Burr's windows, and she found herself vaguely wondering if Nicholas were at his books— those books that never failed him. He had that consolation at least—his books were more to him than she had been.

She was not conscious of anger; she felt only an indifferent weariness—a nervous shrinking from the brutality of his rage. His face as she had seen it rose suddenly before her, and she put her hand to her eyes as if to shut out the sight. She saw the clear streak of the highway, the gray pasture, the solitary star overhanging the horizon, and she felt the dead leaves blown against her cheek from denuded trees far distant. And lighted by a glare of memory she saw his face—she saw the convulsed features, the furrow that cleft the forehead like a seam, the heavy brows bent above the half-closed eyes, the spasmodic working of the drawn mouth. She saw the man in whom, for its brief instant, evil was triumphant—in whom that self-poise, which had been to her as the secret of his strength, was tumultuously overthrown.

A great fatigue weighed upon her, as if she had emerged, defeated, from a physical contest. Her hands trembled, and something throbbed in her temple like an imprisoned bird.

As she sat in the silence, the door opened softly and Miss Chris came in, bearing a lamp in her hand.

" Eugie," she said, peering into the darkness, " are you there? "

Eugenia lowered the window and came over to the hearth rug, where she stood blinking from the sudden glare of the lamp. There were some half-extinguished embers amid the ashes in the fireplace, and she threw on fresh wood, watching while it caught and blazed up lightly over the old brass andirons.

Miss Chris set the lamp on the table and came over to the fire. She carried her key basket in her hand, and the keys jingled as she moved. Her smooth, florid face had a fine moisture over it that showed like dew on a well-sunned peach.

" You aren't worrying about Nick Burr, Eugie," she said with the amiable bluntness which belonged to her. " I wouldn't let it worry me if I were you."

Eugenia turned with a flash of pride.

" No, I am not worrying about him," she answered.

Miss Chris lifted a vase from the mantel-piece, dusted the spot where it had stood, and replaced it carefully.

" Of course, I know you've seen a good deal of

him of late," she went on; "but, as I told Tom, I
knew it was nothing more than your being playmates together. He's a good boy, and I don't believe that scandal about him any more than I would
about Bernard; but he's Amos Burr's son, after all,
though he has raised himself a long way above him,
and, as poor Aunt Griselda used to say, ' When all's
said and done, a Battle's a Battle.' "

Eugenia was looking into the fire.

" Yes," she repeated slowly, " a Battle's a Battle,
after all."

" That's right, dear. I knew you'd say so. I always declared that you were more of a Battle than
all the rest of us put together—if you do look the
image of a Tucker. Tom was telling me only last
week that he'd leave you as free as air and trust the
name in your hands sooner than he would in his
own—and he has a great deal of family pride, you
know, though he was so wild in his youth. But I
remember my father once saying: ' A Battle may go
a long way down the wrong road, but he'll always
pull up in time to turn.' "

Her beautiful eyes shone in the firelight, and her
placid mouth formed a round hole above her
dimpled chin, giving her large face an expression
almost infantile. She took up the key basket, which
she had placed on the mantel-piece, cast a glance at
the pile of logs to see if it had been replenished, felt
the cover on the bed, after inquiring if it sufficed,
and, with a cheerful " good-night," passed out, closing the door behind her.

Eugenia did not turn as the door closed. She
stood motionless upon the hearth rug, looking down

17

into the fire. Something in the huge old fireplace, with its bent andirons supporting the blazing logs, in the increasing bed of embers upon the bricks, in the sharp odour of the knot of resinous pine she had thrown on with the hickory, brought before her the winter evenings in Delphy's little cabin, when they sat upon three-legged stools and roasted early winesaps. She saw the negro faces in the glow of the hearth, and she saw Nicholas and herself sitting side by side in the shadow. His childish face, with its look of ancient care, came back to her with the knotted boyish hands that had carried and fetched at her bidding. The whole wistful little figure was imaged in the flames, melting rapidly into the boy, eager to act, ardent to achieve, who had bidden her good-bye on that November afternoon, and, dissolving again, to reappear as the strong man who had come upon her in Uncle Ish's little shanty, bearing the old negro's bag upon his shoulder.

She had loved him for his strength, his vigour, his gentleness—and she still loved him.

Of the men that she had known, who was there so ready to assist, so forgetful of services which he had rendered? There was none so powerful and yet so kind—so generous or so gentle. An impulse stirred her to cross the fields to his door and fling herself into the breach that divided them; but again the phantom in the flames grew dim and then sent out the face that she had seen that afternoon—convulsed and quivering, with its flitting sinister likeness to Amos Burr. A voice that seemed to be the voice of old dead Aunt Griselda—of her whole dead race that had decayed and been forgotten, and come to life again in her—spoke suddenly from the silence:

"When all's said and done, a Battle's a Battle."

The resinous pine blazed up, the pungent odour filled the large room, and from the lightwood sticks tiny streams of resin oozed out and dripped into the embers, turning the red to gray.

Mingling with the crackling of the flames there was a noise as of the soughing of the wind in the pine forests.

The hearth grew suddenly blurred before her eyes; and a passion of grief rose to her throat and clutched her with the grip of claws. For an instant longer she stood motionless; then, turning from the fire, she threw herself upon the floor to weep until the daybreak.

VII

When Nicholas left Eugenia it was to stride blindly towards his father's gate. The rage which had stunned him into silence before the girl now leaped and crackled like flame in his blood. His throat was parched and he saw red like a man who kills.

Passing his home, he kept on to Kingsborough, and once within the shadow of the wood, he broke into a run, flying from himself and from the goad of his wrath. As he ran, he felt with a kind of alien horror that to meet Bernard Battle face to face in this hour would be to do murder—murder too mild for the man who had lied away his friend's honour for the sake of the whiteness of his own skin. It was the injustice that he resented with a holy rage—the hideous fact that a clean man should be spotted to save an unclean one the splashing he merited.

And Eugenia also—he hated Eugenia that he had kept her image untarnished in his thoughts; that he had allowed the desire for no other woman to shadow it. He had held himself as a temple for the worship of her; he had permitted no breath of defilement to blow upon the altar—and this was his reward. This—that the woman he loved had hurled the first stone at the mere lifting of a Pharisaical finger—that she had loved him and had turned from him when the first word was uttered—as she would not have turned from the brother of her blood

had he been damned in Holy Writ. It was for this
that he hated her.

The light of the sunset shining through the wood
fell dull gold on his pathway. A strong wind was
blowing among the trees, and the dried leaves were
torn from the boughs and hurled roughly to the
earth, when they sped onward to rest against the
drifts by the roadside. The sound of the wind was
deep and hoarse like the baying of distant hounds,
and beneath it, in plaintive minor, ran the sighing of
the leaves before his footsteps. Through the wood
came the vague smells of autumn—a reminiscent
waft of decay, the reek of mould on rotting logs,
the effluvium of overblown flowers, the healthful
smack of the pines. By dawn frost would grip the
vegetation and the wind would lull; but now it
blew, strong and clear, scattering before it withered
growths and subtle scents of death.

Out of the wood, Nicholas came on the highway
again, and turned to where the afterglow burnished
the windows of Kingsborough. He followed the
road instinctively—as he had followed it daily from
his childhood up, beating out the impression of his
own footsteps in the dust, obliterating his old, even
tracks by the reckless tramp of his delirium.

When he reached the college grounds he paused
from the same dazed impulse and looked back upon
the west through the quiet archway of the long brick
building. The place was desolate with the desolation of autumn. Through the funereal arch he saw
the sunset barred by a network of naked branches,
while about him the darkening lawn was veiled with
the melancholy drift of the leaves. The only sound

of life came from a brood of turkeys settling to roost in a shivering aspen.

He turned and walked rapidly up the main street, where a cloud of dust hung suspended. Past the court-house, across the green, past the little white-washed gaol, where in a happier season roses bloomed—out into the open country where the battlefields were grim with headless corn rows—he walked until he could walk no further, and then wheeled about to retrace heavily his way. His rage was spent; his pulses faltered from fatigue, and the red flashes faded from before his eyes.

When he reached home supper was over, and Nannie sat sewing in the little room adjoining the kitchen.

"You're late for supper," she said idly as he entered. "Sairy Jane's gone to bed with a headache and ma's in a temper. I'll get you something as soon as I've done this seam."

"I've had supper," he answered shortly, adding from force of habit, "where's ma?"

Nannie motioned towards the kitchen and drew a little nearer the lamp, while Nicholas left the room in search of his stepmother.

Marthy Burr, a pile of newly dug potatoes on the floor beside her, was carefully sorting them before storing them for winter use. The sound ones she laid in a basket at her right hand, those that were of imperfect growth or showed signs of decay she threw into a hamper that was kept in the kitchen closet.

"You ought to make Jubal do this," said Nicholas as he entered.

" I wouldn't trust the thickest skinned potato in the field in his hands," returned Marthy sharply. " He an' yo' pa made out to store 'em last year, an' when I went to look in the first barrel, the last one of 'em had rotted."

" Let them rot," said Nicholas harshly. " I be damned if I'd care. You don't eat them, anyway."

" I reckon if I was a man I might consarn myself 'bout the things that tickle my own palate—an' 'taters ain't one of 'em," was his stepmother's retort. " But, being a woman, it seems I've got to spend my life slavin' for other folks' stomachs. But you're yo' Uncle Nick Sales all over again; ' Don't you get up befo' day to set that dough, Marthy,' he'd say, but when the bread came on flat as a pancake, he'd look sourer than all the rest."

" What was my Uncle Nick Sales like ? " asked Nicholas indifferently. He knew the name, but he had never heard the man's story.

" All book larnin' an' mighty little sense—just like you," replied his stepmother with repressed pride in her voice. " Could read the Bible in an outlandish tongue an' was too big a fool to come in out of the rain. He used to sit up all night at his books—an' fall asleep the next day at the plough. He was the wisest fool I ever see."

" Poor fool! " said Nicholas softly. It was the epitaph over the unmarked grave of that other member of his race who had blazed the thorny path before him. A strange, pathetic figure rose suddenly in his vision—a man with a great brow and a twisted back, with brawny, knotted hands—an unlearned student driving the plough, an ignorant philosopher dragging the mire.

"Poor fool!" he said again. "What did his learning do for him?"

"It killed him," returned his stepmother shortly.

She stood before him wiping her gnarled hands on her soiled apron. His gaze fell upon her, and he wondered angrily whence sprung her indomitable energy—the energy that could expend itself upon potatoes. Her face was sharpened until it seemed to become all feature—there were hollows in the narrow temples, and where the pale, thin hair was drawn tightly over the head he could trace the prominent bones of the skull.

As he looked at her his own petty suffering was overshadowed by the visible tragedy of her life— the sordid tragedy where unconsciousness was pathos. He reached out quickly and took a corner of her apron in his hand. It was the strongest demonstration of affection he had ever made to her.

"I'll sort them, ma," he said lightly. "There's not a speck in the lot of them too fine for my eyes." And he knelt down beside the earthy heap.

But when he went up to his room an hour later and lighted his kerosene lamp, it was not of his stepmother that he was thinking—nor was it of Eugenia. His stiffened muscles contracted in physical pain, and his brain was deadened by the sense of unutterable defeat. The delirium of his anger had passed away; the fever of his skin had chilled beneath the cold sweat that broke over him—in the reaction from the madness that had gripped him he was con-

scious of a sanity almost sublime. The habitual
balance of his nature had swung back into place.

He got out his books and arranged them as usual
beside the lamp. Then he took up the volume he
had been reading and held it unopened in his hands.
He stared straight before him at the whitewashed
wall of the little room, at the rough pine bedstead,
at the crude washstand, at the coloured calendar
above.

On the unearthly whiteness of the wall he beheld
the pictured vision of that other student of his race
—the kinsman who had lived toiling and had died
learning. He came to him a tragic figure in mire-
clotted garments—a youth with aspiring eyes and
muck-stained feet. He wondered what had been his
history—that unknown labourer who had sought
knowledge—that philosopher of the plough who had
died in ignorance.

" Poor fools ! " he said bitterly, " poor fools ! " for
in his vision that other student walked not alone.

The next morning he went into Kingsborough at
his usual hour, and, passing his own small office,
kept on to where Tom Bassett's name was hung.

It was county court day, and the sheriff and the
clerk of the court were sitting peaceably in arm-
chairs on the little porch of the court-house. As
Nicholas passed with a greeting, they turned from
a languid discussion of the points of a brindle
cow in the street to follow mentally his powerful
figure.

" I reckon he's got more muscle than any man in
town," remarked the sheriff in a reflective drawl.
" Unless Phil Bates, the butcher, could knock him

out.   Like to see 'em at each other, wouldn't you?"
he added with a laugh.

The clerk carefully tilted his chair back against
the wall and surveyed his outstretched feet.   "Like
to live to see him stumping this State for Congress,"
he replied.   "There goes the brainiest man these
parts have produced since before the war—the people want their own men, and it's time they had 'em."

Nicholas passed on to Tom's office, and, finding
it empty, turned back to the judge's house, where
he found father and son breakfasting opposite each
other at a table bright with silver and chrysanthemums.

They hospitably implored him to join them, but
he shook his head, motioning away the plate which
old Cæsar would have laid before him.

"I wanted to ask Tom if he had heard this—this
lie about me," he said quickly.

Tom looked up, flushing warmly.

"Why, who's been such a blamed fool as to tell
you?" he demanded.

"You have heard it?"

"It isn't worth hearing.   I called Jerry Pollard
up at once, and he swore he was all wrong—the girl
herself exonerates you.   Nobody believed it."

Nicholas crushed the brim of his hat in a sudden
grip.

"Some believe it," he returned slowly.   He sat
down at the table, smiling gratefully at the judge's
protestations.

"They aren't all like you, sir," he declared.   "I
wish they were.   This world would be a little nearer
heaven—a little less like hell."

There was a trail of lingering bitterness in his voice, and in a moment he added quickly: " Do you know, I'd like to get away for a time. I've changed my mind about caring to live here. If they'd send me up to the legislature next year, I'd make a new beginning."

The judge shook his head.

" I doubt the wisdom of it, my boy," he said. But Tom caught at the suggestion.

" Send you," he repeated. " Of course; they'll send you from here to Jericho, if you say so. Why, there's no end to your popularity among men. Where the ladies are concerned, I modestly admit that I have the advantage of you; but they can't vote, God bless them! "

" You're welcome to all the good they may bring you, old boy," was Nicholas's unchivalrous retort.

" Oh, you're jealous, Nick! " twitted Tom gaily. " They don't take kindly to your carrot locks. Now, I've inherited a way with them, eh, dad? "

The judge complacently buttered his buckwheats. There was a twinkle in his eyes and a quiver at the corner of his classic mouth.

" It was the only inheritance I wasn't able to squander in my wild oats days," he returned. " May you cherish it, my boy, as carefully as your father has done. It would be a dull world without the women."

" And a peaceable one," added Nicholas viciously.

" We owe them much," said the judge, pouring maple syrup from the old silver jug. " If Helen of Troy set the world at war, she made men heroes."

" You can't get the pater to acknowledge that the

fair things are ever wrong," put in Tom protestingly.
" He would have proved Eve's innocence to the Almighty. If a woman murdered ten men before his
eyes he'd lay the charge on the devil and acquit
her."

The judge shook his head with a laugh.

" I might merely argue that the queen can do no
wrong," he suggested.

When Tom had finished his breakfast, Nicholas
walked with him to his office, and, seeing Bessie
Pollard, red-eyed and drooping in her father's door,
he lingered an instant and held out his hand. There
was defiant sympathy in his act—disdain of the
judgment of Kingsborough—and of General Battle,
who was passing—and pity for a bruised common
thing that looked at him with beautiful, mindless
eyes.

" You aren't looking bright to-day," he said
kindly, " but things will pull through, never fear
—they always do, if you give them time."

Then he responded coolly to the general's cool
nod, and, rejoining Tom, they went on arm in arm.
In his large-minded manhood it had not occurred to
him to connect the girl with the wrong done upon
him—he knew her to be more weak than wicked,
and, in her soft, pretty sadness, she reminded him of
a half-drowned kitten.

During the next few months he frequently passed
Eugenia in the road. Sometimes he did not look at
her, and again he met her wistful gaze and spoke
without a smile. Once he checked an eager movement towards her because he had met Bernard just
ahead—and he hated him; once he had seen the

carriage in the distance and had waited in a passionate rush of remorse and love to hear her laughter as she talked with Dudley Webb. They had faced each other at last with resolute eyes and unswerving wills. On his side was the pride of an innocent man accused, the bitterness of a proud man on an inferior plane; on hers, the recollection of that wild evening in the road, and the belated recognition of the debt she owed her race.

In the winter she went up to Richmond and he slowly forced himself to renounce her. He began to see his old dream as it was—an emotional chimera; a mental madness. As the year grew on he watched his long hope wither root and branch, until, with the resurrection of the spring, it lay still because there was no life left that might put forth. And when his hope was dead he told himself that his unhappiness died with it, that he might throw himself single-hearted into the work of his life.

VIII

The year passed and was done with—leaves budded, expanded, fell again. Eugenia watched their growth, fulfilment, and decay as she had watched them other seasons, though with eyes a thought widened by experience, a shade darkened by tears. At first she had suffered wildly, then passively, at last resignedly. The colour rebloomed in her cheek, the gaiety rang back to her voice, for she was young, and youth is ever buoyant.

There was work for her to do on the place, and she did it cheerfully. She studied farming with her father and overhauled the methods of the overseer, to the man's annoyance and the general's delight. "She tells me Varly isn't scientific," roared the general with rapturous enjoyment. "A scientific overseer! She'll be asking for an honest politician next."

"I'm sure Varly is a very respectable man," protested Miss Chris in her usual position of defence. "The servants were always devoted to him before the war—that says a good deal."

"There's not a better man in the county," admitted the general, "or a worse farmer. Here I've let him go down hill at his own gait for more than thirty years, to be pulled up in the end by a chit of a girl. I wouldn't, if I were you, Eugie. He's old and he's slow."

"Oh! I'll promise not to hurt him," returned

Eugenia. " I save him a lot of hard work, and he likes it."

She drew on her loose dogskin gloves and went out to overlook the shucking of the corn.

With the exercise in the open air she had gained in suppleness and brilliancy. It was the outdoor work that saved her spirit and her beauty—that gave her endurance for the indoor monotony and magnified the splendid optimism of her saddest hour. She was a woman born for happiness; when the Fates failed to accord it she defied them and found her own.

In the autumn news came that Nicholas was elected to the General Assembly. The judge brought it, riding out on a bright afternoon to chat with the general before the blazing logs.

" The lad has a future," said the judge with a touch of pride. " Brains don't grow on blackberry vines ; " then he laughed softly. " Cæsar voted for him," he added.

The general slapped his knee.

" Cæsar is a gentleman," he exclaimed. " He was the first darkey in Kingsborough to vote the Democratic ticket. I walked up to the polls with him and the boys cheered him. You weren't there, George."

The judge shook his head.

" They called it undue influence," he said; " but, on my honour, Tom, I never spoke a political word to Cæsar in my life. Of course he'd heard me talk with Tom at dinner. He'd heard me say that the man of his race who would dare to vote with white men would be head and shoulders above his people, a man of mind, a man that any gentleman in the county would be proud to shake by the hand—but seek to influence Cæsar! Never, sir!"

"Now, there's that Ishmael of mine," said the general aggrievedly. "He no sooner got his vote than he cast it just to spite me. I told the fool he didn't know any more about voting than the old mule Sairy did, and he said he didn't have to know 'nothin' cep'n his name.' He forgot that when they challenged him at the polls, but he voted all the same —voted in my face, sir."

They lighted their pipes and sang the praises of that idyllic period which they called "before the war," while Eugenia crept away into the shadows.

She was glad that Nicholas would go; glad, glad, glad—so glad that she wept a little in the cold of a dark corner.

A week later Dudley came down, and she met him with a friendliness that dismayed and disarmed him. Could a woman be so frankly cordial with a man she loved? Could she face a passion that inspired her with such serene self-poise? He questioned these things, but he did not hesitate. He was of a Virginian line of lovers, and he charged in courtship as courageously as his father had charged in battle. He was magnificent in his youthful ardour, and so fitted for success that it seemed already to cast a prophetic halo about his head.

"You are superb," Eugenia had said, half insolently, looking up at him as he stood in the firelight. "How odd that I never noticed it before."

"You are looking at yourself in my eyes," he returned gallantly.

She shook her head.

"There are so many women who like handsome men, it's a pity you can't fall in love with one," she said coldly.

"Am I to infer that you prefer ugly men?" he questioned.

"I—oh! I am too good-looking to care," she replied.

She sprang up suddenly and stood beside him. "We do look well together," she said with grave audacity.

He laughed. "I am flattered. It may weigh with you in your future plans. Come, Eugie, let me love you!"

But her mood changed and she dragged him with her out into the autumn fields.

In the last days of November a long rain came— a ruinous autumnal rain that beat the white roads into livid streams of mud and sent the sad dead leaves in shapeiess tatters to the earth. The glory of the fall had brought back the glory of her love; its death revived the agony of the long decay.

At night the rain throbbed upon the tin roof above her. Sometimes she would turn upon her pillow, stuffing the blankets about her ears; but, muffled by the bedclothes, she heard always the incessant melancholy sound. She heard it beating on the naked roof, rushing tumultuously to the overflowing pipes, dripping upon the wet stones of the gutter below, sweeping from the earth dead leaves, dead blossoms, dead desires.

In the day she watched it from the windows. The flower beds, desolated, formed muddy fountains, the gravel walk was a shining rivulet, the sycamore held three yellow leaves that clung vainly to a sheltered bough, the aspen faced her, naked—only the impenetrable gloom of the cedars was secure—sombre and inviolate.

On the third day she went out into the rain; splashing miles through the heavy roads and returning with a glow in her cheeks and the savour of the dampness in her mouth.

Taking off her wet garments she carried them to the kitchen to be dried. With the needed exercise, her cheerful animation had returned.

In the brick kitchen a gloomy group of negroes surrounded the stove.

"Dar's gwine ter be a flood an' de ea'th hit's gwine ter pass away," lamented Aunt Verbeny, lifting the ladle from a huge pot, the contents of which she was energetically stirring. "Hit's gwine ter pass away wid de men en de cattle en de crops, en de black folks dey's gwine ter pass des' de same es dey wuz white."

"I'se monst'ous glad I'se got religion," remarked a strange little negro woman who had come over to sell a string of hares her husband had shot. "De Lawd He begun ter git mighty pressin' las' mont', so I let 'im have His way. Blessed be de name er de Lawd! Is you a church member, Sis Delphy?"

"Yes, Lawd, a full-breasted member," responded Delphy, clamping the declivity of her bosom.

"I ain' got much use fur dis yer gittin' en ungittin' er salvation," put in Uncle Ish from the table where he was eating a late dinner of Aunt Verbeny's providing. "Dar's too much monkeyin' mixed up wid it fur me. Hit's too much de work er yo' j'ints ter make me b'lieve hit's gwine ter salivate yo' soul. When my wife, Mandy, wuz 'live, I tuck 'n cyar'ed her long up ter one er dese yer revivals, en' ole Sis Saphiry Baker come 'long gittin' happy, en fo' de Lawd she rid 'er clean roun' de chu'ch. Naw, suh, de religion I wanter lay holt on is de religion uv rest."

" I ain' never sarved my Lawd wid laziness," put in Aunt Verbeny reprovingly. " When He come arter me I ain' never let de ease er my limbs stan' in de way. Ef you can't do a little shoutin' on de ea'th, you're gwineter have er po' sho' ter keep de Lawd f'om overlookin' you at Kingdom Come."

The strange little woman faced them proudly. " My husband, Silas, got religion in de night time," she said, " an' he bruck clean thoo de slats. De bed ain't helt stiddy sence."

Eugenia emerged from the dusk of the doorway, where she had lingered, and Delphy rose to take the dripping clothes.

" Des' look at her!" exclaimed Aunt Verbeny at the girl's entrance. " Ain't she a sight ter mek a blin' man see?" Then she added to the strange little woman, " Dar ain' no lack er beaux roun' yer, needer."

Uncle Ish grunted.

" I ain' seen 'em swum es dey swum roun' Miss Meely," he muttered, while Aunt Verbeny shook her fist at him behind the stranger's back. " De a'r wuz right thick wid 'em."

" I reckon dis chile'll be mah'r'd soon es she sets her min' on it," returned Delphy indignantly. " She ain' gwineter have ter do much cuttin' er de eye-lashes, needer.   De beaux come natch'ul."

" Dar's Marse Dudley, now," said Aunt Verbeny. " I ain' so ole but my palate hit kin taste a gent'mun a mile off.   Marse Dudley ain' furgit de times I'se done roas' him roas'in' years when he warn' mo'n er chile.   Hit's ' how's yo' health, Aunt Verbeny? ' des' de same es 'twuz den."

Eugenia laughed and flung the heap of garments into Delphy's arms.   " The rain's over," she said; " but, Uncle Ish, you'd better get Congo to fix you up for the night.   It is too wet for your rheumatism," and she ran singing upstairs to where the general was dozing in the sitting-room.   " Wake up, dad! it's going to clear! "

The general started heavily from his sleep.   There was a dazed look in his eyes.

" Clear? " he asked doubtfully, " has it been raining? "

Eugenia shook him into consciousness.

" Raining for three whole days, and I believe you've slept through it.   Now the clouds are break-ing."

" What is it the Bible says about ' the winter of our discontent '?—that's what it is."

" Not the Bible, dear—Shakespeare."

" It's the same thing," retorted the general testily. His speech came thickly as if he held a pebble in his mouth, and the swollen veins in his face were livid.

Eugenia bent over him in sudden uneasiness. " Aren't you well, papa? " she asked.   " Is anything the matter? "

The general laughed and pinched her cheek.

" Never better in my life," he declared, " but I'll
have to be getting new glasses. These things aren't
worth a cent. Find them, Eugie."

Eugenia picked them up, wiped them on his silk
handkerchief, and put them on his nose.

" You've slept too long," she said. " Come and
take a walk in the hall."

She dragged him from his chair, and he yielded
under protest.

" You forget that two hundred pounds can't skip
about like fifty," he complained.

But he followed her to the long hall, and they
paced slowly up and down in the afternoon shadows.
At the end of ten minutes the general declared that
he felt so well he would go back to his chair.

" I'll get the ' Southern Planter ' and read to
you," said Eugenia. " Don't go to sleep."

She ran lightly upstairs and, coming down in a
moment, called him. He did not answer and she
called again.

The sitting-room was in dusk, and, as she entered,
the firelight showed the huge body of the general
lying upon the hearth rug. A sound of heavy snor-
ing filled the room.

She flung herself beside him, lifting the great head
upon her lap; but before she had cried out Miss
Chris was at her elbow.

" Hush, Eugie," she said quickly, though the girl
had not spoken. " Send Sampson for Dr. Bright,
and tell Delphy to bring pillows. Give him to me."

Her voice was firm, and there was no tremor in
her large, helpful hands.

When Eugenia returned, the general was still lying

upon the hearth rug, his head supported by pillows.
Miss Chris had opened one of the western windows,
and a cool, damp air filled the room. The rain had
begun again, descending with a soft, purring sound.
Above it she heard the laboured breathing from the
hearth rug, and in the firelight she saw the regular
inflation of the swollen cheeks. The distended
pupils stared back at her, void of light.

As she stood motionless, her hands clenched before her, she followed the soft, weighty tread of Miss
Chris, passing to and fro with improvised applica-
tions. The light fall of the rain irritated her; she
longed for the relentless downpour of the night.

At the end of an hour the roll of wheels broke the
stillness, and she went out to meet the doctor, passing, with a shiver, the unconscious mass on the floor.

They carried him to his bed in the chamber next
the parlour, and through the night and day he lay
an inert bulk beneath the bedclothes. Miss Chris
and Eugenia and the servants passed in and out of
his room. One of the dogs came and sat upon the
threshold until Eugenia put her arms about his neck
and drew him away. She had not wept; she was
white and drawn and silent, as if the shock had
dulled her to insensibility. During the afternoon of
the next day she persuaded Miss Chris to rest, and,
softly closing the door, sat down in a chair beside
her father's bed. It was the high white bed that had
known the marriage, birth, and death of a century
of Battles. In it her father was born; beside it,
kneeling at prayer, her mother had died. The
stately tester frame had seen generations come and
go, and had remained unchanged. Now its stiff

white curtains made a ghastly drapery above the
purple face.

Eugenia sat motionless, her thoughts vaguely
circling about the still figure before her. It was not
her father—this she felt profoundly—it was some
strange shape that had taken his place, or she was
held by some farcical nightmare from which she
should awake presently with a start. The half-used
glasses on the little table beside her; the candle
burned down in the socket, and overlooked; the
tightly corked phials of useless drugs; the strong
odour of mustard from the saucer in which a plaster
had been mixed—these things struck upon her fal-
tering consciousness with a shock of horrible reality.
The odour of the mustard was more real than the
breathing of the body on the bed.

As she sat there, she thought of her mother—the
pale, still woman who had lain beautiful and dead
where her father was dying now. She came to her
as from a faded miniature, wistful, holy, at rest—
blessed and above reproach. Her heart went out to
her as to one standing near, hidden by the long white
curtains—nearer than Aunt Chris asleep upstairs,
nearer than Bernard, who was coming to her, nearer
than the great form on the bed. Closer than all
other things was that spiritual presence. Then she
thought of her old negro mammy, who had died
when she was but a baby—her mother's nurse and
hers. She recalled the beloved black face beneath
the snowy handkerchief, the restful bosom in blue
homespun, the tireless arms that had rocked her into
slumber. Then of Jim, the dog, true friend and
faithful playmate. All the lives that she had loved

and had been bereft of gathered closer, closer in the
gray shadows.

Her gaze passed to the window, seeking in the sad
landscape the little graveyard where they were lying.
The rain came between her and the clouded hill—
descending softly and insistently between her eyes
and the end of her search.   Against the panes the
dripping branches of the shivering mimosa tree beat
themselves and moaned.   A chill seized her and, rising, she went to the hearth, noiselessly piling wood
upon the charred and waning logs, which crumbled
and sent up a thin flame.   She hurried to the bed and
sat down again, her eyes on the blanket that rose
and fell with the difficult breath.   As she looked at
the large, familiar face, tracing its puffed outline and
gross colouring, it resolved itself into her earliest
remembrance—throughout her childhood he had
been her slave and she his tyrant.   What wish of
hers had he ever ignored?   With what demand had
he ever failed to comply?   At the end of the long
life what had remained to him except herself—the
single compensation—the one reward?   The pity of
it smote her as with a lash.   He had lived with such
fine bravery, and he had had so little—so little, and
yet more than myriads of the men that live and die.
That live and die!   About her and beyond her she
seemed to hear the rushing of great multitudes—the
passing of the countless souls through the gates of
death.

With a cry she threw herself upon her knees, beseeching the dull ears.

Six hours later he died, and when the rain ceased

and the sun came out they buried him beside his wife
in the little graveyard. For days after the funeral
Eugenia wandered like a shadow through the still
rooms. Bernard had come and gone, carrying with
him his short, sharp grief. Miss Chris had put aside
her own sorrow and gone back to the management
of the house ; only the girl, worn, idle, tragic,
haunted the reminders of her loss. Coming upon
the general's old slouch hat on the rack, she had
grasped it in sudden passionate longing ; at the sight
of his half-filled pipe she had rushed from the room
and from the house. The faint scent of tobacco
about the furniture was a continual torture to her.
In the great chamber next the parlour she would sit
for hours, staring at the cold white bed, shivering
before the fireless hearth. The place chilled her like
a vault ; but she would linger wretchedly until led
away by Miss Chris, when she would sob upon
that broad, unselfish bosom.

December passed ; the unsunned earth turned itself for a winter rest. January came, swift and
changeful. With February a snowstorm swept
from the north, driving southward. At first they
felt it in the air ; then the swollen clouds chased overhead ; at last the white flakes arrived, falling, falling,
falling. Through the night the storm made a glist-
ening mantle for the darkness ; through the day it
hid sombre sky and sombre earth in a spotless veil.
It covered the far country to the distant forests ; it
weighted the ancient cedars until their green
branches bent to earth ; it wrapped the gravelled
walk in a winding sheet ; it filled the hollows of the
box bushes until they hardened into hills of ice. The

snow was followed by cold winds. The ground froze in the night. Long icicles formed on the naked trees, the window panes bore a lacework of frost.

One afternoon, when the landscape was white and hard, Eugenia went out into the deserted sheep pasture where the dead oak stood. A winter sunset was burning like a bonfire in the west, and as far as the red horizon swept an unbroken waste of snow. The rail fences shone silver in their coat of frost, and from the blackened tree above her pendants of ice were shot with light. Across the field a flock of gaunt crows flew, casting purple shadows.

Eugenia leaned against the oak and stared vacantly at the landscape—at the sunset, and at the waste of snow, across which flitted the demoniac shadows of the crows. Her eyes saw only the desolation and the death ; they were sealed to the grandeur.

A sense of her own loneliness swept over her with the loneliness of nature. Her own isolation—the isolation of a strong soul in pain—walled her apart as with a wall of ice. That assurance of human companionship on which she had based her future seemed suddenly annihilated. She was alone and life was before her.

Then, as she turned her gaze, a man's figure broke upon the field of snow, coming towards her. It was Dudley Webb, and in the resolute swing of his carriage, in the resistless ardour of his eyes, he seemed to reach her from east and west, from north and south, surrounding her with a warmth of summer.

As he looked at her he held out his arms.

" Eugie—poor girl! dear girl! "

In the desolation of her life he stood to her as the hearth of home to a wanderer in the frozen North.

For an instant she held back, and then, with a sob, she yielded.

" I must be loved," she said.   " I must be loved or I shall die."

Around them the winter landscape reddened as the sunset broke, and above their heads the crows flew, cawing, across the snow.

BOOK IV

THE MAN AND THE TIMES

BOOK IV

THE MAN AND THE TIMES

I

The Democratic State Convention had taken an hour's recess. From the doors of the opera house of Powhatan City the assembled delegates emerged, heated, clamorous, out of breath. The morning session, despite its noise, had not been interesting —awaiting the report of the Committee on Credentials, the panting body had fumed away the opening hours. Of the fifteen hundred representatives of absent voters, the favoured few who had held the floor had been needlessly discursive and undeniably dull. There had been overmuch of the party platform, and an absence of the wit which is the soul of political speaking; and, though the average Virginia Convention is able to breast triumphantly the most encompassing wave of oratory, the present one had shown unmistakable signs of suffocation. At the end of the third speech, metaphor had failed to move it, and alliteration had ceased to evoke applause. It had heard without emotion similes that concerned the colour of Cleopatra's hair, and had yawned through perorations that ranged from Socrates to the Senior Senator, who sat upon the stage. Attacks upon the " cormorants and harpies that roost in Wall Street " had roused no thrill in the mind of the majority that knew not rhetoric. The most patient of the silent members had observed that " after all, their business was to nominate a candidate for governor," while the unruly spirits, as they brandished palm-leaf fans, had wished " that blamed committee would come on."

Now, after hours of restless waiting, they emerged, stiff-kneed and perspiring, into the blazing sunshine that filled the little street. Once outside, they opened their lungs to the warm air in an attempt to banish the tainted atmosphere of the interior ; but the original motive of expansion was lost in a flow of words. On the sidewalk the crowd divided into streams, pulsing in opposite directions. Heated, noisy, pervasive, it surged to dinners in hotels and boarding-houses, and overflowed where Moloney's restaurant displayed its bill of fare. It came out talking, it divided talking; still talking, it swept a roaring sea of flesh, into the far-off buzz of the distance. In a group of three men passing into the lobby of the largest hotel, there was a slender man of fifty years, with a well-knit figure, half closed, indifferent eyes, and an emphatic mouth. In the insistent hum of words about him, his voice sounded in a brisk utterance that carried a hint of important issues.

" Oh, I don't think Hartley's much account," he was saying. " I'd bet on a close shave between Webb and Crutchfield, with Webb in the lead. Small will get the lieutenant-governorship, of course. Davis ought to be attorney-general, but he'll be beaten by Wray. It's the party reward.

Davis is the better lawyer, by long odds, but Wray
has stuck to the party like a burr—I don't mean
a pun, if you please."

The younger of his two companions, a spirited
youth with high-standing auburn hair, laughed up-
roariously.

"The trouble is they're afraid Burr won't stick to
the party," he protested. "Major Simms, who is
marshalling Crutchfield's forces, you know, said to
me last night—' Oh, Burr's all right when you let
him lead, but he's damned mulish if you begin to
pull the other way.'"

The third man, a sunburned farmer, with a
dogged mouth overhung by a tobacco-stained mus-
tache, assented with a nod.

"There's not a better Democrat in Virginia than
Nick Burr," he said. "If the party's got anything
against him it had better out with it at once. He
made the most successful chairman the State ever
had—and he's honest—there's not a more honest
man in politics or out."

"Oh, I know all that," broke in the auburn-haired
young fellow, whose name was Dickson; "I'd back
Burr against any candidate in the field, and I'm
sorry he kept out of it. I hoped he'd come forward
with you to manage his campaign, Mr. Galt," he
said to the first speaker.

Galt waived the remark.

"Perhaps he thought his chances too slim for a
walkover," he said in non-committal fashion, as
Burr's best friend. "I hear, by the way, that the
delegation from his old home is instructed to vote
for him on the first ballot, whether or not."

19

" He has a great name down in my parts," put in the farmer. " The people think he has the agricultural interests at heart. They wanted to send him to Congress in Webb's place, you know."

" Yes, I know," said Galt. " Hello, Bassett," as Tom Bassett joined him. " Where've you been? Lost sight of you this morning."

" Oh, I was out with the Committee on Credentials. A member? I should say not. I wanted to hear that Madison County case, so I got made sergeant-at-arms. By the way, Dick," to Dickson, " I hear you held the floor for five minutes this morning and got off five distinct stories that landed with Columbus."

" Nonsense. I didn't open my mouth—except to call ' time ' on the men who did. There's our orator now."

He bowed to an elderly gentleman with a sharply pointed chin beard and the type of face that was once called clerical.

" Some one defined oratory the other day," said Galt, " as the fringe with which the inhabitants of the Southern States still delighted to trim their politics—so I should call the gentleman of to-day ' a political tassel.' He's ornamental and he hangs by a thread."

And he passed into the lobby arm-in-arm with Tom Bassett.

The place was swarming with delegates: delegates from country districts, red-faced farmers in flapping linen coats and wide-brimmed hats; delegates from the cities, dapper, well-groomed, cordial-voiced; delegates of the true political type, shaven, obse-

quious, alert; delegates of the cast that belongs
at home, outspoken, honest-eyed, remote; stout
delegates, with half-bursting waistbands, thin delegates, with shrunken chests. In the animated throng
there was but one condition held in common—they
were all heated delegates. In one corner a stout
gentleman in a thin coat, with a scarlet neck showing above his wilted collar, held a half-dozen lis-
teners with his eyes, while he plied them with
emphatic sentences in which the name of Crutchfield
sounded like a refrain. Moving from group to
group, portly, unctuous, insinuating, a man with an
oily voice was doing battle in the cause of Webb.

The throng that passed in and out of the lobby
was continually shifting place and principles. One
instant it would seem that Crutchfield triumphed in
a majority sufficient to overwhelm the platform; a
moment more and the Webb men were vociferously
in the ascendant. At the time it resolved itself into
a question of tongues.

"This is thick," said Ben Galt, dodging the straw
hat with which a perspiring politician was fanning
himself and gently withdrawing himself from the
arms of a scarlet individual in a wet collar to collide
with his double. "Let's go to dinner. Ah! there's
the Lion of Democracy—how are you, Judge?"

The Lion, a striking figure, with a graceful, snow-
white mane and a colossal memory, held out a tireless hand. "Well met, Ben," he exclaimed in effu-
sive tones. "I've been on the outlook for you all
day. One moment—your pardon—one moment—
Ah, my dear sir! my dear sir!" to a countryman who
approached him with outstretched hand, "I am de-

lighted.   Remember you?   Why, of course—of
course!   Your name has escaped me this instant;
but I was speaking of you only yesterday.   No,
don't tell me! don't tell me.   I remember.   Ah,
now I have it—one moment, please—it was after
the battle of Seven Pines.   You lent me a horse after
the battle of Seven Pines.   Thank you—thank you,
sir.   And your charming lady, who made me the
delicious coffee.   My best regards to her."

The great man was surrounded, and Galt and Bassett, leaving him to his assailants, passed into the
dining-room.

Glancing hastily down the long room filled with
small, overcrowded tables, they joined several men
who were seated near an open window.

"Hello, Major.   Glad to see you, Mr. Slate!
How are things down your way, Colonel?"

A tired negro waiter, with a napkin slung over
his arm, drew back the chairs and deposited two
plates of lukewarm soup before the newcomers, after
which he lifted a brush of variegated tissue paper
and made valiant assault upon the flies which over-
ran the tables.   Stale odours of over-cooked food
weighted the atmosphere, and waiters bearing enormous trays above their heads jostled one another as
they threaded their difficult ways.   Occasionally the
clamour of voices was lost in the clatter of breaking
dishes.   Tom Bassett pushed his plate away and
mopped his large forehead.   He appeared to have
developed without aging in the last fifteen years
—still presenting an aspect of invincible respecta-
bility.

"It's ninety-two degrees in the shade, if it's any-

thing," he declared, adding, " Has anybody seen
Webb to-day?"

The colonel, whose name was Diggs, nodded with
his mouth full, and, having swallowed at his leisure,
proceeded to reply, holding his knife and fork poised
for service. He was fair to the point of insipidity,
and his weak blue eyes bulged with joviality.

"Shook hands with him at the train last night,"
he said. " Hall was a day ahead of time. Great
politician, Hall. Working for Webb like a beaver.
Here, waiter! More potatoes."

" I went to sleep last night to the music of Webb's
men," said Galt, "and I awoke to the tune of
Crutchfield. I don't believe either side went to
bed. My wonder is whom they found to work on."

Slate, a muscular little man, with a nervous affection about the mouth that gave him an appearance of
being continually on the point of a surprising utterance, hesitated over, caught, and finally landed his
speech. " They're dead against Webb down my
way," he said. " Our delegation is instructed to
vote for anybody that favours retrenchment, unless
it's Webb—they won't have Webb if he moves to
run the State on the two-cent system. If we'd cast
a quarter of a vote for him they'd drum us out of
the district. It's all because he voted for that railroad bill in Washington last winter. We hate a
railroad as a bull hates a red flag."

Major Baylor, a courtly gentleman, with a face
that bore traces of a survival of the old Virginian
legal type, spoke for the first time.

" Fauquier stands to a man for Dudley Webb,"
he said. " He has a large following in my section,

and I understand, by the way, that if Hartley withdraws after the first ballot, it will mean a clear gain for Webb in the eighth district. He's safe, I think."

"Oh, we're Crutchfield strong," laughed the colonel good-humouredly, reaching for a toothpick from the glass stand in the centre of the table. "We think a man deserves something who hasn't missed a convention for fourteen years."

There was a spirit of ridicule tempered with good-humour about the group, which showed it to be, in the main, indifferent to the result—an attitude in vivid contrast to the effervescent partisanship of the leaders. With the exception of the colonel, whose heart was in his dinner, they appeared to be unconcerned spectators of the events of the day.

"Hall was telling me a good story on Webb last week," said Diggs, as he waited for his dessert. "It was about the time he seconded the nomination of Reed for attorney-general—ever hear it?"

"Fire away!" was Galt's reply, as he leaned back in his chair. The colonel's stories were the platform which had supported him throughout a not unsuccessful social career.

"It was when Webb was a young fellow, you know, just beginning to be heard of as an advocate. He was at his first convention, eager to have his say, hard to keep silent; and he was asked to second the nomination of Reed, a boyish-looking chap of twenty-six. He didn't know Reed from Adam, but he was ambitious to be heard just then—and he'd have spoken for the devil if they'd have given him a chance. Well, he launched out on his speech in fine style. He began with Noah—as they all did in

those days—glided down the centuries to Seneca
and Cæsar, touched upon Adam Smith and Jefferson, and finally landed in the arms of Monroe P.
Reed. There he grew fairly ecstatic over his subject. He spoke of him as ' the lawyer sprung, full-armed, from the head of learning,' as the ' nonpareil
Democrat who clove, as Ruth to Naomi, to the immortal principles of Virginia Democracy,' and in a
glorious period, he rounded off ' the incomparable
services which Monroe P. Reed had rendered the
deathless cause of the Confederacy!' In an instant
the house came down. There was a roar of laughter,
and somebody in the gallery sang out: ' He was at
his mother's breast!'

"For a moment Webb quailed, but his wits never
left him. He faced the man in the gallery like
Apollo come to judgment, and his fine voice rang
to the roof. 'I know it, sir, I know it,' he thundered, ' but Monroe P. Reed was one of the stoutest breastworks of the Confederacy. I have it from
his mother, sir!'

"Of course the house went wild. He was the
youngest man on the floor, and they gave him an
ovation. Since then, he's learned some things, and
he's become the only orator left among us."

The colonel finished hurriedly as his apple pie was
placed before him, and did not speak again during
dinner.

"He is an orator," said Galt. "He doesn't use
much clap-trap business either. I've never heard
him drag in the Medes and Persians, and I could
count his classical quotations on my fingers. Personally, I like Burr's way better—it's saner and it's

sounder—but Webb knows how to talk, and he has a voice like a silver bell—Ah, here he is."

As he spoke there was a stir in the crowd at the doorway and Dudley Webb entered and took the nearest vacant seat.

The first impression of him at this time was one of extreme picturesqueness. A slight tendency to stoutness gave dignity to a figure which, had it been thin, would have been insignificant, and served to accentuate a peculiar grace of curve which prevented his weight from carrying any suggestion of the coming solidity of middle age. His rich, rather oily hair, worn longer than the fashion, fell in affected carelessness across his brow and lent to his candid eyes an expression of intensity and eloquence. His clear-cut nose and the firm, fleshy curve of his prominent chin modified the effect of instability produced by his large and somewhat loosely moulded lips. The salient quality of his personality, as of his appearance, was an ease of proportion almost urbane. His presence in the overcrowded room diffused an infectious affability. Though he spoke to few, he was at once, and irrepressibly, the friend of all. He did not go out of his way to shake a single hand, he confined his conversation, with the old absorption, to the men at his table—personal supporters, for the most part; but there was about him a pacific emanation—an atmosphere at once social and political, which extended to the far end of the room and to men whose names he did not know.

He talked rapidly in a vibrant, low-toned voice, with frequent gestures of his shapely hands. His

laugh was easy, full, and inspiriting—the laugh of a
man with a vital sense of humour.   As Galt watched
him, he smiled in unconscious sympathy.

"But for Burr, I think I'd like to see Webb
governor," he said.   "After all, it is something to
have a man who looks well in a procession—and he
has a charming wife."

II

The gas light and electric light illuminating the opera house fell with a curious distinction in tone upon the crowd which filled the building and overflowed through darkened doors and windows. Beneath the electric jets the faces were focussed to a white hush of expectancy, which mellowed into a blur of impatient animation where the dim gas flickered against the walls.

Since the birth of Virginia Democracy, the people had not witnessed so generous an outpouring of delegates. In a State where every man is more or less a politician, the convention had assumed the air of a carnival of males—the restriction of sex limiting it to an expression of but half the population.

The delegations from the congressional districts were marshalled in line upon the floor and stage, their positions denoted by numbered placards on poles, while in the galleries an enthusiastic swarm of visitors gave vent to the opinions of that tribunal which is the public. A straggling fringe of feet, in white socks and low shoes, suspended from the red and gilt railings of the boxes, illustrated the peculiar privileges enjoyed in the absence of the feminine atmosphere. From stage to gallery the play of palm-leaf fans produced the effect of a swarm of gigantic insects, and behind them rows of flushed and perspiring faces were turned upon the gentleman who held the floor.

A composite photograph of the faces would have resulted in a type at once alarming and reassuring —alarming to the student of individual endeavour, reassuring to the historian of impersonal issues. It would have presented a countenance that was unerringly Anglo-Saxon, though modified by the conditions of centuries of changes. One would have recognised instinctively the tiller of the soil—the single class which has refused concessions to the making of a racial cast of feature. The farmer would have stamped his impress indelibly upon the plate—retaining that enduring aspect which comes from contact with natural forces—that integrity of type which is the sole survival of the Virginian pioneer.

In the general face, the softening influences of society, the relaxing morality of city life would have appeared only as a wrinkle here and there, or as an additional shadow. Beneath the fluctuating expression of political sins and heresies, there would have remained the unaltered features of the steadfast qualities of the race.

The band in a far corner rolled out "Dixie," and the mass heaved momentarily, while a cloud of tobacco smoke rose into the air, scattering into circles before the waving of the palm-leaf fans. Here and there a man stood up to remove his coat or to stretch his hand to the vendor of lemonade. Sometimes the fringe of feet overhanging the boxes waved convulsively as a howl of approbation or derision greeted a fresh arrival or the remarks of a speaker. Again, there would rise a tumultuous call for a party leader or a famous story teller. It was a jovial, unkempt, coatless crowd that spat tobacco juice as recklessly as it applauded a fine sentiment.

As an unwieldy gentleman, in an alpaca coat, made his appearance upon the platform, there was an outburst of emotion from where the tenth delegation was seated. The unwieldy gentleman was the Honourable Cumberland Crutchfield, a popular aspirant to the governorship.

When Galt entered the hall, an athletic rhetorician was declaiming an eulogy which had for its theme the graces of his candidate. " You came too soon," observed a man seated next a vacant chair, which Galt took. " You should have escaped this infliction."

" My dear fellow, I never escaped an infliction in my life," responded Galt serenely. " I cut my teeth on them—but here's another," and he turned an indifferent gaze on the orator, who had risen upon the platform. " Good Lord, it's Gary! " he groaned. " Now we're in for it."

" Mr. Chairman and gentlemen of the convention," Gary was beginning, " it is my pleasant duty to second the nomination of the Honourable Cumberland Crutchfield of the gallant little county of Botetourt. Before this august body, before this incomparable assemblage of the intellect and learning of the State, my tongue would be securely tied (" I'd like that little job," grunted the man next to Galt) did not the majesty of my subject loosen it to eloquence. Would that the immortal Cicero (" Now we're in for it," breathed Galt) in his deathless orations had been inspired by the illustrious figure of our fellow-countryman. Gentlemen, in the Honourable Cumberland Crutchfield you behold one whose public service is an inspiration, whose private life is a benediction—one who has borne without abuse the grand old title of the Cæsar of Democracy, and I dare to stand before you and assert that, had Cæsar been a Cumberland Crutchfield, there would have been no Brutus. Gentlemen, I present to you in the Honourable Cumberland Crutchfield the Vested Virgin of Virginia!"

The chairman's gavel fell with a thud. In the uproar which ensued hats, fans, sticks filled the air. The tenth delegation rose to a man and surged forward, but it was howled down. "Go it, old man!" sang the boxes, where the fringe of feet was wildly swaying, and "He's all right!" screeched the galleries. To a man who may be made fun of a Virginia convention can be kind, but in the confusion Gary had sauntered out for a drink.

After his exit the seconding motion flowed on smoothly through several tedious speeches ; and when the virtues of Mr. Crutchfield had been sufficiently exploited Major Baylor requested the nomination of Dudley Webb. He spoke warmly along the old heroic lines.

"The gentleman whom I ask you to nominate as your candidate for governor stands before his people as one of the foremost statesmen of his day. The father fell while defending Virginia; the son has pledged his splendid ability and his untiring youth to the same service. From a child he has been trained in the love of country and the principles of Democracy. In his veins he carries the blood of a race of patriots. From his mother's breast he has imbibed the immortal milk of morality. He has laboured for his people in a single-hearted service that seeketh not its own. There is no man rich enough to buy the good-will of Dudley Webb; there is none so poor——"

" That he hasn't a vote to sell him!" called a voice from the pit.

In an instant a chorus of yells rang out from stage to gallery. The man who spoke was knocked down by a Webb partisan, and assailant and assailed were hustled from the house.

When the uproar was subdued, the thin voice of Mr. Slate sounded from the platform.

" What he doesn't sell he buys," he cried in his nervous, penetrant tones. " Twelve years ago he was accused of lobbying with full hands in the legislature. He was the lobbyist of the P. H. & C. railroad. The charge was passed over, not disproved. What do you say to this, Major?"

In the effort to restore order the chairman grew purple, but the major turned squarely upon his questioner.

" I say nothing, sir. It is unnecessary to assert that a gentleman is not a criminal at large."

A burst of applause broke out.

" I repeat the charge," screamed Slate.

" It is false!" retorted the major.

" It's a damned lie!" called a dozen voices.

" Nick Burr knows it. Ask him!" answered Slate.

From a peaceable assemblage the convention had passed into pandemonium. Two thousand throats made, in two thousand different keys, a single gigan-

tic discord. The pounding of the chairman was a
faint accompaniment to the clamour. In the first
lull, a man's voice with a dominant note was heard
demanding recognition, and at the sight of his towering figure upon the platform there was a short
silence.

" It's Nick Burr! " called a man from Burr's district. " Let's hear Nick Burr."

There was a protest on the part of the Webb faction. Burr and Webb were looked upon as rivals.
" He hates Webb like the devil! " cried a delegate,
and " It's pie for Burr! " sneered another. But as
he moved slightly forward and faced the chairman
a sudden hush fell before him.

Among the men surrounding him his powerful
figure towered like a giant's. His abundant red
hair, waving thickly from his bulging forehead, redeemed by its single note of colour the rigidity of
his features. His eyes—small, keen, deeply set beneath heavy brows—flashed from a dull opacity to
an alert animation. But in the first and last view of
his face it was the mouth that marked the man; the
straight, thin lips would close or unclose at their
own will, not at another's—the line of the mouth,
like the line of the hard, square jaw, was the physical
expression of his character. He was called ugly,
but it was at least the ugliness of individuality—the
ugliness of an unpolished force—of a raw, yet dis-
ciplined energy. Now, as he stood at his full height
upon the stage, his personality was felt before his
words were uttered. He had but one attribute of
recognised oratory—a voice; and yet a voice so
little vibrant as to seem almost without inflections.

It was resonant, far-reaching, incisive; but it rang abruptly and without mellowness.

" Mr. Chairman," he began, and his words were heard from pit to gallery. " It is perhaps unnecessary for me to state that I do not rise as an advocate of Mr. Webb. I am neither his personal friend nor his political supporter, but in the year alluded to by the gentleman from Nottoway I was upon a committee appointed to investigate the charges which the gentleman from Nottoway has seen fit to revive." A silence had fallen in which a whisper might have been heard. Every eye in the building was turned to where his outstanding mop of hair shone red against the smoke-stained wall. " The charges were thoroughly investigated and emphatically withdrawn. The gentleman from Nottoway has been misinformed or his memory has misled him—since there was abundant evidence brought before the committee to prove the suspicions against Mr. Webb's methods as a lobbyist to be absolutely without foundation.

" I have made this statement because I believe myself to be in a better position to disprove this old and forgotten charge than any man present. As I am a recognised opponent of Mr. Webb's political ambition my testimony to the integrity of his personal honour may be of additional value."

In the thunder of applause that shook the building he turned for the first time towards the house. The cheers that went up to him brought the animation to his eyes. The faces in the pit were hidden behind a sea of handkerchiefs and hats—it was the response which a Virginia audience makes to a brave or a

generous action. "Hurrah for honest Nick!" yelled
the floor, and "Go in and win yourself!" shouted a
delegate from his own district.

He spoke again, and they were silent.

"Men of Virginia, in the naming of your governor, let us have neither subterfuge nor slander.
Better than the love of party is the love of honesty
—and the Democracy of Jefferson cannot thrive
upon falsehood. Fair means are the only means,
honest ends are the only ends. The party owes its
right to existence to the people's will; when its life
must be prolonged by artificial stimulants it is fit
that it should die. It is not the people's master,
but the people's servant; if it should usurp the oppressor's place, it must die the oppressor's death.

"For fifteen years I have worked a Democrat
among you, and it is not needed that I should put
in words my love for the party I have served; but I
say to you to-day that if that party were doomed to
annihilation and a lie could save it, I would not
speak it."

He sat down and the uproar began again. Beyond the party were the people, and he had touched
them. With the force of his personality upon it he
had become suddenly the hero of the house. "Honest Nick! Honest Nick!" shouted the galleries, and
the cry was echoed from the pit. When order was
restored Major Baylor completed his speech; it was
seconded by a sensible young congressman, and the
oratory was cut short by a call for votes.

In a flash the chairmen of the different delegations
were stung into action. A buzz like that of bees
swarming rose from the pit and white slips of paper

20

fluttered from row to row. The Webb leaders were whipping their faction into an enthusiasm that drowned the roll call. At last, with the reading of the ballot, there was silence, followed by applause. Webb led slightly in advance of Crutchfield; Burr came next, Hartley last. With the surprise of the third name, round which there had been a rally of uninstructed delegations, a cheer went up. In the clamour Burr had risen to ask that his name be withdrawn, but the chorus of his newly formed followers howled him down. Then Hartley was dropped from the race and a second ballot ordered. The excitement in the building could be felt like steam. The heat was rising and a nervous tension weighted the atmosphere. Through the clouds of tobacco smoke the records of changes sounded distinctly. The Hartley delegation that Webb had counted on divided and went two ways; the county of Albemarle passed over to Burr; the city of Richmond broke its vote into three equal parts.

Each change was received with a roar by the opposing factions—while the clerks stumbled on, making alteration upon alteration. On the floor and the stage the chairmen thickened in the fight. Ben Galt had sprung suddenly into life as Burr's manager, and in the aisle Tom Bassett, in his shirt sleeves, with a tally sheet in his hand, was inciting his battalion to victory. About him the Webb men were summing up the votes needed to bring in their leader. The noise had a dull, baying sound, as if the general voice were growing hoarse. The odour of good and bad tobacco was dense and stifling. In the midst of the clamour a drunken man rose to move that the convention consider the subject in prayer.

Upon the reading of the second ballot the confusion deepened. The name of Crutchfield went down, and Burr and Webb ran hotly neck to neck. Then the Crutchfield party, which had held bravely together, began to go over, and, as each change was made, a shout went up from the successful force. Hall and Galt had established themselves on opposite sides of the stage and were working with drawn breath. Galt, with a cigar in his mouth and a fan in his hand, was the only cool man in the house. He had caught the wave of popular enthusiasm before it had had time to break, and he was giving it no ground upon which to settle. Tom Bassett in the centre aisle was cheering on his workers. He was superb, but the Webb men were not behind him; it was still neck to neck. Then, at last, with the third ballot, Burr led off, and the voting was over.

There was a call upon the name of the successful candidate, but before he stood up the Honourable Cumberland Crutchfield rose to eulogise the wisdom of the convention in nominating the man he had tried to defeat. The Cæsar of Democracy was beaming, despite his disappointment—a persistent beam of the flesh.

" Gentlemen, you have made your decision, and it is for me to bow to its wisdom. In the Honourable Nick Burr your choice has fallen upon the man who will most incite to ardour each individual voter. His record is a glorious one,"—for an instant he wavered; then his imagination took a blinded leap. " He was born a Democrat, he lives a Democrat, he will die a Democrat. In the life of his revered and lamented father, the late Alexander P. Burr, he has a shining example of unshaken conviction and unswerving loyalty to principle. Gentlemen, you have chosen well, and I pledge myself to uphold your nominee and to be the foremost bearer of your banner when it waves in next November from the line of Tennessee to the Atlantic Ocean."

He sat down amid ecstatic cheers and Nicholas Burr came forward.

His face was grave, but there was the light of enthusiasm in his eyes and his head was uplifted.

"There's a man who has capitalised his conscience," sneered a Webb follower with a smile.

Across the hall Ben Galt was lighting a cigar, the tattered remains of his fan at his feet. "There's a statesman that came a century too late," he remarked to Tom Bassett. "He's a leader, pure and simple, but he's out of place in an age when every man's his own patriot."

III

The successful man was returning to Kingsborough. He had spent the week in Richmond, where he had lived for the past ten years, and he was now going back to receive the congratulations of the judge—as he would have gone twice the distance.

It was the ordinary car of a Southern railroad, and leaning his head against the harsh, bristly plush of the seat, he had before him the usual examples of Southern passengers.

Across the aisle a slender mother was holding a crying baby, two small children huddling beside her. In the seat in front of him slouched a mulatto of the new era—the degenerate descendant of two races that mix only to decay. Further off there were several men returning from business trips, and across from them sat a pretty girl, asleep, her hand resting on a gilded cage containing a startled canary. At intervals she was aroused by the flitting figure of a small boy on the way to the cooler of iced water. From the rear of the car came the amiable drawl of the conductor as he discussed the affairs of the State with a local drummer, whose feet rested upon a square leathern case.

Nicholas Burr leaned back and closed his eyes, crossing his long legs which were cramped by the limited space. He had already exchanged pleasantries with the conductor, and he had chatted for twenty minutes with a farmer, who had gone back at last to the smoking-car.

The low, irregular landscape was as familiar to him as his own face. He knew it so well that he could see it with closed eyes—could note each change of expression where the daylight shifted, could tell where the thin cornfields ended and the meadows rolled fresh and green, could smell the stretch of young pines above the smoke of the engine, and could follow to their ends the rain-washed roads that crawled with hidden heads into the blue blur of the distance. He knew it all, but he was not thinking of it now.

He was thinking of the day, fifteen years ago, when he had left Kingsborough to throw himself and his future into the service of his State. He had told himself then, fresh from the influence of Jefferson and the traditions of Kingsborough, that he had but one love remaining—the love of Virginia. Now, with the bitterer wisdom of experience, that youthful romance showed half foolish, half pathetic. To the man of twenty-three it had been at once the inspiration and the actuality. His personal life had turned to ashes in an hour, and he had told himself that his public one, at least, should remain vital. He had pledged himself to success, and it came to him now that the cause had been won by his single-heartedness—by the absolute oneness of his desire. There had been a sole divinity before him, and he had not wandered in the way of strange gods. He had given himself, and after fifteen years he was gaining his recompense—a recompense for more work than most men put into a lifetime.

He smiled slightly as he thought of the beginning. In the beginning his sincerity had been laughed at, his ardour had met rebuff. He had gone to Richmond to meet an assembly of statesmen; he had found a body of well-intentioned, but unprofitable servants. They were men to be led, this he saw; and as soon as his vision was adjusted he had determined within himself to become their leader. The day when a legislator meant a statesman was done with; it meant merely a man like other men, to be juggled with by shrewder politicians or to be tricked by more dishonest ones. They plunged into errors, and lived to retrieve them; they walked blindfold into traps, and with open eyes struggled out again. For he found them honest and he found them faithful where their lights led them. He remembered, with a laugh, a New Englander who, after a fruitless winter spent in scenting the iniquities of the ruling party, had angrily exclaimed that "if politicians were made up of knaves and fools, Mason and Dixon's was the geographical line dividing the species." Nicholas had retorted, "If to be honest means to be a fool, we are fools!" and the New Englander had chuckled homeward.

That was his first winter and he had been nobody. Ah, it was hard work, that beginning. He had had to fight party plans and personal prejudices. He had had to fight the recognised leaders of the legislature, and he had had to fight the men who pulled the strings—the men who stood outside and hoodwinked the consciences of the powers within. He had had to fight, and he had fought well and long.

He recalled the day of his first decisive victory—

the day when he had stood alone and the people—the great, free people, the beginning and the end of all democracies—had rallied to his standard. He had won the people on that day, and he had never lost them.

But he was of the party first and last. In his youth he had believed in the divine inspiration of the Jeffersonian principles as he believed in God. On the Democratic leaders he had thought to find the mantle of Apostolic Succession. He had believed as the judge believed—with the passionate credulity of an older political age. Time had tempered, but it had not dissipated, his fiery partisanship. He sat to-day with the honours of a party upon him —honours that a few months would see ratified by a voice nominally the people's. He laughed now as he remembered that Galt had said that in five years Dudley Webb would be the most popular man in the State. "When Senator Withers stops delivering orations, there'll be a call for an orator, and Webb will arise," he had prophesied. "They don't need him now because the senator gets off speeches like hot cakes; but mark my words, the first time Webb is asked to make an address at the unveiling of a Confederate statue, there won't be a man to stand up against him in Virginia. He's a better speaker than Withers—only the public doesn't know it, and there'll be hot times when it finds it out."

The train was slackening for a wayside station. Outside a man was driving a plough across a field where grain had been harvested. Nicholas followed with his eyes the walk of the horses, the purple-brown trail of the plough, the sturdy, independent figure of the driver as he passed, whistling an air. Over the Virginian landscape—the landscape of a country where each ragged inch of ground wears its strange, distinctive charm, where each rotting " worm fence " guards a peculiar beauty for those who know it—lay the warm hush of full-blown summer.

The man at the plough aroused in Nicholas Burr a sudden exhilaration as of physical exertion. It brought back his boyhood which had brightened as he had passed farther from it, and he felt that it would be good on such an afternoon to follow the horses across fields that were odorous of the up-turned earth.

The train went on slowly, with the shiftless slouch of Southern trains, the man at the plough vanished, and Nicholas returned to his thoughts.

The years had been almost breathless in their flight. He had put himself to a purpose, and he had lost sight of all things save its fulfilment. The success that men spoke of with astonished eyes—the transformation of the barefooted boy into the triumphant politician, had a firm foundation, he knew, though others did not. It was his capacity for toil that had made him—not his intellect, but his ability to persevere—the power which, in the old days, had successfully carried him through Jerry Pollard's store. As chairman of the Democratic Party, men had called his campaigns brilliant. He alone knew the tedious processes, the infinite patience from which these triumphs had evolved—he alone knew the secret and the security of his success.

The train stopped with a lurch.

"Kingsborough, sir!" said the conductor with a friendly touch upon his arm.

He started abruptly from his reverie, lifted his bag, and left the car. On the platform outside a group of stragglers recognised him, and there was a hearty cheer followed by frantic handshakes. The incident pleased him, and he spoke to each man singly, calling him by name. The sheriff was one of them, and the clerk of the court, and the old negro sexton of the church. There was a fervour in their congratulations which brought the warmth to his eyes. He was glad that the men who had known him in his poverty should rise so cordially to approve his success.

He left the station, walking rapidly to the judge's house. He had frequently returned to Kingsborough, but to-day the changes of the last fifteen years struck him with a sensation of surprise. The wide, white street, half in sunshine, half in shadow, trailed its drowsy length into the open country where the roads were filled with grass and dust. He noticed with a pang that the ivy had been torn from the church and that the glazed brick walls flaunted a nudity that was almost immodest. He had remembered it as a bower of shade—a gigantic bird's nest. He saw that ancient elms were rapidly decaying, and when he reached the judge's garden he found that the syringa and the lilacs had vanished. The garden had faced the destroyer in the plough, and trim vegetables thrived where gaudy blossoms had once rioted.

As he opened the gate he saw old Cæsar bending above the mint bed, and he went over to him.

"Dar ain' nuttin better ter jedge er gent'mun by den his mint patch," the old negro was muttering, "an' dis yer one's done w'ar out all dose no 'count flow'rs, des' like de quality done w'ar out de trash. Hi! Marse Nick, dat you?" he shook the proffered hand, his kindly black face wrinkling with hospitality. "Marse George hev got de swelled foot," he said in answer to a question, "an' he ain' tech his julep sence de day befo' yestiddy. Dis yer's fur you," he added, looking at the bunch in his hand.

"You're a trump, Cæsar!" exclaimed Nicholas as he ascended the steps and entered the wide hall, through which a light breeze was blowing.

The library door was open and he went in softly, lightening instinctively his heavy tread. The judge was sitting in his great arm-chair, his white head resting against the cushioned back, his bandaged foot on a high footstool.

"Is it you, my boy?" he asked, without turning.

Nicholas crossed the room and gripped the outstretched hand which trembled slightly in the air, the usual rugged composure of his face giving place to frank tenderness.

"I'm sorry to see the gout's troubling you again," he said.

The judge laughed and motioned to a chair beside his desk. His fine dark eyes were as bright as ever, and there was a youthful ring in his voice.

"I'm paying for my pleasures like the rest of us," he responded. "The truth is, Cæsar makes me live too high, the rascal—and I go on a bread-and-milk diet once in a while to spite him." Then his tone changed; he pushed aside a slender vase of "safrano" roses which shadowed Nicholas's face and regarded him with genuine delight. "It's good news you bring me," he exclaimed. "I haven't had such news since they told me the Democratic Party had wiped out Mahonism. And it was a surprise. We thought Dudley Webb was too secure for the chances of the 'dark horse.' Well, well, I'm sorry for Dudley, though I'm glad for you. How did you do it?"

Nicholas laughed, but his face was grave. "Ben Galt says I worked up a political 'revival,'" he replied. "He declares my methods were for all the world the counterpart of those employed in a Methodist camp meeting, but he's joking, of course. It was a distinct surprise to me, as you know. I had declined to offer myself as a candidate for the nomination, because I believed Webb to be assured of victory. However, the Crutchfield party proved stronger than we supposed, and they came over to my side. I was the 'dark horse,' as you say."

"It's very good," commented the judge. "Very good."

"Galt is afraid that what he calls 'the political change of heart' won't last," Nicholas went on, "but he knows, as I know, that I am the choice of the people and that, though a few of the leaders may distrust me, the Democratic Party as a body has entire confidence in me. You will understand that, had I doubted that the decision was free and untrammelled, I should not have accepted the nomination."

The judge nodded with a smile. "I know," he said, "and I also know that you were not born to be a politician. You will bear witness to it some day. You should have stuck to law. But have you seen Dudley?"

The younger man's face clouded. When he spoke there was a triumphant zest in his voice. His deeply-set eyes, which had at times a peculiarly opaque quality, were now charged with light. The thick red locks flared above his brow.

" He spoke pleasantly to me after the convention," he answered. " It was a disappointment to him, I know—and I am sorry," he finished in a forced, ex-clamatory manner, and was silent.

The judge looked at him for a moment before he went on in his even tones.

" His wife was telling me," he said. " She was down here a week or two before the convention. It seems that they are both anxious to return to Rich-mond to live. She's a fine girl, is Eugie. It was a terrible thing about that brother of hers, and she's never recovered from it. I can't understand how the boy came to commit such a peculiarly stupid forgery."

A flash of bitterness crossed the other's face; his voice was hard.

" He has missed his deserts," he returned harshly.

" Oh, I don't know, poor fellow," murmured the judge, flinching from a twinge of gout and settling his foot more carefully upon the stool. " He has been a fugitive from the State for years and a stranger to his wife and children. There was al-ways something extraordinary in the fact that he escaped after conviction, and I suppose there was a kind of honour in his not breaking his bail. At least, that's the way Eugie seems to regard it—and it is such a pitiful consolation that we might allow her to retain it. She tells me that Bernard's wife has been in destitute circumstances. It's a pity! it's a pity! I had always hoped that Tom Battle's boy would turn out well."

The younger man met his eyes squarely and spoke in an emotionless voice.

"I should like to see him serving his sentence," he said.

An hour later he left the judge's house and walked out to his old home. Since his father's death the place had undergone repairs and improvements. The lawn had been cleared off and sown in grass, the fences had been mended, and the house had been painted white. It could never suggest prosperity, but it had assumed an appearance of comfort.

In the little room next the kitchen he heard his stepmother scolding a small negro servant, and he broke in good-humouredly upon her discourse.

"All right, ma?" he called.

Marthy Burr turned and came towards him. She had aged but little, and her gaunt figure and sharp face still showed the force of her indomitable spirit.

"I declar' if 'tain't you, Nick!" she exclaimed.

He took her in his arms and kissed her perfunctorily, for he was chary of caresses. Then he lifted Nannie's baby from the floor and tossed it lightly.

"Nannie's spending the day," explained his stepmother with an attempt at conversation. "She would name that child Marthy, an' it's the best lookin' one she's got."

The baby, a pink-cheeked atom in a blue gingham frock, made a frantic clutch at the vivid hair of the giant who held her, and set up a tearful disclaimer. Nicholas returned her to the rug, where she attempted to swallow a string of spools, and looked at his stepmother.

"Where's that dress I sent you?" he demanded.

Marthy Burr sat down and smoothed out the creases in her purple calico.

"Laid away in camphor," she replied with a diffidence that was rapidly waning. "Marthy, if you swallow them spools, you won't have anything to play with."

Nicholas looked about the common little room —at the coarse lace curtains, the crude chromos, the distorted vases—and returned to his question.

"You promised me you'd wear it," he went on.

"Wear my best alpaca every day?" she demanded suspiciously. "I wouldn't have it on more'n an hour befo' one of them worthless niggers would have spilt bacon gravy all over it. There ain't been no peace in this house since you sent those no 'count darkies here to help me. If yo' pa was 'live, he'd turn them out bag an' baggage befo' sundown. Lord, Lord, when I think of what yo' poor pa would say if he was to walk in now an' find them creeturs in the kitchen."

Her stepson smiled.

"Now, if you'll sit still a moment, I'll tell you a piece of news," he said.

"You ain't thinkin' of gettin' married, air you?" inquired Marthy Burr with sudden keenness.

"Married!" He laughed aloud. "I've no time

for such nonsense.   Listen—no, let the baby alone, she isn't choking.   If the Powers agree, and the Democratic Party triumphs in November, I shall be Governor of Virginia on the first of January."

His stepmother looked at him in a dazed way, her glance wandering from his face to the baby with the string of spools.   There was a pleased light in her eyes, but he saw that she was striving in vain to grasp the full significance of his words.

"Well, well," she said at last.   "I al'ays told Amos you wa'nt no fool—but who'd have thought it!"

IV

The Capitol building at Richmond stands on a slight eminence in a grassy square, hiding its gray walls behind a stretch of elms and sycamores, as if it had retreated into historic shadow before the ruthless advance of the spirit of modernism. In the centre of the square, whose brilliant green slopes are intersected by gravelled walks that shine silver in the sunlight, the grave old building remains the one distinctive feature of a city where Iconoclasm has walked with destroying feet.

A few years ago—so few that it is within the memory of the very young—the streets leading from the Capitol were the streets of a Southern town— bordered by hospitable Southern houses set in gardens where old-fashioned flowers bloomed. Now the gardens are gone and the houses are outgrown. Progress has passed, and in its wake there have sprung up obvious structures of red brick with brownstone trimmings. The young trees leading off into avenues of shade soften the harshness of an architecture which would become New York, and which belongs as much to Massachusetts as to Virginia.

The very girls who, on past summer afternoons, flitted in bareheaded loveliness from door to door, have changed with the changing times. The loveliness is perhaps more striking, less distinctive; with the flower-like heads have passed the old grace and the old dependence, and the undulatory walk has quickened into buoyant briskness.   It is all modern —as modern as the red brick walls that are building where a quaint mansion has fallen.

But in the Capitol Square one forgets to-day and relives yesterday.   Beneath the calm eyes of the warlike statue of the First American little childen chase gray squirrels across the grass, and infant carriages with beruffled parasols are drawn in white and pink clusters beside the benches.   Jefferson and Marshall, Henry and Nelson are secure in bronze when mere greatness has decayed.

To the left of the Capitol a gravelled drive leads between a short avenue of lindens to the turnstile iron gates that open before the governor's house. Here, too, there is an atmosphere of the past and the picturesque.   The lawn, dotted with chrysanthemums and rose trees, leads down from the rear of the house to a wall of grapevines that overlooks the street below.   In front the yard is narrow and broken by a short circular walk, in the centre of which a thin fountain plays amid long-leaved plants. The house, grave, gray, and old-fashioned—the square side porches giving it a delusive suggestion of length—faces from its stone steps the thin fountain, the iron gates, beyond which stretches the white drive beneath the lindens, and the great bronze Washington above his bodyguard of patriots.   Between the house and the city the square lies like a garden of green.

It was on a bright morning in January that Ben Galt entered one of the iron gateways of the square and walked rapidly across to the Capitol.

He ascended the steep flight of stone steps, and paused for an instant in the lobby which divided the Senate Chamber from the House of Delegates. The legislature had convened some six weeks before, and the building was humming like a vast bee-hive.

In the centre of the tesselated floor of the lobby, which was fitted out with rows of earthenware spittoons, stood Houdon's statue of Washington, and upon the railing surrounding it groups of men were leaning as they talked. Occasionally a speaker would pause to send a mouthful of tobacco juice in aimless pursuit of a spittoon, or to slice off a fresh quid from the plug he carried in his pocket.

Galt, stopping behind a stout man with sandy hair, tapped him carelessly on the shoulder.

" Eh, Major? " he exclaimed.

The major turned, presenting a florid, hairy face, with small, shrewd eyes and an unpleasant mouth. His name was Rann, and he was the most important figure in the Senate. It was said of him that he had never made a speech in his life, but that he was continually speaking through the mouths of others. He could command more votes in both branches than any member of the Assembly, but his ambition was confined to the leadership of the men about him; he had been in the State Senate fifteen years, and he had never tried to climb higher, though it was reported that he had sent a United States senator to Washington.

" Ah, we'll see you oftener among us now," he said as he wheeled round, holding out a huge red hand, " since your friend sits above." He laughed, with a motion towards the ceiling, signifying the direction of the governor's office. "By the way, I was sorry about that bill you were interested in," he went on; "upon my word I was—but we're skittish just now on the subject of corporations. Charters are dangerous things—you can't tell where they're leading you, eh?—but, on my word, I was sorry."

"So was I," responded Galt with peculiar dryness —adding, with the frankness for which he was liked and hated, "I'd been dining that committee for weeks. Seven of them swore to back me through, and the eighth man said he'd go as the others went. My mind was so easy I lost sight of them for six hours, and every man John of them voted against the bill. I believe you got in a little work in those six hours."

Rann laughed and lowered one puffy eyelid in a blandly unembarrassed wink. "Oh, we don't like corporations," he replied, "I think I remarked as much. How-de-do, Colonel? Where'd you dine last night? Missed you at table."

The colonel was Diggs, and, after a curt nod in his direction, Galt pushed his way through the lobbyists and glanced into the House of Delegates, where an animated discussion of an oyster bill was in progress.

Owing to the absolute supremacy of the Democrats, the body presented the effect of a party caucus rather than a legislative branch of opposing elements. The few Republicans and Populists were lost in the ruling faction.

Galt was nodding here and there to members who

recognised him, when his arm was touched by a lank countryman who was standing near.

" Eh? " he inquired absently.

" I jest axed you if you reckoned we paid that gentleman over yonder for talking that gosh about oyschers? "

Galt bowed.   " Why, I suppose so," he responded gravely.   " It's a good day's work.   Am I to presume that you are not interested in oysters? "

" An' he gits fo' dollars a day for saying them things," commented the other shortly.   " I tell you 'tain't wo'th fo' cents, suh."

He lifted his bony hand and gave a tug at his scraggy beard.   In a moment he spoke again.

" Can you p'int out the young fellow from Goochland? " he inquired.   " That's whar I come from."

Galt pointed out the representative in question, and smiled because it was a man who had dined with him the evening before.

" That he? " exclaimed the countryman contemptuously.   " Why, I've been down here sence Saturday, an' that young spark ain't opened his mouth. I ain't heerd him mention Goochland sence I come."

" Oh, there's time enough," ventured Galt good-humouredly.   " He's young yet, and Goochland is immortal! "

" An' I reckon he gits fo' dollars same as the rest," went on the stranger reflectively, " jest for settin' thar an' whittlin' at that desk.   I used to study a good deal about politics fo' I come here, but they air jest a blamed swindle, that's what they air."

He turned on his heel, and in a moment Galt

entered the elevator and ascended to the office of the chief executive.

Reaching the landing he crossed a small gallery, where hung portraits of historic Virginians—governors in periwigs and lace ruffles and statesmen of a later age in high neckcloths. At the end of a short passage he opened the door of the anteroom and faced the private secretary, who was busy with his typewriter.

The secretary glanced up, recognised Galt, and gave a cordial nod.

"The governor's got a gentleman in just now who called about the boundary line between Virginia and Maryland," he said as Galt sat down. "He wants to see you, though, so you'd better wait. For a wonder there's nobody else here. Two-thirds of the legislature were up a while ago."

He spoke with an easy intimacy of tone, while the click of the typewriter went on rapidly.

Galt nodded in response and, as he did so, the door opened and the caller came out.

"You're the very man!" exclaimed a hearty voice, and Nicholas Burr was holding out his hand. "Come in. You're the only human being I know who is always the right man in the right place. How do you manage it?"

He sat down before his desk, pushing aside the litter of letters and pamphlets. "I should like you to glance over this list of appointments," he went on.

"It is what I dropped in about," responded Galt.

He flung himself into an easy chair and stretched his long legs comfortably before him. He did not

take the list at once, but sat staring abstractedly at
the freshly papered green walls above the large La-
trobe stove whose isinglass doors shone like blood-
shot eyes.

It was a long cheerful room with three windows
which overlooked the grassy square. There was a
bright red carpet on the floor, and before the desk
lay a gaudy rug enriched with stiff garlands. In
one corner a walnut bookcase was filled with papers
filed for reference, and the shelves across from it were
lined with calf-bound " Codes of Virginia." Among
the pictures on the pale-green walls there were
several of historic subjects—Washington among his
generals and Lee mounted upon Traveller. Over
the mantel hung an engraving of the United States
Senate with Clay for the central figure. Beside the
desk a cracker box was filled with unanswered
letters.

" Yes, I dropped in about that," repeated Galt, his
gaze returning to the rugged features of the man at
the desk. " You're not looking well, by the way."

The other laughed. " The office seekers have
been at me," he replied; " but I'm all right. What
were you going to say? "

His large, muscular hand lay upon the desk, and
as he spoke he fingered an open pamphlet. His
penetrating eyes were on Galt's face.

Galt lifted the list of names and read it in silence.

" A-ahem! " he said at last and laid it down; then
he took it up again.

" I have given a good deal of attention to the edu-
cational boards," continued the governor slowly.
" I do not think it is sufficiently realised that only

men of the highest ability should be placed in control of institutions of learning."

"Ah, I see," was Galt's comment. In a moment he spoke abruptly:

"I say, Nick, has it occurred to you to ascertain the direction in which the influence of these men will go in the next senatorial election?"

The other hesitated an instant. "Frankly, I have done my best to put such questions aside," he answered.

Galt squared round suddenly and faced him; there was a decisive ring in his voice.

"The next election comes in two years," he said quietly. "I have it on excellent authority that Withers will not seek to succeed himself. His health has given out and he is going to the country. Now, remove Withers, and there are two men who might take his place in the Senate. You know whom I mean?"

"Yes, I know."

Galt went on quickly:

"You want the senatorship?"

"Yes, I want it."

"Very good. Now, Webb and yourself will run that race, and one of you will lose it. It's going to be a hot race and a hard winning. There'll be some pretty unpleasant work to be done by somebody. You've been in the business long enough to know that the methods aren't exactly such as you can see your face in."

"All the more need for clean men," broke in Nicholas shortly.

"Just so. But the man who spends his days in

the bathtub doesn't walk about where mud is fling-
ing. I'm an honest man, please God. You're an
honest man, and that's why a lot of us are running
you with might and main and money. But there's
an honesty that verges on imbecility, and that's the
kind that talks itself hoarse when it ought to keep
silent. Save your talking until you get to the Senate,
and then let fly as much morality as you please;
it won't hurt anybody there, heaven knows. You
are the man we need, and a few of us know it, though
the majority may not. But for the next two years
give up trying to purify the Democratic Party. The
party's all right, and it's going to stay so."

"It has been my habit to express my convictions,"
returned the other quickly.

"Then drop the habit," replied Galt with an affectionate glance that softened the shrewd alertness of
his look. "My dear and valued friend, a successful
politician does not have convictions; he has emotions. Convictions were all right when Madison
was President, but that gentleman has been in heaven these many years, and they don't thrive under
the present administration. A party man has got
to be a party mouthpiece. He may laugh and weep
with the people, but he has got to vote with the
party—and it's the party man who comes out on
top. Why, look at Withers! Hunt about in his
senatorial record and you'll find that he has voted
against himself time out of number. You and I
may call that cowardliness, but the party calls it
honour and applauds every time. That applause
has kept him the exponent of the machine and the
idol of the people, who hear the fuss and imagine it

means something.   Now Webb is like Withers, only
smarter.   He is just the man to become a sounding
brass reflector, and there's the danger."

" And yet I defeated him! " suggested the
governor.

Galt laughed, with a wave of his thin, nervous
hand.

" My dear governor, you are the one great man in
State politics, but that unimportant fact would not
have landed you into your present seat had not the
little revivalistic episode befuddled the brains of the
convention."

Nicholas shook his head impatiently.   " You
make too much of that," he said.

" Perhaps.   I want to impress upon you that you
have a hard fight before you.   The Webb men are
already putting in a little quiet work in the legislature—and they have even been after the guards at
the penitentiary.   Major Rann is your man, and he
tells me the Webb leaders are the quietest, most
insidious workers he has ever met.   As it is, he is
your great card, and his influence is immense.
Webb would give his right hand for him."

The governor tossed the hair from his brow with
a quick movement.

" I have the confidence of the people," he said.

" The people!   How long does it take a clever
politician to befuddle them?   You aren't new to the
business, and you know these things as well as I do
—or better.   I tell you, when Dudley Webb begins
to stump the State the people will begin to howl for
him.   He'll win over the women and the old Con-
federates when he gets on the Civil War, and the

rest will come easy. There won't be need of bogus ballots and disappearing election books when the members of the Democratic caucus are sent up next session."

" What do you want?" demanded the governor abruptly. He leaned forward, his arms on the desk.

Galt tapped the list of appointments significantly.

" As a beginning, I want you to scratch out a good two-thirds of these names. The others will go all right. The men I have cross marked are not all Webb men to-day, but they will throw their influence on Webb's side when the pull comes."

Nicholas took up the list and reread it carefully. " The men I have named I believe to be best suited to the positions," he returned. " One, you may observe, is a Republican—that will call for hostile criticism—but he was beyond doubt the best man. I regret the fact that the majority of these men are Webb partisans, but I wish to make these appointments for reasons entirely apart from politics."

Galt had risen, and he now stood looking down upon the governor with a smile in his eyes.

" So it goes?" he asked, pointing to the sheet of paper.

The other nodded.

" Yes, it goes. I am not a fool, Ben. I wish things were different—but it goes."

" And so do I," laughed Galt easily. " You won't mind my remarking, by the way, that you are a brick, but a brick in the wrong road. However, you hold on to Rann, and the rest of us will hold on to you. Oh, we'll see you to-night at Carrie's coming-out affair, of course. The child wouldn't have you absent for worlds. If my wife and daughter represented the community you might become Dictator of Richmond. Good morning!"

As he crossed the little gallery where the portraits hung there was an abstracted smile about the corners of his shrewd mouth.

V

" Juliet! " called Galt as he swung open his house
door.

It was his habit to call for his wife as soon as he
crossed the threshold, and she was accustomed to
respond from the drawing-room, the pantry, or the
nursery, as the case might be. This evening her
voice floated from the dining-room, and following
the sound he stumbled over a shadowy palm and
came upon Juliet as she put the last touches to a
long white table, radiant with cut glass and roses.

She wore a faded blue dressing-gown, caught
loosely together, and her curling hair, untouched
by gray, fell carelessly from its coil across her full,
fair cheek. She had developed from a fragile girl
into a rounded matron without losing the peculiar
charm of her beauty. The abundant curve of her
white throat was still angelic in its outline. As she
leaned over to settle the silver candelabra on the
table, the light deepened the flush in her face and
imparted a shifting radiance to her full-blown loveliness.

" How is it, little woman? " asked Galt as he put
his arm about the blue dressing-gown. " Working
yourself to death, are you? "

Since entering his home he had lost entirely the
air of business-like severity which he had worn all
day. He looked young and credulous. Juliet

laughed with the pettish protest of a half-spoiled wife and drew back from the table.

" It is almost time to dress Carrie," she said, " and the ice-cream hasn't come.   Everything else is here. Did you get dinner downtown ? "

" Such as it was—a miserable pretence.   For heaven's sake, let's have this over and settle down. I only wish it were Carrie's wedding; then we might hope for a rest."

" Until Julie comes out—she's nearly fourteen. But you ought to be ashamed, when we've been working like Turks.   Eugenia cut up every bit of the chicken salad and Emma Carr made the mayonnaise—she makes the most delicious you ever tasted.   Aren't those candelabra visions?   Emma lent them to me, and Mrs. Randolph sent her oriental lamps.   There's the bell now!   It must be Eugie's extra forks; she said she'd send them as soon as she got home."

" Good Lord!" ejaculated Galt feebly.   "You are as great at borrowing as the children of Israel."

His comments were cut short by the entrance of Eugenia's silver basket, accompanied by an enormous punch bowl, which she sent word she had remembered at the last moment.

" Bless her heart!" exclaimed Juliet.   " She forgets nothing; but I hope that bowl won't get broken, it is one somebody brought the general from China fifty years ago.   Eugie is so careless.   She invited the children to tea the other afternoon and I found her giving them jam on those old Tucker Royal Worcester plates."

She broke off an instant to draw Galt into the

reception rooms, where her eyes roved sharply over the decorations.

" They look lovely, don't they? " she inquired, re-arranging a bowl of American Beauty roses. " I got that new man to do them Mrs. Carrington told me about—Yes, Carrie, I'm coming! Why, I de-clare, I haven't seen the baby since breakfast. Un-natural mother! "

And she rushed off to the nursery, followed by Galt.

An hour later she was in the drawing-room again, her fair hair caught back from her plump cheeks, her white bosom shining through soft falls of lace.

" I wonder how a man feels who isn't married to a beauty," remarked Galt, watching her matronly vanity dimple beneath his gaze. He was as much her lover as he had been more than twenty years ago when pretty Juliet Burwell had put back her wedding veil to meet his kiss. The very exactions of her petted nature had served to keep alive the passion of his youth; she demanded service as her right, and he yielded it as her due. The unflinching shrewdness of his professional character, the hard-ness of his business beliefs, had never entered into the atmosphere of his home. Juliet possessed to a degree that pervasive womanliness which vanquishes mankind. After twenty years of married life in which Galt had learned her limitations and her minor sins of temperament, he was not able to face her stainless bosom or to meet her pure eyes without believing her to be a saint. In his heart he knew Sally Burwell to be a nobler woman than Juliet, and yet he never found himself regarding Sally through

an outward and visible veil of her virtues.   Even
Tom Bassett, who was married to her, had lost the
lover in the husband, as his emotions had matured
into domestic sentiment. Galt had seen Sally wrestle
for a day with one of her father's headaches, to be
rewarded by less gratitude than Juliet would receive
for the mere laying of a white finger on his temple
—Sally's services were looked upon by those who
loved her best as one of the daily facts of life; Juliet's
came always as an additional bounty.

To Galt himself, the different developments of
the two women had become a source of almost
humorous surprise. After her marriage Sally had
sunk her future into Tom's; Galt had submerged
his own in Juliet's.   Behind Tom's not too remarkable success Galt had seen always Sally's quicker
wit and more active nature; to his own ambitions,
his love for Juliet had been the retarding influence.
He had been called "insanely aspiring" in his profession, and yet he had sacrificed his career without a murmur for the sake of his wife's health.   He
had sundered his professional interests in New
York that he might see the colour rebloom in
her cheek, and neither he nor she had questioned
that the loss was justified.   In return she had rendered him a jealous loyalty and an absorbing wifehood, and he had found his happiness apart from his
ambition.

Now she dimpled as he looked at her and he
pinched her cheek.

"The mother of six children!" he exclaimed;
"they're changelings."   He looked at Carrie, who
was flitting nervously from room to room.

" It's a shame she didn't take after you," he added.
" She carries the curse of my chin."

" She's splendid!" protested Juliet. " I never
had such a figure in my life; Sally says so. Carrie
is a new woman, that's the difference."

" But the old lady's good enough for me," finished
Galt triumphantly; then he melted towards his
daughter. " I dare say she's stunning," he observed. " Come here, Carrie, and bear witness that
you're as handsome as your parents."

Carrie floated up, a straight, fine figure in white
organdie, her smooth hair shining like satin as it
rolled from her brow. Her mouth and chin were
too strong for beauty, but she was frank and clean
and fresh to look at.

" Oh, I am just like you," she declared, " and I'm
not half so pretty as mamma. There's the bell.
Somebody's coming!"

There was a rustle of women's skirts on the way
upstairs, and in a moment several light-coloured
gowns were fringed by the palms in the doorway.

When the governor entered, several hours later,
the rooms were filled with warmth and laughter and
the vague perfume of women's dresses mingled with
the odour of American Beauty roses. An old-
fashioned polka was in the air, and beyond the fur-
thest doorway he saw young people dancing. The
red candles were burning down, and drops of wax
lay like flecks of blood upon the floor. Near the
entrance, a small, dark woman was leaning upon a
marble table, and as she saw him she held out a
cordial hand. She was plain and thin, with pale,
startled eyes and a mouth that slanted upward at one

22

corner, like a crooked seam. She spoke in an abrupt, skipping manner that possessed a surprising fascination.

" Behold the conquering hero! " she exclaimed, her pale eyes roving from side to side. " I suppose if you were never late, you would never be longed for."

" My dear Miss Preston," protested pretty little Mrs. Carrington, who was soft and drowsy, with eyes that reminded one of a ruminating heifer's.

" I assure you, I have been positively longing to have you gratify my curiosity," declared Miss Preston. " You know you do such dear, eccentric things that we couldn't exist without you—at least I couldn't because I should perish of boredom. No, you shan't escape just yet, so stop looking at that beautiful Mrs. Galt. You must tell me first if it is really true that you once carried a woman out of a burning building in your right hand. It is so delightful to be strong, don't you think? "

The governor regarded her gravely. Before her animated chatter his gravity became almost grotesque. " The only burning building I was ever in was a burning smoke-house," he returned quietly. " I never carried a woman out of anything in either hand."

There was a bored expression in his eyes, and he glanced beyond the group to where Juliet stood surrounded.

" Pardon me," he said in a moment, and passed on.

In the crowd about him, where pretty women were as plentiful as pinks in a garden bed, he moved awkwardly, with the hesitating steps of a man who is uncertain of his pathway. His powerful frame and the splendid vigour in his daring strides seemed out of place amid a profusion of exotics that trembled as he passed. His appearance suggested the battlegrounds of nature—high places, or the breadth of the open fields; at the plough he would have been grandly picturesque, in the centre of a throng of graceful men and women he loomed merely large and ill at ease. Above his evening clothes his face showed rough, rather than refined, and his stubborn jaw gave an impression of heaviness.

As he reached Juliet she uttered an exclamation of pleasure and held out her hand. " Emma, you have heard of my Sunday-school scholar," she said to a girl beside her. " My prize scholar, I mean. Sally, have you seen the governor? "

Emma Carr, a pink-and-white girl who bore herself with the air of an acknowledged belle, bowed, with a platitude that sounded original on her lovely lips, and Sally Bassett turned with a hearty handshake.

" And he is our Nick Burr! " she exclaimed. " Tom, where are you? "

She spoke with an impulsive flutter which he had remembered as the sparkle of mere girlish liveliness. Now he saw that it had degenerated into a restlessness that appeared to result from a continued waste of nervous energy. She looked older than Juliet, though she was in fact much younger, and her face was drawn and heavily lined as if by years of ill-health. Her physical strength was prodigious; one perceived it with the suddenness of surprise. Much the same impression was produced by her youthful manner in connection with her worn features; yet, in spite of her faded prettiness, there was a singular charm in her unabated vivacity.

She darted off in pursuit of Tom, to be arrested by the first newcomer she encountered, and Nicholas was responding gravely to Juliet's banter when his eyes fell full upon Eugenia Battle as she stood at a little distance.

He had not seen her for fifteen years, and he started quickly as if from an unsuspected shock. She was talking rapidly in her fervent voice, the old illumination in her look. Her noble figure, in a straight flaxen gown, was drawn against a background of green, her head was bent forward on her long white neck, her kindly hands were outstretched. She had developed from a girl into a woman, but to him she was unchanged. Her face was, perhaps, older, her bosom fuller, but he did not see it—to him she appeared as the resurrected spirit of his youth. Miss Carr was speaking and he made some brief rejoinder. Eugenia had turned and was looking at him; in a moment he heard her voice.

" Are old friends too far beneath the eyes of your excellency? " she asked, and he heard the soft laugh pulse in her throat.

Her hand was outstretched, and he took it for an instant in his own.

" I am very glad to see you," he remarked lamely as he let it fall—so lamely that he bit his lip at the remembrance. " You are looking well," he added.

" Of course—a woman always looks well at night," she answered lightly. " And you," she laughed again, her kindly, unconscious laugh; " you are looking—large."

He did not smile. "I have no doubt of it," he responded, and was silent.

Juliet Galt broke in with an affectionate protest. "Eugie is as great a tease as ever," she said. "She will be the death of my baby yet. I tell her to choose one of her own size, but she never does. She always plagues those smaller than herself—or larger."

But Eugenia had turned away to greet a stranger, and in a moment Nicholas drew back into a windowed embrasure where the lights were dim.

Suddenly a voice broke upon his ear addressing Juliet Galt—the vibrant tones of Dudley Webb. He had come in late and was standing in mock helplessness before Juliet and Carrie, his plump white hand vacillating between the two.

"I am at a loss!" he exclaimed with an appealing shrug of his shoulders. "Which is the débutante?"

Juliet laughed, her cheeks mantling with a pleased blush.

"You're a sad flatterer, Dudley! Isn't he, Eugie?"

Eugenia turned with a questioning glance.

"Oh, it's just his way," she returned good-humouredly. "A kindly Providence has decreed that he should cover over my deficiencies."

Dudley protested affably, and ended by giving a hand to each. In the crowded rooms he had become at once the picturesque and popular figure. His magnetism was immediately felt, and men and women surrounded him in small circles, while his pleasant words ran on smoothly, accompanied by the ring of his infectious laugh. The luminous pallor of his clear-cut, yet fleshy face, was accentuated by the sweep of his dark hair that clung closely to his forehead. He seemed to have brought with him into the heated rooms the spirit of humour and the zest of life.

From the deep embrasure Nicholas Burr watched curiously the flutter of women's skirts and the flicker of candle light on shining heads. Eugenia moved easily from group to group, the straight fall of her flaxen gown giving her an added height, the dark coil of hair on the nape of her long neck seeming to rise above the shoulders of other women. She was never silent—for one and all she had some ready words, and her manner was cordial, almost affectionate. It was as if she were in the midst of a great family party, held together by the ties of blood.

In a far corner Juliet Galt and Emma Carr, the prettiest women in the room, sat together upon a corn-coloured divan, and in front of them a file of men passed and repassed slowly on their way to and from the dining-room, pausing to exchange brief remarks and drifting on aimlessly. Near them a fair, pale gentleman, robust and slightly bald, with protruding eyes and anæmic lips, had flung himself upon a gilded chair, a glass of punch in his hand. He had danced incessantly for hours in the adjoining room, and at last, wearied, winded, with a palpitating heart, he had found a punch bowl and a gilded chair.

Through the doorway floated music and the

laughter of young girls intoxicated with the dance. In the hall, some had sought rest upon the stairway, and sat in radiant clusters, fanning themselves briskly as they talked. There was about them an absence of coquetry as of self-consciousness; they were frank, cordial-voiced, almost boyish.

The governor stepped suddenly from the embrasure and ran against Ben Galt, who caught his arm.

" I've been searching the house for you," he exclaimed, " after landing my twelfth matron in the dining-room." Then catching sight of the other's face, he inquired blandly:

" Bored? "

" I am."

Galt gave a comprehending wink.

" So am I. These things are death. I say, don't go! Come into the library and we'll lock the door and have supper shoved in through the window, while we talk business. I've a decanter of the finest Madeira you ever tasted behind the bookcase. Juliet will never know, and I don't care a continental if she does. I'm a desperate man!"

" I was just going," replied the governor. " I'm not up to parties; but lead off, if it's out of this."

VI

It was one o'clock when the governor left Galt's house, and turning into Grace Street strolled leisurely in the direction of the Capitol Square. The night was sharp with frost and a rising wind drove the shadows on the pavement against darkened house-fronts, while behind a far-off church spire, a wizened moon shivered through a thin cloud. On the silence came the sound of fire bells ringing in the distance.

The bronze Washington in the deserted square shone silver beneath the moonlight, and down the frozen slopes the trees stretched out stiffened limbs. From the governor's house a broad light streamed, and quickening his pace he entered the iron gate, which closed after him with a rheumatic cough, and briskly ascended the stone steps. As he drew the latch-key from his pocket he was thinking of his library, where the firelight fell on cheerful walls and red leathern chairs, and with the closing of the door he crossed the hall and entered the first room on the left.

A red fire burned in the grate, and the furniture reflected the colour until the place seemed pervaded by a visible warmth. The desk in the centre of the room, the shining backs of law books, the crimson rugs, the engravings on the walls, the easy chair drawn up before the hearth, presented to him as he entered now the security of individual isolation. He

had felt the same sense of restfulness when he had
ascended, after the day's work, to the little whitewashed attic of his father's house. To-night he
liked the glow because it suggested warmth, but he
could not have told off-hand the colour of the carpet
or the subjects of the engravings on the wall; and
had he found a white pine chair in place of the red
leathern one, he would have used it without an ad-
mission of discomfort. In the midnight hours he
liked the empty house about him—the silence and
the safeguard of his loneliness. The deserted reception-rooms at the end of the hall pleased him by their
stillness and the cold of their fireless grates. Even
the stiff, unyielding furniture, in its fancy dress of
satin brocade, soothed him by its remoteness when
he passed it wrapped in thought.

He flung himself into the easy chair, raised the
light by which he read, and unfolded a newspaper
lying upon his desk. As he did so an article which
concerned himself caught his eye, and he read it
with curious intentness.

"THE MAN WITH THE CONSCIENCE.

REFUSES TO RECOMMEND THE PROPOSED RESTRICTION OF THE SUFFRAGE.

ATTACHES HIS SIGNATURE TO SEVERAL BILLS.—TO
AMEND AND RE-ENACT THE CHARTER OF THE
TOWN OF CULPEPER—TO ESTABLISH A
FERRY ACROSS THE PIANKITANK."

He reread it abstractedly, pondering not the
future of Culpeper or of the Piankitank River, but
the title by which he was beginning to be known:

" The Man with the Conscience!" He had been
in office less than a month, and three times within
the last week he had been called " The Man with
the Conscience." Once a member of the Senate
had declared on the floor that the " two strongest
factors in present State politics are found to be in
the will of the people and the conscience of the governor." The morning papers had reported it, and
when, several days later, he had vetoed a bill providing to place certain powers in the hands of a
corporation that was backed by large capital, he
had been hailed again as " The Man with the Conscience!" Now he wondered as he read what the
verdict would be to-morrow, when his refusal to
sign a document which lay at that moment upon his
desk must become widely known. He had refused,
not because the bill granted too great rights to a
corporation, but because it needlessly restricted the
growth of a railroad. Would his refusal in this instance be dubbed "conscience" or "inconsistency"?

At the moment he was the people's man—this he
knew. His name was cheered by the general voice.
As he passed along the street bootblacks hurrahed!
him. He had determined that the governorship
should cease to represent a figurehead, and for right
or wrong, he was the man of the hour.

He laid the paper aside, and lifting a pipe from his
desk, slowly lighted it. As the smoke curled up, it
circled in gray rings upon the air, filling the room
with the aroma of the Virginia leaf. He watched
it idly, his mind upon the pile of unopened letters
awaiting his attention. Above the mantel hung a
small oil painting of a Confederate soldier after Ap-

pomattox, and it reminded him vaguely of some
one whom he had half forgotten.   He followed the
trail for a moment and gave it up.   Higher still was
an engraving of Mr. Jefferson Davis, with the well-
remembered Puritan cast of feature and the severe
chin beard.   Beneath the pictures a trivial ornament
stood on the mantel and beside it a white rose in
water breathed a fading fragrance.   A child who
had come to feed the squirrels in the square had
put the rose in his coat, and he had transferred it
to the glass of water.

He turned towards his desk and took up several
cards that he had not seen.   So Rann had called
in his absence—and Vaden and Diggs.   As he
pushed the cards aside, he summoned mentally the
men before him and weighed the possible values of
each.   Why had Rann called, he wondered—he had
an object, of course, for he did not pay so much as a
call without a purpose.   The name evoked the man
—he saw him plainly in the circles of gray smoke—
a stout, square figure, with short legs, his plaid socks
showing beneath light trousers; a red, hairy face,
with a wart in his left eyebrow, which was heavier
than his right one; a large head, prematurely bald,
and beneath an almost intellectual forehead, a pair of
shrewd, intelligent eyes.   Rann was a match for any
man in politics, he knew—the great, silent voice,
some one had said—the man who was clever enough
to let others do his talking for him.   Yes, he was
glad that Rann would back him up.

The remaining callers appeared together in his
reverie—Vaden and Diggs.   They were never mentioned apart, and they never worked singly.   They

were honest men, whose honesty was dangerous because it went with dull credulity. In appearance they were so unlike as to make the connection ludicrous. Vaden was long, emaciated, with a shrunken chest in which a consumptive cough rattled. His face was scholarly, pallid, pleasant to look at, and there was a sympathetic quality in his voice which carried with it a reminder of past bereavements. Beside the sentimental languor which enveloped him, Diggs loomed grotesquely fair and florid, with eyes bulging with joviality, and red, repellent, almost gluttonous lips. He was a teller of stories and a maker of puns.

They were both honest men and ardent Democrats, but they were in the leading strings of sharper politicians. Perhaps, after all, the fools were more to be feared than the villains.

Somewhere in the city a clock rang the hour, and, as his pipe died out, he rose and went to his desk.

The next morning Vaden and Diggs dropped in to breakfast, and before it was over he had ascertained that they were seeking to sound him upon his attitude towards the recent National Party Platform. As he dodged their laboured cross-examination he laughed at the overdone assumption of indifference. Before they had risen from the table, Rann joined them, and the conversation branched at once into impersonal topics. Diggs told a story or two, at which Rann roared appreciatively, while Vaden fingered his coffee spoon in pensive abstraction.

As they left the dining-room, which was in the basement, and ascended to the hall, Diggs glanced into the reception-rooms and nodded respectfully at the brocaded chairs.

"I like the looks of that, governor," he said, "but it's a pity you can't find a wife. A woman gives an air to things, you know." Then he cocked an eye at the ceiling. "This old house ain't much more than a fire trap, anyway," he added. "The trouble is it's gotten old-fashioned just like the Capitol building over there. My constituents are all in favour of doing the proud thing by Virginia and giving her a real up-to-date State House. Bless my life, the old Commonwealth deserves a brownstone front—now don't she?"

He appealed to Rann, who dissented in his broad, if blunt, intelligence.

"I wouldn't trade that old building for all the brownstone between here and New York harbour," he declared.

The governor laughed abstractedly, but a week later he recalled the proposition as he sat in Juliet Galt's drawing-room, and repeated it for the sake of her frank disgust.

"I shall tell Eugie," she exclaimed. "Eugie finds everything so new that she suffers a perpetual homesickness for Kingsborough."

"There's nobody left down there except the judge and Mrs. Webb," broke in Carrie; "and you know she gets on dreadfully with Mrs. Webb—now doesn't she, Aunt Sally?"

"She never told me so," laughed Sally, "but I strongly suspect it. I don't disguise the fact that I consider Mrs. Webb to be a terror, and Eugie's a long way off from saintship."

"I hardly think that Mrs. Webb would consent to join our colony," observed Nicholas indifferently.

" May Kingsborough long enjoy her rule," added Juliet. " I hear that she has grown quite amiable towards the judge since she prophesied that he would have chronic gout and he had it."

" It would be so nice of them to marry each other," suggested Carrie with an eye for matrimonial interests. " You needn't shake your head, mamma. Aunt Sally said the same thing to Uncle Tom."

She was standing on the hearth rug in her walking gown, slowly fastening her gloves. Sally looked at her and laughed in her nervous way.

" Well, I confess that it did cross my mind," she admitted. " Tom, like all men, believed Mrs. Webb to be a martyr until I convinced him that she martyred others."

" Oh, he still believes it behind your back," said Nicholas.

Juliet turned upon him frankly. " It's a shame to destroy wifely confidence," she protested. " Sally hasn't been married long enough to know that the only way to convince a husband is to argue against oneself."

Her head rested upon the cushions of her chair, and her pretty foot was on the brass fender. There was a cordial warmth about her which turned the simple room into home for even the casual caller. The matronly grace of her movements evoked the memory of infancy and motherhood; to Nicholas Burr she seemed, in her beauty and her abundance, the supreme expression of a type—of the joyous racial mother of all men.

Her youngest child, a girl of three, that she called " baby," had come in from a walk and was standing at her knee in white cap and cloak and mittens, her hand clutching Juliet's dress, her solemn eyes on the governor. He had tried to induce her to approach, but she held off and regarded him without a smile.

" Now, now, baby," pleaded Juliet, " who fed the bunnies with you the other day? "

" Man," responded the baby gravely.

" Who gave you nice nuts for the dear bunnies? "

" Man."

" Who carried you all round the pretty square? "

" Man."

" Who gave you that lovely picture book full of animals? "

" Man."

" Then don't you love the kind man? "

" Noth."

" Yes, you do—you've forgotten. Go and speak to him."

The child approached gravely to make a grab at his watch-chain; he lifted her to his knee, and friendship was established. They were at peace a moment later when a voice was heard in the hall, and the curtains were swung back as Eugenia Webb entered, tall and glowing, her head rising from a collar of fur. She brought with her the breath of frost, and the winter red was in her cheeks, fading slowly as she sat down and threw off her wraps. He saw then that she looked older than he thought and that her elastic figure had settled into matronly lines.

She raised her spotted veil and drew off her gloves.

" I mustn't talk myself out," she was saying

lightly, "because Dudley means to make me bring him to call this evening. I can't induce him to come by himself—he simply won't. He considers my mission in life to be the combined duties of paying his calls and entertaining his legislators. We had six senators to dinner last night, and we pay six visits this evening. Come here, Tweedle-dee," to the baby. "Come to your own Aunt Eugie and give her a kiss."

The child looked at her thoughtfully and shook her head.

"Kith man," she responded shortly.

The swift red rose to Eugenia's face. Nicholas was looking at her, and her eyes flashed with the old anger at a senseless blush.

"That's right, old lady," said the governor to the child. "Tell her you'd rather kiss a man every time."

"Of course she had," replied Eugenia half angrily. "She's going to be her mother all over again."

Juliet laughed her full, soft laugh. "Now, Eugie," she protested gaily, "my sins are many, but spare me a public confession of them."

"She takes after her aunt," put in Sally frankly. "I always liked men better, and I think it's unwomanly not to—don't you, governor?"

Nicholas put the child down and rose.

"I'm afraid my womanliness is only skin deep," he returned, "but I wouldn't give one honest man for all the women since Eve."

"Behold our far-famed gallantry!" exclaimed Sally.

Eugenia looked up, laughing. She had seized upon the child, and he saw her dark eyes above the solemn blue ones.

" I'm afraid you aren't much of a politician, Governor Burr, if you tell the truth so roundly," she said. " The first lesson in politics is to lie and love it; the second lesson is to lie and live it. Oh, we've been in Congress, Dudley and I."

She moved restlessly, and her colour came and went like a flame that flickers and revives. He wondered vaguely at her nervous animation—she had not possessed a nerve in her girlhood—nor had he seen this shifting restlessness the other night. It did not occur to him that the meeting with himself was the cause—he knew her too well—but had his presence, or some greater thing, aroused within her painful memories of the past?

As he walked down Franklin Street a little later he contrasted boldly the two Eugenias he had known—the Eugenia who was his and the Eugenia who was Dudley Webb's. After fifteen years the rapture and the agony of his youth showed grotesque to his later vision; men did not love like that at forty years. He could see Eugenia now without the quiver of a pulse; he could sit across from her, knowing that she was the wife of another, and could eat his dinner. His passion was dead, but where it had bloomed something else drew life and helped him to live. He had loved one woman and he loved her still, though with a love which in his youth he would have held to be as ashes beside his flame. There were months—even years—when he did not think of her; when he thought profoundly

23

of other things; but in these years the thrill of no woman's skirts had disturbed his calm. And again, there were winter evenings—evenings when he sat beside the hearth, and there came to him the thought of a home and children—of a woman's presence and a child's laugh. He could have loved the woman well had she been Eugenia, and he could have loved the child had it been hers; but beyond her went neither his vision nor his desire.

Now he swung on, large, forceful, a man young enough to feel, yet old enough to know. He entered his door quickly, as was his custom, impatient for his work and his fireside. On his desk lay the papers that had been brought over by his secretary, and he ran his fingers carelessly through them, gleaning indifferently the drift of their contents. As he did so a light flashed suddenly upon him, and the meaning of Eugenia's restlessness was made clear, for upon his desk was an application for the pardon of Bernard Battle.

VII

The paper was still in his hand when the door behind him opened.

"A lady to see you, suh."

"A lady?" He turned impatiently to find himself facing Eugenia Webb. She had come so swiftly, with a silence so apparitional, that he fell back as from a blow between the eyes. For a moment he doubted her reality, and then the glow in her face, the mist on her furs, the fog of her breath, proclaimed that she had followed closely upon his footsteps. She must have been almost beside him when he hurried through the frost.

"You wish to speak to me?" he asked blankly, as he drew a chair to the hearth rug. "Will you not sit down?"

There was an unfriendly question in his eyes, and she met it boldly with the old dash of impulse.

"They told me that to-morrow would be too late," she said. "I went to Ben Galt's to ask him to come to you in my place, but he is out of town. I found you there instead. It is a matter of life and death to me, so I came."

She sat down in the chair he had drawn up for her, her muff fell to the floor, and he placed it upon the desk where the petition lay unrolled. As he did so he saw the list of names that presented the appeal —judge, jury, prosecuting attorney, all were there.

She followed his gaze and moved slightly towards

him. " It can't be true that you—that you will not——" she said.

He was stirring the fire into flame, but as she broke off he turned squarely upon her.

" I have not looked into the case," he answered harshly.

He was standing beside his own hearthstone and he was at ease. There was no awkwardness about him now; his height endowed him with majesty, and in his inflexible face there was no suggestion of heaviness. He looked a man with a sublime self-confidence.

Her colour beat quickly back, warming her eyes.

" Oh, I am so glad," she said. " When you know all you will do as we ask you, because it is right and just. If he did not serve that two years' sentence he has served six years of poverty and sickness. He is a wreck—we should not know him, they say—and he has not seen his wife and children for——"

He raised his hand and stopped her. A rising anger clouded his face, and, as she met his eyes, she slowly whitened.

" And you ask me—me of all men—to show mercy to Bernard Battle? Was there not a governor of Virginia before me? "

She shook her head.

" Oh, it was different then—he did not know, and we did not know, everything. For years we had not heard from him——"

" So my predecessor refused? " he asked.

She bowed her head. " But it is *so* different now—every one is with us."

He was looking her over grimly in an anger that

seemed an emotional reversion to the past—as he felt himself reverting with all his strength to the original savage of the race.   The hour for which he had starved sixteen years ago was unfolding for him at last.   He gloated over it with a passion that would sicken him when it was done.

"When you came to me," he said slowly, "did you remember——"

She had risen and was standing before him, her hands hidden in the fur upon her bosom.   She was pleading now with startled eyes and cold lips—she who had turned from him when the first lie was spoken—she was pleading for the man who had blackened his friend's honour that he might shield his own—she was pleading though she knew his baseness.   The very nobility of her posture—the nobility that he had found outwardly in no other woman—hardened the man before her.   The cold brow, the fervent mouth, the fearless eyes, the lines with which Time had chastened into womanliness her girlish figure—these had become the expression of an invincible regret.   As he faced her the iron of his nature held him as in a vise, for life, which had made him a just man, had not made him a gentle one.

But her spirit had risen to match with his.   "He wronged you once," she said; "let it pass—we have all been young and very ignorant; but we do not make our lives, thank God."

He looked at her in silence.

Then, as he stood there, the walls of the room passed from before his eyes, and the gray light from the western window was falling upon the white road beyond the cedars.   The vague pasture swept to the

far-off horizon where hung the solitary star above
the sunset. From the west a light wind blew, and
into their faces dead leaves whirled from denuded
trees far distant. But surest of all was this—he
hated now as he hated then. "As for him—may
God, in His mercy, damn him," he had said.

"Because he wronged you do not wrong yourself," she spoke fearlessly, but she fell back with an
upward movement of her hands. The man was before her as the memory had been for years—she
knew the distorted features, the convulsed, closed
mouth, the furrow that cleft the forehead like a scar.
She saw the savage as she had seen it once before,
and she braved it now as she had braved it then.

"You are hard—as hard as life," she said.

"Life is as we make it," he retorted. He lifted
her muff from the desk and she took it from him,
turning towards the door. As he followed her into
the hall he spoke slowly: "I shall read the papers
that relate to the case," he said. "I shall do my
duty. You were mistaken if you supposed that your
coming to me would influence my decision. Personal appeal rarely avails and is often painful."

He unlatched the outer door and she passed out
and descended the steps.

When he returned to the fire he was shivering
from the draught let in by the opening doors, and,
lifting the fallen poker, he attacked almost fiercely
the slumbering coals. The physical shock had not
tempered the rage within; he felt it gnawing upon
his entrails like a beast of prey. Once only in his
life had he found himself so powerless before a de-
vouring passion, and then, as now, he had glutted

it with wounded love. Then, as now, he had hated
with a terrible desire.

The application lay upon his desk, and he pushed
it out of sight. He could not read it now—he wondered if the time would ever come when he could
read it. The thought smote him with the lash of
fear—the fear of himself. He who an hour ago had
held his assurance to be beyond assault was now
watching for the death of his hate as he might have
watched for the death of a wolf whose fangs he had
felt.

Lifting his head, he could see through the cur-
tained window the chill slopes of the square and the
circular drive beneath the great bronze Washington. Beyond the distant gates rose the church
spires of the city, suffused with the pink flush of
sunset. The atmosphere glowed like a blush upon
the perspective, which was shading through variations of violet remoteness. All was frozen save the
winter sunset and the advancing twilight.

He turned from the window and faced the painting of the Confederate soldier. For a moment he
regarded it blankly, then, pushing aside Eugenia's
chair he threw himself into one across from it. He
was thinking of Bernard Battle, and he remembered
suddenly that he must have hated him always—that
he had hated him long ago in his childhood when the
weak-faced boy had headed a school faction against
him. True, Dudley Webb had incited the attempt at
social ostracism, but he bore no resentment against
Dudley—on the contrary, he was convinced that he
liked him in spite of all—in spite, even, of Eugenia.
With the inflexible fairness that he never lost, he

knew that, with Eugenia, Dudley had not wronged
him. It had been a fight in open field, and Dudley
had won. He had even liked the vigour of his
wooing, and some years later, when they had met, he
had given the victor a hearty handshake. He distrusted him as a politician, but he liked him as a man.

And Bernard Battle. That was an honest hate,
and he hugged it to him. Before him still, so vivid
that it seemed but yesterday, hovered the memory
of that wild evening in the road, and the unforgotten
sunset faced him as he hurried through the wood.
In the acuteness of his remembered senses he could
hear the dead leaves rustle in his pathway and could
smell the vague scents of autumn drifting on the
wind. Through all the years of public life and passionate endeavour he had not lost the memory of
that bank of clouds, nor missed one breath from the
sharp mingling of autumn odours. To this day
the going down of the sun in red and gold awoke
within him the impulse of revenge, and the effluvium of rotting flowers or the tang of pines revived
the duller ache of his senseless rage.

On that evening he had buried his youth with his
youthful passion. The hours between the twilight
and the dawn had seen his emotions consumed and
his softer side laid waste. Since then he had not
played saint or martyr; he had gone his way among
women, and he had liked some good ones and some
bad ones—but the turn of Eugenia's head or the
trick of her voice had haunted him in one and all.
He had followed the resemblance and had found the
vacancy; he had been from first to last a man of one
ideal. His nature had broadened, hardened, rung

metallic to the senses; but it had not yielded to the shock of fresh emotions. He had loved one woman from her childhood up.

And again she rose before him as in that Indian summer when he knew her best—her beauty flaming against the autumn landscape, " clear as the sun, and terrible as an army with banners." He saw her red or pale, quivering or cold, always passing from him in a splendour of colours that was like the clash of music.

That was sixteen years ago and it seemed but yesterday. He had lost her, and yet he had not been unhappy, for he had learned that it is not gain that makes happiness nor loss that kills it. Life had long since taught him the lesson all great men learn—that happiness is but one result of the adjustment of the individual needs to the Eternal Laws. A man had once said of him, " Burr must think a lot of life; he bears it so blamed well. He's the happiest man I know," and Burr, overhearing him, had laughed aloud:

" Am I? I have never thought about it."

He did not think about life, he lived it; this was the beginning and the end of his success.

The face of Eugenia faded slowly into the firelight, and he rose and shook himself like a man who awakes from a nightmare. There was work for him at his desk, and he settled to it with sudden determination.

A week later the papers were still in his desk. He told himself at first that he would send them to Kingsborough to Judge Bassett and abide by his decision; but the course struck him as cowardly and he put it from him. The work was his and he would do it. Then for a week longer he went on his way and did not think of them. His days were filled with work and it was easy to leave disturbing thoughts alone; what was not easy was to consider them judicially.

At last Galt spoke of the matter, and he could not refuse to listen.

" By the way, I am hearing a good deal about that Battle pardon," Galt said. " You are looking into the matter, I suppose? "

The other shook his head.

" I have not done so as yet," he answered. " I am waiting."

" Don't wait too long or the poor devil may apply higher. He's ill, I believe, and if he insists on returning to the State, as they say he will, the law can't help but arrest him. It's a sad case. So far as I can see he was a catspaw for the real criminal and didn't have sense enough to hold on to a share of the money after he sold himself. His sister has been to see you, hasn't she? She's a superb woman, and it was a good day for Dudley Webb when he married her."

He looked up inquiringly.

" Ah, what were you saying ? " asked the governor.

That night he locked himself in with the papers and plunged into the case. He read and reread each written word until he was in possession of the minutest detail. In another instance he knew that the reasons for granting the pardon would have seemed sufficient, and he would probably have had it made out at once. As it was, he admitted the force of the appeal, but something stronger than himself held him back. Above the name before him he saw the girlish face of the man he hated—saw it accusing, defying, beseeching—and beyond it he saw the gray road and the solitary star above the sunset. In the silence his own voice echoed, "As for him—may God, in His mercy, damn him."

He locked the papers away again. "I cannot do it," he said.

Several days later he sent for a member of the legislature from the town where the crime was committed. He questioned him closely, but without result—the people up there were tired of it, the man said—at first they had been wrought up, but six years is a long time, and they didn't care much about it now. As the governor closed the interview he realised that he had hoped a bitter hope that his revenge might be justified. When the door had shut, he went back to the case again, and again he left it. "It ought to be done, but, God help me, I cannot do it," he said.

The next morning, while he was at work in his office in the Capitol, his secretary came in to tell him that Miss Christina Battle was in the anteroom. He rose hurriedly. "I will see her at once," he said, and he opened the door as Miss Chris came in, panting softly from her ascent in the elevator.

She had changed so little that he took her hand in sudden timidity, recalling the days when he had sold her chickens before her hen-house door. But when he had settled her in one of the cane rocking chairs beside the stove, his confidence returned and he responded heartily to her beneficent beam. Her florid face, shining large and luminous above the stiff black strings of her bonnet, reminded him of illustrations he had seen in which the sun is endowed with human features and an enveloping smile.

"This is the greatest honour my office has brought me," he said with sincerity.

She laughed softly, smoothing her black kid glove above her plump wrist.

"I don't know what they mean by saying you aren't a lady's man, Governor Burr," she returned. "I am sure old Judge Blitherstone himself never turned a prettier compliment, and he lived to be upwards of ninety and did them better every day of his life. They used to say that when Mrs. Peachy Tucker dropped in to see him as he was breathing his last, and told him to look forward to the joys of heaven and the communion of saints, he replied, 'Madam, if you remain with me I shall merely pass from one heaven to another,' and they were his last words."

The governor smiled into her beautiful, girlish eyes. "Men have spoken worse ones," he said, her kindliness warming him like a cordial.

"It was good of you to come," he added.

"Not a bit of it," protested Miss Chris with emphasis. "It's all about that poor, foolish boy—he's still a boy to me, and so are you for that matter. You know how wicked he has been and how miserable he has made us all, for you can't stop loving people just because they are bad. Now you are a good man, Governor Burr, and that's why I came to you. You'll do right if it kills you, and whatever

you do in this matter is going to be the right thing.
You can't help being good any more than he can
help being bad, and I hope the Lord understands
this as well as I do—I don't know, I'm sure—sometimes it looks as if He didn't; but we'd just as well
trust Him, because there's nothing else for us to do.

"Now the foolish boy wronged you more than he
wronged us; but you'll forgive him as we forgave
him, when you know what he's suffered.   It's better
to be sinned against than to sin, God knows."

Her eyes were moist and her lips trembled.   The
governor crossed to where she sat and took her
hand.

"Dear Miss Chris," he said, "women like you
make men heroes."   And he added quickly, "The
pardon is being made out.   When it is ready I will
sign it."

She looked at him an instant in silence; then she
rose heavily to her feet, leaning upon his arm.
"You're a great man, Nick Burr," she said softly.

An hour later Nicholas Burr looked calmly down
upon his signature that meant freedom for Bernard
Battle.   He had won the victory of his life, and he
was feeling with a glow of self-appreciation that he
had done a generous thing.

VIII

Miss Chris, in her hired carriage, rolled leisurely into Franklin Street, where pretty women in visiting gowns were going in and out of doorways. She leaned out and bowed smilingly several times, but she was not thinking of the gracefully dressed callers or of the houses into which they went. When Emma Carr threw her a kiss from Galt's porch, she responded amiably; but she was as blind to the affectionate gesture as to the striking beauty of the girl in her winter furs.

Up the quiet street the leafless trees made a gray vista that melted into transparent mist. The sunshine stretched in pale gold bars from sidewalk to sidewalk, and overhead the sky was of a rare Italian blue. But for the frost in the air and the naked boughs, it might have been a day in April.

Presently the carriage turned into Main Street, halting abruptly while a trolley car shot past. " Please be very careful," called Miss Chris nervously, gathering herself together as they stopped before a big gray house that faced a gray church on the opposite corner. A flight of stone steps ran from the doorway to a short tesselated entrance leading to the street, where two scraggy poplars still held aloft the withered skeletons of last year's tulips. The Webbs had taken the house because the box bushes in the yard reminded Eugenia of Battle

Hall, while Dudley declared it to be the best breathing space he could get for the money.

"We done git back, Mistis," announced the negro driver, descending from his perch, and at the same instant the door of the house flew open and Eugenia ran out, bareheaded, followed by Dudley.

"I saw you from the window, Aunt Chris," she cried, "and now I want to know the meaning of this mystery. Dudley suspects you of having a lover, but I am positive that you've stolen a march on me and have been to market. What a pity I confessed to you that I couldn't tell brains from sweetbreads."

"Let me get there, Eugie," said Dudley, as Miss Chris emerged with the assistance of the driver. "Take my arm, Aunt Chris, and I'll hoist you into the house before you know it."

"Well, I declare," remarked Miss Chris, carefully stepping forth. "I don't know when I've had such a turn. These street car drivers have lost all their manners. If we hadn't pulled up in time, I believe he would have gone right into us. And to think that a few years ago we never got ready to go to market until the car was at the door. Betty Taylor used to call to the driver every morning to wait till she put on her bonnet—and time and again I've seen him stop because she had forgotten her list of groceries. Now, if you weren't standing right on the corner, I actually believe they'd go by without you."

"That's progress, Aunt Chris," responded Dudley cheerfully.

Here the driver insisted upon lending a hand, and

between them they established Miss Chris before the fire in the sitting-room. " I wish you'd make Giles go out and pick up that loose paper that's scattered on the pavement," she said to Eugenia. " It looks so untidy. If I wasn't rheumatic I'd do it myself."

Dudley and Eugenia seated themselves across from her. " Now where have you been, Aunt Chris?" they demanded.

Miss Chris laughed softly as she took off her bonnet and gloves and gave them to Eugenia; then she unfastened her cape and passed it over.

" You'll never find out that, my dears," she returned. " I'm not too old to keep a secret. Why, I've gone and lost my bag. Didn't I carry that bag with me, Eugenia?"

" Of course you did," said Eugenia. " Never mind, I'll make you another." She went out to put away Miss Chris's wraps, and came back presently, laughing.

" Have you found out her secret, Dudley?" she asked. " If she doesn't tell you, it will die with her."

" I know better than to ask," returned Dudley good-humouredly. " That's the reason I'm her favourite. I don't ask impertinent questions, do I, Aunt Chris?"

" Bless you, no," responded Miss Chris serenely, as she stretched out her feet in their cloth shoes.

" You're her favourite because you happen to be a man," protested Eugenia. " She comes of a generation of man spoilers. I believe she thinks I ought to bring you your slippers in the evening— now don't you, Aunt Chris?"

"My dear mother always brought them to my father," replied Miss Chris placidly. "It was her pleasure to wait on him."

"And it is mine to have Dudley wait on me. But you do make an unfair difference between us, Aunt Chris. Why did you call me 'uncharitable' when I said Mrs. Gordon painted immodestly! Dudley said the same thing this morning, and you only smiled."

"It was uncharitable, my dear, and besides it is too palpable to need mention—but men will be men."

Eugenia frowned. "I wish you would occasionally remember that women will be women," she suggested. She wore a scarlet shirtwaist, and the glow from the fire seemed to follow her about.

"I won't have Aunt Chris bullied, Eugie," declared Dudley as he rose. "Well, I'm off again. I may bring a legislator or two back to dinner. What have we got?"

"The Lord knows," replied Eugenia desperately. "Our third cook this month for one thing, and Congo refuses to serve dinner in courses. He says 'dar's too much shufflin' er de dishes for too little victuals.'"

Dudley laughed at her mimicry.

"Oh, I suppose we'll do," he said. "By the way, don't forget to call on Mrs. Rann to-day."

Miss Chris was gazing placidly into the fire. As Dudley turned with his hand on the door knob, she looked up.

"I was surprised to find the Capitol so dirty," she observed regretfully.

24

Dudley swung round breathlessly.

"Well, I am—blessed!" he gasped.

"So that's where you've been!" cried Eugenia. She threw herself beside Miss Chris's chair. "What did he say, Aunt Chris?" she implored.

Miss Chris blushed with confusion.

"Well, if I haven't let it out!" she exclaimed. "Who'd have thought I couldn't keep a secret at my age." Then she patted Eugenia's hand. "He's a good man," she said softly, "and it's all right about Bernard."

"I knew it would be," said Dudley quickly. "You know, Eugie, I always told you he'd do it."

But Eugenia had turned away with swimming eyes. "I must tell Lottie," she said hurriedly. "Oh, Aunt Chris, how could you keep it? To think the children are at school!"

Dudley, with an afterthought, turned from the door and gave her an affectionate pat on the shoulder. "It's fine news, old girl," he said cheerfully, and Eugenia smiled at him through her tears.

As he went out she followed him into the hall and slowly ascended the stairs. On the landing above she entered a room where Bernard's wife was lying on a wicker couch, cutting the pages of a magazine.

"Lottie, I've good news for you," she exclaimed, "the best of news."

Lottie tossed aside the magazine and raised herself on her elbow. She had a pretty, ineffectual face and a girlish figure, and, despite her faded colouring, looked almost helplessly young. Her round white hands were as weak as a child's.

"I'm sure I don't know what it can be," she returned. "You look awfully well in that red waist, Eugie. I think I'll get one like it."

Eugenia picked up a child's story book from the rug and laid it on the table; then she stood looking gravely down on the younger woman.

"Can't you guess what it is?" she asked.

Lottie looked up with a nervous blinking of her eyes. She had paled slightly and she leaned over and drew an eiderdown quilt across her knees.

"It—it's not about Bernard?" she asked in a whisper.

"Yes, it is about Bernard. You may go to him and bring him home. You may go to-morrow. Oh, Lottie, doesn't it make you happy?"

Lottie drew the eiderdown quilt still higher. She was not looking at Eugenia, and her mouth had grown sullen. "I don't see why you send me," she said. "Why can't Jack Tucker bring him home? He's with him."

"But I thought you wanted to go," returned Eugenia blankly.

"I haven't seen him for six years," said Lottie, her face still turned away. "He is almost a stranger—and I am afraid of him."

"Oh, Lottie, he loves you so!"

"I don't know," protested Lottie. "He has been so wicked."

Eugenia was looking down upon her with dismayed eyes.

"Don't you love him, Lottie?" she asked.

For a moment the other did not reply. Her lips trembled and her knees were shaking beneath the eiderdown quilt. Then with a slow turn of the head she looked up doggedly. " I believe I hate him," she answered.

A swift flush rose to Eugenia's face, her eyes flashed angrily, she took a step forward. " And you are his wife!" she cried.

But Lottie had turned at last. She flung the quilt aside and rose to her feet, her girlish figure quivering in its beribboned wrapper. There were bright pink spots in her cheeks.

" Yes, I am his wife, God help me," she said.

Eugenia had drawn back before the childish desperation. Lottie had never revolted before— she had thought Eugenia's thoughts and weakly lived up to Eugenia's conception of her duty. She had been meek and amiable and ineffectual; but it came to Eugenia with a shock that she had never admired her until to-day—until the hour of her rebellion.

She spoke sternly—as she might have spoken to herself in a moment of dear, but dismal failure.

" Hush," she commanded. " You are one of us, and you have no right to desert us. It is because you are his wife that my home is yours and your children's. I am only his sister, and I have stood by him through it all. Do you think, if his sins were twenty times as great, that I should fall away from him now?"

Lottie looked at her and laughed—a little heartless laugh.

" Oh, but I am not a Battle," she replied bitterly. " Battle sins are just like other people's sins to me."

Then she raised her pretty, nerveless hands to her throat.

"I have wanted to be free all these years," she said. "All these years when you would not let me forget Bernard Battle—when you shut me up and hid me away, and made me old when I was young. And now—just as I am beginning to be happy with my children—you tell me that I must go back to him and start afresh."

Her voice grated upon Eugenia's ears, and she realised more acutely than her pity the fact that Lottie was common—hopelessly common. For an instant she forgot Bernard's greater transgressions in the wonder that a Battle should have married a woman who did not know how to behave in a crisis—who could even chant her wrongs from the housetop. At the moment this seemed to her the weightier share of the family remissness. The loyalty of the Battle wives had been as a lasting memorial to the Battle breeding—which, after all, was more invincible than the Battle virtue.

She crossed to the window and stood looking out upon the winter sunshine falling on the gray church across the way. On the stone steps a negro nurse was sitting, drowsily trundling back and forth before her a beruffled baby carriage. Nearer at hand, in the yard on the left of the tesselated entrance below, a pointed magnolia tree shone evergreen beside the naked poplars, and a bevy of sparrows fluttered in and out amid the sheltering leaves.

"Oh, you will never understand," wailed Lottie. She had flung herself upon the couch and was sobbing weakly. "It is so different with you and Dudley."

Eugenia turned and came back. "I do understand," she returned gently, and before Lottie could raise her lowered head she left the room.

She had promised Dudley that the calls should be made, and she put on her visiting gown without a thought of shirking the fulfilment of her pledge. From the day of her marriage she had zealously accepted the obligations forced upon her by Dudley's political aspirations, and Mrs. Rann became to-day simply a heavier responsibility than usual. Her world was full of Mrs. Ranns, and she braved them with dauntless spirits and triumphant humour. As she buttoned her gloves on the way downstairs she was conscious of a singularly mild recognition of the fact that the world might have been the gainer had Mrs. Rann abided unborn.

But the fresh air restored her courage, and by the time she sat in Mrs. Rann's drawing-room, face to face with her hostess, she was at ease with herself and her surroundings. She gave out at once the peculiar social atmosphere of her race; she uttered her gay little nothings with an intimate air; she laughed good-humouredly at Mrs. Rann's gossip, and she begged to see photographs of Mrs. Rann's babies. It was as if she had immediately become the confidential adviser of Mrs. Rann's domestic difficulties.

Mrs. Rann, herself, was little and plain and obsolete. She appeared to have been left behind in the sixties, like words that have become vulgar from disuse. She wore bracelets on her wrists, and her accent was as flat as her ideas. Before the war —and even long after—nobody had heard of the Ranns; they had arrived as suddenly as the electric lights or the trolley cars. When Miss Chris had alluded to them as " new people," and Juliet Galt had declared that she " did not call there," Dudley had thrown out an uncertain line to Eugenia. " Rann is a useful man, my dear," he had said. " He may be of great help to me," and the next day Eugenia had left her card. Where Dudley's ambitions led she cheerfully followed.

" We are politicians," was her excuse to Juliet, " and we can't afford to be exclusive. Of course, with Emma Carr and yourself it is different. You may exclude half society if you please, and, in fact, you do; but Dudley and I really don't mind. He wants something, and I, you know, was born without the instinct of class."

So she sat in Mrs. Rann's drawing-room and received her confidences, while Juliet and Emma Carr were gossiping across the street.

" The greatest trouble I have with Mr. Rann when he comes to town," said Mrs. Rann, " is that he refuses to wear woollen socks. I don't know whether Mr. Webb wears woollen socks or not."

Eugenia shook her head.

" I've no doubt he would be a better and a wiser man if he did," she responded.

" Then he doesn't catch cold when he puts on thin ones with his dress suit. Now Mr. Rann says woollen socks don't look well in the evening—and he takes cold every time he goes out at night. He won't even let me put red flannel in the soles of his shoes."

" Then he's not the man I thought him," said Eugenia as she rose. " Do you know, the baby is so pretty I stopped her carriage. If she were mine I shouldn't let her grow up."

Mrs. Rann glowed with pride, and in the depths of her shallow eyes Eugenia read a triumphant compassion. This little vulgar countrywoman, upon whom she looked so grandly down, was pitying her in her narrow heart.

She flushed and turned away.

" You have never had a child? " asked the little common voice.

Eugenia faced her coldly. " I lost one—a week old," she replied, and she hated herself that she was proud of her seven days' motherhood. She had mourned the loss, but she had never vaunted the possession until now.

As she left the house her name was called by Juliet Galt from her window across the way. " Come over, Eugie," she cried. " We've been watching you," and as Eugenia ascended the steps the door was opened and she was clasped in Emma Carr's arms. " We've shut our eyes and ground our teeth and put ourselves in your place," she said. " Oh, Eugie, she's worse than the dentist! "

" I went to the dentist's first," was Eugenia's reply.

She followed Miss Carr into the drawing-room and sank into the window-seat beside Juliet, who was bending over her embroidery frame. Then she laughed—a full, frank laugh.

" You dear women," she said, " if you knew the lot of a politician's wife, you'd—marry a footman."

" Provided he were Dudley Webb," returned Emma Carr. She seized Eugenia's hand and they

smiled at each other in demonstrative intimacy.
" You know, of course, that we are all in love with
your husband—desperately, darkly in love—and
you ought to be gray with jealousy. If I were
married to the handsomest man in Virginia I'd get
me to a nunnery."

" That's not Eugie's way," said Juliet, snapping
off her silk. " If she went, she'd drag him after."

" Oh, he's just Dudley," protested Eugenia.
" I'd as soon be jealous of Aunt Chris—and he's
waiting at home this instant with his senators come
to judgment on my dinner. If I were free, I'd spend
the day with you, Juliet, but I've married into
servitude."

IX

When Eugenia went upstairs that night she softly opened Lottie's door and glanced into the room. By the sinking firelight she saw Lottie lying asleep, her hand upon the pillow of her younger child, who slept beside her. The pretty, nerveless hand, even in sleep, tremored like a caress, for whatever Lottie's wifely failings, as a mother she was without reproach. Lottie—vain, hysterical, bewailing her wrongs—was the same Lottie now resting with a protecting arm thrown out—this Eugenia admitted thoughtfully as she looked into the darkened room where the thin blue flame cast a spectral light upon the sleepers. From this shallow rooted nature had bloomed the maternal ardour of the Southern woman, in whom motherhood is the abiding grace.

Eugenia closed the door and crossed the hall to Miss Chris, who was reading her Bible as she seeded raisins into a small yellow bowl. The leaves of the Bible were held open by her spectacle case which she had placed between them; for while her hands were busy with material matters her placid eyes followed the text.

"I thought I'd get these done to-night," she remarked as Eugenia entered. "I'm going to make a plum pudding for Dudley to-morrow. Where is he now?"

"A political barbecue, I believe," responded Eugenia indifferently as she knotted the cord of her flannel dressing-gown. She yawned and threw herself into a chair. "I wonder why everybody spoils Dudley so," she added. "Even I do it. I am sitting up for him to-night simply because I know he'll want to tell me about it all when he comes in."

"It's a good habit for a wife to cultivate," returned Miss Chris, shaking the raisins together. "If my poor father stayed out until four o'clock in the morning he found my mother up and dressed when he came in."

"I should say it was 'poor' grandmamma," commented Eugenia drily. "But Dudley won't find me after midnight." Then she regarded Miss Chris affectionately. "What a blessing that you didn't marry, Aunt Chris," she said. "You'd have prepared some man to merit damnation."

"My dear Eugie," protested Miss Chris, half shocked, half flattered at the picture. "But you're a good wife, all the same, like your mother before you. The only fault I ever saw in poor Meely was that she wouldn't put currants in her fruit cake. Tom was always fond of currants——" in a moment she abruptly recalled herself. "My dear, I don't say you haven't had your trials," she went on. "Dudley isn't a saint, but I don't believe even the Lord expects a man to be that. It doesn't seem to set well on them."

"Oh, I am not blaming Dudley," returned Eugenia as leniently as Miss Chris. "We live and let live—only our tastes are different. Why, the chief proof of his affection for me is that he always describes to me the object of his admiration—which means that his eyes stray, but his heart does not, and the heart's the chief thing, after all."

"I'm glad you aren't jealous," said Miss Chris. "I used to think you were—as a child."

"Oh, I was—as a child," replied Eugenia. Her kindly face clouded. It was borne in upon her with a twinge of conscience that the absence of jealousy which had become the safeguard of Dudley's peace proved her own lack of passion. What a hell some women—good women—might have made of Dudley's life—that genial life that flowed as smoothly as a song. In the flights and pauses of his temperament what discord might have shocked the decent measure of their marriage? Persistent passion would have bored him; exacting love would have soured the charm of his radiant egotism. It was because she was not in love with him, that her love had wisely meted out to him only so much or so little of herself as he desired—and with a sudden arraignment of Fate she admitted that because she had failed in the first requirement of the marriage sacrament, she had made that sacrament other than a mockery. Out of her own unfulfilment Dudley's happiness was fulfilled.

"Yes, Dudley suits me," she said absently, "and, what's the main thing, I suit Dudley."

"Well, well, I'm glad of it," returned Miss Chris, but in a moment Eugenia was kneeling beside her, her hand upon the open Bible.

"Dear Aunt Chris, you haven't told me all," she said.

"All?" Miss Chris wavered. "You mean about Bernard?"

" I mean about the governor." She closed the
Bible and pushed it from her. " Do you think he
is quite, quite happy ? "

Miss Chris laughed in protest.

" Do I believe him to be pining of hopeless love?
No, I don't," she retorted.

" Oh, not that ! " exclaimed Eugenia impatiently.
She appeared vaguely to resent Miss Chris's assurance. She was feminine enough to experience an
irrational jealousy at the idea of a vacancy which
she had done her best to create. It destroyed an
example of the permanence of love.

" I don't suppose anybody could be happy on
politics," observed Miss Chris. " It doesn't seem
natural." And she slowly added : " I wish some
good woman would marry him."

" I don't ! " said Eugenia sharply. She rose with
a spring from the rug, and left Miss Chris to her
reflections and her raisins. In her own room she
sat down before the fire and loosened her hair from
the low coil on her neck. She drew out the hairpins one by one, until her hands were full, and the
thick black rope fell across her bosom. Then she
tossed the pins upon her bureau and shook a veil
over her face and shoulders. As she settled herself
into her chair she glanced impatiently at the clock.
Dudley was late, and she listened for his footsteps
with the composure of a woman from whom the
flush of marriage has passed away. His footsteps
were as much a part of her days as the ticking of the
clock upon the mantel. If the clock were to stop
she would miss the accustomed sound, but so long
as it went on she was almost unconscious of its pres-

ence.   Her affection for Dudley had grown so into
her nature that it was like the claim of kinship—
quiet, unimpassioned, full of service—the love that
is the end of many happy marriages, the beginning
of few.

As she sat there she fell vaguely to wondering
what her lot would have been had her pulses fluttered to his footsteps as they came and went.   She
would have known remorseless waitings and the
long agony of jealous nights—all the passionate self-
torture that she had missed—that she had missed,
thank God!   She made the best of her life to-day,
as she would have made the best of blows and
bruises.   It was the old buoyant instinct of the Battle blood—the fighting of Fate on its ground with
its own weapons.   She had insisted strenuously
upon her own happiness—and she had found it not
in the great things of life, but in the little ones.   She
was happy because happiness is ours in the cradle
or not at all—because it is of the blood and not of
the environment.

During the first years of her marriage she had
intensely sought the relief of outside interests.   She
had worked zealously on hospital boards and had
exhausted herself in the service of the city mission.
Then a new call had quivered in her life, and she had
let these things go.   With the passion of her nature
she had pledged herself to motherhood, and that, too,
had foiled her—for the child had died.   Looking
back upon the years she saw that those months of
tranquil waiting were the happiest of her life—those
monotonous months when each day was as the day
before it, when her hands were busy for the love that

would come to her, and her heart warmed itself before the future. The child was hers for a single week, and afterwards she had put her grief away and gone back to the old beginning. She had given herself to little kindnesses and trivial interests, for the fulfilment of her nature had withered in the bud.

The key turned in the door downstairs and in a moment she heard Dudley in the hall. As her door opened she looked up brightly. " Up, old girl? " he asked cheerfully, and as he came to the fire he bent to kiss her.

" Did you make a speech? and what did you say? " she inquired.

" Oh, they got a good deal out of me," he responded with a genial recollection which he proceeded to unfold. His eyes shone and his face was flushed. As he stood on the hearth rug before her she admitted with a sigh of satisfaction his physical splendour. The glow of his personality warmed her into an emotion half maternal. She regarded him with the eyes of tolerant affection.

" Oh, yes, I think I made a friend of Diggs," he was adding complacently as he flecked a particle of cigar ash from his coat. " He got off a capital story, by the way. I'd give it to you, but I'm half afraid —you're so squeamish."

" His jokes don't amuse me," returned Eugenia indifferently. " Who else was there? "

" Well, the governor was very much there. He did some stiff talking. I say, Eugie, do you know, I believe he used to have a pretty strong fancy for you—didn't he? "

Eugenia looked at him with a laugh. "Oh, a fancy?" she repeated.

She moved away, gathering her hair from her shoulders; but in a moment she came back again and rubbed her cheek against Dudley's arm as she used to rub it against General Battle's old linen sleeve. "Dudley," she said with a sudden break, "the baby would have been ten years old to-night— do you remember?"

Dudley was looking into the fire; his face grew grave, and he patted Eugenia's head. "You don't say so! Poor little chap!" he exclaimed.

They were both silent. Dudley's eyes were still on the flame, but the shadow lifted from his brow. Eugenia's lips quivered and grew firm. She gently drew herself away and began braiding her hair, but her hands were unsteady.

In a moment Dudley spoke again. "It was a great pity I lost that governorship," he said abstractedly.

A week after this Eugenia went with Juliet Galt to the Capitol to hear a speech in which Dudley was interested. The Senate Chamber was crowded, and as the atmosphere grew oppressive while Dudley's gentleman held the floor, she rose and went out into the lobby where a noisy circle pulsed round Houdon's Washington. She had spoken to several acquaintances, and her hand was in the clasp of a house member from her old county, when she started at the sound of a shrill voice rising above the persistent hum of the legislators and the lobbyists.

"I'm a-lookin' for the governor, Nick Burr," it said.

" I didn't know the governor posed as a cavalier," laughed the house member, and as a wave of humour lighted the faces around her, Eugenia turned to find Marthy Burr standing in the doorway. She wore a stiff alpaca dress, and beneath the green veil above her bonnet she cast alert, nervous glances from side to side. Her hands clutched, in a death-like grip, a cotton umbrella and a small, covered basket.

Eugenia hesitated for a single instant, and then took a step forward with outstretched hand, a kindly glow in her face; but as she did so the crowd parted and Nicholas Burr reached his stepmother's side.

" Why, this is a treat, ma!" he said heartily, and he took the umbrella and the basket from her reluctant hands, despite her warning whisper, " thar's new-laid eggs in thar!"

" My dear Mrs. Burr!" exclaimed Eugenia. She lifted her gaze from the homely figure in its awkward finery, to the man who stood beside her. Then she stooped and kissed Marthy Burr on the cheek.

" Do let her come home with me," she said.

Her eyes fell and a wave of colour beat into her face. An instant before she had felt her act to be entirely admirable; now it flamed before her in a mental revelation that she was a sycophant who sought the reward of an assumed virtue. With the reward had come the knowledge—she had found both in Nicholas's eyes; and as she felt the thrust of self-abasement, she felt also that for the sake of that look she would have kissed a dozen Burrs a dozen times.

25

"You are very kind," said the governor. "But you know I have an empty house."

Then he put his arm about Marthy Burr and assisted her down the steps to the walk below. She looked about her with half-frightened, half-defiant eyes, and clung grimly to his powerful figure.

As Eugenia watched them, a quick remembrance shot before her. She saw Nicholas Burr as she had seen him in his youth—ardent, assured, holding out his arms to the future, which was to be love, love, love. Now the future had become the present, and the one affection that remained to him was that of the old, illiterate woman, with the rasping voice. He had lost the thing he had lived for—and he was happy.

BOOK V

THE HOUR AND THE MAN

BOOK V

THE HOUR AND THE MAN

I

On one of the closing days of the legislative session, Ben Galt lounged into the anteroom of the governor's office and cornered the private secretary. "Look here, Dickson, what's the latest demonstration of Old Nickism? I hear he's giving Rann trouble about that bill of his."

Dickson nodded significantly towards the closed door. "Rann's with him now," he replied; "they're having it hot in there. Rann may bluster till he's blue, but he won't make the governor give an inch. That bill's as dead as a door nail. The governor's got a fit of duty on."

"Or his everlasting obstinacy," returned Galt irritably. "His duty does more harm than most men's devilment—it stands like a stone wall between him and his ambition. Of course, that bill is a political swindle, but there isn't another politician in the State who would interfere in Rann's little game."

"Oh, between us, I think Rann's honest enough. He believes he's up to a good thing, but the governor disagrees with him—there's where the row begins."

" What does the governor say about it? "

" Say? " laughed Dickson.   " Why, I asked him
if he would approve the measure and he said ' No! '
That's the beginning and the end of his discourse
—a ' No ' long drawn out."

The door opened abruptly, and Rann put out his
head.   " Will you step in here, Mr. Galt? " he asked,
and his voice was husky with anger.   " With pleasure, my dear Major," responded Galt easily, as he
crossed the threshold and closed the door after him.
" I am always at your service as a peacemaker."

The governor was standing before his desk, his
eyes upon Rann, who faced him, red and trembling.
Galt had seen Burr wear this impassive front before,
and it had always meant trouble.   His eyes were
opaque and leaden, his face as expressionless as a
mask.   He was motionless save for the movement
of one hand that drummed upon the desk.   " If you
possess any influence with the governor," said Rann
to Galt, " will you tell him that his course is ruinous
—ruinous to imbecility?   If he thinks I am going
to throw away a winter's work on that bill he's mistaken his man.   It's taken me the whole session to
get that measure through the legislature, and I'm
not going to have it defeated now by any crack-
brained moralist.   He'll sign that bill or——"

Burr spoke at last.   " Am I the governor of this
State or are you? " he thundered.   His face did not
change, but his powerful voice rang to the full.

Rann gave an ugly little sneer, his cheek purpling.
" I may not be governor, but I made you so," he
retorted.

" Your mistake, my dear Major, was that you

neglected to create him in your own likeness," put in Galt coolly.

"By the people's will I am governor, and governor I'll be," said Nicholas grimly; "as for this bill you speak of, I might have saved you the trouble of working for your pitiable majority. Since you have seen fit to deride my motive, it is sufficient for me to say that the measure will not become a law over my opposition, and I shall oppose it to the death."

Rann was shaking on his short legs and his hands were trembling. "So you defy me, do you, Governor?" he demanded.

"Defy you?" the governor laughed shortly, "I don't trouble to defy you. I laugh at you—the whole lot of you who come to cozen me with party promises. So long as I spoke your speech and did your bidding I might have the senatorship for the asking. I was honest Nick Burr, though I might belie my convictions at every step. So long as I wore the collar of your machine upon my neck my honesty was the hall-mark of the party. Where is my honesty, the first instant that I dare to stand against you? Defy you? Pshaw! You aren't worth defying!"

"Hold on!" said Galt hastily. "Nick, for God's sake, leave our friend alone. You're both good fellows—too good to quarrel——"

"Oh, there's no use," protested Rann, wiping his flaming brow. "I've offered a dozen compromises —but compromise I won't without that bill. Bear witness that I've upheld him from the start. I'd have run him for the presidency itself if I'd had the power, and when I ask a little friendly return he talks about his damned duty. But I tell you, he's signed his own warrant. He's as dead in this State as if his grave was dug. He's held his last office in the Democratic Party."

" I shall certainly not owe my second to you," responded the governor; then he looked vacantly before him. " I have the pleasure to wish you good morning," he said.

When Rann had gone, and the door had slammed after him, Galt turned, with a laugh.

" Shake! " he exclaimed, and as Nicholas grasped his hand, added lightly, " My dear friend, you may as well have a quiet conscience, since you'll never have the senatorship."

Nicholas drew his hand away impatiently. " I'm not beaten yet," he said. " I'll fight and I'll win, or my name's not Burr! Do you think I'm afraid of a sneak like that? Why, he offered me the senatorship as coolly as if he had it in his pocket! "

Galt laughed. " I'm not sure he hasn't; at any rate he's the power of the ring, and the ring's the power of the party."

" Then I'll fight the ring," said Nicholas, " and, if need be, I'll fight the party. So long as right and the people are with me the party may go hang."

" My dear old Nick, history teaches us that the party hangs the people. By the way, you've done Webb a good turn; Rann is going to fight you fair and foul—mostly foul."

" Oh, I'm not afraid of Rann, or of Webb."

" Or yet of the devil! " added Galt. " When I come to think of it, I never called you timid. But wait a few days and Rann will have this little passage reported to his credit. I'll get ahead of him with the story, or I'll find some cocked-up account of it circulating in the lobby. It's easier to blacken the best man than to whiten the worst. Well, I'm going. Good day!"

When the door closed, the governor crossed to the window and stood looking down upon the gray drive beneath the leafless trees. The sun was obscured by a sinister cloud that had blotted out all the fugitive brightness of the morning. A fine moisture was in the air, and the atmosphere hung heavily down the naked slopes, where the grass was colourless and dead. Beyond the gates, the city was lost in a blurred and melancholy distance, from which several indistinct church spires rose and sank in a sea of fog.

But blue and gray were as one to Nicholas. He was not exhilarated by sunshine nor was he depressed by gloom; only the inner forces of his nature had power to quicken or control his moods. His inspiration, like his destiny, lay within, and so long as he maintained his wonted equilibrium of judgment and desire it was, perhaps, impossible that an outside assault should severely shake the foundations of his life.

Now, while the glow of his anger still lingered in his brain, it was characteristic of the man that he was feeling a pity for Rann's disappointment—for the discomfiture of one whose methods he despised. In Rann's place, he felt that he should probably have risen to the charge as Rann rose—implacable, unswerving; but he was not in Rann's place, nor

could he be so long as personal reward was less to
him than personal honour. Yes, he could pity Rann
even while he condemned him. For an instant—a
single instant—he had found himself shrinking from
the combat, and in the shock of self-contempt which
followed he had hurled the shock of his resentment
upon the tempter. In that moment of weakness it
had seemed to him an easy thing to let one's self go;
to yield to a friendly, if distrusted force; to place
gratified ambition above the sting of wounded
scruples. Was he infallible that he should make
his judgment a law, or without reproach that he
should set his conscience as an arbiter?

Then in a sudden illumination he had seen the
betrayal of his sophistry, and he had stood his
ground—for the strong man is not he who is im-
pervious to weaknesses, but he who, scorning his
failures, towers over them. He had felt the temptation and he had wavered, but not for long. In all
his periods of storm and stress he had found that
his nature rebounded in the end. Disquietude
might waste his ardour; but give him time to reor-
ganise his forces, and his moral energy would triumph at the last.

As he looked out upon the great bronze Washington against the sad-coloured sky, he realised, with
a pang like the thrust of homesickness, the isolation
in which he stood. An instinctive need to justify
himself had risen within him, and with it awoke the
knowledge that beyond that uncertain abstraction
which he called "the People," he was an alien
among his kind. Galt was his friend, Tom Bassett
he could count on, a score of others would stand or

fall in his service, but where was the single emotion which bound him to humanity? Where the common claim of kinship which belonged to Galt, to Bassett, and to all mankind? He had known many men, but he knew not one who was not drawn by some connecting link that was apart from patriotism, or ambition, or desire. Then quickly there came to him, not the judge, who was the parent of his intellect, but the withered little woman, who was not even the mother of his body. The only happiness that rose and set in him was that pitiable happiness that could not think his thoughts or speak his speech. It had never occurred to him that he loved Marthy Burr—his kindness had been wholly compassionate—it was the knowledge that she loved him that now illuminated her image. It was the old blind craving born again, to be first with somebody—for there are moods in which it is better to be adored by a dog than to adore a divinity. He beheld Eugenia's womanhood as "A sword afar off"; but with him was the eternal commonplace—his stepmother's sharp, pained eyes and shrivelled hands. He had loved Eugenia until there was nothing left; now he wanted to be loved, if by a dog.

He raised his head and smiled upon the bronze Washington and the sad-coloured sky. In the drive below men were passing, and from time to time he recognised a figure. He saw only men down there, and the thought came to him that his was a man's world—only in the outside circle might he catch the flutter of a woman's dress. He turned and went back to his desk and his work.

Two days later the papers chronicled without

comment his opposition to Rann's bill. He was aware that Rann possessed no uncertain influence with the editors of the " Morning Standard," and he was surprised at the apparent indifference displayed by the curt announcement. Did Rann's resentment hang fire? Or was the press prepared to uphold the governor?

On the morning of the same day a member of the legislature with whom he was slightly acquainted came in to congratulate him upon his stand. His name was Saunders, and he was a man of some ability, whom Nicholas had always regarded as a partisan of Webb.

" I've been fighting that bill this whole session," he said emphatically, " and I'd given up all hope of defeating it when you had the pluck to knock it over. You've made enemies, Governor, but you've made friends, and I'm one of them. Give me the man who dares!" He held out his hand as he rose, and Nicholas responded with a hearty grip. Before the legislature closed he found that Saunders spoke the truth—he had made friends as well as enemies. The inborn Anglo-Saxon love of " the man who dares " was with him—a regard for daring for its own heroic sake. The hour was his, and he braved his shifting popularity as he would brave its final outcome.

II

One afternoon in early May, Dudley Webb came out upon his front steps and paused to light a cigar before descending to the street. A spring of happy promise was unfolding, for overhead the poplars bloomed against an enchanted sky. In the shadow of the church across the way, children were romping, their ecstatic trebles floating like bird-song on the air.

With the cigar between his teeth, Dudley heaved a sudden reminiscent sigh—the sigh of a man who possesses an excellent digestion and a complacent conscience. Things had gone well with him of late —the fact that a trivial domestic interest darkened for the moment his serene horizon proved it to be the solitary cloud of a clear day. The cloud in question had gathered in the shape of no less a person than Mrs. Jane Dudley Webb. She had been on a visit to Richmond, and he had seen her only two hours before safely started on her homeward journey. The truth was that Mrs. Webb and Eugenia had asserted for the past two days an implacable hostility, and Dudley's genial efforts at pacification had resulted merely in diverting a share of the unpleasantness upon his own head. It was a lamentable fact that Eugenia, who was amiable to the point of weakness where members of the Battle family were concerned, found it impossible to harmonise with the elder Mrs. Webb. They had disagreed upon such important subjects as Miss Chris's house-keeping and Dudley's moral welfare, until Eugenia, after an inglorious defeat, had relapsed into silence —a silence broken only upon Dudley's return from the station, when she had unbosomed herself of the declaration that she "couldn't stand his mother, and it was as much as she could do to stand him." Dudley had met this alarming outburst with its logical retort, "Hadn't you better see a doctor, Eugie?" whereupon Eugenia had protested that "if she wasn't fit for an asylum, he needn't thank Mrs. Webb," and had dissolved in tears.

At the moment Dudley had experienced a warm recognition of his generosity in refraining from the use of his own endurance of many Battles, as an illustration of the opposite and virtuous course; but upon later reflection he frankly admitted that the cases were by no means similar. It had not occurred to him, he recalled, to deny that Mrs. Webb was singularly trying, though he wondered, half resent-fully, why Eugenia could not be brought to regard that lady's foibles from his own gently humorous point of view. He was not in the least disconcerted by his mother's solicitude as to the condition of his soul, or by the fact that she still felt constrained to allude to the governor of the State as "a person of low antecedents." Personally, he was inclined to admire—and frankly to admit it—the ability which had brought Burr into prominence from a position of evident obscurity, while he regarded Mrs. Webb's eccentric attitude as a kind of antedated comedy. What he objected to was his wife's inability to grasp the keynote of the situation.

It was pleasant to reflect, however, as he leisurely descended the steps, that he had brought Eugenia round by less heroic measures than an assault upon her family altars. He was glad to think that he had given her a cup of tea instead.

Crossing slowly to Franklin Street, he hesitated an instant on the corner, and turned finally in the direction of his office. There was a nearer way down town, but he always chose this one because experience had taught him that if pretty women were abroad here they would be found. With the same instinct of enjoyment he might have gone out of his way daily to pass the window of a florist.

As he walked on in the spring sunshine he held his handsome head erect, blowing the smoke of his cigar in the scented air. He moved leisurely, finding life too good to be wasted in rushing. The soft atmosphere ; the fragrance of his fine cigar ; the beauty of the women he passed—these sufficed to bring the glow of animation to his smooth, full face.

Once he stopped to shake hands with pretty Emma Carr, detaining her by a jest and a laugh— and again he paused to exchange a word with Juliet Galt, who was at her window. It was only when he turned into the business street again that he brought his mind to bear upon less engaging subjects.

Then it was that he remembered he had delivered the evening before his most successful oration. He had spoken to a large audience upon " Personal Morality in Politics," and he had received an appreciation that was prolonged and thundering. When it was over some one had called him a " greater orator than Withers," to add quickly, " and a better

Democrat than Burr." He could still see the whimsical smile Burr had turned upon the speaker, and he could still feel his own sense of elation.

Well, as for that matter, he was a better Democrat than Burr—if to be a better Democrat meant to place the party will above his personal opinion. After all, what was a party for if not to unite individual effort and to combine individual differences? If organisation was not worth the sacrifice of personal prejudices it might as well dissolve before the next election day. It was, of course, a pity that a man like Burr should dissent from the views of important politicians, but one might as well talk of a ship without officers as of a party without organised leaders. It was a pity from Burr's point of view, he was willing to admit, but so long as Burr would make trouble it was just as well that the ill wind should blow his own side good—he was honestly glad that it had blown Rann's influence in his direction. He had never felt more hopeful of anything in his life than he now felt of the senatorship. Indeed, he was inclined to think that he might have something very like a " walk over."

" Hold on, Webb," a voice called behind him, and a moment later he was joined by Diggs, who congratulated him upon his speech of the evening before. Webb tossed back the congratulations with a laugh. " Yes, it's a popular subject just now," he said. " Since the negroes have stopped voting in large numbers we're even going in for honest elections."

" Well, I reckon it's as well," admitted Diggs. " We used to have some rampant rascality under

the old system, I dare say; it took clever trickery to
bring in the white rule sometimes. We have a large
negro majority down my way, that obliged us to
devise original methods of disposing of it. It was
fighting the devil with fire, I suppose; but self-pres-
ervation was a law long before Universal Suffrage
was heard of. At any rate, I had my hand in it now
and then. Once, I remember, on an election day
when every darkey in the neighbourhood had turned
out to vote, I hit on the idea that the man who was
to carry the returns across the river should pretend
to get drunk and upset the boat. It was a pretty
scheme and would have worked all right, but, will
you believe it, the blamed fool got drunk in earnest,
and when the boat upset he was caught under it and
drowned." He paused an instant and complacently
added: " But we lost those returns, all the same."

Webb threw his cigar stump in the gutter and
turned to Diggs with a laugh. " That reminds me,"
he began, and started a story which he finished on
his office steps.

When he went home some hours later he found
that Eugenia had regained her high good-humour.
She was sitting before the fire in her bedroom, her
hair flowing in the hands of Delphy, who had moved
up from Kingsborough, and was doing a thriving
trade as a shampooer. It was her fortnightly custom to pass from head to head in a round of the
Kingsborough colony, promoting an intimate trend
of gossip among her patrons.

As Dudley entered, she was seeking to induce
Eugenia to consent to an application from one of
the many bottles she carried in an ancient travelling

bag, which had long since descended to her from General Battle.

" Lawd, Miss Euginny, dis yer ain' gwineter hu't you.   Hit ain' nuttin but ker'sene oil nohow.   Miss Sally Burwell des let me souse her haid in it de udder day.   Hit'll keep you f'om gittin' gray, sho's I live."

" You shan't touch me with it, Delphy.   And you ought to be ashamed—I haven't a gray hair.   Have I, Dudley?"

Delphy returned the bottle with a sigh, and applied herself to a vigorous brushing of Eugenia's hair.

" You sho is filled out sence I see you, Marse Dudley," she observed at last.

" Yes, I'm getting fat, Delphy," returned Dudley with a laugh.   " It's old age, you know.   It's a long time since the days when you spanked me with a heavy hand."

" Go 'way f'om yer, Marse Dudley ; you know I ain' never spank you none ter hu't.   En you ain' er bit too fat ter fit yo' skin, nohow."

Dudley regarded her with a kindly, patriarchal eye as he straightened himself against the mantel. " Any news from down your way, Delphy?" he inquired with interest.   " What's become of Moses? Moses was always a friend of mine.   He used to bring me a pocketful of peanuts from every picking he went to."

Delphy shook her head, her huge lips tightening. " He's down wid de purple headache," she replied gloomily, " twel he can't smell de diff'ence between er 'possum en er polecat.   Yes, suh, Mose he's moughty low down, en' ter dis yer day he ain' never

got over Marse Nick Burr's ous'in' you en Miss
Euginny outer de cheer you all oughter had down
yonder at de cap'tol. I ain' got much use fer Marse
Nick myse'f. He's monst'ous hard on po' folks. I
ain' been able to rent out mo'n oner my rooms sence
he's been down dar. Dat's right, Miss Euginny,
yo' hyar's des es dry es I kin git it."

When Delphy had gone, Dudley leaned down
and put his arm about Eugenia as he kissed her.
" All right, Eugie? " he asked cheerfully. Eugenia
returned his caress with a startled pleasure, looking
up at him affectionately, fascinated by the glow
which hung about him.

" Oh, I really don't think I could do without you,
Dudley," she said quickly.

" Well, it's a good thing you don't have to," responded Dudley as he kissed her again.

It was several days after this that Eugenia came to
him one evening as he stood before the fire and
laid her cool cheek against his arm.

" Oh, Dudley," she said breathlessly, " I am so
happy—so absurdly happy."

She raised her head and Dudley, looking at her
in the firelight, found her more beautiful than she
had been even in the radiant days of her girlhood.
He had seen that high resolve in her face but once
before, and he grasped the meaning now as then—
it was the dawn of motherhood that enveloped her.
She had heard the call of the generations in the end
—the appeal of the race that moved her nature
more profoundly than did the erratic ardours of the
individual. There was a clear light in her eyes,
and her features had taken an almost marble-like

nobility. The look in her face reminded him of moments in the old days at Battle Hall, when she had wrapped the wandering general in a tenderness that was maternal. With a sudden penetrant insight into her heart, he realised that her natural emotions were her nobler ones—that as child and mother the greatness of her nature assumed its visible form. He drew her closer, the best in him responding to the mystery he beheld dimly in her eyes. For ten years they had not touched natures so nearly; it was the vital breath needed to vivify a union which was not rooted in the permanence of an enduring passion.

And as the months went on the wonder deepened in Eugenia's eyes. The old restlessness was gone; she was like one who, having looked into the holy of holies, keeps the inward memory clear. She was in the supreme mental state—attained only by religious martyrs or maternal, yet childless, women long married—when physical pain loses its relative values before the exaltation of an abiding vision. And, above all, she was what each woman of her race had been before her—a mother from her birth.

III

From the day of the child's birth it did not leave Eugenia's sight. Her eyes followed it when it was carried about the room, and she watched wistfully the dressing and undressing of the round little body. She knew each separate frock that she had made before its coming, and each day she called for a different and a daintier one. " I must make new ones," she said at last, " he is such a beauty!" And she would hold out her arms for him, half dressed as he was, and, as he lay beside her, fresh and cool and fragrant as a cowslip ball, she would cover the soft pink flesh with passionate kisses. Her motherhood was an obsession, jealous, intense, unreasoning.

They had named him after the general—Thomas Battle Webb, but to Eugenia he was " the baby," the solitary baby in a universe where birth is as common as death. And, indeed, he was a thing of joy— the nurse, Dudley, Miss Chris, all admitted it. There was never so round, so rosy, so altogether marvellous a baby, and never one that laughed so much or cried so little. " He was born with a silver spoon in his mouth," declared Miss Chris. " I can see his luck already in his eyes."

At first Eugenia had been tortured by a fear that the little life would go out as the other had done; but, as the weeks went on and he lived and fed and fattened, her fear was lost in the wondering rapture of possession. Nothing so perfectly alive could cease to be.

When she was well again she dismissed the nurse and took, herself, entire charge of the child. "There are no mammies these days," she had said in reply to Dudley's remonstrances, "and I can't trust him with one of the new negroes—I really can't. Why, I saw one slap a baby once." So she bathed and dressed him in the mornings and rocked him to sleep at midday and at dark, and in the brightness of the forenoon gave him an airing on the piazza that overlooked the back garden. From the time of her getting up to her lying down he left her arms only when he was laid asleep in the little crib beside her bed.

But, for all this, he was a healthy, hearty baby, with a round bald head, great blue eyes like china marbles, and a ridiculous mouth that would not shut over the pink gums and hide the dimples at the corners. He did not cry because, as yet, he hadn't seen the moon, and the lamp had been carefully emptied and given to him as soon as he was big enough to hold out his hands. Pins had not stuck him, because Eugenia had guarded against the danger by sewing ribbons on his tiny innumerable slips. And he was as amiable as his elders are apt to be so long as they are permitted to regard the visible universe as a possible plaything.

At this time it was Eugenia's custom to hold him on her lap while she ate her meals, or to leave Miss Chris in charge if the small tyrant chanced to be asleep. Miss Chris had become a willing servitor;

but she occasionally felt it to be her duty to put a modest check upon Eugenia's maternal frenzy.

" My dear, there were ten of us," she remarked one day, " and I am sure we never required as much attention as this one."

" And nine of you died," Eugenia solemnly retorted.

Miss Chris was compelled to assent; but she immediately added: " Not until we had reached middle age. Belinda died youngest, and it was of pneumonia, at the age of forty-one. You don't think neglect during her infancy had anything to do with it, do you? Nobody ever accused my poor dear mother of not looking after her children."

But Eugenia stood her ground. " One can never tell," was all she said, though a moment later she wiped her eyes and sobbed: " Oh, papa! If papa could only see him! He would be so proud."

" Of course, darling," said Miss Chris. " He was always fond of children. I remember distinctly the way he carried on when his first child was born— but he lost him of croup before he was a month old."

She left the room to see after the housekeeping, and Eugenia hugged the baby to her bosom, and cried over him and kissed him, and thought his eyes were like her father's—though, for that matter, the general's were gray and watery, with weak red lids that blinked. The baby gurgled and showed his gums still more and clutched the lace upon his mother's breast until it hung in shreds. It was a new gown, but neither Eugenia nor the baby cared for that—if he had wanted to pull her hair out, strand

by strand, she would have submitted rather than
have brought a wrinkle to his cloudless brow.

A little later she took him out upon the sidewalk,
after swathing him from head to foot in a light-blue
veil that floated about her like a strip of sky.   It was
here that Juliet Galt found her, as she was passing,
and, throwing back her pretty head, she laughed
until the tears came.

" O Eugie, Eugie, if you had six! " she gasped.

Eugenia flinched slightly at her merriment. " But,
Juliet, I can't trust him with a nurse. Why, you
told me only the other day that your faithful old
Fanny called Elizabeth an ' imp of Satan.' "

Juliet only wrung her hands and laughed the
more. " It's too funny," she panted at last; " but
I'm sure if Fanny said it about Elizabeth it was true
—she never tells stories."   Then she rippled off
again. " Oh, my poor Dudley! How does he en-
dure it? Why, Ben would ship the babies off to
boarding school if I attempted this."

" Dudley tries to be good about it," replied Eugenia, " but he hates it awfully."

Juliet went by, and Eugenia kept up her slow
promenade until Dudley came up to dinner.   Then
she followed him into the house and upstairs to her
room, where he turned upon her reproachfully :

" I say, Eugie, I wish you'd stop this sort of thing.
It isn't fair to me, you know."

" How absurd, Dudley! "

" But it isn't. People will begin to say that I'm
bankrupt or a beast.   If you will go parading round
like this, for heaven's sake hire a servant or two to
follow after ; it'll look more decent."

Eugenia's response was far from satisfactory, and the next morning, before going to his office, he drew Miss Chris aside and unburdened himself into her sympathetic ear. "You don't think Eugie's a—a —exactly crazy, do you, Aunt Chris?" he wound up with, for Miss Chris was on his side, and he knew it.

"I don't wonder you ask, Dudley, I really don't," was her comforting rejoinder. "Why, she actually had the face to tell me yesterday that I'd never had any children, so I couldn't advise her. It is provoking. I don't pretend to deny it."

Dudley took up his hat and carefully examined the inside lining. "Well, I'll settle it," he said at last, and went out.

The next day, when Eugenia went upstairs from dinner, she found Delphy in a nurse's cap and apron, installed in a low chair before the fire, jolting the baby on her knees with a peculiar rhythmic motion.

Eugenia fell back, regarding her with blank amazement. "Why, Delphy, where did you come from?" she exclaimed. "I didn't know you were in service. Whom are you nursing for?"

Delphy responded with a passive nod. "I'se nussin' for Marse Dudley," she retorted.

"But I don't want a nurse, Delphy. I take care of the baby myself. I like to do it."

Delphy kept up her drowsy jolting, shaking at the same time an unrelenting head. "Go 'long wid you, honey," she returned. "I ain' oner yo' new-come niggers. I'se done riz mo' chillun den you'se got teef in yo' haid, en I ain' gwine ter have Marse Dudley's chile projecked wid 'fo' my eyes. You ain' no mo' fitten ter nuss dis chile den Marse Dudley hisse'f is."

" O Delphy!" gasped Eugenia reproachfully. She made a dart at the baby, but he raised a shrill protest, which caused her hopelessly to desist. " O Delphy, you've come between us! " she cried.

" I 'low ef I hadn't you'd 'a' run plum crazy," was Delphy's justification. " Dis yer chile's my bizness, en yourn it's down yonder in de parlour wid Marse Dudley."

Eugenia wavered and stood irresolute. Delphy's authority, rooted in superior knowledge, appeared to be unshakable, but she made a last desperate effort. " Suppose he should get sick without me, Delphy? "

Delphy positively snorted. " Ef you wanter raise dis yer chile, Miss Euginny," she replied, " you'd des better let me alont. Hit's a won'er you ain' been de deaf er him 'fo' I got yer wid yo' sto' physicks en yo' real doctahs es dunno one baby f'om anur when dey meet 'im in de street. I reckon, ef he'd got de colic you'd have kilt 'im terreckly, you en yo' sto' physicks en yo' real doctahs! Now, you'd des better dress yo'se'f an' go down yonder ter de parlour."

But as she finished Dudley strolled in and stood beaming down upon his offspring as it lay, round and pinkly impressive, in Delphy's lap. " Fine boy, eh, Delphy? " he inquired proudly.

" Dat 'tis, suh," responded Delphy heartily, " an' he's des de spit er you dis ve'y minit."

The following morning Dudley went to Washington for several days, and Eugenia was left with Miss

Chris and the child.   Lottie and the little girls were with Bernard, who was dragging to a tedious end in Florida, where he had been ordered as a last resource.   Poor, pretty, ineffectual Lottie had succumbed to the unrelenting pressure of her duty.   She had sacrificed herself from sheer lack of the force necessary to withstand fate.

During Dudley's absence Eugenia gave herself up to as much of the baby as Delphy grudgingly allowed her, sewing, in the long intervals, on tiny slips as delicate as cobwebs.   Even this occupation was not wholly a peaceful one.   " Des wait twel he begin ter crawl, en' den whar'l dose spider webs be? " propounded Delphy in the afternoon of the third day. " Dey'll be in de ash-ba'r'l er at de back er de fireplace, en dat's whar dey b'long.   Marse Dudley ain' never wo' no sech trash ner is you yo'se'f."

Eugenia did not respond.   She seated herself beside the window, and with one eye on her child and one on her work sewed silently, her white hands gleaming amid the laces in her lap.   The training of her slave-holding ancestors was strong upon her, and she regarded Delphy's liberty of speech as an inherent right of her position.   The Battle servants had always spoken their minds to their mistresses in a manner which caused them to become hopeless failures when they hired themselves into strange families, where the devotion of their lives could not be offered in extenuation of the freedom of their tongues.

So when Eugenia spoke, after a placid pause, it was merely to suggest that the baby's head was hanging too far over Delphy's knee.   " That can't be healthful, Delphy," she said, half timidly. Delphy grunted and adjusted matters with a protest. " Hit's de way yourn done hung en Miss Meely's done hung befo' you," she muttered. Eugenia turned to the window and looked out upon the back yard, where the horse-chestnut tree was a mass of bloom, delicate as a cloud. In the beds below, roses were out in red and white, and against the gray wall of the stable at the end of the brick walk purple flags were flaunting in the shadow. Across the city, beyond the tin roofs and the chimney-pots, the sun was going down in a mist as sheer as gauze, and the surrounding atmosphere was charged with opalescent lights.

Her eyes rested upon it with a quick sense of its beauty; then the sunset lost itself in the round of her thoughts. She had missed Dudley, and she was glad that he was coming home to-night. For the first time during the fifteen years of her marriage she experienced a vague uneasiness at his absence. A year ago she had not known a tremor of loneliness when he was away—but then the child was unborn. Now, in some subtle way, the child's existence was bound and rebound in Dudley's. The two stood together in her thoughts; she could not separate them—the child was but a smaller, a closer, a dearer Dudley—a Dudley of her dreams and visions, the ideal ending to life's realities.

As she sat beside the window, her eyes wandering from the sunset to the baby asleep in Delphy's lap, she wondered that she had never before suffered this incipient thrill of nervous fear. Was it that her affection for her child had revivified all lesser emotions? Or was it that with supreme love came the vague, invincible perception of supreme loss? Did great happiness bear within itself the visible reflection of great sorrow? Her life before this had been more peaceful—it had been also less complete. With the coming of her heart's desire had awakened her heart's inquietude—both had dawned after years of restless waiting and uncertain wandering. It was borne in upon her, with something like a pang, that the fulness of life had blossomed for her only when her first youth was withered, when she had long since relinquished high expectations or keen desire. She had set her young mind and her quick passion on a far-away good, she had shed vain tears over the lack of it; yet, in the end, she found compensation where she would least have sought it—in the things which made up her destiny. She had learned the wisdom of acceptance, and Fate had rewarded her, not by yielding to her what she had called her heart's necessity, but by fitting her heart to the necessity that was already hers. She had not known the fulfilment of her young ideals, but she was content at last with an existence which was a personal surrender to older realities. For herself she asked now only busy days of domestic interests and the unbroken serenity of middle age—but, despite herself, another life was before her, for she lived again in her child.

The twilight fell. She put her work aside, and, coming to the hearth rug, took the baby from Delphy's arms. He was in his night-dress, and his big blue eyes were drugged with sleep. As Eugenia took him he gave a whimpering cry and clutched her with his little hands before he nestled into the lace at her bosom.

Some hours later, while Eugenia awaited Dudley in the dining-room, Miss Chris came in to see that his late supper was in preparation. " The train is over-due," she said, with a glance at the clock. " He will be hungry when he gets in. He always is."

Eugenia looked up anxiously. " I am beginning to feel alarmed," she replied. " Can anything have happened, do you think? He is an hour late."

Miss Chris shook her head as she refilled the sugar-bowl. " Why, he's often late," she rejoined. " I never knew you to be nervous before. What is it? "

" Oh, I don't know," said Eugenia. She rose and stood looking at the clock, her brow wrinkling. " If he isn't here in five minutes I'm going to the station," she added, and went upstairs for her wraps.

When she returned Miss Chris resorted to argument. " Don't be absurd, Eugie," she urged. " You can't go alone. It's too late and too far."

" But I sent for a carriage," replied Eugenia decisively. " If anything happens to the baby come after me," and a moment later she rolled away, leaving Miss Chris transfixed upon the doorstep.

As the carriage passed along the lighted streets she smiled at the recollection of the face Miss Chris had turned upon her. Well, she was absurd, of course, but one couldn't go through life being reasonable. And if anything were to happen to Dudley she would always remember that she had refused to go to walk with him the afternoon before he went away, because the baby was crying for the flames

and couldn't be left with Delphy. Dudley was pro-
voked about it, but men never understood these matters. He had even gone so far as to declare that
his son would get only his deserts if he were to cry
himself hoarse; and she had felt impelled to resent
so hard-hearted an utterance. How could the baby
know that the fire was the only thing in the world
he couldn't have for his own?

When she drew up at the station the train was just
coming in, and she rushed through the waiting-
room to the gate from which the passengers were
streaming. As she reached it Dudley came through,
talking animatedly to the man who walked beside
him. "That was the very point, my dear sir——"
he was saying, when he caught sight of Eugenia,
and paused abruptly, domestic affairs asserting their
supremacy in his mind. "Why, Eugie!" he gasped.
"What's happened?"

Eugenia seized his arm impatiently. "Oh, you
were so late, Dudley," she cried, half angrily. "You
made me miserable—it wasn't right of you!"

She hesitated an instant and, looking up, found
that his companion was Nicholas Burr. His eyes
were upon her, and he lifted his hat without speaking, but Dudley at once turned to him.

"You are old friends with Mrs. Webb, Governor,"
he said lightly, "but you don't know the ways of a
woman who thinks her husband may lose himself
between Washington and Richmond."

Nicholas met the impatient flicker in Eugenia's
eyes and laughed.

"Oh, she hardly fancied you had fallen over-
board," he returned. "It's too difficult in these

days.   I trust you have had no great anxiety, Mrs. Webb."

And he passed on, his bag in his hand.

When Dudley and Eugenia were in the carriage she held herself erect and attacked him with asperity. " You might at least not laugh at me," she said.

For reply he smiled and flung his arm about her. " My darling girl, it's one of the things that make life worth living," he retorted.   " When I cease to laugh at you I'll cease to love you—and that's a long way off."

IV

The campaign which would decide the election of a United States Senator was warming to white heat. On the last day of October Tom Bassett, dropping into Galt's office, greeted him with the exclamation: " So you've taken to the stump!"

Galt put aside his papers and rose with a laugh, holding out his hand. " My dear fellow, may I ask where you have spent the last fortnight? Is it possible that my oratorical fame has just penetrated to your retreat?"

Tom sat down, and taking off his hat, ran his hand through his hair with an exhausted gesture. " Oh, I've been West. I got back last night, and I'm off to New York in an hour. So it's a fact that you've been on the stump?"

" It is! I don't mean to allow the Webb men to do all the talking. You heard about my joint debate with Diggs at Amelia Court-house, didn't you? That, my dear Tom, was the culminating point of my glorious career. I squared him off as nicely as you please, and with no rough edges either."

But Tom refused to be impressed. " Oh, anybody could do up Diggs," he said. " I hear, however, that you had some hot words between you."

Galt shook his head. " Ah, the words were as nothing to the drinks that followed," he sighed. " Diggs mayn't be much on speeches, but he's great

27   4¹7

on cocktails. It was a glorious day!" Then he
grew serious. "When he was fairly wound up I
got a good deal out of him," he said. "We came
down on the train together, and I found out that he
was against Burr simply because the Webb men
had told him that he pledged himself to them when
he allowed them to send him to the Legislature. It's
all rot, of course; his constituents are strong for
Burr, but he's a good deal of a fool, and Rann has
put it into his head that he must do the 'honest
thing' by coming out for Webb. He has a great
idea of party honour, so out he's come."

"Rann's a born organiser," commented Tom.

"Ah, there's where we aren't even with him. He
and his assistants have been drilling their forces ever
since he had that clash with Burr, and the discipline's
so good they are beginning to convince the people
that the opinions of a dozen men represent the principles of the party. What Burr aims at, of course,
is to organise the mass of Democratic voters as
effectively as Rann has organised the ring."

"That's a tough job," said Tom, "but if it's to
be done, Burr's the man to do it. As it is, I haven't
a doubt that the majority is with us."

"Well, I live in hope," returned Galt easily. "It
seems to me there's a clear chance of our having a
good deal over half the votes in the caucus. Now,
grant that there'll be a hundred and twenty regular
Democratic votes——"

"Of which Webb already claims sixty-five."

"Claims!" growled Galt. "He may claim the
whole confounded lot if he wants to. The question
is—will he get them?"

"He will if Rann can manage it. It isn't mere party bitterness that actuates that man—there's a good deal of personal spite mixed with it. He hates Burr."

"Oh, I dare say. But he overreached himself when he tried to get control of the committee. They decided in favour of Saunders in the last Southside contest, and Saunders is pledged to Burr."

Tom drew out his watch and moved towards the door, but having reached it, he swung round with a question: "Seen Webb since your debate?" he inquired.

Galt nodded. "I had a chat with him in the lobby at the 'Royal' last night, and I must admit that, so far as Webb's concerned, this campaign is a particularly decent one. He can't help being a gentleman any more than he can help being a demagogue. Both instincts are in the blood."

"Yes, I rather think you're right. Well, good-bye. I'll see you Tuesday."

He ran downstairs, breaking into a whistle on the way, and Galt, after a moment's hesitation, took up his hat and followed him. He had an appointment with Burr's campaign manager, who had his head-quarters at the Royal Hotel.

It was there that Galt found him, holding a jubilant gathering in his rooms. He was absolutely sanguine of success, and when Galt left an hour later, he sought to impart to him his emphatic confidence. "My dear sir, I can conclusively prove to you that we shall win," he said, one eye on Galt and one on a reporter who had just entered. "I can prove it to you in figures—and figures never lie.

There is not the faintest doubt that Burr will have seventy votes by the meeting of the caucus."

" Glad to hear it," was Galt's response; but in passing through the lobby on his way out he encountered an equal assurance in the opposite camp. Rann, who was the centre of a small group, broke away and came towards him.

" I suppose the governor has reconciled himself to defeat, eh, Mr. Galt? "

Galt shook his head with a laugh. " Defeat! Why, Major, we're just beginning to enjoy our triumph. Burr has his seventy votes in his hand and he keeps it closed."

Rann flushed angrily, his mouth twitching. " If you will come this way, sir, I can prove to you on paper—on paper, sir—that Webb has his majority as plain as if the caucus was over. Seventy votes! Why, bless my soul, he must have counted in every Republican and Independent that will be sent up. Seventy votes! I tell you he won't have forty— not forty, sir! "

" Ah, he laughs best that laughs last, my dear Major."

And he left the hotel, walking rapidly in the direction of the Capitol. Once or twice he stopped to speak to an acquaintance who wanted his opinion of Burr's chances, and to such inquiries his response was invariably an expression of perfect conviction. But when alone his uncertainty appeared—and he acknowledged to himself that he was afraid of Rann's last card. What it was he did not know, but he knew that when the time came it would be well played. Bassett was right—it was not party bitterness that moved Rann, it was personal hatred.

The square was flooded with sunshine, and down the green slopes gray squirrels were feeding from the hands of children. Overhead the elms were russet from a sharp frost, and the golden leaves of the sycamores shone against the leprous whiteness of the branches.

Near a fountain he came upon his own small daughter building huts of pebbles. As she saw him she gave a shrill scream and caught his knees in a tight embrace. He raised her in his arms for a kiss, and then spoke cordially to the old negro janitor of the Capitol, who was watching him. " Is that you, Carter? Good-morning!"

" Well, I declar, boss, I ain' seen you fur a mont' er Sundays."

" You must have been looking at the clouds, Carter."

" Naw, suh, I'se been lookin' right out yer, an' I ain' seen you. Is you gwine ter 'lect de gov'nor?"

Galt was holding his daughter high enough to reach the branches of an elm. " I'm trying to, Carter," he returned good-humouredly, " but I can't do it by myself. Won't you lend a hand?"

" I'll len' 'em bofe, if you want 'em, boss. I'se been stedyin' 'bout dis bizness, an' I'se got a plan all laid out in my haid. Dey's a lot er coloured folks in dis State, suh."

" That's so, man."

" An' dey's all got a vote des de same es de white?"

Galt laughed. " Sure's you live," he replied.

" Well, I'se gwine ter git my friend Bob Viars ter

git up er meetin' er all de coloured folks roun' in Cumberland County, an' I'se gwine ter put on de bes' I'se got an' git up on de platform an' Bob's gwine tell 'em I'se de janitor er de Capitol dat knows all de ways de laws are made—an' when Bob says dat, I'se gwine ter bow an' flirt my hank'chif."

Galt nodded.   " Oh, I see," he said.

" Den I'se gwine say I'se come ter tell 'em ter 'lect de gov'nor 'case he's de bes' man in de State an' de greates' gent-man dey's ever lay eyes on— an' I'se gwine flirt my hank'chif some mo'."

" What else ? " said Galt.

" I'se gwine tell 'em I kin prove de gov'nor's de bes' man in de State by 'splainin' er de tarif—dat I kin prove it by 'splainin' er de tarif so dey'll unnerstan' it ev'y word—an' when I flirt my hank'chif dat time, Bob's gwine call out ' Yo' time's up, boss! ' an' I'se gwine answer back, ' Naw 'tain't, Bob, des lemme 'splain de tarif. I'se got de 'splanification er de tarif right on de tip er my tongue,' an' Bob's gwine holler out, ' Not anudder word, boss, not anudder word! ' an' he gwine shuffle me right spang out."

Galt put down his daughter and shook Carter's hand.   " If you ever get out of a job, my man," he said, " go into politics.   Is the governor in his office ? "

" I'se des dis minit seen him come out fer dinner."

" All right, I'll find him," and he went on to the governor's house.

Nicholas was in his library, a law-book open before him.   When he saw Galt he turned from his desk and motioned to a chair beside him.   " Come in, Ben, and sit down.   I'm glad to see you."

Galt threw himself into the chair. "I've just seen Ryan," he said, "and I never met a more sanguine man. He doesn't give Webb a chance."

"Ah, is that so?" asked the governor; his tone was almost indifferent, but in a moment he leaned forward and spoke rapidly:

"I fear there's trouble in Kingsborough, Ben. They've brought a negro there to the gaol from Hagersville, where there were threats of a lynching."

"The devil! Well, you aren't afraid that Kingsborough will turn lawless? My dear friend, there isn't enough vitality down there to make one first-class savage."

Nicholas fell back again, his vivid hair drawing the superb outline of his head on the worn leather against which he leaned.

"Oh, I'm not afraid of Kingsborough," he returned, "but Hagersville is only three miles distant, and the country people are much wrought up. God knows they have reason to be."

"Ah, the usual thing."

"I don't know the details—but there is sufficient evidence against the man, they say, to hang him twenty times. He's as dead as if the noose had left his neck—but he must die by law. There hasn't been a lynching in the State since I've been in office."

He spoke quietly, but Galt saw the anxiety in his face and met it bravely.

"Nonsense, my dear Nick, don't let your hobby run away with you. If there had been any danger they'd have got the wretch away. By the bye, Tom

Bassett has gone to New York. I saw him this morning."

" Yes, he dropped in last night. You haven't seen this, I dare say—it's a copy of Diggs's speech at Danville. So they have fallen on my private life at last."

He handed Galt a typewritten sheet, watching him closely as he read it. " This looks as if they feared me, doesn't it? " he asked.

Galt's reply was an oath of sudden anger. " This is Rann! " he cried. " I see his mark! " A flush of red rose to his face and his voice came again in a long-drawn whistle of helpless rage. " The scoundrel! " he said sharply. " He's raked up that old Kingsborough scandal of Bernard Battle's and made you the man. Oh, the sneaking scoundrel! "

His passion appeared in quick contrast to the other's composure. He was resenting the slander with a violence that he would not have wasted on it had it touched himself—for the fame of his friend was a cause for which his easy-going nature would spring at once into arms.

Burr came over to him and laid a hand on his shoulder. " When you come to think of it, Ben," he said, " it's no great matter."

" Then what steps have you taken about it? "

Nicholas's arm fell to his side. " I have done nothing. What's the use? "

Galt strode to the window and back again to the fireplace. His eyes were blazing. " The use? Why, man, use or no use, I'll send the last one of them to hell, but they'll stop it! It's Rann—Rann

from the beginning. I'd take my oath on it—
but I'm his match, and he'll find it out. I'll have
Diggs retract this lie by six o'clock this evening or
I'll——"

He checked himself abruptly. "How long have
you had this?"

"A half-hour. The speech goes in the evening
papers."

"A half-hour! And you sit here snivelling about
your lynching. Why, what are the necks of ten
such devils worth to your good name? When I
come to think of it, I'd like to lend a hand at a
lynching myself. If I had Rann here——"

The governor laughed dryly. "To tell the truth,
my dear fellow, I don't take it seriously. The people know me."

Galt uttered an angry exclamation and flung out
his hand. "Oh, give over, Nick," he implored.
"Don't drive me to frenzy! I can't stand much
more."

He took up a sheet of paper and wrote several
lines in pencil. "After all, I've been thinking to
some purpose," he said. "Judge Bassett is the man
we need. I'll telegraph to him from your office,
and I'll have his reply scattered broadcast. If it
riddles Webb like shot, I'll have it out."

"Oh, it isn't Webb," said Nicholas. He was
looking into the fire, but as the door closed behind
Galt he turned and seated himself at his desk. The
law-book he had been reading lay to one side, and
he opened it and followed up the question that per-
plexed him. His face was grave, but his eyes were
shot with light. When Galt came back he entered

slowly and hesitated an instant before speaking, then he said:

"There's bad news, Nick. The judge has had a stroke of paralysis. He is now unconscious. Tom can't be reached, and you——"

Nicholas took out his watch. "I have fifteen minutes in which to make that train," was his answer. "Will you tell Dickson to repeat all messages?" Then, as Galt followed him into the hall, he looked back and spoke again. "Until to-morrow," he said, and went out.

Galt delivered the message to Dickson and walked uptown to Webb's house, where he expected to find him. He had not lunched, and he remembered suddenly that Nicholas had also gone hungry; but the thought brought a smile as he rang Webb's bell. "Oh, for once in a lifetime a man may be heroic," he said. Then he entered the house and found, not Dudley, but Eugenia.

At the sound of his name she had risen and come swiftly forward with outstretched hand. Her face was white and her eyes heavy with anxiety, but he felt then, as always, the calm nobility of her carriage. In the added fulness of her figure her beauty showed majestic.

He took her hand, holding it warmly in his own. "My dear Eugenia, if you are in trouble, remember that I am an ignoble edition of Juliet."

"Oh, I want you, not Juliet," she said. "I have sent for Dudley, but he has not come—I took the paper at the door by chance—and I find that Colonel Diggs has brought up that old dead lie about the governor. He dares to say that the people of Kings-

borough believe it—the coward! They never believed it—it is false—as false as the lie itself. Oh,
if I were a man I would kill him for it, but I am a
woman, and you——"

"Kill him!" He laughed harshly. "We don't
kill men who blacken our friend's honour; we wait
till they attack our own lives—that's our code for
you. If it were otherwise, I should act upon it with
pleasure. But I came to see Webb about this thing.
Where is he?"

"Oh, he is coming."

She sat down, keeping her excited eyes upon him.
"It was Bernard, my own brother," she said passionately. "You know this, and the world must
know it. The world shall know it if I have to utter
it from the housetops. Oh, I have sinned enough
in ignorance; now I will speak."

She bit her lips to keep back the quick tears, tap-
ping her foot upon the floor. The red was in her
cheeks and her eyes were as black as night. Her
bosom quivered from the lash of her scorn.

"But you must keep out of it, my dear Eugie.
Dudley and I will manage it. We'll see Diggs and
get a retraction from him—that's sensible and simple. There's no scandal the better for dragging a
woman into it."

She stopped him fiercely. "Then I give you fair
warning. If you do not stop it, I shall. Ah, here's
Dudley!"

She met him as he entered the room, clasping her
hands upon his arm. "Dudley, have you seen it—
this falsehood?"

He let her hands fall from his arm and drew her

with him to the fireside. " Yes; I have seen it," he answered, and as he shook hands heartily with Galt he made a casual remark about the weather.

" Oh, Dudley, what does the weather matter?" cried Eugenia. " No, don't sit down. You are to go at once to Colonel Diggs and tell him everything —and not spare any one—and you may tell him also that—I despise him! "

He smiled at her vehemence—it was so unlike Eugenia. " I didn't know you took so much interest in these things," he said lightly. " I thought the baby had cured you."

But she caught his hand and held it in her own. " Don't, Dudley," she implored. " You know what it means to me. You know all."

His face softened as he met her eyes; but instead of replying to her appeal he turned with a question to Galt. " Can I do any good?" he asked. " I am willing, of course, to do what I can."

" I was going to ask you to see Diggs," said Galt quietly. " We shall endeavour to keep his speech out of the morning papers, but it has already appeared in the evening issue. You might secure a card from him retracting his statements. I hardly think he knew them to be false."

" I'll go at once," replied Dudley. He went into the hall and took up his hat, but as Galt opened the door he lingered an instant and looked at his wife. She came to him, her eyes shining, and in a flash he realised that to Eugenia it was a question of his own honour as well as of the governor's. With a smile he lifted her chin and met her gaze. " Are you satisfied, my lady?" he asked; but before she could respond he had joined Galt upon the pavement.

There he paused to light a cigar, while Galt hesitated and looked at his watch. " I suppose I may leave it in your hands," suggested the older man. " Diggs isn't on the best of terms with me, you know."

Dudley took the cigar from his mouth and threw the match over the railing into the grass. " Oh, I'll do my best," he answered readily, " and I'll see that the statements are delivered to the newspapers at once. I am as much interested in it as you are. It was a dirty piece of work." And leaving Galt, he quickened his pace as he crossed the street.

Diggs was at his hotel and somewhat relieved at the sudden turn of affairs. " Honestly, I hated it," he frankly admitted. " It's the kind of job I'd like to wash my hands of. But Major Rann took oath on the truth of the story, and he convinced me that I owed it to the community to expose Burr's character. I don't know why I believed it, except that it never occurs to one to doubt evil. However, I'm glad you called. I assure you I'll take more pleasure in retracting the statements than I did in making them."

He wrote the notes and gave them into Dudley's hands. " If they don't get in to-morrow's issue, they must wait over till election day. It's a pity this is Saturday—but you'll have them in, I dare say."

" Yes; I'll take them down," said Dudley. He descended in the elevator, walking rapidly when he reached the pavement. Diggs's parting words came back to him and he repeated them as he went. To-

morrow's was the last paper before election day.
If the speech were reported in the morning issue and
Burr's friends made no denial, there would be, as
far as the country voters were concerned, a silence
of two days.   The contest was not yet decided, this
he knew—it would be a close one, and a straw's
weight might turn the scales of public favour.   Rann
realised this too, for he did not fling slime at men for
nothing—there was a serious purpose underneath
the last act of his play.   He was doing it for the
sake of those Democrats whose constituents were
divided against themselves, and he was trusting to
himself to hold the votes that came his way when the
cloud should have passed from Burr again.   It was
all so evident that Dudley held his breath for one
brief instant.   The whole scheme lay bare before
him—he had but to drop these letters into the nearest box, and Rann's purpose would be fulfilled.   In
the howl of reprobation that followed the hounding
of Burr his own hour would come.   And granted
that the governor was cleared before the meeting of
the caucus—well, men are easier to keep than to
win—and he might not be cleared after all.

A clock near at hand struck the hour.   He raised
his head and saw the " Standard " office across the
street—and the temptation passed as swiftly as it
had come.   The instinct of generations was stronger
than the appeal of the moment—he might sin a great
sin, but he could never commit a meanness.

With sudden energy he crossed the street and ran
up the stairs.

V

Again he was returning to Kingsborough. The familiar landscape rushed by him on either side— green meadow and russet woodland, gray swamp and dwarfed brown hill, unploughed common and sun-ripened field of corn. It was like the remembered features of a friend, when the change that startles the unaccustomed eye seems to exist less in the well-known face than in the image we have carried in our thoughts.

It was all there as it had been in his youth—the same and yet not the same. The old fields were tilled, the old lands ran waste in broomsedge, but he himself had left his boyhood far behind—it was his own vision that was altered, not the face of nature. The commons were not so wide as he had thought them, the hills not so high, the hollows not so deep—even the blue horizon had drawn a closer circle.

A man on his way to the water-cooler stopped abruptly at his side. " Well, I declar, if 'tain't the governor! "

Nicholas looked up, and recognising Jerry Pollard, shook his outstretched hand. " When did you leave Kingsborough? " he inquired.

" Oh, I jest ran up this morning to lay in a stock of winter goods. Trade's thriving this year, and you have to hustle if you want to keep up with the tastes of yo' customers. Times have changed since I had you in my sto'."

"I dare say. I am glad to hear that you are doing well. Was the judge taken ill before you left Kingsborough?"

"The judge? Is he sick? I ain't heard nothin' 'bout it. It wa'n't more'n a week ago that I told him he was lookin' as young as he did befo' the war. It ain't often a man can keep his youth like that— but his Cæsar is just such another. Cæsar was an old man as far back as I remember, and, bless you, he's spryer than I am this minute. He'll live to be a hundred and die of an accident."

"That's good," said the governor with rising interest. "Kingsborough's a fine place to grow old in. Did you bring any news up with you?"

"Well, I reckon not. Things were pretty lively down there last night, but they'd quieted down this morning. They brought a man over from Hagersville, you know, and befo' I shut up sto' last evening Jim Brown came to town, talkin' mighty big 'bout stringin' up the fellow. Jim always did talk, though, so nobody thought much of it. He likes to get his mouth in, but he's right particular 'bout his hand. The sheriff said he warn't lookin' for trouble."

"I'm glad it's over," said the governor. The train was nearing Kingsborough, and as it stopped he rose and followed Jerry Pollard to the station.

There was no one he knew in sight, and, with his bag in his hand, he walked rapidly to the judge's house. His anxiety had caused him to quicken his pace, but when he had opened the gate and ascended the steps he hesitated before entering the hall, and his breath came shortly. Until that instant he had not realised the strength of the tie that bound him to the judge.

The hall was dim and cool, as it had been that May afternoon when his feet had left tracks of dust on the shining floor. Straight ahead he saw the garden, lying graceless and deserted, with the unkemptness of extreme old age. A sharp breeze blew from door to door, and the dried grasses on the wall stirred with a sound like that of the wind among a bed of rushes.

He mounted the stairs slowly, the weight of his tread creaking the polished wood. Before the threshold of the judge's room again he hesitated, his hand upraised. The house was so still that it seemed to be untenanted, and he shivered suddenly, as if the wind that rustled the dried grasses were a ghostly footstep. Then, as he glanced back down the wide old stairway, his own childhood looked up at him—an alien figure, half frightened by the silence.

As he stood there the door opened noiselessly, and the doctor came out, peering with shortsighted eyes over his lowered glasses. When he ran against Nicholas he coughed uncertainly and drew back. " Well, well, if it isn't the governor! " he said. " We have been looking for Tom—but our friend the judge is better—much better. I tell him he'll live yet to see us buried."

A load passed suddenly from Nicholas's mind. The ravaged face of the old doctor—with its wrinkled forehead and its almost invisible eyes—be-

28

came at once the mask of a good angel. He grasped
the outstretched hand and crossed the threshold.

The judge was lying among the pillows of his
bed, his eyes closed, his great head motionless.
There was a bowl of yellow chrysanthemums on a
table beside him, and near it Mrs. Burwell was
measuring dark drops into a wineglass. She looked
up with a smile of welcome that cast a cheerful light
about the room. Her smile and the colour of the
chrysanthemums were in Nicholas's eyes as he went
to the bed and laid his hand upon the still fingers
that clasped the counterpane.

The judge looked at him with a wavering recognition. "Ah, it is you, Tom," he said, and there
was a yearning in his voice that fell like a gulf between him and the man who was not his son. At
the moment it came to Nicholas with a great bitterness that his share of the judge's heart was the share
of an outsider—the crumbs that fall to the beggar
that waits beside the gate. When the soul has entered the depths and looks back again it is the face
of its own kindred that it craves—the responsive
throbbing of its own blood in another's veins. This
was Tom's place, not his.

He leaned nearer, speaking in an expressionless
voice. "It's I, sir—Nicholas—Nicholas Burr."

"Yes, Nicholas," repeated the judge doubtfully;
"yes, I remember, what does he want? Amos
Burr's son—we must give him a chance."

For a moment he wandered on; then his memory
returned in uncertain pauses. He looked again at
the younger man, his sight grown stronger. "Why,
Nicholas, my dear boy, this is good of you," he ex-

claimed. " I had a fall—a slight fall of no conse-
quence. I shall be all right if Cæsar will let me fast
a while. Cæsar's getting old, I fear, he moves so
slowly."

He was silent, and Nicholas, sitting beside the
bed, kept his eyes on the delicate features that were
the lingering survival of a lost type. The splendid
breadth of the brow, the classic nose, the firm, thin
lips, and the shaven chin—these were all downstairs
on faded canvases, magnificent over lace ruffles, or
severe above folded stocks. Over the pillows the
chrysanthemums shed a golden light that mingled
in his mind with the warm brightness of Mrs. Burwell's smile—giving the room the festive glimmer
of an autumn garden.

A little later Cæsar shuffled forward, the wineglass in his hand. The judge turned towards him.
" Is that you, Cæsar? " he asked.

The old negro hurried to the bedside. " Here I
is, Marse George; I'se right yer."

The judge laughed softly. " I wouldn't take five
thousand dollars for you, Cæsar," he said. " Tom
Battle offered me one thousand for you, and I told
him I wouldn't take five. You are worth it, Cæsar
—every cent of it—but there's no man alive shall
own you. You're free, Cæsar—do you hear, you're
free! "

" Thanky, Marse George," said Cæsar. He passed
his arm under the judge's head and raised him as
he would a child. As the glass touched his lips the
judge spoke in a clear voice. " To the ladies! " he
cried.

" He is regaining the use of his limbs," whispered

Mrs. Burwell softly. " He will be well again," and
Nicholas left the room and went downstairs. At
the door he gave his instructions to a woman servant. " I shall return to spend the night," he said.
" You will see that my room is ready. Yes, I'll be
back to supper." He had had no dinner, but at
the moment this was forgotten. In the relief that
had come to him he wanted solitude and the breadth
of the open fields. He was going over the old
ground again—to breathe the air and feel the dust
of the Old Stage Road.

He passed the naked walls of the church and followed the wide white street to the college gate.
Then, turning, he faced the way to his father's farm
and the distant pines emblazoned on the west.

A clear gold light flooded the landscape, warming
the pale dust of the deserted road. The air was keen
with the autumn tang, and as he walked the quick
blood leaped to his cheeks. He was no longer conscious of his forty years—his boyhood was with him,
and middle age was a dream, or less than a dream.

In the branch road a fall of tawny leaves hid the
ruts of wheels, and the sun, striking the ground like
a golden lance, sent out sharp, fiery sparks as from
a mine of light. Overhead the red trees rustled.

It was here that Eugenia had ridden beside him
in the early morning—here he had seen her face
against the enkindled branches—and here he had
placed the scarlet gum leaves in her horse's bridle.
The breeze in the wood came to him like the echo of
her laugh, faded as the memory of his past passion.
Well, he had more than most men, for he had the
ghost of a laugh and the shadow of love.

Passing his father's house, he went on beyond the fallen shanty of Uncle Ish into the twilight of the cedars. At the end of the avenue he saw the rows of box—twisted and tall with age—leading to the empty house, where the stone steps were wreathed in vines. Did Eugenia ever come back, he wondered, or was the house to crumble as Miss Chris's rockery had done? On the porch he saw the marks made by the general's chair, which had been removed, and on one of the long green benches there was an E cut in a childish hand. At a window above —Eugenia's window—a shutter hung back upon its hinges, and between the muslin curtains it seemed to him that a face looked out and smiled—not the face of Eugenia, but a ghost again, the ghost of his old romance.

He went into the garden, crossing the cattle lane, where the footprints of the cows were fresh in the dust. Near at hand he heard a voice shouting. It was the voice of the overseer, but the sound startled him, and he awoke abruptly to himself and his forty years. The spell of the past was broken—even the riotous old garden, blending its many colours in a single blur, could not bring it back. The chrysanthemums and the roses and the hardy zenias that came up uncared for were powerless to reinvoke the spirit of the place. If Eugenia, in her full-blown motherhood, had risen in an overgrown path he might have passed her by unheeding. His Eugenia was a girl in a muslin gown, endowed with immortal youth—the youth of visions unfulfilled and desire unquenched. His Eugenia could never grow old —could never alter—could never leave the eternal sunshine of dead autumns. In his nostrils was the keen sweetness of old-fashioned flowers, but his thoughts were not of them, and, turning presently, he went back as he had come. It was dark when at last he reached the judge's house and sat down to supper.

He was with the judge until midnight, when, before going to his room, he descended the stairs and went out upon the porch. He had been thinking of the elections three days hence, and the outcome seemed to him more hopeful than it had done when he first came forward as a candidate. The uncertainty was almost as great, this he granted; but behind him he believed to be the pressure of the people's will—which the schemes of politicians had not turned. Tuesday would prove nothing—nor had the conventions that had been held; when the meeting of the caucus came, he would still be in ignorance—unaware of traps that had been laid or surprises to be sprung. It was the mark to which his ambition had aimed—the end to which his career had faced—that now rose before him, and yet in his heart there was neither elation nor distrust. He had done his best—he had fought fairly and well, and he awaited what the day might bring forth.

Above him a full moon was rising, and across the green the crooked path wound like a silver thread, leading to the glow of a night-lamp that burned in a sick-room. The night, the air, the shuttered houses were as silent as the churchyard, where the tombstones glimmered, row on row. Only somewhere on the vacant green a hound bayed at the moon.

He looked out an instant longer, and was turning
back, when his eye caught a movement among
the shadows in the distant lane. A quick thought
came to him, and he kept his gaze beneath the heavy
maples, where the moonshine fell in flecks. For a
moment all was still, and then into the light came
the figure of a man. Another followed, another,
and another, passing again into the dark and then
out into the brightness that led into the little gully
far beyond. There was no sound except the baying
of the dog; the figures went on, noiseless and orderly
and grim, from dark to light and from light again
to dark. There were at most a dozen men, and they
might have been a band of belated workmen returning to their homes or a line of revellers that had
been sobered into silence. They might have been
—but a sudden recollection came to him, and he
closed the door softly and went out. There was
but one thing that it meant; this he knew. It meant
a midnight attack on the gaol, and a man dead before morning, who must die anyway—it meant
vengeance so quiet yet so determined that it was
as sure as the hand of God—and it meant the defiance of laws whose guardian he was.

He broke into a run, crossing the green and following the path that rose and fell into the gullies as
it led on to the gaol. As he ran he saw the glow of
the night-lamp in the sick-room, and he heard the
insistent baying of the hound.

The moonlight was thick and full. It showed the
quiet hill flanked by the open pasture; and it showed
the little whitewashed gaol, and the late roses bloom-
ing on the fence. It showed also the mob that had

gathered—a gathering as quiet as a congregation at prayer. But in the silence was the danger—the determination to act that choked back speech—the grimness of the justice that walks at night—the triumph of a lawless rage that knows control.

As he reached the hill he saw that the men he had followed had been enforced by others from different roads. It was not an outbreak of swift desperation, but a well-planned, well-ordered strategy; it was not a mob that he faced, but an incarnate vengeance.

He came upon it quickly, and as he did so he saw that the sheriff was ahead of him, standing, a single man, between his prisoner and the rope. "For God's sake, men, I haven't got the keys," he called out.

Nicholas swung himself over the fence and made his way to the entrance beneath the steps that led to the floor above. He had come as one of the men about him, and they had not heeded him. Now, as he faced them from the shadow he saw here and there a familiar face—the face of a boy he had played with in childhood. Several were masked, but the others raised bare features to the moonlight—features that were as familiar as his own.

Then he stood up and spoke. "Men, listen to me. In the name of the Law, I swear to you that justice shall be done—I swear."

A voice came from somewhere. "We ain't here to talk—you stand aside, and *we'll* show you what we're here for."

Again he began. "I swear to you——"

"We don't want no swearing." On the outskirts

of the crowd a man laughed. " We don't want no swearing," the voice repeated.

The throng pressed forward, and he saw the faces that he knew crowding closer. A black cloud shut out the moonlight. Above the pleading of the sheriff's tones he heard the distant baying of the hound.

He tried to speak again. " We'll be damned, but we'll get the nigger!" called some one beside him. The words struck him like a blow. He saw red, and the sudden rage upheld him. He knew that he was to fight—a blind fight for he cared not what. The old savage instinct blazed within him—the instinct to do battle to death—to throttle with his single hand the odds that opposed. With a grip of iron he braced himself against the doorway, covering the entrance.

" I'll be damned if you do!" he thundered.

A quick shot rang out sharply. The flash blinded him, and the smoke hung in his face. Then the moon shone and he heard a cry—the cry of a well-known voice.

" By God, it's Nick Burr!" it said. He took a step forward.

" Boys, I am Nick Burr," he cried, and he went down in the arms of the mob.

They raised him up, and he stood erect between the leaders. There was blood on his lips, but a man tore off a mask and wiped it away. " By God, it's Nick Burr!" he exclaimed as he did so.

Nicholas recognised his voice and smiled. His face was gray, but his eyes were shining, and as he steadied himself with all his strength, he said with a laugh. "There's no harm done, man." But when they laid him down a moment later he was dead.

He lay in the narrow path between the doorstep and the gate where roses bloomed. Some one had started for the nearest house, but the crowd stood motionless about him. "By God, it's Nick Burr!" repeated the man who had held him.

The sheriff knelt on the ground and raised him in his arms. As he folded his coat about him he looked up and spoke.

"And he died for a damned brute," was what he said.

VI

It was the afternoon of election day, and Eugenia sat in her drawing-room with Sally Bassett.

Outside there was the sound of tramping feet, for the people were giving him burial. They had been passing so for half an hour and they still went on, on, on—he was going to his grave in state.

"There are the drums," said Sally, turning her ear. "All Virginia has come to town, I believe. The whole city is in mourning, and by and by they will put up his statue in the Capitol Square—but if he had lived, would he have had the senatorship?"

"Ah, who knows?" said Eugenia. She played idly with the spoon of her teacup, her eyes on the coals.

"As you say—who knows?" murmured the other. "And, after all, it is perhaps better that he died just now. He would have tried to lift us too high, and we should have fallen back. He was a hero, and the public can't always keep to the heroic level."

There were tears in her voice.

Eugenia turned from her and said nothing.

After Sally had gone she still sat with her cup in her hand before the fire. Her child was rolling on the floor at her feet, but she did not stoop to him. She was not thinking—she was merely resting from emotion—as she would rest for the remainder of her days.

The sound of tramping feet died away. The cars passed once more, and along the block a boy went whistling a tune. Everything was beginning again —everything would go on as it had gone since the dawn of time, and she would go with it. The best or the worst of it was that she would go happily— neither regretting nor despairing, but filled to the finger-tips with the cheerful energy of a busy life.

Suddenly she caught up her child with a frantic rapture and held him to her bosom, kissing the small hands that reached up to her lips. This was her portion, and even to-day she was content.

An hour later Dudley found her sitting there when he entered, and as he straightened himself against the mantel he looked down on her with an affectionate gaze.

"He was a great man," he said simply, and his generous spirit rang in his voice.

"Yes, he was a great man," repeated Eugenia. She looked up at her husband as he stood before her —buoyant with expectation, mellowed by the glow of assured success. He smiled into her face, and she smiled back again with quick tenderness. Then she bent above her child and kissed his lips, and the sunlight coming from the day without shone in her eyes.